Praise for

"Charming, wry, and emotionally resonant. Dimova's propulsive, assured prose captures a fresh, gritty world bursting with wonderful characters—and monsters galore!" —Allison Saft, *New York Times* bestselling author of *A Far Wilder Magic*

"Sharply written, utterly imaginative, by turns terrifying and hopeful—a wonderful read." —Lilith Saintcrow, *New York Times* bestselling author of *Working for the Devil*

"There's no safety when the Foul Days come for you: this book will drag you in and not let you go until dawn." —Marie Brennan, award-winning author of *A Natural History of Dragons*

"A fast-paced murder mystery in a Balkan-inspired fantasy world where your ex can be a literal monster. Charming, clever, and compulsively readable, this debut is wholly original and monstrously fun." —Rebecca Schaeffer, author of the Market of Monsters series

"A sure-footed, swift-paced race against time, *Foul Days* brings Slavic folklore to terrifying life. This is a brilliant modern fantasy that's not afraid to show its teeth." —Ed McDonald, author of The Redwinter Chronicles

"An incredible story filled with monsters and magic which deserves not only to be read, but savored." —Maelan Holladay, author of *The Storm Gathers*

"A fast-paced thrill ride with immersive world-building and a snarky but realistic main character who you just can't help but root for." —Frances White, author of *Voyage of the Damned*

"A phenomenal blend of danger and delight from an exciting new voice in fantasy . . . Will leave you breathlessly awaiting the sequel long before you reach that final page." —Kamilah Cole, author of *So Let Them Burn*

BY GENOVEVA DIMOVA

THE WITCH'S COMPENDIUM OF MONSTERS

Foul Days

*Monstrous Nights**

*Coming October 2024

GENOVEVA DIMOVA

FOUL DAYS

The Witch's Compendium
of Monsters

BOOK 1

TOR PUBLISHING GROUP
NEW YORK

FOUL DAYS

Copyright © 2024 by Genoveva Dimova

Interior illustrations by Rhys Davies

A Tor Book
Published by Tom Doherty Associates / Tor Publishing Group
120 Broadway
New York, NY 10271

www.torpublishinggroup.com

Tor® is a registered trademark of Macmillan Publishing Group, LLC.

The Library of Congress Cataloging-in-Publication Data is available upon request.

ISBN 978-1-250-87731-4 (trade paperback)
ISBN 978-1-250-90010-4 (ebook)

Our books may be purchased in bulk for promotional, educational, or business use. Please contact your local bookseller or the Macmillan Corporate and Premium Sales Department at 1-800-221-7945, extension 5442, or by email at MacmillanSpecialMarkets@macmillan.com.

First Edition: 2024

Printed in the United States of America

0 9 8 7 6 5 4 3 2 1

FOUL DAYS

1

It was nearly midnight on New Year's Eve, but the city inside the Wall didn't celebrate. The people there knew the birth of a new year was— like any birth—difficult, painful, and dangerous.

Only one pub, nestled in the snowdrifts between Chernograd's tall spires, was open that night. It was packed but hushed. The patrons huddled close together, rubbing shoulders as they lifted their glasses. The corner table, hidden in a cloud of pipe smoke, was particularly quiet. It was Kosara's turn to bet, and she took her time.

Being the best at cards wouldn't be enough to win tonight: she had to be the best at cheating. And to cheat, she needed that damned fireplace to burn brighter.

"Well?" Roksana said, plum rakia dripping down her chin. It landed on the table, glistening in the dim electric lamplight like droplets of amber. The two golden beads tying her thick braids glinted, contrasting against her tanned skin. Her fingers drummed on the deck of cards, ready to deal. "Are you in?"

All three of them—Roksana, Malamir, and the stranger—had their eyes fixed on Kosara. *Don't let the corners of your mouth twitch. Don't swallow too loudly, don't rub the sweat off your palms on your trousers, try to calm down your heartbeat . . .*

"Give me a second," she said. "I'm thinking."

"For fuck's sake, Kosara!" Roksana slammed her tankard on the table. Several of the patrons at the other tables jumped. It was distressing seeing a woman her size lose her temper. "We haven't got all night."

Kosara didn't let Roksana's raised voice intimidate her. She could pretend all she wanted, but Kosara knew she wasn't truly angry. It was clear to her that Roksana's mind wasn't in the game at all. Her eyes kept darting to the clock, whose hands crept closer and closer to midnight.

"Shush, you old grump." Kosara looked down at her cards. *The queen of clubs,* she thought automatically, *a woman with black hair and black eyes. It must be me.* She also held a king of clubs and a five of diamonds. If only she could replace her five with an ace, she'd be holding the second-strongest combination in a game of Kral.

Kosara cast a glance towards the pile of logs in the fireplace. They'd been smouldering there for what felt like hours, occasionally hissing and sending a wisp of smoke into the air. She could gently encourage them, but was it worth the risk of getting caught?

For a long moment, the only sounds were the gramophone playing quietly in the corner and the soft gurgling of Roksana's pipe.

No risk, no gain. Kosara quietly clicked her fingers under the table. The fire cracked. Flames enveloped the logs.

She looked around. Roksana's eyelids were half-shut as she pulled on her pipe. She'd left the last few buttons of her shirt open, and her many evil-eye and brass-bell necklaces peeked from underneath. Malamir and the stranger were both preoccupied with their own thoughts, biting their lips, rearranging their cards, counting their tokens.

At Kosara's feet, her shadow grew larger, darker, and stronger from the light of the roaring flames. She did her best not to let her gaze follow it as it slid under the table.

"Oh my God!" Kosara said, her gaze fixed on the barred window: on the snow whirling outside, the searchlights piercing the sky, and beyond them, the shadow of the Wall. From a distance, it looked like granite, dark and solid. Close up, it resembled something alive— swirling and rippling, as if thousands of fingers tried to break through from the other side.

Any other day, her opponents would have seen right through Kosara's obvious distraction attempt. Tonight, their eyes immediately followed hers.

"Are they here already?" Roksana's fingers slowly drew out her pistol from its holster. It seemed strangely small in her large hand.

Malamir's leather trousers squeaked as he fidgeted in his seat. Kosara almost felt guilty when she saw the panic in his face. Almost.

"They can't be here," he mumbled. "It's too early."

The stranger kept pulling on his polka-dot neckerchief, as if he'd tied it too tightly. His eyes darted between the window and Roksana's pistol. His mouth hung half-open, as if a question was just about to roll out of it. In the end, he swallowed it hard.

Kosara's shadow extended one dark finger over the table's edge and flicked through the deck so quickly it was a blur, until it found the card it looked for. It disappeared back under the table.

"I can't see anything," Malamir said, his large eyes made even larger by the thick lenses of his glasses, blinking fast.

"No." Suspicion crept into Roksana's voice. "Me neither."

The shadow handed Kosara the ace under the table. She quickly swapped it for the five.

"Oh no, sorry." Kosara tried to sound genuinely nervous. She didn't have to pretend much. "I must have imagined it. Perhaps it was a stray cat."

Malamir gave her a pointed look over the golden rims of his glasses. She would have felt bad, if she wasn't certain he also cheated. As did the stranger: no one had that much luck. And if all of them were cheating, she reasoned, it was as if no one was.

"Sorry," she said again. "We're all a bit on edge tonight, aren't we?"

Roksana's pipe bobbed up and down in her mouth as she considered this. The smoke grew so thick it made Kosara's eyes water. The air seeped with the stench of spilled beer, full ashtrays, and too many people in too tight a space, but beneath that floated the sweet odour of seer's sage. Kosara would recognise it anywhere—a potent sedative she used in all her potions for good dreams. It came in wafts every time Roksana pulled on her pipe, sliding into Kosara's nostrils and making her eyelids heavy.

She would have called Roksana on trying to put them all to sleep, but she knew better than to argue with the dealer.

"Should we get back to the game, then?" Kosara gave her a winning smile.

Roksana sighed and returned the pistol to its holster. "You never told me if you're in."

"I'm in."

"Wasn't that difficult, was it? Malamir?"

"It's getting late." Malamir's watch slid between his trembling fingers and swung on its chain. Kosara felt a strong compulsion to double her bet.

Would you look at that! A hypnotising watch. Kosara had never seen one of those in the wild before.

"Where did you get that from?" she asked.

Malamir grinned, his white teeth glinting. "My watch? It's nice, isn't it? I won it at cards."

No wonder the old rascal was doing so well. If he hadn't already given up, Kosara would have gladly ratted him out to Roksana. As it was, she stashed this information in case it came in handy later.

"Alright," Roksana said. "And what about you, mister . . ."

"My name isn't important," said the stranger.

Kosara rolled her eyes. He was trying *way* too hard with the "dark and mysterious" act. He didn't utter a word unless it was to raise the bet. When he wasn't inspecting his cards, he stared at Kosara, as if he waited for her to do something. As if he'd never seen a witch before.

"So, Mr. My-name-isn't-important." Roksana chuckled at her own joke. "Are you in?"

"I might be in." The stranger twisted the knot of his neckerchief. The toes of his red brogues tapped on the dusty floor. "I might be in, if we make things a bit more interesting."

Kosara looked down at her pile of tokens. She'd done well tonight. The silver ones were enough for her to eat like a queen for a month. With the bronze ones she could buy that dress she'd spotted in the tailor's window: velvet and black as midnight. With the iron tokens she'd order everyone in the pub a drink tomorrow—to celebrate, if they survived tonight.

She scratched the scar on her cheek, three raised scrapes. Every self-respecting witch had a few battle scars. "How much?"

"I don't want your money," said the stranger.

"What do you want, then?"

Slowly, he untied his neckerchief. Roksana whistled.

On a thin chain around the stranger's neck hung a string of black beads. He brushed them with his palm, and they trembled like candle flames in the wind.

Kosara bit her lip hard, almost to blood. The stranger wore a necklace of witches' shadows.

"I want your shadow," he said.

Through the haze of seer's sage smoke and alcohol, Kosara felt the sharp sting of alarm. She shook her head so quickly, her hair hit her across the face. "No. I can't."

"Think about it. You'll bet one shadow. I'm offering you"—he weighed them in his hand—"eleven. It's a good deal."

"I'm a witch. Without my shadow, I'm nothing."

"You're a mediocre witch. I'm offering you true power."

A mediocre witch. She'd be offended if it wasn't true. She could heat up her coffee with a snap of her fingers and ask her shadow to fetch her coat. On a good day, she could conjure a firework or two. Parlour tricks.

If she won, she'd become a real witch, like the ones from the old fairy tales. She'd pay all the inns, cafes, and restaurants with alchemists' gold. She'd weave herself a dress from moonlight. She'd turn the river into wine and give the entire city a free drink.

But if she lost . . .

Everyone knew what happened to witches who'd lost their shadows: they slowly turned into shadows themselves. It could take years or even decades, but it was unavoidable. Was it worth betting her corporeal body for the possibility of almost unlimited power?

"Come on, Kosara," said the stranger. "Just think what you could do with so much magic. You could cross the Wall and escape this cursed city. Wouldn't that be wonderful?"

Kosara chewed on her lip. The stranger had read her completely wrong. She didn't want to cross the Wall, which—she was aware—made her a minority in Chernograd. She couldn't leave her city to be ravaged by its monsters while she lived happily ever after on the other side.

No, what she truly wanted was for the monsters to be dealt with, once and for all. And with such power, she could finally achieve that.

"Don't do anything stupid, doll." Malamir's horrified eyes searched hers.

"No risk"—Roksana shot a cloud of smoke at her—"no gain."

"Well?" said the stranger. "I've been told you can't resist a good gamble."

"Who told you that?" Kosara asked.

"One of your friends."

Kosara raised her eyebrows at Roksana and Malamir. She would hardly call them "friends." More like good acquaintances.

Roksana smirked, her face half-hidden behind a curtain of smoke. "Wasn't me."

"Me neither," Malamir said quickly. "I'd never."

"How many years have we known each other?" Roksana asked. "I've never said a bad word about you."

"Me neither," added Malamir. "Never."

Kosara let out a puff of air through her nostrils. *Dirty liars.* They were lucky she liked them.

She looked down at her cards, blurring slightly in her trembling fingers. Her hand was nearly unbeatable. The only way the stranger could win was if he held a queen, a king, and an ace of spades.

Kosara had bet on much worse chances before, but she'd never bet anything so precious.

"Come on, Kosara," the stranger said again.

He wouldn't give up easily. A witch's shadow couldn't be stolen—it had to be given willingly. He'd already convinced eleven other witches to give him theirs.

Kosara downed her glass of plum rakia in one go. It burned her tongue and seared her throat, but it did nothing to calm her nerves.

"Kosara, doll." Malamir rested a hand on her shoulder. She didn't look at him. In the corner of her eye, she saw his hypnotising watch swinging in the dark hollows of his coat. "I really don't think this is a smart—"

"Stop pestering her, for fuck's sake," Roksana snapped. "It's her decision. Our Kosara knows what she's doing."

Do I? Kosara struggled to keep her hands steady. Her heart thumped in her ears, fast and loud. So loud, she almost didn't hear the chiming of the clock.

It was midnight.

For a bizarre second, Kosara felt relieved—she didn't need to decide tonight. Then her heart beat even louder. It was midnight.

"Well?" said the stranger. "What do you say?"

Kosara gave him a grim look. "We'll have to continue the game some other time."

"Why?"

"It's midnight."

"So?"

He had to be joking. There was no way he didn't know.

"What's the matter? What's going on?"

Kosara nodded towards the window. At first, it was quiet. The only noise was the distant hissing and popping of fireworks on the other side of the Wall. Chernograd slept under its blanket of snow.

Then the nightmare began.

The spotlights grew brighter, moving faster and faster, frantically searching the black sky. A siren sounded, so loud even the curtain of snow couldn't dampen its wails.

The monsters descended on the walled city. High in the sky, their oily wings glistened in the moonlight, and their eyes shone like lanterns. As they landed, their curved talons screeched against the cobblestones.

Kosara quickly patted her trousers' pockets, to make sure all her talismans were ready. There was one she itched to try, crafted from a rabbit's paw and a cockerel's comb—it would choke anyone or anything who tried to land a hand on her.

Let them come. Her eyes were fixed on the window. The streetlights flickered, revealing and hiding the dark shadows of the monsters. *Let them come.*

There was a scratch at the door and a low purr.

"Is that a stray cat?" the stranger asked, the words tumbling out fast. "Please tell me that's just a—"

The purr grew into a growl. Something heavy slammed against the door. The hinges creaked, straining under the pressure. Talons slashed at the wood, sinking deep enough for their sharp tips to protrude on the other side.

Malamir crossed himself. Roksana cocked her gun.

"What the hell is that?" the stranger shouted.

Kosara's fingers gripped the talisman in her pocket, the magic words ready on her lips. If the ward she'd drawn in front of the door didn't work . . .

A loud shriek sounded, as if from an animal that had been badly burned.

Kosara smiled. The ward had done its job. That had been its first test tonight, undoubtedly the first of many. She tiptoed closer to the window, careful to stay hidden behind the curtain.

Several furry figures dashed across the street, leaving deep tracks in the fresh snow. One could mistake them for children in the dark— that was how small they were—if it wasn't for their teeth the size of daggers. As they ran past the milliner's, all the mirrors in the shop window shattered.

"Karakonjuls," she said when she returned to her seat. "They're gone now. They must have smelled easier prey elsewhere."

"*Kara*-what?" the stranger asked. "What are those? Some kind of feral dogs?"

Roksana laughed loudly, her golden tooth glinting. "Where have you seen a horned, blood-sucking dog? The varkolaks are the dogs."

"No, they're not," Kosara snapped. "The varkolaks transform into *wolves*. Christ, Roksana, you're a monster hunter, you should know that."

Another loud noise came from outside. The stranger jumped. "And what was that?"

Something thumped on the roof, making the light swing. Dust rained from the ceiling.

"A yuda, most likely," Kosara said. "They sometimes nest on the roofs." The stranger still looked petrified, so she added, "Nothing to worry about, unless you hear them calling your name."

"Why?"

"It means you'll die. Didn't you receive your educational pamphlet?"

"My what?"

Simply unbelievable. The Witch and Warlock Association released one every year, containing detailed information on the different types of monsters and how to fight them. Kosara had spent hours licking all the envelopes shut before they got sent out to every household in Chernograd.

Yet, year after year, she discovered that no one bothered to read them.

Chernograd would never get rid of its monsters if it kept refusing to listen to its witches. Yes, it was much easier to buy an "anti-monster" necklace from a charlatan than to carve aspen stakes and distil holy water, but the difference was, the latter worked, while the former didn't.

The stranger swallowed, his Adam's apple bouncing. "Wait, you're trying to tell me that there's some kind of large prophetic bird—"

"Half woman, half bird." Kosara listened. Actually, it didn't sound much like a yuda. It seemed to be hooves, rather than talons, drumming on the roof tiles. "Or it could be a samodiva. They like riding those damned gold-horned deer of theirs all over the place."

That last sentence, she had to shout. The barkeep banged on the ceiling with the handle of his rifle until whatever had landed there flew away.

The stranger looked around, as if he couldn't believe no one else was making the sort of scene he was. The other patrons kept drinking in silence.

"What the hell is a samodiva?" he asked.

"Beautiful women who force you to dance with them," Kosara said.

"That doesn't sound that bad."

"Until you die from exhaustion."

"Oh." A drop of sweat rolled down the stranger's forehead and landed in his eye. He blinked fast. "But why? Why are all the monsters here?"

Roksana laughed. "It's New Year's Eve, in case you haven't noticed."

"What does that have to do with it?"

"The Foul Days have begun," Malamir said gravely, as if reciting from some ancient tome. He'd had a brief stint as an actor back in the day, and he'd never shaken off his taste for the dramatic. "The New Year was born, but it hasn't been baptised yet. The monsters roam the streets freely."

Kosara narrowed her eyes at the stranger. "You've never heard of these monsters before? Really?"

"I have," the stranger said. "Of course I have. But I didn't realise they just fell down from the sky like that. Like, like, the world's sharpest-toothed hailstorm."

"Not all of them do," Kosara said. "Those are the intruders. The karakonjuls, the samodivas, the yudas . . . Oh, and the rusalkas."

"The rusalkas?"

"Fish people," Roksana supplied.

"Not quite," Kosara said. "But close enough."

"Right," the stranger said. "So those are the intruders."

Malamir continued in his grave tone, "They are only allowed to come here during the Foul Days, when the boundary between our world and theirs is hair-thin."

"And the rest?" asked the stranger.

"The rest are our homegrown monsters," Kosara said. "They simply become more active during the Foul Days—and more powerful. All the upirs rise from their graves, all the wraiths wake up, all the varkolaks transform into wolves . . ."

"I don't know how you manage to keep them all straight."

"It's quite easy, really." Kosara squinted at the stranger. This went way beyond educational pamphlets. Had he slept through every New Year's Eve? "I can't believe you don't know any of this."

"I'd heard rumours, of course, but I'd assumed you people were all exaggerating. You're known for being superstitious folk. No offence."

You'd be superstitious too if it was a matter of life and death.
Knowing your amulets from your talismans could save your skin in
a monster attack.

Then Kosara realised what the stranger had said. *You people . . .*

"You're from the other side of the Wall, aren't you?" she asked.
When the stranger remained silent, she knew she was right.

Now that she thought about it, he obviously wasn't a local. He
seemed older than her, maybe mid-thirties, but his skin was smooth
and unscarred. He wore a light coat—in the middle of winter! Instead
of boots, he had on a pair of suede brogues. His feet would freeze in
the snow outside.

Poor bastard. Of all days, he'd decided to come to Chernograd on
New Year's Eve. He was either very brave or completely clueless. Judging by what she'd seen so far, Kosara would bet on clueless.

"The other side of the Wall?" Malamir pushed his glasses up his
nose with one long index finger. "How did you get here?"

"That's none of your business," the stranger snapped.

Kosara measured him with her eyes. *How, indeed?* How had the
clueless foreigner ended up on this side of the Wall, with eleven witches'
shadows tied around his neck?

Crossing the Wall was dangerous. Its tentacles slashed at the air
high above it, preventing anyone from flying over. Its roots sank deep
into the ground, stopping anyone from burrowing under.

But dangerous didn't mean impossible. There were amulets that
could teleport you across, and talismans which protected you from
the Wall's wrath. Neither came cheap. Kosara knew several people
who'd traded everything they owned to escape Chernograd.

The rich crossed the Wall all the time, she'd heard, coming back
with silk-woven foreign clothes and strange-smelling imported alcohol to serve at their exclusive parties. Kosara had little chance to
encounter "the rich" to ask them. They were about as rare in Chernograd as a sober man on a Friday night.

She'd never met anyone, however, who'd crossed the Wall in the
opposite direction. Someone from Belograd.

The Belogradeans were all cowards. That was why they'd built the

Wall in the first place: to keep the monsters out of their precious city. The people they'd trapped with them be damned.

In fact, Kosara suspected the Belogradeans saw it as a bonus. What better way for rich Belograd to get rid of its poor neighbours once and for all? For them, Chernograd was a cancerous growth that needed to be isolated before it could infect the rest of the world.

The stranger shifted in his seat. "So, what are you going to do?"

Kosara shrugged. "What we do every New Year's Eve. We'll sit tight and wait for it to pass."

"We'll do our best to survive," Malamir said.

Roksana raised her glass in the air. "Personally, I intend to get absolutely plastered."

"As I said"—Kosara flashed her a quick look—"what we do every New Year's Eve."

"For how long?" the stranger asked.

"Until the first rooster's crow on Saint Yordan's Day," Malamir said. "Saint Yordan the Baptist."

"Twelve days," Kosara added since the stranger still seemed confused.

"Twelve days!" The stranger's voice grew higher and higher pitched. "You mean to tell me that for the next twelve days monsters will roam the streets and you'll just sit here and drink?"

"It's as good a place to barricade in as any," Kosara said. "Plenty of bedrolls, tinned food, bright lights to keep the yudas away, garlic to scare off the upirs."

"Plenty of booze," Roksana added.

The stranger looked around the pub. "You're all insane! How can you be so calm?"

Believe me, I'm anything but. Kosara was pleasantly surprised the stranger couldn't hear the thumping of her heart.

Roksana patted the stranger on the shoulder, making him stagger. "You'll get used to it soon enough."

"I really don't think I will."

"You'll be fine," Kosara said. "We'll all be fine."

Yes, the monsters were terrifying, but they weren't unbeatable.

They all had their weaknesses: karakonjuls hated riddles they couldn't answer, yudas couldn't stand to see their own image in the mirror, samodivas were easily distracted by music. It came down to knowing what those weaknesses were, and no one knew monsters better than a witch. Kosara had a talisman ready for any possible turn of events, any possible enemy . . .

Any, except for one. One of the monsters couldn't be defeated, as she knew from painful experience. One of them made shivers run down her spine and cold sweat break on her skin, and she'd be glad to never see him again—

"Is this all the monsters, then?" the stranger asked, his fist still tight around his neckerchief. He must have seen something in Kosara's face. "Have all of them come?"

"No," Kosara said. "That's not all of them."

"Why, what's left?"

"*Who's* left." Kosara took a deep breath. How ridiculous that she couldn't even utter his name without bracing herself first. As if by simply saying it, she might summon him. "The Zmey. The Tsar of Monsters."

She couldn't stop herself from glancing out the window, half-expecting to see his pale face framed by the dark street.

He wasn't there. Of course he wasn't there yet. The Zmey always arrived last.

Sometimes, Kosara wondered if he did it just to torture her. If he waited a tad longer each year because he knew she'd let herself hope that, maybe this time, he wouldn't come.

But surely, the Tsar of Monsters had more important things to do than to torture her?

"What's so special about him?" the stranger asked. "That Zmey of yours? Is he the biggest and most monstrous of them all?" He giggled nervously.

I'm glad you're finding the humour in the situation, Belogradean.

"No." Kosara gripped the talisman in her pocket even tighter. "He's the most human."

2

Earlier that day, Kosara took out a lock of the Zmey's hair, carefully pressed between two sheets of paper in an old spell book. She'd kept it on her bedside table all year, worried that if she let it out of her sight for too long, it might disappear.

It hadn't been easy to obtain. Kosara and the Zmey had developed an annual ritual in the last seven years, ever since she'd left his palace. Every year, she did her best to avoid him. Every year, he found her. He'd smile his handsome smile and ask in his sweetest voice, "How about a game of cards?"

The wager? A lock of hair.

It wasn't simply a sentimental keepsake. For a witch, a lock of hair had power. It meant that if she won, Kosara would finally have a weapon she could use against him. Not strong enough to hurt him, but perhaps strong enough to keep him away.

Which was why the Zmey enjoyed the game so much. He always won—until last year.

Kosara walked downstairs to the kitchen and hung her cauldron over the hearth. The room was aglow with the light of the fire, reflecting in the copper pots and pans hanging on the walls. The brighter it grew, the darker the shadows became, her own swirling and whirling around them.

Sweat beaded on Kosara's skin, the droplets mirroring the flames, as if she were covered in hundreds of small fires. She'd stripped down to her underwear, and her chemise clung to her wet skin. Instead of subduing the hearth, she stoked it. She needed all the power she could get.

It wasn't as if anyone else was around to complain about the heat. Kosara lived alone.

There was a loud bang from one of the upstairs bedrooms.

It wasn't as if anyone else *alive* was around, Kosara corrected herself. The ghost of her sister haunted a bedroom upstairs.

A few more bangs followed. Strange, Nevena wasn't this active usually. Perhaps she could feel the heat after all, or the magic Kosara wielded.

"Nevena!" Kosara shouted. "Will you please stop it? I'm trying to concentrate."

The banging continued. Kosara sighed. No point trying to reason with kikimoras.

First, Kosara fished inside a bucket of salty water for two rusalka ink sacs. She pierced them with her knife, letting the dark liquid drip into the cauldron, hissing as it hit the copper surface.

Then, she rummaged for the rest of the ingredients among the many jars and bottles scattered around the kitchen. Aspen tree sap served as a binder, a rusty nail used to kill a karakonjul as a mordant, thyme oil and soda ash as preservatives. Finally, she threw the lock of the Zmey's hair into the cauldron.

The mixture came to a boil fast, large bubbles rising to the surface and popping, splattering the walls with sticky black liquid.

As she watched it, Kosara wondered if she was making a mistake. What if her attempt to keep the Zmey away angered him too much?

He'd told her before that if she ever tried to defy him again, he'd take more than a lock of her hair. He'd take her. He'd force her back under his control. He liked her knowing that her freedom was conditional on his goodwill.

No, she decided. She was toeing the line, but she wasn't crossing it. He'd see this as a challenge—a part of their game of cat and mouse. Next year, he'd arrive prepared to fight her spell, but by then, Kosara would have devised a different one to throw at him.

Or maybe her spell wouldn't be strong enough to stop him. He'd laugh that annoyingly pleasant laugh of his, like hundreds of chiming bells, and then she'd have to sit through another card game. She'd squirm under his icy stare for hours, as he threw stronger and stronger cards on the table. Finally, she'd chop off a lock of hair to give him, and the missing chunk would remind her of him whenever she looked at herself in the mirror.

Kosara sighed. She had to make sure her spell would hold. She'd spent all year preparing it: a ward strong enough to keep the Zmey out. She'd read every book on the subject she could get her hands on. She'd practised all the runes. It *would* hold.

Unless someone invited the Zmey in, that was. But who would do that?

At last, Kosara took the cauldron off the fire and emptied the liquid into a glass vial. She wiped her forehead with the back of her hand. Then, she put out the fire with a click of her fingers.

The kitchen went dark, only the flickering of the gas lamps remained. The cold from outside immediately began to seep through the walls.

Kosara got dressed: black woollen trousers, a warm sweater, her long coat, leather boots she'd worn so often the soles were starting to rub through. She couldn't do the spell in her house—it would be the first place the Zmey would look for her after he arrived at midnight.

"Bye, Nevena!" Kosara shouted.

The ghost remained silent. Sometimes, Kosara wondered if Nevena could even understand her.

Most ghosts were little different from the people they'd been while still alive. But Nevena wasn't like most ghosts. She was a kikimora: a wraith who rose from the blood spilled after a murder. All that was left of the sister Kosara remembered was her pain and her anger.

Kosara sighed and opened the front door. She braced herself against the winter wind, burying her chin in the neckline of her sweater. After the warmth of the kitchen, stepping outside felt like diving into a cold swimming pool.

She stumbled through the muddy snowdrifts, past dark houses and snow-covered gardens, gripping the vial of inky liquid in her pocket. Her bag hung heavy on her shoulder, filled with notes and sketches copied from spell books.

Granite spires rose high above, icicles hanging off their elaborately carved buttresses. Their grand shapes were a reminder of Chernograd's more prosperous past before the Wall was built. Now, their stonework was black with dirt and soot, and their arches were crumbling.

In the distance, magic factories coughed dark smoke out of their long chimneys, contrasting against the white streets and the pale sky. Most of them manufactured medicine, cosmetics, or perfumes for export over the Wall to Belograd. Ironically, few in Chernograd could afford their products.

People in dark clothes passed Kosara, their grim faces peeking over ugly hand-knitted scarves and even uglier hand-knitted jumpers. Their coats were more like patchwork blankets, sewn together so they'd last another winter. Occasionally, a horse-drawn carriage flew past, spraying muddy water over the pavements. The swearing of the now-soaked pedestrians was drowned out by the drumming of the horse's hooves.

Kosara elbowed her way through the crowds gathered in front of the Main Street shops. It was the last day of the year: the last chance to stock up on holy water and aspen stakes in peace, to melt any remaining family heirlooms into silver bullets, to hire a witch to draw a protective ward around the house's doors and windows. Customers and merchants bargained quietly, in tense whispers, as if shouting would break whatever fragile peace they still had until midnight. Some of them clutched steaming cups of coffee, brown and thick as mud, and others were already well into their wine, their breath coming out in pungent plumes.

Finally, Kosara reached the pub. The barkeep, Bayan, waited for her in front of it, only a thin sliver of his face visible between his karakonjul fur hat and his scarf. He narrowed his eyes at her in question.

Kosara nodded at him, and he unlocked the door.

She went to her knees on the icy ground. Then, she unscrewed the lid from her vial, dipped her finger in it, and began drawing.

"Kosara!" a familiar voice called outside the bar, just after midnight. He didn't shout, but his words nevertheless carried over the wind's howling, the monsters' cries, and the people's screams. "Kosara!"

The blood rushed to Kosara's head. Her nails left crescents in the soft skin of her palms.

He was here already. How the hell had he found her so fast?

She looked down at the ward she'd drawn. Half of it was visible on the floor inside, arching around the door and windows: a series of runes drawn in black ink. The other half was outside. If Kosara had done her job right, no amount of snow or hail or rubbing of shoes would erase it for the next twelve days.

She'd hoped to have an hour or two to test it on lesser monsters, like the karakonjuls. To recharge it if needed, or maybe try a different recipe if this one proved too weak—but the Zmey was here already.

"Kosara!" His voice came closer and closer. It sent shivers down her spine.

Calm down, for God's sake. It would be the same as every year. He'd come, he'd make her feel small, weak, and helpless, and then he'd leave.

But, for some reason, this time it felt different. There was something in his voice—something she hadn't heard in a long time. Something taut like a guitar string.

Anger.

"Kosara!"

His shadow ran past the window. He wiped the frost away with his palm and peeked inside.

His eyes were the bright blue only found in the centre of a flame, and his hair was like molten gold. When his gaze fell on the mirror above the bar, it shattered.

"Here you are."

The doorknob rattled.

Kosara inhaled sharply. She watched, petrified, as the lines of her ward twisted and strained under the pressure, but they didn't break. For now.

After a few long seconds, the doorknob fell still. Kosara didn't dare exhale yet. The Zmey hit the door with his shoulder.

The ward blurred as if it barely held itself together. As if any minute, its runes would melt and leak between the floorboards like dirty rainwater disappearing down the gutter.

Kosara couldn't take her eyes off it. Her body was glued to the chair. Her movements were sluggish, the air thick as treacle.

The Zmey hit the door again. The ward kept shifting on the floor. But it didn't break.

It didn't break.

Kosara let out a tiny sigh of relief. The ward was holding. She looked around the pub: at the confused faces of the patrons, at her nervous companions around the table, and at Bayan the barkeep, who gave her a thumbs-up.

After a while, the Zmey stopped banging on the door. There was a long, silent moment.

And then he laughed. Kosara shrank in her seat, his voice ringing in her ears.

"Good one, my little Kosara. Good one."

"I'm not little," Kosara spat out, mostly to check if she still had her voice. "And I'm not yours. What do you want?"

"How about you invite me in? It's awfully cold out here." He let his voice tremble, as if from a shiver. Kosara didn't believe him for a second. She's seen how the snowflakes landing on his skin evaporated with a hiss.

"What do you want?" Kosara repeated, careful to keep her voice steady. She was a witch. Witches weren't afraid of monsters.

A useless witch. The voice in her mind sounded an awful lot like the Zmey's. *A weak witch. You're nothing without me, Kosara.*

The real Zmey, the one outside her mind, laughed again. As if they were simply two friends sharing a joke. "I'd like you to explain why you'd ever think it was a good idea to cheat me."

Kosara's mouth filled with the metallic taste of blood.

He knew. Dear God, he knew.

Of course she'd cheated him at cards last year—she'd never have won otherwise—but she'd taken every precaution to make sure he wouldn't catch her. And he hadn't, not until a year later.

Kosara hadn't told anybody she'd cheated. At least, she was fairly certain she hadn't. She did have the tendency to run her mouth when she'd had a bit too much to drink, but she wouldn't have told anyone *that*. Would she?

She cast a glance at Malamir, playing with the ends of his sleeves, and at Roksana, pulling on her pipe quickly, letting out cloud after cloud of sweet-smelling smoke.

"Who told you?" Kosara asked the Zmey, the talisman hot and heavy in her hand. If he uttered one of their names, she wouldn't hesitate. She'd use it against them.

"Nobody needed to tell me, my dear Kosara. I'm the Tsar of Monsters, remember? I know everything that happens in my city."

This city isn't yours.

Kosara loosened her grip around the talisman. Perhaps the Zmey was telling the truth. Perhaps she hadn't been as smooth as she'd thought last year. It wouldn't be the first time.

"Come on, you cheating hag." The Zmey raised his voice. He was losing his patience. "Invite me in."

The other patrons watched Kosara and waited for her next move, mild curiosity on their faces, as if this was nothing but a play at the theatre. After all, it wasn't them who'd angered the Zmey. He wasn't like the other monsters, hungry for human flesh and blinded by bloodthirst. He wouldn't bother them if they stayed out of his way.

"Very well," the Zmey said once it became obvious Kosara had no intention of getting up from her seat. "Since Kosara here is being so rude, will one of you good people please invite me in?"

The other patrons' murmurs filled the pub. Their eyes pierced Kosara. She wrapped her arms around herself, as if appearing as small as she could might turn her invisible.

"You, Stamen!" the Zmey shouted towards a large man sitting next to the fire. "How come you're all alone? Where's the wife?"

Stamen's fingers gripped his glass so hard, Kosara was worried he'd break it. His mouth was a small, trembling *o*.

"Wait, let me guess," said the Zmey. "You had another fight, didn't you? She's staying with her sister. The house on Iglika Street with the roses on the balcony? Maybe I'll pay her a visit later. Unless you'd like to invite me in?"

Stamen looked at Kosara. His fingernails dragged along the chair's armrest as he tried to pull himself up.

"No, wait, Stamen . . ." Kosara began, but she didn't know how to finish the sentence. She couldn't threaten him—she had some semblance of morals.

How had she not even considered that this might happen? She'd assumed the other people in the pub would be as desperate to keep the Zmey out as she was. Except, the rest of them didn't know what he was capable of. Kosara was the only one in all of Chernograd who knew him.

The only one he'd left alive, anyway.

"You stay right where you are," Bayan growled at Stamen. "I don't want him in my pub."

Stamen staggered in his place, his eyes fixed on the rifle in Bayan's hand. Kosara flashed Bayan a grateful smile. He didn't return it.

Roksana leaned closer, the smell of her pipe smoke surrounding Kosara like a sticky, dizzying cloud. "Maybe you should open that door before the Zmey hurts someone."

Kosara turned to her, startled. "If I open that door, he'll hurt *me*."

"No, he won't. You know him. He cares about you."

"The Zmey cares about nobody but himself, Roksana."

Roksana shrugged and leaned back in her chair, her fingers casually resting on the handle of her pistol.

"You don't understand," Kosara said. "He's angry with me. You've never been around when he's been angry with me."

"Why, what would he do?"

Kosara's fingers automatically brushed her neck. Her bruises had long healed, but she still felt the Zmey's ghostly touch there. "He'll take me back to his palace."

"Surely he wouldn't do it against your w—"

"He would."

Finally, Roksana fell silent.

"And what about you, Maria?" This time, the Zmey addressed a woman knitting in the corner. The clicking of her needles immediately stopped. "Your little girl is at her dad's tonight, isn't she? I'd bet your ex was too cheap to pay for proper wards. After all, that's why you left him . . ."

Maria shot up from her seat. "Don't you dare—"

"What was that? You're going to invite me in?"

The barkeep held onto Maria's forearm to stop her from going to the door. Good old Bayan, Kosara knew she could rely on him—

He turned to Kosara, gripping his rifle. "You have sixty seconds to get out."

Goddamnit.

"To get out?" She tried for a disarming smile, but her face was too tense. She must have looked like she bared her teeth at him. "Come on now, Bayan, you can't throw me out to the dogs like that."

"Fifty-nine, fifty-eight, fifty-seven—"

"Bayan, *please*—"

"Bayan," came a voice from a nearby table. "You can't do this." Kosara recognised a young woman who'd recently applied to be her apprentice. Kosara had turned her down—she was a mediocre witch. What could she possibly teach a student?

To Kosara's surprise, several other voices from the nearby tables rose in agreement.

"The girl's right," said Sava the baker, standing up from his seat and crossing his large arms in front of his chest. "You can't."

"This is none of your concern," Bayan barked. "It's not your business he's going to set on fire."

"You agreed to give us all refuge here." Sava took a step forwards. Kosara frantically gestured at him to sit back down. He was a big man and might have looked intimidating, but the only reason he could stand up on his dodgy knees was the poultice Kosara brewed him every week. He'd be helpless in a fight.

Bayan considered him over the barrel of his rifle. "The circumstances have changed." And then he added, stressing each word, "Fifty-six, fifty-five, fifty-four—"

The stranger coughed in his fist. Kosara jumped. She'd almost forgotten he was there.

"I believe I can help," he said.

"How?"

"I can take you beyond the Wall. He'll never get you there. But it will cost you."

"How much?"

"I think you know."

My shadow.

Kosara's first instinct was to refuse. She couldn't leave Chernograd. Every year, there were fewer and fewer witches willing to fight the monsters. It was a profession with a rather high death rate.

Besides, the people here needed her to protect them from the Zmey. She *knew* him. Whenever he was about to strike a particular neighbourhood, she was always there first, evacuating the people and the animals. Whenever he'd set his eyes on yet another young girl, Kosara was the one who warned her family to be careful.

Not that it always worked.

"—forty-six, forty-five—"

She also couldn't leave Nevena. Whatever small part of her sister was still left, it was here. She'd be so lonely without Kosara.

"—forty-two, forty-one—"

And to lose her shadow? She'd die without it. She'd spend a few years or decades as a useless, defenceless witch, and then, she'd fade into a shadow herself.

"—thirty-nine, thirty-eight—"

On the other hand, if the Zmey got her, she was as good as dead. She couldn't go back to his palace. Never again.

"Kosara, don't—" Malamir started.

"Leave her alone," Roksana snapped. "It's her decision."

Kosara squeezed her eyes so hard, colourful spots danced in front of her vision. She could still see the Zmey's teeth, sharp like a dog's, bared in a smile. She could smell the sulphur on his breath, coming out in clouds in the frigid night. She could feel his fingers, always scalding hot, wrapped around her neck, squeezing and not letting go, no matter how much she pleaded.

Her vision would get blurry, every breath would burn, and one thought would shine bright in her half-conscious mind: *I'm going to die.*

Kosara looked down at her shadow. *Don't,* screamed a desperate little voice in her mind, *you'll regret it.*

But there was also the other voice, the one stuck on repeat: *I'm going to die, I'm going to die, I'm going to die—*

Her city would have to do without her. She was probably giving herself too much credit, anyway—Chernograd was a survivor. The absence of a single witch wouldn't be enough to crush it.

And Nevena? Nevena was dead.

"—twenty-nine, twenty-eight, twenty-seven—"

Kosara grabbed her shadow in her fist. At first it tried to fight, twisting and turning and sliding between her fingers. Then it fell still. She rolled it in her palms until it was small and black like a jet bead.

Without giving herself enough time to hesitate, she placed it in the stranger's open hand. As soon as her fingers let go of it, something pulled on her navel, so abruptly she nearly fell. She stood in the middle of the room, surrounded by light. When she lifted her arm, on the wall behind her, her shadow didn't raise its arm in reply.

What. Have. I. Done.

She'd done what she had to do.

"—seventeen, sixteen, fifteen—"

The Zmey slammed his fists against the door. "If you don't let me in *right now,* you'll all regret it."

The stranger threw his neckerchief in her face. "Tie it over your eyes."

It felt like it took her hours, with her hands shaking so badly.

"I'll put something on your foot," he said. Her left boot came off. The cold air tickled her toes. "Give me your hands." He grabbed them between his palms and dragged her after him, turning and kicking her heels, as if in a peculiar dance. Then he mumbled something. A spell?

"—five, four, three—"

It suddenly hit her: she was leaving Chernograd. *Wait!* She wanted to shout. *I'm not ready! I've changed my mind!*

Too late.

Her body shook. Her ears rang. For a second, she hung in the air, weightless. Then, her feet crashed against the hard ground. A warm breeze hit her face. It smelled like imported spices and exotic flowers, like distant winds and sea salt.

Belograd.

The stranger lifted her left foot up in the air and slid off the amulet he'd put there. Kosara leaned on his shoulder so she wouldn't lose her balance. One second, his hand was around her waist, and then he took a step back. Kosara staggered, disoriented with her eyes covered, but managed not to fall.

"Can I take it off now?" she asked, and without waiting for an answer, she pulled the neckerchief off her eyes with twitching fingers.

Her left boot rested next to her on the white cobblestones. The stranger was gone.

In the sky above, fireworks flashed. The beating drums were deafening. Laughing people in bright clothes pushed against Kosara.

She could feel the absence of her shadow at her completely nonmagical fingertips.

What have I done. . . .

Kosara stumbled backwards until her body hit something hard. A wall. The stones were wet and cold against her back. She leaned on them, shut her eyes, and breathed deeply until her heart stopped leaping like a frightened bunny.

This had been a terrible mistake. This city, it felt all wrong. It even smelled wrong. She didn't belong here. She was a witch—she belonged in Chernograd.

Though could she even call herself a "witch" now that she'd traded her magic away?

If only she hadn't been such a coward. If only she'd found the strength to face the Zmey. Tears prickled behind her shut eyelids.

Get a grip of yourself, she thought sternly. The last thing she needed was to show weakness in front of this new, strange city.

She was a witch and she'd fought countless monsters. She could handle Belograd, even without her magic. It wasn't as if she was planning on staying long, anyway.

She'd made a snap decision in a moment of desperation, but it had worked, hadn't it? She'd escaped the Zmey. All she had to do now was to find the stranger again and get him to bring her back to Chernograd. She'd convince him to give her magic back. The *how* was still a bit fuzzy, but there had to be something he'd trade for it.

And if he refused? She'd steal it. Years of cheating at cards had given her very nimble fingers.

Then, she'd hide from the Zmey until the Foul Days were over. She'd have a year to figure out how to face him.

Yes, because hiding from him worked so well this time, a little voice chimed in her mind.

Shut up, she thought at it.

Her eyes flew open. She let the bright lights of Belograd rush back into her vision. The crowd pushed past her like a stream. Their loud voices grated in her ears. Their heavy perfumes made her head spin.

Someone shoved a glass of mulled wine in her hands and shouted, "Happy New Year!"

3

Day One

As Kosara pushed her way through the crowd, shiny shoes stepped on her feet and elbows draped in silk shoved her. Occasionally, a stranger grabbed her by the hand and tried to drag her into a dance. They screamed at her—congratulations for New Year's Eve, most likely—but she couldn't hear them over the incessant crackle and pop of the fireworks. Their faces lit up in different colours: blue, green, purple, blue again, green . . .

I'd rather fight an army of karakonjuls than this.

Her adrenaline was starting to recede, and all of a sudden, she was freezing. The wind cut straight through her shirt and burrowed deep into her bones. She mumbled a spell and clapped her hands, fully expecting a flame to appear between them and warm her fingers. When nothing happened, she swore under her breath.

Right. She'd traded her magic away.

Thankfully, no one spotted her clapping like a madwoman. Kosara felt terribly conspicuous already—with her black clothes, she was the only dark spot around. The local fashion was for bright colours and embroideries, beads and pearls and precious stones. She found it difficult not to stare.

How come none of these clothes ever made it over the Wall? Chernograd imported most of its fabrics from Belograd. Did the Belogradeans send over only their ugliest products on purpose?

Kosara kept walking, her neck getting sore from looking around. It was like being in a parallel version of Chernograd. The houses were built in the same style, with tall windows and pointed roofs, but rather than covered in dirt and soot, they shone, freshly plastered and brightly painted. The cobblestones were so clean they gleamed. The people seemed so *happy*. Which most likely tied back to the biggest difference: there were no monsters.

It felt . . . off. Kosara had never experienced a New Year's Eve which didn't end in a monster invasion.

She had to admit, it was a relief not having to check every dark corner for a lurking karakonjul, or to occasionally stop and listen for the flapping of yuda wings. However, she knew very well the peace on this side of the Wall was bought with the suffering of the people on the other. Her people.

She couldn't enjoy it. It wasn't *right*.

She had to get back home.

A gust of wind hit her, and she shivered. With a sigh, Kosara admitted to herself that finding the stranger would have to wait until tomorrow. There were more pressing matters—for starters, she had to find somewhere to sleep tonight if she didn't want to freeze to death out in the street.

But even before that, she had to eat. The scents wafting from the stalls at every corner made her mouth water: hot chocolate and roasted chestnuts, cardamom-infused wheat, honey biscuits, sizzling koftas and shish kebabs. Some smells she didn't recognise—of spices she'd never tasted and herbs that didn't feature in any of her herbology books. On the counters rose mountains of colourful fruits, cakes dripping with syrup, and boiled sweets that glinted like jewels. It was a far cry from the tins of jellied meat that had awaited her back in Bayan's pub.

She approached one stall cautiously. A piece of lamb the size of her arm rotated on a skewer in front of the coal rack. The seller stretched flatbreads over a large stone dome, occasionally wiping the sweat off her forehead with her apron.

"How much?" Kosara asked.

"Two grosh for a small one, three for a large."

Kosara swore internally. Her stomach let out a pleading growl. A queue was forming behind her.

"Well?" the seller asked.

Kosara gave her an appraising look. Fine wrinkles framed her mouth. *Late fifties or early sixties.* A gold band glinted on her left ring finger. *Married.* One of her hands pressed at her temple, and her eyes were bloodshot from the lack of sleep. *And unwell.*

"How about instead of paying, I tell your fortune?" Kosara asked.

"How about you get out of the way of the paying clients?"

"Your vision is swimming. Your head hurts, and even the thought of food is making you sick. Which is very unfortunate since you've been cooking all night. Am I right?"

The seller licked her dry lips. "Maybe."

A woman in the queue behind Kosara clapped her hands. "This is fascinating! What's wrong with her?"

She has a migraine.

"It's a curse," Kosara said. "Someone's jealous of you, and they've paid a witch to curse you."

"What would anyone be jealous of?" The seller waved her hand, encompassing the stall. "I'm not exactly rolling in it."

Kosara's eyes fell on the wedding band again. "Your partner."

"You know what, Mariam, he *is* a looker," said the woman from the queue. Several other voices rose in agreement. Kosara couldn't have hoped for a better audience.

Mariam pointedly ignored them. "What should I do?"

Get some sleep, keep hydrated, have a nice warm cup of tea. "You have to keep vigil for three days. Burn a candle in your bedroom and make sure it never goes off. You can't leave it even for a minute."

"Stay home for three days! But what about my stall?"

"Find someone else to mind it. There's no other way."

"Get your husband to mind it, Mari!" shouted the woman from the queue. "I, for one, would start coming twice as often."

Mariam gave her a dark look. The woman giggled and raised her nearly empty glass of mulled wine in the air.

"Burn a candle," Mariam turned back to Kosara. "Is that all?"

"No. You also need to make a potion by boiling a thumb-sized piece of ginger in a pint of holy water, and you have to take it every morning and evening."

"And you're sure that would lift the curse?"

"Positive."

Mariam hesitated for a moment. Then, she sliced a piece of lamb and wrapped it in a steaming flatbread. Before she handed it to Kosara, she drizzled garlic yogurt all over it. "Perhaps I need a holiday," she said. "Thank you."

"No," Kosara salivated so much she could barely speak, "thank *you*."

"Oooh, do me next!" said the woman from the queue. After all her help, Kosara could hardly refuse.

"Me next!" came another voice from the crowd.

"And me!"

Kosara spent the next half hour prescribing potions, breaking curses, and predicting tall, dark strangers. By the end of it, her pockets were full of grosh. The flatbread seller had long closed her stall and gone home to drink ginger tea, but the queue didn't disperse. More and more people joined it, lured by the promise that a *real* witch from Chernograd would tell their fortune.

It seemed that sticking out like a sore thumb wasn't such a bad thing, after all. It attracted a rather large clientele. Kosara was aware witches were rare on this side of the Wall, but she'd never thought the Belogradeans would be so desperate for one.

Good thing Vila can't see me now! Kosara's old teacher would've been so disappointed to find her favourite student reduced to a charlatan in the streets of Belograd.

For a moment, something half-forgotten wiggled in Kosara's stomach. Guilt. She quickly suppressed it. She had no other trade than witchcraft, and she had to eat.

Belograd didn't need real witches, anyway. There were no monsters here. The locals themselves didn't know how good they had it, the spoiled brats. Their problems seemed so minuscule: "Help, Miss Witch, my daughter-in-law always forgets my name day" or "Oh no, it's going to rain next Wednesday when my date and I were meant to be going stargazing." Try stargazing while fighting off upirs, why don't you? Try eating name-day cake while hungry varkolaks nibble on your calves!

Kosara was exactly what their made-up problems needed—a charlatan. She would have stayed all night and squeezed those Belogradean suckers out of their last grosh, if she hadn't been so tired. Her eyelids grew heavier with every blink.

"Thanks for your business, everyone," she said finally. "I'm afraid I have to wrap up for tonight. It's getting late."

"Where can we find you?" shouted a tall man from the back of the queue. He stooped, his hand pressed against the small of his back. *Devil's claw would help the pain,* Kosara thought automatically, *as would white willow bark.*

"I don't know," Kosara said. "I just arrived. I have nowhere to stay."

At this, the crowd grew notably silent. *So, this is how it is.* They were happy to ask for her help, but none of them wanted to let a witch from Chernograd into their home.

"There's a hotel just down the road. . . ." someone mumbled.

Kosara looked down at her purse. It was much fuller than it had been half an hour ago, but she knew it wouldn't be enough.

The buildings around her were tall and imposing. Plaster cherubs played the harp around the windows, and marble tritons supported the entrance archways on their muscly shoulders. The gentlemen passing by wore fine silks and linen. Precious stones and pearls glinted on the necks and wrists of the ladies. She'd found herself in a posh neighbourhood.

"Bah, a hotel!" A tall woman leaned on the wall of the bakery, the flame of her cigarette flickering like a firefly. White handprints covered her apron, and flour coated her hair. When Kosara heard her accent, she felt like running to her and hugging her—which, obviously, she didn't do. The woman was from Chernograd. Kosara would probably get slapped if she touched her.

"You can stay in my attic room," the woman said. "Two grosh a night, what do you say, hen? It's full of dust and spiders. Since you're a witch, you'd probably feel at home."

Kosara couldn't believe her luck. She was so grateful, she chose to ignore that last dig. "Sounds perfect."

The two of them weaved their way through the crowd. Kosara had to pretend not to hear the questions shouted after her: "How do you break a family curse?" and "Will I get married soon?" and "About that tall dark stranger . . ."

As Kosara's new landlady led her through the city, the white cobblestones gave way to grey asphalt and potholes filled with muddy water. The buildings were just as tall, but a lot less grand, with poky stairwells peeking through the open doorways and plaster peeling in large chunks off the facades. The streets grew so narrow, the two of them had to press themselves against the wall whenever one of Belograd's horseless carriages passed by.

Kosara had read about them, but she'd never seen one. With their bulbous metallic bodies, they reminded her of oversized beetles. They left a trail of black smoke and the stink of chemicals behind them.

"I'm Gizda, by the way," the landlady said after a while.

"Kosara."

"How did you end up in Belograd, Kosara?"

"It was kind of an accident."

"Ha!" Gizda barked, her ruddy face showing no signs of amusement. "An accident!"

Kosara knew how ridiculous she sounded. People spent their entire life savings to come to Belograd. It wasn't something you simply stumbled into.

"No, honestly," she said. "I didn't want to leave Chernograd."

"Really?"

"Really. I'm a witch. I belong in Chernograd."

"Please, hen. Don't give me that patriotic nonsense. You're a witch: you can't convince me you aren't happy you're on this side of the Wall, telling gullible fools' fortunes, rather than on the other, fighting monsters."

Kosara bit her lip. Of course she was happy she wasn't fighting monsters.

But if not her, who would? What would her colleagues think when they heard she'd escaped?

What did the Zmey think?

That he'd won. Again. That was what he would think. That he'd finally managed to chase her away from her city.

"I did consider crossing the Wall once," Kosara said carefully. "A few years back. I even had the money saved. But then I changed my mind."

"Why?"

Kosara hesitated. The first reason had been that she'd lost all the money she'd saved, but there was also something else. "Because I don't feel like I'd have a purpose here. What would I do? Tell gullible fools their fortunes? That's it?"

"What's your purpose over in Chernograd, if I may ask?"

"I can help over there. I know how to fight the monsters."

"And do people listen to you? Or do they get swept up by louder charlatans who promise easy solutions?"

"Well . . ." Kosara hesitated. "Some listen. We've been doing a yearly survey with the Witch and Warlock Association, and we've been noticing a slow but steady drop in the number of deaths from monster attacks every year, and—"

"Right, okay. But you're on this side of the Wall now. You can forget about all that. It's not your problem anymore. Aren't you happy?" Gizda studied her face insistently, as if this was some sort of test.

Kosara shook her head. "I traded too much to cross the Wall."

She saw the question in Gizda's eyes. Still, she knew it wouldn't come out. They were both from Chernograd: they respected each other's right to keep secrets.

Gizda sighed. "I know what you mean, hen, I really do. I scrimped and saved all my life to pay the smugglers for passage across. All that money wasted."

"You don't like it here?"

"It's a city like any city. I don't hate it. But was it worth it?" She shrugged her broad shoulders. A pause, and then she started talking quickly. "My brother emigrated as soon as he finished school. He was barely eighteen when he paid the smugglers to take him across. He kept sending us letters, though, he never forgot us. It was he who convinced me I had to move. If you ask him, it's all sunshine and roses here."

"What if I ask you?"

Gizda pulled on her cigarette. "It appears to be at a first glance, doesn't it? Listen to me, hen. Belograd is like a fairground version of a city, but there are razors hidden in the candy floss, and the toffee apples are poisonous. They don't want us here. That's what it all boils down to. They'd rather we stayed behind our Wall where we belong."

"They claim the Wall was built to keep the monsters out. . . ." Kosara said, careful to neither agree nor disagree with the statement. Gizda obviously had a lot of strong opinions on the subject, and Kosara really wanted to have somewhere to sleep tonight.

"Bah, the monsters! If that's the case, why didn't they make it so the Wall only keeps the monsters out? Do you know what the punishment is if they catch you trafficking people into Belograd? Life imprisonment!"

Kosara started speaking without really thinking. Every primary school child knew why. "They were afraid we'd spread the diseases caused by the monsters on this side of the Wall. Lycanthropy, mostly." She saw Gizda's face, and quickly added, "Or at least that's what they claim."

"You can't convince me they had the magical power to build a giant Wall around our city in one night but couldn't spare the resources to find a cure for lycanthropy. They simply didn't want to. To them, we're as bad as the monsters. You know why? Because we're poor."

Kosara chewed on her lip. "I only just got here. . . ."

"Just you wait. You'll see I'm right. But since you reminded me, you need to go and register at the police station. They'll have to put you under quarantine."

"What? Why?"

"To make sure you aren't infected, of course. Every new arrival from Chernograd goes through the quarantine during their first full moon here."

"And what if I am infected?"

It was a hypothetical question, but the suspicion in Gizda's eyes made Kosara wish she'd never asked. The landlady was silent for a few long, uncomfortable seconds. "If you're infected, they shoot you."

A chill ran down Kosara's spine, one that not even her thermal vest could protect her from. She automatically raised her fingers to the scar on her cheek. Nevena's face floated to the front of her mind, mascara-tinged tears welling in her eyes. *Just shoot me*, Nevena whispered. *If I turn, just shoot me.*

"I can't be quarantined," Kosara said loudly enough to drown the voice in her head. "I have things to do."

"Don't we all? Listen, it's up to you, but I strongly suggest you go voluntarily. Otherwise, they'll arrest you. After the fuss you caused today, I don't think you can hide for long."

Kosara hadn't even considered that. She sighed. "I'll think about it."

The streetlights grew dimmer and sparser until the two of them walked in almost complete darkness. Kosara fidgeted, her fingers grasping one of the talismans in her pocket. She couldn't help but imagine the Zmey's pale eyes peering at her from the dark alleyways, even though she knew he was just as trapped on the other side of the Wall as she was on this one.

She hated the way her hands shook, and her heart raced at every noise. Before she lost her shadow, she'd have never been afraid to walk the streets after dark, even in this strange city. In fact, she'd have probably hoped someone would attack her so she could try her newest talisman.

Now, her talismans were useless. Her evil eye beads were nothing but pretty trinkets. Her boiled egg amulet was simply a tasty snack. She was helpless.

Someone whistled. Kosara turned towards the sound. Two bright lights gleamed in the distance.

"What the hell . . ." She staggered backwards until her back hit the wall.

The lights flew towards her, unnaturally fast, unnaturally bright. Kosara could see it now: they were the eyes of an enormous monster. Its body glinted in the moonlight, sliding over the ground. Black steam rose in its wake.

Kosara watched it, too terrified to move. Her hand gripped the boiled egg talisman so hard it broke. Yolk ran out between her trembling fingers.

A hoarse sound pierced the night. Kosara jumped about a foot in the air, her back scraping against the rough wall. It took her a moment to realise it had been Gizda's laughter.

"Calm down, hen!"

Kosara's mouth gaped open. *Calm down?* Couldn't she see the monster?

"It's called a train," Gizda said. "It's a kind of horseless carriage—"

The end of the sentence got drowned by loud hissing and screeching, as the train passed over the bridge above their heads. Its windows shone, and inside it, people sat, talking and laughing, and snoring with their cheeks pressed against the windows.

A train! Kosara let go of the breath she'd been holding. *Of course* it was a train.

She'd read about trains in plenty of romance novels. They were often the scenes of dramatic chases over the roofs of the carriages, and hushed love confessions in the dark compartments. She'd just never thought they would be so big, so loud, or so bright.

But then again, everything in Belograd seemed to be big, loud, and bright.

Kosara looked down at her ruined talisman. She let the egg fall to the ground. It would make a fine dinner for one of Belograd's many stray cats.

"Sorry. I thought . . ." Kosara cleared her throat. Gizda must have taken her for an uneducated, provincial fool. "I thought it was a monster. It's been a long day."

"Don't worry about it. The first time I saw them, I nearly pissed myself, too." Gizda laughed again. "We're almost there. I should have maybe mentioned the room is near the train station. I hope you don't mind the noise."

Kosara shrugged. She was so exhausted, she doubted anything could keep her awake.

Finally, they reached a dilapidated house squeezed between two taller buildings. Gizda led Kosara up the narrow stairwell soaked in a familiar cocktail of smells: dirt, mildew, and Chernogradean sour cabbage.

The attic room was barely big enough for both of them to fit standing next to the rickety bed. The wind slammed against its only window and whistled in the chimney. Gizda reached and pulled on a cord, making the electric bulb hanging from the ceiling crack and sizzle, filling the room with bright yellow light.

Kosara gasped despite herself. How posh was that! In Chernograd, you only got electricity in public buildings.

"I know, I know, it's a mess," Gizda said, obviously misunderstanding Kosara's reaction. She waved a hand towards the old clothes scattered over the bed and the miscellaneous objects in boxes on the floor. "As my mum used to say, it looks like Lamia has been through it, though it beats me what that's supposed to mean. But it should do you for a few days. There are extra blankets in the wardrobe. I keep old clothes there too, feel free to help yourself."

"Thank you," Kosara said. Gizda looked at her as if she was a charity case. Which, Kosara supposed, she was. "I had no time to pack . . ."

"Don't worry about it. We Chernogradeans have to help each other. God knows no one else would. Do you know anyone on this side of the Wall? I can ask around for them if you want."

"I don't. . . ." Kosara said, but then she realised that wasn't entirely true. There was someone. He still owed her quite a lot of money, and besides, she was certain he was involved with smugglers. Maybe he knew the stranger.

Kosara couldn't wait to see the look on his face when she turned up at his doorstep.

"Do you know Sevar Tabakov? He's about my height, dark hair—"

Gizda clapped her hands in front of her chest. "Of course I know Sevar! Why didn't you tell me you're Sevar's friend?"

"I'm not exactly his—"

"Oh dear, how exciting is this? You've arrived right on time—his engagement party is the day after tomorrow. Or"—Gizda checked her watch—"I suppose, tomorrow. Everyone's going."

"He's getting married?" Kosara said, but the real question she wanted to ask was, *He's found someone stupid enough to marry him?*

"Yes, to a Belogradean girl, can you believe it? I heard her parents are furious. Anyway, I'll give you the address." Gizda buried her arm in her bag, rummaging for a piece of paper and a pen. "He'll be so happy to see you, I'm sure, he's such a lovely boy."

Internally, Kosara rolled her eyes, but she didn't bother saying anything. She had to admit Sevar could be charming. Otherwise, he wouldn't have managed to swindle her out of her life savings.

Roksana had introduced her to Sevar a couple of years after Kosara had escaped the Zmey's grasp. A couple of years after Nevena's death. Sevar had sensed Kosara's vulnerability, and he'd done precisely what every good con man did: he'd mercilessly exploited it.

"There you go, hen." Gizda handed her a note with the address. "I'll let you get your beauty sleep now. I'll be downstairs. If you need anything, don't hesitate to ask. I can't believe you never told me you're Sevar's friend!"

Kosara forced a smile. It immediately fell off her face once she shut the door behind Gizda's broad back.

She walked to the window and peeked through the dusty curtains. Her room was as basic as they got, but she had to admit the view was magnificent. At nearly four in the morning, Belograd didn't sleep. The multihued lanterns decorating its market stalls and shop windows shone brightly. Streetlights framed the roads like garlands. The tall towers and onion domes of churches, mosques, and palaces glinted in the moonlight: green copper, burnished brass, and bright, shining gold.

Kosara smiled despite herself. She'd just had a terrible day. Scratch that, it had been a disaster of a day. But there was a silver lining—she could at least ruin Sevar's engagement party tomorrow. And hopefully, he'd tell her where to find the stranger.

She rested her forehead against the cold window frame. Her mind cleared somewhat. Away from the Zmey's threatening presence and Belograd's bustle, for the first time in what felt like hours, she started *thinking*.

The Zmey had found her so quickly: only minutes after midnight. How convenient that the stranger had just the right thing to help her escape, for the mere price of all her magic powers. Why would the clueless foreigner ever think it was a good idea to come to Chernograd on New Year's Eve, casually wearing a necklace of witches' shadows?

It was obvious. Someone had ratted her out to the Zmey. Someone had placed the stranger in the right position at the right time, with the sole purpose of stealing her shadow.

She'd been lured into a trap, and she'd enthusiastically leaped headfirst into it.

Kosara swore under her breath and sank her fingernails into her palms. She'd find the rat, whoever they were. And once she did, she'd show them what a witch could do with a rabbit's paw and a cockerel's comb.

And then, she'd have to face the Zmey. But this time, she'd plan it better. This time, she'd make sure to consider everything that could possibly go wrong. He would never catch her unprepared again.

She was done living in fear in her own goddamned city.

And how exactly would you do that, my little powerless witch? The familiar voice sounded in her head—the one that spoke with the Zmey's warm baritone.

I'll figure it out, she thought. *I have all the time in the world.*

Do you, though? What about when the shadow sickness gets you?

Kosara shoved that voice deep within herself, deep enough that she wouldn't have to listen to it.

She *would* figure it out.

4

Day Two

When Kosara arrived, the engagement party was in full swing: it raged in the house, spilled into the garden, and finally diffused somewhere up the street. The guests sat under the fig trees, smoking and laughing, keeping warm with mulled wine. She walked past a moustached man playing the accordion while a woman danced with—Kosara blinked to make sure she wasn't imagining things—a large brown bear.

"Don't worry!" the man shouted when he caught Kosara staring. "She's tame! And so is the bear!"

Kosara groaned audibly and kept walking. She'd been in Belograd for nearly two days now, though, granted, she'd spent most of the first day sleeping. She still wasn't used to the Belogradeans' willingness to engage complete strangers in meaningless conversation.

She stood near the door, not quite finding the courage to go in. It had been years since she'd last seen Sevar. Was she really about to walk into his house and ruin one of the most important days of his life?

At a table nearby towered a pile of sweets: sesame halwa with pistachios, pumpkin pastries dripping with honey syrup, multicoloured pieces of lokum rolled in coconut flakes. Kosara ate a few, more out of nervousness than hunger. Then she stuffed a lot more in her pockets for later. She doubted she'd get the chance to con her way into a dinner again, and she also didn't like the idea of imposing on Gizda's hospitality. The landlady had invited her in for a meal the previous evening, and Kosara felt like she already owed her enough.

This was all new to her. Pistachios? Coconut? Those were rare treats back home. Chernograd got most of its food imported from Belograd, arriving on unmanned hot-air balloons over the Wall. There wasn't usually room for anything besides necessities.

She'd just bitten into a piece of walnut baklava when a warm hand landed on her shoulder.

"Hi there," said a young woman. Dimples appeared in the corners of her mouth as she smiled. "Are you one of Sevar's friends?"

Kosara chewed as quickly as she could, the honey syrup momentarily gluing her mouth shut. Finally, she managed to swallow. "What gave it away?"

"You're dressed as if you're going to a funeral. Honestly, you Chernogradeans, it wouldn't kill you to add a pop of colour!" The woman laughed. She herself was dressed entirely in pops of colour—sunflower yellows and turquoise blues and grass greens. Her wide trousers swished as she walked. "Come on in, what are you doing standing outside? I'm sure Sevar can't wait to see you."

Kosara forced a smile. *I wouldn't be so sure.*

The living room was so cramped, Kosara wouldn't have been able to make her way through it if it wasn't for the woman dragging her forwards by the hand. A band played in the corner, enthusiastically pulling on guitar strings and violently slamming on drums. Kosara could barely hear them over the chatter.

Groups of people sat on silken cushions scattered all over the floor, smoking shisha and spitting clouds of scented smoke: sour cherry and dark chocolate, bitter cinnamon, and sweet vanilla. Heavy woollen rugs covered the floor and tapestries hung on the walls, trapping the smells and sounds and the heat of all those bodies inside the room. Kosara's head spun.

How could Sevar afford all this? The rugs, the tapestries, the mahogany furniture and the silken cushions, the imported alcohol and tobacco? Evidently, he had done well for himself on this side of the Wall.

"I'm Nur, by the way." The woman looked back at Kosara. "Sevar's fiancée."

Oh no, you poor thing.

"And you are . . ." Nur said.

"Kosara!" someone shouted.

Kosara recognised his voice. Sevar shoved his way through the crowd towards her. He stopped a few steps short, his eyes fixed on her, and his nostrils flared.

He'd grown older. The buttons of his shirt strained against his pot belly. His hair had started to turn white at his temples. Looking at him, Kosara realised how much she must have changed over the last half a decade, too.

"What are you doing here?" Sevar asked. And then, not giving her a chance to reply, "I don't have the money. With the wedding and everything, you've picked a very bad time—"

"I don't need your money," Kosara said. She did. She needed money badly. But more than that, she needed answers. "I just want to talk."

Nur let out a nervous laugh. "I'd better leave you to it." She stepped backwards. "You seem to have a lot to talk about, and I have guests to greet."

Sevar watched her disappear in the crowd. Then he turned to Kosara. "I'm so happy you finally crossed the Wall, you know. Just like you always dreamed."

Don't you dare. . . . "You have no idea what I dream of."

He smiled a warm smile, and for a second, she remembered why she used to like him—but only for a second.

"Come on," he said. "You used to always tell me about how once you'd escaped, you'd open a workshop on this side of the Wall. With soft carpets, crystal chandeliers, and a smoke machine, right? You'd only offer your services to a select clientele: you'd foretell big profits to rich magnates, and predict academic successes to young intellectuals, and promise tall, dark strangers to aristocratic ladies. . . ."

Kosara squirmed, listening to her young foolishness thrown back at her. It had only been after Sevar had left without her that she'd realised her problems weren't tied to Chernograd. Escaping the city wouldn't have helped her escape them.

"Never mind that," Kosara said. "I'm looking for a man. A smuggler. He helped me cross the Wall. I'm wondering if you might know him."

Sevar's smile finally faltered. "Why would I know him?"

"You were friends with smugglers back in the day. I thought you might have heard something. He's tall, scrawny, wears a necklace of witches' shadows."

Sevar's eyes widened. He glanced down at the floor, where Kosara didn't cast a shadow. "Oh, Kosara, I'm so sorry! I had no idea. I can't believe I've been blabbering about your workshop, rubbing salt in the wound—"

"Do you know this man or not?" Kosara snapped. She couldn't stand him pitying her.

Sevar ran his hand through his hair. "Listen, Kosara, I'm not that guy anymore. I don't associate with smugglers. I'm getting married, Nur and I are thinking about starting a family, I don't want any trouble. . . ."

Lies. Kosara had spotted the labels on the bottles of wine the guests were drinking—it was all Chernogradean. The cigarettes they smoked were thick and smelly: Chernogradean. The magazines on the living room table were Chernogradean. The books on the shelves? Chernogradean.

He was foolish to be so obvious about it. Smuggling was illegal.

But then, Sevar had always been like that. He used to get out of any trouble with a charming smile, and occasionally, a few banknotes slipped into the right hand. He was never afraid of the consequences because he never faced them. Of course he'd show off his smuggled goods in front of his Belogradean friends.

"Sevar, please," Kosara said. "I need to find this man quickly. If you know anything at all, tell me."

Sevar licked his lips. He realised how dire the situation was, she could see it in those big, deceptively honest eyes of his. He might have been a crook and a scam artist, but he wasn't heartless.

"I don't associate with smugglers anymore," he said, "but back in the day, after I crossed the Wall—"

Using my savings.

"—I was here all alone—"

Because you abandoned me in Chernograd.

"—with no money, so I did a few odd jobs for someone. You know Konstantin Karaivanov?"

Kosara laughed. "Do I know Chernograd's most famous smuggler? Who doesn't?"

She'd done a few odd jobs for him herself. Living in Chernograd, it was difficult to avoid him.

"I thought you would. Konstantin had me deliver smuggled talismans and amulets to a swanky boutique on the Main Street. It's called the Witch's Cauldron." Sevar saw her face and shrugged. "Tacky, I know. But that's where all of Chernograd's smuggled magic tends to end up once it crosses the Wall. If this guy has your shadow, I can't imagine where else he'd try to pawn it."

"I don't know if he'd pawn it. He seemed like . . ." Kosara hesitated. "Almost like he was collecting them."

"Even if he doesn't, they would've heard of him. A witch's shadow is just the sort of thing those people would love to get their dirty paws on."

Kosara gave him a sideways smile. *Dirty paws.* A bit rich coming from him.

"It's on the Main Street, did you say?" she asked.

"Across from the big pharmacy near the fountain."

"Thank you."

"You're welcome, old friend. You'd better go there at once."

Oh no, you're not getting rid of me that easily. "It's eight in the evening. Surely they're shut." Kosara took a glass of mulled wine from a nearby tray. "I think I'll stay for a while. It's lovely to see you're doing so well after all these years. Are those rugs from Phanarion? They must have cost a fortune."

"Kosara . . ."

"Maybe if you sold a few of them, you'd be able to give me my money back."

"I told you. Wait until after the wedding. I'll pay you back, I promise."

"No offence, but I don't believe your promises anymore. Maybe I'll mention it to Nur, she seems reasonable. . . ."

Sevar paled. He took a step sideways, as if to block Kosara's way towards Nur. As if that would stop her.

"Honestly, Kosara, have you not grown up at all over the past five years?"

"Have *I* not grown up? You stole my money. You made me believe you'd buy us passage to Belograd. I packed my bags and waited for you to show up all night, and you never did. You crossed the Wall without me!"

At last, he had the decency to blush. "Are you really still upset about that? It was half a decade ago."

"Of course I'm still upset! Does Nur know she's marrying a scam artist? Perhaps she deserves to."

This time, he took a step towards Kosara. "Don't you dare go near her," he hissed. "This is why I left you behind, Kosara. Because you never let things go. There wouldn't have been enough room for all your emotional baggage to come with us to Belograd. Wherever you go, the ghosts from your past go with you."

Kosara couldn't believe what she was hearing. "I only have one ghost and you know as well as I do she can't leave my house in Chernograd."

"I was speaking *metaphorically*. It's not just Nevena, you know. You're still completely hung up on that Zmey of yours—"

A loud clap sounded. Sharp pain ran up Kosara's arm. It took her a second to realise she'd slapped Sevar so hard, she'd hurt her own hand. Five red fingers bloomed on his cheek.

His hand slowly rose to rub them. His eyes were wide with shock.

"Sevar!" Nur's cheery voice came as if from very far. Kosara was so angry, her ears buzzed.

She forced a smile, and so did Sevar. Kosara suspected they both looked equally fake.

"Am I interrupting something?" Nur appeared, a bottle of mulled wine in her hand. She took a swig, then refilled Kosara's empty glass.

"Not at all, darling," Sevar grabbed her by the waist and spun her before she'd seen the hand impression on his cheek. She leaned her head on his chest.

"Another one of your friends just arrived," Nur said. "I told her you're in the living room. Here she is! Easy to spot, isn't she?"

She was—she towered at least a head above the other guests. Her hair glistened waxy in the lamplight, gathered in two long braids. Her black silken shirt was tucked into a pair of wide poturi, and her many brass-bell necklaces jingled with her every step. A pipe hung from the corner of her mouth, sending clouds of seer's-sage-scented smoke towards the ceiling.

Roksana. What the hell was she doing here?

"Sevar, my friend!" A broad smile split Roksana's face as she approached, her arms spread. Then she spotted Kosara. The smile froze. "Kosara?"

"Roksana."

"Would you look at that?" said Nur, already slipping away into the crowd. "More guests arriving. I'll see you in a bit."

"I'll come and help you, darling!" Sevar stumbled and nearly fell in his rush to run after her.

Roksana and Kosara glared at each other for a long moment. Kosara struggled to place the monster hunter's familiar face in this strange new environment. In the background, the band started a cheerful tune, the flute player's cheeks growing redder by the second.

"What are you doing here?" Roksana asked, stealing Kosara's line.

"No, what are *you* doing here?"

Roksana pulled on her pipe and spat a cloud of smoke in Kosara's face. Kosara's eyelids grew heavy. She shook her head to dispel the effect of the seer's sage—she wasn't going to be distracted that easily.

"Sevar's been my best friend since we were little," Roksana said. "You can't expect me to miss his engagement party."

Kosara was surprised by how much that hurt. They weren't close—she'd never let anyone close after what happened with her sister—but nevertheless, she liked Roksana. The monster hunter had been there for her after Nevena's death, always ready to fix her a stiff drink and play a round of cards with her, no questions asked.

"He stole my money, Roksana," Kosara said. "Your friend is a thief."

"Oh, please don't make me take sides." Roksana tried to put a hand on her shoulder, but Kosara took a step back. "I told you, I've known Sevar since we were in diapers. He's like my brother. He's a good guy, deep down."

"I thought you already took my side, after you let me dribble and cry all over your shoulder that night Sevar left me in Chernograd."

"That was five years ago, Kosara. You know he needed the money to escape, what with his debts and everything. . . . But I promise you, he's changed. Perhaps realising what he did to you was the catalyst."

Kosara rolled her eyes. She didn't want to be anyone's *catalyst*. Besides, Sevar wouldn't have been in debt if he hadn't wasted his money on drink, gambling, and useless trinkets.

"How did you even get here?" Kosara asked. "Did the stranger offer you a deal too?"

"Oh no, Sevar gave me a lift in his hot-air balloon."

Kosara swore internally. The lying bastard! "I don't associate with smugglers anymore," Sevar had told her. In a way, she supposed it was true: he didn't associate with them, he *was* one.

Which, of course, meant that he'd been able to come back for her this entire time. "I'm so happy you finally crossed the Wall." Yeah, right. He'd hoped to never see her again. Kosara had assumed that old wound had long scabbed over, but she felt it again now, stinging.

And then, there was this big stupid idiot right in front of her.

"Are you insane?" she asked, her voice higher pitched than she'd intended.

Roksana grinned, her gold tooth glinting. "Not our best idea, I admit. You know how they always say crossing the Wall by air is terribly dangerous? They aren't joking. I can't tell you how many times we nearly got killed. I lost count at ten."

"You would've deserved it. Honestly, Roksana! You risked your life crossing the Wall in a hot-air balloon to go to that waste of breath's engagement party?"

"I told you, the guy's like my brother. Besides, since when are you so upset about people crossing the Wall? The Belogradeans would just love it if we stayed behind our Wall, nice and quiet, wouldn't they? If it depended on me, I'd raze the whole bloody thing to the ground."

"I'm not upset you crossed it! I'm upset you risked your life doing it." Kosara measured Roksana with her eyes. There had been something about that last comment which rang truer than the rest. "Why did you cross the Wall, really?"

Roksana hesitated. "Promise not to tell?"

Kosara stepped closer to her. "I promise."

"I wanted to see it from up close. After you got taken away, and I realised I'd never gone anywhere near it—"

"See it up close? Why?"

Roksana shrugged. "We've all been living in such fear of it, you know? It's like a giant monster that's captured Chernograd and wouldn't let go. Well, I'm a monster hunter. I know that even the scariest monster can be defeated."

Kosara scoffed. Utter nonsense. The Wall wasn't a monster; for starters, as far as she was concerned, it wouldn't simply crumble into dust because you shot it with a silver bullet.

Roksana was obviously still not telling the whole truth. Fine. She could keep her secrets.

"You're an idiot," Kosara said. "What would seeing it from up close even do?"

Roksana laughed. "It did nothing. Other than show me it's just as dangerous as everyone says. You're right, I am an idiot. Don't worry, I've learned my bloody lesson. I'll figure out a smarter way to cross back. I've got quite a bit of money saved, and—"

"You're going back?" Kosara asked. For some reason, she was surprised, even though she herself planned on returning to Chernograd as soon as possible. Most people were happy to have escaped.

"Of course I'm going back. I'm a monster hunter, Kosara! What would I do on this side of the Wall?"

"You could retrain as a pest exterminator?"

"Very funny. No, I'm going back home as soon as I can. I don't like it here. It's all too . . . nice."

"Too nice?"

"Yes. It's all new and tidy and shiny. And the people are so friendly, it's kind of sinister. Why are they always smiling? What are they hiding that's so funny? You can come with me if you want. I can't imagine they need a witch on this side of the Wall."

Kosara scoffed. "You'd be surprised."

She herself hadn't expected just how much Belograd relied on Chernogradean magic. In the pharmacies, half of all medicines and cosmetics were imported from Chernograd. The jewellery shops were full of amulets and talismans. The perfumeries stank strongly of magic.

Kosara was aware, of course, that the city imported tonnes of magical objects from Chernograd every year. She had a few colleagues back home who were paid government wages to produce them. However, seeing all the magic on this side of the Wall had still come as a shock.

At the same time, it made sense. If Belograd didn't need Chernograd's magic, it would have probably left them to starve to death long ago.

Roksana pulled on her pipe and exhaled a cloud of smoke in Kosara's face again. Kosara stifled a yawn. God, she was so tired of all of them. If only she could curl up on one of those cushions on the floor and forget about Sevar, and the stranger, and her shadow.

"Come on," Roksana said. "Let's get you another glass of wine. You look like you need it." Roksana took her by the hand, and Kosara let her. As much as she hated to admit it, she was happy to see the monster hunter. She desperately needed someone familiar in this strange new city.

Roksana led her to a pile of cushions tucked away in the corner. Kosara sank in between them. Roksana poured two glasses of wine and handed one to her.

Kosara took a large gulp, then leaned her head against the wall.

"I'm so glad to see you're all right," Roksana said. "It all happened so fast. I kept thinking I should've done something to stop him—"

"The Zmey or the stranger?"

"Either bloody one."

"There was nothing you could have done. It was my decision to give my shadow to the stranger." *My stupid, idiotic decision.* "I'm trying to find him and get it back, but I don't even know where to start looking."

Roksana pressed her shoulder against Kosara's. "Give it time. I'm sure someone must know something. He's a smuggler who walks around with a necklace of witches' shadows. People would notice."

"I don't have time. I need to get back to Chernograd." Kosara sighed. "I wish the stranger had never come to our pub last night."

"I know."

Kosara rested her head on Roksana's shoulder. The sweet smell of seer's sage filled her nostrils. The band played a slow song, and the guests got up to dance. The women whirled, their skirts colourful circles floating through the room. The men's legs moved so fast, kicking and crossing over, they were almost invisible.

Kosara did her best not to pay attention to Nur and Sevar, staring intently into each other's eyes, their bodies pressed close together. *For God's sake, get a room!*

She pitied the poor girl, tying herself to Sevar forever. He had the spine of a snake and the moral compass of a vulture. But beneath the pity, coiling deep in the pit of Kosara's stomach, lurked a different feeling. One she was too embarrassed to ever admit out loud. Jealousy.

"You don't have to look at her like that," Roksana said.

Kosara startled, warm blood rushing to her cheeks. "Sorry, what?"

"You don't have to look at her with such pity. That girl knows what she's getting into."

"She does?"

"The two of them were made for each other. You know how they could afford those carpets? She robbed a bank. A whole bloody bank! On her own. With a toy gun."

"No way." Kosara glanced at Nur with newfound respect. This perhaps showed something was amiss in Kosara's own moral compass.

Roksana continued, "Sevar says they met when they were pickpocketing the same man at the market. Their fingers touched over the wallet in his back pocket."

"That has got to be a joke."

Roksana shrugged. "Knowing those two, I wouldn't be surprised if it was true."

Kosara's eyes followed Nur and Sevar drifting through the room, bright smiles shining on their faces. Even crooks and criminals eventually found someone who cared about them. There had to be something encouraging in that.

Or perhaps Kosara should have felt more discouraged: she was an even more dire case than those two. Maybe she was destined to live alone, with only the ghosts from her past to keep her company.

Sensing her mood, Roksana offered her another refill, and Kosara accepted it, even though she knew it was a bad idea.

"It's lucky I met you tonight, actually," Roksana said. "I need your expertise as a witch."

Kosara pushed herself up. "What's wrong?"

"Nothing's wrong. It's just personal interest. Have you ever heard of something called a Lamia?"

"I . . ." Kosara hesitated. She could vaguely recall hearing the name, but for the life of her, she couldn't remember where. "Not really. What is it?"

"A monster. I read about it in an old book. It's said to have caused great destruction in Chernograd back in the day. It's also supposedly unbeatable because if you cut one of its heads, another three grow in its place."

"That sounds like good news for a monster hunter. Think of all the eyes, horns, and ears you can sell. It's a renewable resource."

Roksana's face suggested she was in no mood for jokes. "Are you sure you've never heard of it?"

"Certain. You know I know my monsters."

Though now that she thought about it, she did remember an odd gap she'd spotted in the old bestiary Vila had given her, right between "karakonjul" and "kikimora." The remains of the torn page were blackened and left soot marks on Kosara's fingers. As if it had been burned.

"Hmm." Roksana played with the end of her braid, her golden rings glinting. "Fine, then. I have another question. What can you tell me about embedding magic?"

The pleasant haze the wine had created in Kosara's mind dissipated. Embedding was old, dark magic: one of those that was most dangerous because it truly worked. It hadn't been practised in a very long time. In fact, Kosara suspected the only witch who still remembered how to do it in all of Chernograd was Vila.

Kosara was aware of the theory, of course. Vila believed you couldn't condemn something you didn't know.

"It's not done anymore," Kosara said quickly. "It's not been done in a long time. Why? Do you suspect someone—"

"No, no. I told you, I'm just curious."

"If you have a wraith in your house who's been embedded—"

Roksana laughed. "Don't worry, nothing like that! I just read about it in that same old book."

"That must be some book," Kosara muttered.

"Well, what do you know?"

"It's pretty gruesome."

"So I figured. From what I gather, the main idea is to embed a living person in the walls of a building to protect it from evil spirits."

Kosara shuddered. She poured herself another glass of wine and took a big gulp.

Chernogradean magic wasn't pretty. It had nothing in common with the beautiful Tarot cards and eye-catching crystal balls the Belogradean charlatans seemed to favour. However, there were certain things even a witch from Chernograd would never do.

She took a deep breath. "That's the idea, yes."

"The book mentioned the construction of the Devil's Bridge. Now, I know Chernograd like the palm of my bloody hand, and I've never heard of such a bridge."

"It's not a real bridge. That's just an old story."

"It is? Do you know it?"

"I know it." Kosara racked her wine-soaked brain, trying to remember the details. "Before the Wall was built, Chernograd was surrounded by a river. We could reach Belograd with boats, but the waters were treacherous, and sailing was dangerous. The then-mayor hired the most famous architect in town, Master Manol, to build a bridge to connect the two cities. Manol and his eight brothers began the construction, but there was a problem: whatever they managed to erect during the day,

collapsed into the water at night. The nine brothers quickly realised—
the Devil had cursed the new bridge."

"Funny," Roksana said. "My book claimed it was Lamia destroying
the bridge overnight."

"No, I'm pretty sure it was the Devil in the version my mum used
to tell. Hence, 'The Devil's Bridge.' Anyway, the brothers realised
there was only one solution. They had to embed a young woman in
the bridge to protect it."

Roksana groaned. "A young woman. Of-fucking-course."

"Each morning, the brothers' wives came to the bridge to bring
them breakfast. So, the brothers agreed on a fair way to pick the victim: whoever's wife arrived first the next day would be the one they'd
embed in the bridge. Manol's brothers couldn't bear to keep the terrible secret. They all warned their wives not to come. Manol was too
honourable and said nothing to his wife."

"Honourable! More like bloody stupid."

"Well, yeah. Early the next morning, Manol's wife arrived with the
food basket in one arm and their baby son in the other. When she saw
the brothers' faces, she immediately knew what was about to happen.
She didn't cry, and she didn't beg. She only asked for one thing—that
when they embed her in the bridge, they leave one of her breasts out,
so she could feed her baby."

Kosara stopped talking. Uncomfortable silence followed. The stories from Chernograd had the uncanny ability to kill the mood at
every party.

"Personally," she said after a while, "I don't think the story is meant
to be taken literally. It's a metaphor for the ridiculous sacrifices women
are expected to make for their husbands' careers."

Roksana took a drink of wine. A few drops stayed in the fine hairs
above her upper lip. "You're probably right. Thanks, anyway."

Kosara gave the monster hunter a long look. Roksana was puffing on her pipe, eyebrows furrowed. She'd gotten herself in trouble
again, Kosara could tell, otherwise she wouldn't be on this side of the
Wall, asking about embedding magic and mythical monsters. Perhaps she'd accepted a contract to kill an embedded wraith—the most

dangerous type of ghost, and the most bloodthirsty. She'd done stupider things before.

Or perhaps she'd been paid to find that Lamia of hers, and she was trying to figure out how to lure it. It would be pointless, Kosara was certain. Lamia was obviously mythical. It wouldn't be the first time a monster had turned out to be nothing but a figment of someone's overactive imagination. A few years back, a group of merchants at the market were convinced they'd spotted a dragon circling Chernograd. It turned out it had been the local aero club's latest experimental craft, which they'd unwisely painted green.

In any case, Kosara had no energy to prod for more information. She was in enough trouble herself. She'd let herself relax tonight, but tomorrow, she had to start untangling this whole mess. Hopefully, the Witch's Cauldron boutique would have some answers for her.

Day Three

It was a sunny morning, but the Witch's Cauldron was dark. Layers of silk mesh enveloped the lights on the ceiling, making them glimmer like stars on a foggy night. The gramophone played a slow piano ballad. A few well-dressed men and women tried on expensive necklaces and richly decorated hats, ran ring-encrusted fingers over the fine fabrics, and turned around in front of the tall mirrors.

It looked like the last place Kosara would expect to find her shadow.

She quickly flicked through a rail of dresses. They were all black, but not like her worn, faded black: they were sleek satin, intricate lace, and soft velvet. Precious stones gleamed on their necklines and cuffs.

Several staff members walked between the clothes racks, their heels clicking against the parquet floor. Kosara sensed one of them getting closer and closer, but she didn't turn around until she heard the woman's horrified voice, "Oh, darling! Not those!"

"Excuse me?"

"These won't suit you at all. Come!" She grabbed Kosara by the forearm and dragged her to the discounted rack. Her fingers searched the clothes until they settled on something suspiciously reminiscent of a black sack. She measured it against Kosara's torso. "There you go!"

Kosara placed the sack back on the rail. She squinted towards the staff member's name badge. "Actually, Bistra, I'm not interested in clothes."

"I can tell," Bistra said.

"I'm not interested in clothes *today*. I was wondering if you have something a bit more . . . authentic."

"We've got a collection of rusalka scale jewellery."

"More authentic." Kosara leaned closer. "I'm a witch."

Kosara felt it again—the pang of guilt in the pit of her stomach. She didn't quite understand why. She *was* a witch. All her knowledge and all her experience were still there, she only lacked her magic powers temporarily. A pianist didn't stop being a pianist just because he got a wrist cramp.

"Oh," Bistra said. "Oh!" She looked around. "Please wait here. I'll be back in a minute."

She walked away, leaving Kosara to stand awkwardly in the middle of the shop. Nearby, a middle-aged woman tried on a "varkolak fur" vest, wildly searching for the second sleeve hole with her arm and missing. The fur looked more like it came from a fox. In the corner, a group of girls loudly discussed the necklaces made from braided samodiva hair. If they were real, they'd light up the whole room.

Kosara couldn't believe her eyes. The Belogradeans had turned Chernograd into a fashion trend. The monsters were terrifying, otherworldly creatures—they weren't chic accessories. They certainly weren't, as a nearby poster of an upir-tooth necklace proclaimed, "a great way to add edge to your prom outfit."

"Oh my God," a voice sounded from behind Kosara's back. She turned around. A teenaged girl rushed towards her, her ponytail bobbing up and down behind her back. "Are you a witch?"

"Um." Kosara saw no point in denying it. "Yes."

"From Chernograd? A real witch? Oh my God!" The girl produced a crumpled receipt and a pen from her bag. "Can I have an autograph?"

"Um, sure." Kosara had never been asked for one before. She added way more flourish to her signature than she normally would.

"This is so exciting! My great-granny was a witch, look!" The girl pulled out a vial hanging on a long cord from under her shirt. The glass was old and cloudy, but Kosara could just make out something black hidden inside. "It's a good-luck amulet. Isn't it cool?"

"Is this a shadow?" Kosara asked, trying not to sound horrified.

"The tiniest little piece. My granny had a lot of grandchildren. She left us all a bit of herself before she died."

"How nice of her." Kosara gave the girl a stilted smile. The Belo-gradeans would probably think it a silly superstition, but in Chernograd, it was believed that splitting your shadow was the same as splitting your soul. No witch would ever do it unless she absolutely had to.

"Actually," the girl continued, "I'm a member of the Friends of Chernograd Society. You should totally come and give us a talk one day! We meet every Wednesday evening in the community hall on Lale Street."

"Give you a talk about what?"

"Chernograd, witchcraft, the Wall . . . I'm so glad you've made it through the Wall, by the way. We've been sending petitions to the government for years, trying to convince them to evacuate the human population from Chernograd, but it's been no use."

To *evacuate* them?

"But Chernograd is our home," Kosara mumbled.

"Sorry, what?"

"I said Chernograd is my home."

"You can't mean that. It's full of monsters."

Kosara did mean it. Chernograd was where she'd grown up. Where her house was, and her work, and her family—what was left of it, at least.

Some monsters were a part of families, too. You couldn't convince people they had to "evacuate" and leave Uncle Dimitar behind, just because he grew a bit hairier during the full moon. Aunty Kalina shouldn't have to stay alone in the house simply because she hap-pened to have died fifty years ago.

"No," the teenaged girl insisted. "You can't mean that. Once the Royal Council lets us, we'll evacuate everyone. You'll see."

The Royal Council? She couldn't mean *that* Royal Council: the twelve wizards who'd erected the Wall in the first place a hundred years ago.

"Surely the Royal Council are all dead. . . ." Kosara said.

"Most of them did get replaced, you're right, but believe it or not, Grand Magus Kliment is still going. They wheel him out every New Year's Eve to give a speech on the radio about the dangers of letting the Chernogradeans come here and"—the girl shaped air quotes with her fingers—"*steal our jobs*. Complete nonsense. Chauvinistic propaganda."

Kosara could tell the girl was about to launch into another passionate defence of Chernograd. Thankfully, she spotted Bistra rushing through the crowd towards her.

"Follow me," Bistra mouthed.

"Excuse me," Kosara said to the teenager.

"Every Wednesday at seven!" the girl shouted after her. "We have wine and cheese!"

Bistra led Kosara through the boutique, ably navigating the maze of fabric and precious stones. In the back of the shop, a small door nestled in between two overflowing clothes racks. Bistra selected a key hanging on a chain around her neck, unlocked the door, and gestured at Kosara to follow her through.

This room was arranged more like a museum than a shop. Only the soft glow of the display cases broke up the darkness. Inside them real samodiva hair gleamed, real upir teeth dripped venom, and real varkolak fur glistened, waxy in the electric light. When Kosara read the price labels, her head started spinning.

"I am so sorry about earlier," Bistra said. "I didn't realise you were a witch. I love your shoes, by the way."

Kosara looked down at her muddy boots. "Thanks?"

"Very bohemian chic. I should have immediately known you are a witch, you have such a unique sense of style."

Kosara sensed there was a thinly veiled insult somewhere in between the pleasantries, but she couldn't put her finger on it.

"In fact," Bistra continued, "me and the other girls love to play a game whenever someone walks in the shop. We call it, 'Witch or Bag Lady,' ha-ha."

There was the insult.

"Ha-ha," Kosara said without smiling.

Bistra, on the other hand, was all smiles. "What can I help you with today? We've got a large collection of amulets and talismans, the best in all of Belograd, if I say so myself. For example, we just received a seer's eye. They're very rare, as I'm sure you know."

Kosara heard herself saying, "Can I see it?" She wasn't entirely sure why. Some macabre curiosity.

Bistra slid on a pair of cotton gloves and unlocked one of the display cases. She handed Kosara a ring embedded with an eye instead of a stone. A couple of thin blood vessels ran down the eyeball before disappearing into the silver setting. Kosara waved her hand in front of the eye, and it followed her movement. She shuddered.

"How much?" Kosara asked.

"Two hundred ninety-five."

"It doesn't seem to be in the best condition."

"Four dioptres short-sighted," Bistra admitted. "But it does catch the eye as a fashion accessory, if you'll pardon the pun. What about two hundred ninety?"

"I'll think about it," Kosara said, doing her best impression of a person who had more money than sense. "Actually, what I'm here for is a witch's shadow."

For a brief second, something flashed in Bistra's eyes. Confusion? Fear? She covered it up with another smile. "What a lucky coincidence! You've come right on time. We're expecting a large delivery very soon."

Kosara kept her face neutral, despite her heart climbing in her throat. "Oh, how wonderful. How many can I buy for my collection? Twelve?"

"Now that's just freaky! That's exactly how many we're getting."

So, Sevar had been right. The stranger was about to sell the shadows. It took a con artist to know a con artist, Kosara supposed.

"Are you a bit of a seer yourself?" Bistra asked.

"A little bit," Kosara said. And then she inhaled deeply and found the courage to ask, "How much do they cost?"

Bistra's smile grew brighter. "Ten thousand grosh each. But if you want all twelve, I'm sure we can work out a bulk price—"

Kosara found it impossible to focus on the rest of the sentence.

Ten. Thousand. Grosh. She couldn't even imagine that much money in one place.

How would she ever get ten thousand grosh?

Robbing a bank? Too risky. Taking out a loan from one of Chernograd's gangsters? Even riskier. Selling a kidney? Perhaps the healthiest option.

There had to be someone out there looking for a witch's kidney. She could always start a rumour it was great for acne, or warts, or weight loss. Who needed two kidneys, anyway?

Or maybe there was another way. If she could see the stranger herself, try to convince him to make a deal with her . . .

"Can I speak to your supplier?" she asked. "I'd like to ask them a few questions about the shadows."

"That won't be necessary." Bistra saw right through her. "We'll take care of your order for you. Believe me, you're in safe hands with us. We've worked with some very important clients. We even do home deliveries, so you don't have to lift a finger."

Who knew buying smuggled magical objects was as easy as ordering a new hat from the milliners?

"In that case, can I give you my address?" Kosara said. "So you can contact me when you receive the shadows."

"Certainly. Just a second." Bistra opened a drawer hidden under the upir-teeth display and pulled out a leather-bound notebook. Its pages were covered top to bottom in tiny handwriting: a list of names, addresses, and phone numbers.

The stranger's name and address must have been in there somewhere. Only an arm's length away. Kosara craned her neck to take a peek inside, but Bistra turned it away from her.

"Your name?" Bistra asked, her pen ready.

"Kosara Popova. I live on—"

The clicking of heels sounded from the hallway. Bistra swore under her breath.

The door flew open. At the threshold stood a tall woman, made even taller by a pair of impossibly high stilettos. She also wore—Kosara did a double take to make sure she wasn't seeing things—a cape. Black velvet with a red silk lining. It whispered against the parquet as she marched towards them.

"What's going on here? Give me that!" The tall woman grabbed the key hanging around Bistra's neck and pulled it sharply until the chain undid itself.

Bistra's smile didn't falter. "Um, this is Kosara, Mistress Ruseva. She's a witch, and she—"

"She isn't a witch. How many times have I told you to ask before bringing people here?" Ruseva dropped the key in her cape's inside pocket.

"You were out for lunch," Bistra said, her smile still on her face. Her eyes, however, were welling up. "I was simply trying to take initiative, as we discussed during my last career progression meeting. She said she was a witch—"

"I'm standing right here!" Kosara said. "And I am a witch."

Ruseva wrinkled her nose, as if Kosara was something she'd found stuck to her sole. "Don't lie to me, darling. You're not a witch. You know how I know?"

Kosara bit her lip. She had no idea what had given her away. It was too dark in the boutique for anyone to notice her shadow missing.

In Chernograd, witches were relatively common. Kosara suspected this was because of the city's proximity to the monsters' realm. After all, the first witches had learned magic to fight the monsters.

Everywhere else magic users were becoming rarer and rarer, ever since the Wall was built. Which is why the next thing Ruseva said came as a complete surprise.

"I know because I am a witch."

Damn it. That was just Kosara's luck.

"I can smell another witch's magic from miles away," Ruseva continued. "You don't smell of magic, but of cheap perfume and sour cabbage."

And you smell of casual xenophobia and a superiority complex.

Kosara didn't clench her fists, didn't swing, and didn't punch Ruseva in her big, self-important nose. Instead, she smiled. "We'll speak again."

As she walked towards the door, she bumped into Ruseva shoulder-first, making the tall woman stagger.

"Excuse me." Kosara placed the key for the room in her coat's pocket.

———————

The shutters came rattling down. The clicking of heels faded into the distance.

The boutique grew eerily quiet: the only sound was the tapping of the stray cats' nails on the ceramic tiles as they darted across the roof. Kosara stretched, and the cracking of her neck sounded thunderously loud.

She couldn't tell how late it was. She'd lost track of time, hiding behind a rack of discounted silk shawls from last year's collection, waiting for the boutique to shut. The sickly sweet scent of the perfume the fabric was drenched in made her dizzy. At one point, she almost got caught by an overzealous bargain hunter who seemed determined to go through the entire rack. The only thing that saved her was the bargain hunter's toddler who'd started crying for ice cream.

Kosara cracked her neck again and rubbed her stiff shoulders. This had better be worth it.

She felt her way around the boutique in the darkness, bumping into velvet walls and barely crawling through narrow silk tunnels. Still a bit disoriented, she turned in what she thought was the right direction. Her body slammed into a mannequin.

Kosara reached to stop it. Too late.

It tumbled and crashed onto the floor. One of its necklaces caught on her outstretched fingers. It snapped, sending hundreds of glass beads clanking across the room.

Kosara froze. A second passed, then another. Nothing happened.

She allowed herself to exhale. *Damn you, Kosara, and your clumsy sausage fingers.*

She kept walking, slower and more cautious. Finally, she reached the door hidden in the back of the boutique. The key turned in the keyhole with a satisfying click.

Kosara crossed the room, careful not to touch any of the shiny display cases. She'd read enough detective novels to know leaving fingerprints was a very bad idea.

The address book was still in the same drawer, thank God. Kosara leaned closer to the glowing display case and flipped to the last page. She saw her own name there, under the heading, "interested in witches' shadows." "Kosara Pop" was all Bistra had managed before Ruseva had interrupted her.

Kosara read through the names, not entirely sure what she was looking for. Her heart beat faster whenever she stumbled upon the word "witch." It soon became obvious the boutique sold a large quantity of witch's hats, dresses and ruby-red slippers, witch's wands and cauldrons and herb clippers, witch's teeth—*ew*—and warts—*double ew*—and nail clippings—honestly, who'd pay money for *that*?

And then, just as Kosara was starting to lose hope, her eyes fell on the next entry, under yesterday's date: *Enquiry about 12 witches' shadows. Send M to check it out.* There was also a second note from the same day: *Witches' shadows still unavailable. Send M again tomorrow.*

Send M *where*?

Kosara flicked through the notebook frantically, back and forth, searching for more clues. *Come on.* There had to be an address in there somewhere. *Come on!*

At last, in the margin of a random page, she found a hastily scribbled note: *Witch sh. at 19 Tombul St. Tell M!!!*

Yes! Nineteen Tombul Street. She allowed herself to do a small triumphant dance. *Yes!*

Now, all she had to do was to tiptoe back out of this room, crawl out of the boutique through the window, and take a trip to Tombul Street, wherever the hell that was. Her shadow was so close, she could taste the spells on her tongue. *Yesss!*

Kosara opened the drawer again. Just as she was about to stuff the notebook back inside, she noticed something wet and shiny glistening on her fingertips. The smell was unmistakable. Paint.

The smile froze on her face. She kneeled down and looked at the drawer more closely. Just as she'd suspected: a freshly painted series of symbols glistened on the underside of the handle. She'd somehow avoided them when she first opened the drawer, but the second time, her luck had run dry.

They weren't like the symbols she knew from Chernograd—sharp and angular. They were elegant, flowing together seamlessly. She couldn't read them, but she could guess their meaning. They spelled an alarm.

The notebook slid from her fingers and fell to the floor with a thud.

Kosara rushed towards the exit, her heart thumping in her ears. She'd barely made a step when the door slammed open. Ruseva stood in the door frame for a dramatic second, her cape billowing and her arm outstretched, pointing at Kosara.

"Did you really think I wouldn't notice the key missing?" Her voice echoed in the room. "Gentlemen!"

Ruseva stepped sideways, holding her cape so it billowed just right. Police officers in navy-blue uniforms flooded the room. One of them clicked a pair of handcuffs open.

Kosara swore under her breath. Amazingly, in all her years of barely legal dealings, she'd never been arrested before. She knew there was something she was supposed to say, something Roksana had taught her a long time ago, about lawyers and presence and speaking, or not speaking or . . .

Her brain felt like scrambled eggs.

"I will only speak in the presence of my lawyer," she finally managed.

She didn't have a lawyer. She couldn't afford a lawyer.

The police officer with the handcuffs took that as a cue to advance towards her. His fingers clenched around her wrists. They were burning hot. So hot, she couldn't shake the feeling of déjà vu, from the time she'd spent with the Zmey.

Suddenly, she felt like a trapped animal. *Run!* her mind shouted, but run where? She was surrounded by blue uniforms.

"That won't be necessary, Constable Petrov." A dark-haired man entered the room, his bright-red coat contrasting against the sea of blue. Judging by the silence that fell among the police officers, he outranked them. A few saluted.

He tipped his hat to Kosara, as if he'd met her at the local dance hall, not in the middle of breaking and entering.

"I'm sure Miss Popova will come with us voluntarily." He flashed her a bright smile.

Who the hell is this guy?

"Detective Sergeant Asen Bakharov," he said, as if reading her thoughts. "From the Supernatural Investigations Unit."

"I am—"

"I know who you are." He gestured towards the door. "Please, after you."

As Kosara walked out, she could feel Ruseva's angry gaze on the back of her neck.

"Make sure to search her!" Ruseva shouted. And then, under her breath, "Thieving Chernogradean scum."

6

Day Four

The Supernatural Investigations Unit was housed in what seemed to be a repurposed storage cupboard. The desk only fit in it diagonally, and if Bakharov had sat in one of the chairs next to it, he wouldn't have been able to shut the door. Instead, he leaned on the desktop with his arms crossed and gestured at the chair across from him.

Kosara sat down and gripped the armrest so her fingers would stop trembling.

Calm down, damn it. Being calm was her only way out of this. She hadn't touched anything in the boutique, so they couldn't pin a burglary on her. Right?

Her best bet was to pretend she didn't realise she'd done something wrong. *What do you mean, sneaking into shops after they're shut is illegal in Belograd? It's one of Chernograd's favourite pastimes!* This clueless Belogradean copper would know no better.

Kosara struggled not to fidget in her seat. Her back hurt, and her neck was stiff. One solitary sunbeam squeezed through the tiny window opposite her and blinded her like a spotlight.

She needed her coffee, and a shower, and to brush her teeth. Her mouth tasted like an old ashtray. Her clothes stank of day-old sweat and the nauseating perfume of the Witch's Cauldron. She didn't even want to imagine what her hair looked like.

Detective Bakharov studied her, standing there in his perfectly pressed white shirt. He placed some kind of device on the desk in front of her. "Can you tell me what you were doing in the Witch's Cauldron last night?"

"What's that?" Kosara nodded towards the device.

"It's a voice recorder."

"You're going to capture my voice?"

"It's standard procedure. Don't worry, it's not dangerous."

It's not dangerous? He looked at her as if she was a superstitious fool. The sort of person who refused to have their picture taken out of fear the camera would steal their soul.

Kosara was from Chernograd—that didn't make her an idiot. She simply didn't like the idea that he'd record her, to be able to listen to what she told him over and over again, analysing her every word.

The device glared at her from the desktop, its tiny red light unblinking.

"So," Bakharov said, "can you tell me what you were doing in the Witch's Cauldron last night?"

Kosara inspected a small chip in her nail polish, perfectly casual. "I was just having a look."

"In the middle of the night?"

"I can't stand crowds."

"You don't seem to be grasping the seriousness of the situation. On your answers depends whether you'll get sent back to the holding cell to await sentencing, or allowed to walk free."

Sentencing? Kosara had zero time for any of this nonsense. It was simply unbelievable she'd got caught now, when her shadow waited for her at 19 Tombul Street. She kept repeating the address in her mind, too afraid she might forget it if she stopped: *19 Tombul Street, 19 Tombul Street . . .*

"You can't keep me prisoner." Kosara lifted her gaze and met his, even though the sun made her eyes water. She raised her hand in the air, did an elaborate twist with her wrist, and clicked her fingers. A miniature flame appeared on the tip of her thumb. She'd hidden the trick up her sleeve, just for situations like this. Every witch sometimes utilized a bit of smoke and mirrors. "There are no shackles I can't shatter. There isn't a door I can't unlock. There isn't a jail I can't escape."

"I can see you have no shadow."

"Oh." She put the flame out in her fist. *Maybe not so clueless, after all.*

Bakharov leaned forwards. Perhaps it was because of the sun in her eyes, or due to the lack of sleep, but he suddenly reminded her of Orhan Demirbash, the famous actor. He had the same brown eyes and thick dark hair. "Clever, though," he said. "You used to be a fire witch, didn't you?"

"I *am* a fire witch. How do you know?"

He nodded towards her hands, covered in burn scars.

"Oh," she said without thinking, "that wasn't me."

"Who was it then?"

The Zmey. "Is this in any way relevant to this interrogation?"

Bakharov smiled. "Fair point. Listen, Miss Popova—"

"How do you know my name?"

"One of my responsibilities is keeping an eye on all magic users in Belograd. Especially the new arrivals."

Kosara swore internally. Through her mind went all the times she'd broken the law recently: she'd practised witchcraft without a license, she'd sold fake talismans, she'd accepted payment without issuing receipts . . .

She'd crossed the Wall and refused to enter quarantine.

She took a deep breath, and said, a tad too fast to be believable, "I was just about to come in so you can put me under quarantine, but—"

"Of course you were. We'll get to that later. Firstly, explain to me what you were doing in the Witch's Cauldron last night."

"As I told you, I was just having a look."

"And what was it exactly you were looking for?"

Kosara stared at him. She'd fallen right into that one.

"You don't have to tell me," Bakharov said. "I can guess. Mistress Ruseva is convinced you were there to steal her merchandise, but we searched the room, and we know you went nowhere near any of the objects. We caught you red-handed, holding the boutique's address book. I believe you're looking for your shadow."

Kosara couldn't figure out where this was going. She crossed her arms and said nothing.

"I mean," Bakharov continued, "correct me if I'm wrong, but what other reason would a witch without a shadow have to sneak about a shop which specialises in magical artefacts—"

"Illegally smuggled magical artefacts," Kosara blurted before she could stop herself.

Bakharov smiled at her. He had a nice smile, she had to admit, for a copper. "Precisely! I'm glad we're on the same page. See, Miss Popova, the issue is, we know the boutique smuggles its merchandise from Chernograd. Where else would it all come from? However, we're having a very hard time proving it. Our informants refuse to talk. Our investigations inevitably lead to dead ends. I've spent years working on this case, and I think I might finally have a break."

"You do?" Kosara asked. "What break?"

His smile grew even brighter. "A witness."

Oh no. Kosara sank deeper into her chair. He was offering her a deal. They had a word back in Chernograd for people who made deals with the police. The closest translation she could think of in the Belogradean dialect was "scum."

"I'm well aware your people don't hold the police in particularly high regard," Bakharov said. Honestly, could he read her mind? "And I understand why a newly arrived refugee from Chernograd wouldn't even think to enlist our help to search for her shadow. But if you decide to report your shadow as stolen now—"

Kosara shook her head. He'd got it all wrong. "My shadow wasn't stolen. You can't steal a witch's shadow. I gave it to a man I met playing Kral." She saw his confused face, and added, "It's a card game."

For a second, she wished she hadn't said it. It made her sound like a right fool. But then, who cared about the opinion of some Belogradean copper?

"All right," Bakharov said. "That's a bit of a setback, but not all is lost." He produced a folder from his desk drawer and flicked through its contents until he found a photograph. "Do you know this man?"

Kosara's heart climbed so high up her throat she was worried it might fall out if she opened her mouth.

"Judging by your face, you do," Bakharov said. "What can you tell me about him?"

"He was the man I met playing Kral. The man who took my shadow."

"Where did you meet him?"

"Back in Chernograd."

Bakharov pulled a notepad from his breast pocket and began writing. "And was he, by any chance, wearing bright-red shoes?"

"Yes, I believe he was. Why?"

"As it happens, a pair of red shoes was stolen from the Royal Archaeological Museum a few weeks back."

"Why? Were they expensive?" From what she remembered, they'd looked like a regular old pair of suede brogues.

"I believe the word the curator used was 'priceless.'" Bakharov glanced up at Kosara for a brief second. "I suppose there's no reason not to tell you, since the burglary is on the front pages of every newspaper. The shoes were an invaluable magical artefact, known as 'teleport brogues.' The rumour is, they were made by a wizard from Belograd shortly after the Wall was built, in order to visit his Chernogradean lover."

Kosara couldn't believe her ears. She'd known the Belogradeans had no respect for magic, but this was simply outrageous. A magical artefact this powerful getting buried among dusty vases and old mummies in some *museum*?

"And you just kept them there?" she asked. "In that Royal Museum of yours?"

"Under very strict security, I assure you. The truth is, the Belogradean academic community had long assumed the magic words to activate the shoes died with the man who crafted them. Now we know this is not the case. Irnik Ivanov obviously used them to cross the Wall." Bakharov tapped on the stranger's photograph. *Irnik Ivanov.* Kosara made sure to remember it.

"The thing is," Bakharov continued, "we strongly suspected he was involved in the burglary, since he started working at the museum shortly before it happened. But as far as proof goes, he's done an exceptional job covering his tracks. We have no proof of his involvement with the Witch's Cauldron boutique either, other than a calling card we found on him when he was asked to come in for an interrogation. It's all very flimsy. Unless, of course, you agree to testify."

Here was that disarming smile again. Kosara didn't let herself trust it—he might not have been in uniform, but he was still a police officer. She'd recognise his friendly cop act anywhere.

She chewed on her lip. There was a good reason why he had trouble convincing witnesses to talk. Chernogradean smugglers weren't known for their forgiving nature. Anyone who snitched risked finding themselves at the bottom of the sea with a pair of ankle bracelets made of lead.

"Look, Detective Bakharov—"

"Please, call me Asen."

"I'm not sure I have as much information as you think I have. I didn't even know Irnik Ivanov's name until you just told me it."

He scratched his chin with the end of his pencil. "You might know more than you suspect. Why don't you tell me the entire story? Start with how you met Mr. Ivanov during that Kral game you mentioned."

Kosara saw no reason to hide anything. As far as she was aware, she'd done nothing illegal crossing the Wall—it was Irnik Ivanov who'd committed a crime smuggling her in. Cooperating now would only mean getting out of this mess quicker. She told Bakharov the whole story, only skipping the parts about the Zmey that felt too personal.

As she talked, her eyes darted around the office. She spotted no personal touches: no plant pots on the windowsill, no children's drawings attached to the cupboards, no family photographs on the desk. The walls were bare, except for a pin board hanging next to the door, covered in training certificates, newspaper clippings, and shiny commendation letters from the mayor of Belograd herself.

One of the newspaper articles caught Kosara's eye. On the photograph, Bakharov led an older man towards the station. Despite being handcuffed, the man threw a smile over his shoulder at the camera. Kosara would recognise his self-important smirk anywhere: the man was Konstantin Karaivanov, the infamous Chernogradean smuggler.

Under it hung another newspaper clipping—this one crumpled—which reported on Karaivanov's escape from prison. It looked as if somebody had clenched it in his fist, before flattening it somewhat and pinning it to the board.

I've been working on this case for years. . . . Dear God, Bakharov thought Irnik was involved with Karaivanov's gang, Chernograd's most notorious smuggling circle. Bakharov believed Karaivanov was the one who'd stolen her shadow!

Was it possible? Perhaps. Irnik certainly didn't seem like the mastermind of the operation. Was it likely?

Karaivanov was a greasy little weasel, but he surely knew better than to tread on the toes of Chernograd's magic community. He was well aware that the only thing witches could stand even less than other witches was people who tried to fuck with other witches.

At the same time, he also knew how much a witch's shadow cost.

"As I told you," Kosara said at the end, "I don't think any of this is particularly useful information."

Bakharov kept scribbling in his notepad without looking up at her. "Thank you. You've been very helpful. I trust you'd be willing to repeat your story in court?"

Kosara made a noncommittal harrumph.

"Or would you rather return to the cell?"

Kosara really, truly had no time for this. "I will," she said. Here's hoping she got her shadow back before Karaivanov's cronies got *her*.

"It's important that you lie low until that happens. I can't have my only witness putting herself in danger. I don't know what you found in the Witch's Cauldron, but I don't want you trying to do anything on your own accord. Leave it to us. Will you?"

No way. "I will," she said, smiling. He wasn't the only one in the room who could disarm with a smile.

Bakharov gave her a long look. "Good," he said at last.

"So, when you said I'd be able to walk away free . . ."

"Of course. Right after your quarantine. Give me a second, I'll find a refugee form for you to fill out, and then you'll have forty-eight hours to hand yourself in." He studied her face carefully. Then he added, "I hope you understand the quarantine is for your own good, as much as for the good of Belograd."

Sure. That's why if you discover I'm infected, you'll shoot me. For my own good.

Still, arguing with Bakharov would be a waste of time. It wasn't he who made the rules, he just followed them infuriatingly strictly.

He asked her to sign two copies of at least two dozen different forms and agreements. She confirmed she wasn't a lycanthrope, she swore she had no prior family history of upirism, she promised she'd do her best not to turn into a wraith—as if that was something under her control. . . .

At the end, she formally agreed to return to the police station in forty-eight hours to be detained. *Yeah, right.* Once she got her shadow back, they could do nothing to force her. She was a witch, and there weren't shackles she couldn't shatter.

"Don't even consider trying to hide," Bakharov said. Perhaps she had to work on her poker face. "All our government is asking from you is to stay detained within the station until the full moon is over. Three days, that's all. After that you'll be free to do as you please."

"Of course." She stood up.

Bakharov walked her to the door and extended his hand towards her. "It was a pleasure talking to you."

"Yes," Kosara said, but she couldn't bring herself to say the same. "Well, goodbye."

She made to shake his hand, her eyes still fixed on him. For some reason, she grasped at nothing but air. Her fingertips tingled. It felt like the anticipation right before casting a spell—like an itch in a phantom limb.

Kosara frowned and looked down.

One second, her hand appeared just like it always did—covered in burn scars, dry from the winter air, with calluses at the fingertips from casting spells. Then, for a blink of an eye, it changed, turning midnight black and flat like an ink drawing. Like a shadow.

Kosara stifled a scream. This wasn't possible. This couldn't be happening.

Of course it can, silly. You know this is what happens to witches who've been stupid *enough to trade away their shadows.*

Yes, fine, Kosara admitted, *I knew that.* But it couldn't be happening so *fast.*

She'd thought she had years before the sickness finally caught up with her. Decades. Not four days.

Perhaps she'd imagined it. She'd been through a lot and—

Kosara looked up and met Bakharov's eyes. Immediately, she knew she hadn't imagined it.

"I'm so sorry," he said quickly. For the first time since she'd met him, he seemed flustered. "That's terrible. Awful. I've never seen it manifest so quickly."

Kosara sighed. Of course he knew exactly what he was witnessing. It was a strangely intimate moment to share with a complete stranger. It was, essentially, her death sentence.

And, judging by the pity in his eyes, he knew it. Why did the sickness always have to start at the fingertips, advertising its presence for all to see? Couldn't it begin at her armpit or the small of her back?

"I knew an old witch once," Bakharov said in the same rushed voice. "She traded her shadow for a new liver, she lived for thirty-five years after that. She had twelve grandchildren, and twenty-four great grandchildren, and—"

The man was positively babbling.

"Well, I won't live for thirty-five years," Kosara interrupted him, though she wasn't really listening. She was too busy watching her hands, blinking into shadow every couple of seconds. Tears prickled at her eyes.

She had to get out of there before she started crying in front of this copper.

"Is there anything—" he began.

"No," Kosara said quickly. "I'll see you in forty-eight hours." She shuffled past him and all but ran out the door.

Though she'd tried not to meet his gaze, she could see it in his face: he knew she was lying. There was no way she'd waste time on a quarantine now. She had to move fast. If she didn't get her magic back, she'd be worse than dead.

She'd be a shadow.

Kosara sat on her bed, a fluffy towel balanced on top of her head. Clouds of steam rolled out the open bathroom door, filling the room. She'd scrubbed herself until she was raw, but she could still smell that cheap lemon cleaner they'd used to wash the holding cell.

She had to dry her hair, put clothes on, and hurry to Tombul Street to get her shadow back—but she could do none of these things. She'd wasted most of the day now, and it was too late to make her way to Irnik's end of the city.

In her lap, her fingers kept switching between shadow and flesh. Her borrowed hairbrush lay on the floor at her feet.

Kosara pressed the heels of her hands to her eyes. There had to be something she could do about this. If she didn't, soon the sickness would engulf her whole arm. She'd barely managed to unlock her door—she'd kept dropping the key, letting it fall to the floor with a loud clang. It was a miracle Gizda hadn't come to check what was happening.

Kosara examined her shadowy fingertips. This was some kind of magic, it had to be. It certainly wasn't a normal illness. And every magic, once cast, could be controlled with a lot of focus.

Kosara focused on her fingertips so hard colourful spots danced in front of her vision. Nothing happened.

She swore quietly. What else did magic need? Herbs, and chants, and runes, and magic words . . .

Unbidden, a song came to her mind—one her dad used to sing to her when she was little, when he helped her wash her hands before dinner. *Hey, hands, hey, the two of you, one of you washes the other, and then both of you wash the face. . . .*

Kosara's fingertips stopped tingling. For a long second, the shadow sickness disappeared.

Then, it bloomed again, stronger and darker than before, running all the way from Kosara's hands, up her arms, tickling her collarbone, and finally reaching for her chin.

She jumped up from the bed and ran to the bathroom, her wet feet slapping against the cold tiles. Frantically, she wiped the steam off the mirror.

Her shadow sickness had almost reached her face, its dark tentacles wrapping around her neck. All she'd done was speed the disease up.

Great job, Kosara, she thought bitterly.

But then it hit her. She looked up at the gap in the steamed surface of the mirror and down at her hands. She'd managed to move the sickness off her fingertips. It had worked.

She watched as the sickness drained off her neck, back down her arms, and finally settled over her fingertips again.

"Hey, hands," Kosara half-sang, half-mumbled. "Hey, the two of you . . ."

Her sickness started creeping up her arm again.

Huh. It wasn't ideal, but it worked. She ran a finger over the dark shadows covering her neck. It looked kind of cool, she had to admit. Like an elaborate lace collar, or a tattoo. And the best part was, she could put on a scarf, and nobody would know.

Until it reached her face, that was.

7

Day Five

Tombul Street was as if taken from a postcard: the facades were newly plastered, the cobblestones shone, the rose bushes in the gardens were heavy with blossoms. It was one of those streets where everyone knew each other by name, and no one locked their doors; where the youth didn't smoke, the men didn't swear, and the women went shopping for fun. Kosara advanced carefully, like an explorer in an unfamiliar jungle.

As she walked up the street, dozens of curious eyes followed her. The curtains stirred. The old women knitting and gossiping on the garden benches stared at her. A man pulling on a long-stemmed pipe almost forgot to exhale again and began coughing. A group of children stopped their game of football just to gape at her.

When Kosara finally reached the house at number nineteen, she inhaled and exhaled slowly a few times to calm her heartbeat. Her trembling fingers grasped the knife hidden up her sleeve.

Kosara still wasn't sure what she'd tell Irnik Ivanov. She kept starting arguments in her head, without being able to finish them. *Listen, I know you don't want to piss off Chernograd's most notorious gangster, but . . . Look, I'm aware you've promised my shadow to what seems to be a money-laundering operation on the Main Street, however . . .*

But what? However what? Could she explain how much he'd taken away from her? How taking a witch's shadow was like taking her soul, and living without it caused her to slowly fade into a shadow herself? And if she told him all that, would he care?

Kosara inhaled deeply. There was only one way to find out.

She knocked on the door. No reply. A few seconds later, she knocked again. An old man smoking on the balcony next door threw her a suspicious look.

She tried the handle. It was unlocked.

Of course the door was unlocked. Lucky Irnik lived in such a posh neighbourhood. If this had been the Chernogradean Quarter, she'd have had to deal with at least three locks and a homemade trap on the other side.

Her sweaty hand slid over the knife's handle. *It'll be fine. You're just here to talk. Nothing bad's going to happen.*

She took a few more deep breaths and entered. The first thing she saw was the tapestry-woven carpet, decorated with golden thread, bordered with large tassels, soaked in blood. Then she noticed the body.

Kosara was a witch. She'd bandaged upir bites, dressed samodiva arrow wounds, and stitched limbs torn by varkolaks. She was used to dealing with corpses—sometimes years after their death, when they crawled out of their graves in search of human blood.

She'd never seen anything like this. The stranger lay on his back. She wouldn't have recognised him if it wasn't for his polka-dot neckerchief. He'd been attacked with some kind of curved knife, perhaps, or maybe a dagger. Whatever it was, it had been nasty. It had torn off large chunks from his face.

His murder had been brutal. Senseless. Obviously done in anger.

Kosara winced but she couldn't look away, not yet. She carefully pulled down Irnik's blood-soaked neckerchief. A groan escaped her throat. Only a thin bloody line remained in place of his necklace of shadows. Kosara wouldn't have spotted it among the other bruises, if she hadn't been looking for it. Someone had pulled the necklace off his neck forcefully enough to slice through his skin.

This was why he'd been murdered, she was certain. You didn't walk around with twelve witches' shadows around your neck without attracting some unwanted attention.

The room spun. Acid burned at the back of Kosara's throat.

She dashed out of the house and leaned on the door frame. The cold air prickled her sweaty skin. It smelled of freshly cut grass and coming rain. She inhaled deeply to chase away the stench of death stuck in her nostrils.

Only a couple of days ago, she'd spoken to Irnik. He'd been alive— drinking, playing cards, asking stupid questions. And now he was lying on the floor in a puddle of his own blood. Because of a necklace of witches' shadows.

Kosara waited until her head stopped spinning before returning to the house. She had to concentrate. There was a reason she'd come here. She had to find her shadow.

A blood-splattered telephone lay on the floor near the body, its receiver open. Of course Irnik had been rich enough to afford a telephone. The dial signal echoed in the quiet living room. Kosara knew she ought to phone the police—but not before she'd had a good search around.

She kneeled next to the body. The smell hit her: metallic like blood and putrid like death. Still, she persevered, trying to take small, shallow breaths. It only made her dizzier.

She looked up and saw a kaleidoscope of Kosaras staring back at her from the shattered mirror above the couch. Their faces were ashen, their eyes wide with panic. *Deep breaths,* she reminded herself, *deep breaths.*

Kosara went through Irnik's pockets, as difficult as that was with her fingers switching between shadow and flesh like a semaphore tower. She kept pushing the sickness up her arms, but whenever she got distracted, it returned, darker than before.

All she found were a calling card from the Witch's Cauldron and a pamphlet from the Friends of Chernograd Society. Kosara suspected Irnik had also met the talkative teenager in the boutique.

As she stuffed the papers back into his pocket, something caught her eye. On the floor right next to the body, almost invisible among the rest of the gore, was a drawing. It looked as if someone had dipped their index finger in the pool of blood and hastily scribbled a symbol.

Two interlocking K's. The sign of Konstantin Karaivanov's gang.

Kosara swore loudly. *Of course* Karaivanov was involved in this.

What had poor Irnik done to anger him? Had he tried to double-cross Karaivanov? Had he asked for too much money for the shadows? Kosara couldn't imagine a transgression bad enough to cause this level of carnage.

If Karaivanov was responsible for the murder, chances were, he'd used one of his Chernogradean cronies to do it. Perhaps Kosara ought to ask around. Someone must have heard something—according to Gizda, nothing remained a secret for long in the Chernogradean Quarter.

Pity Roksana had returned to Chernograd. She'd worked for Karaivanov back in the day, when she'd been younger, stupider, and desperate for quick cash. She probably still knew a few people who could give Kosara more information. . . .

For a brief second, a gust of wind rushed through the open door, dispersing the stench of death. A terribly familiar smell lingered in the room.

Seer's sage.

The coppers crawled over the crime scene like hardworking ants. Anywhere Kosara looked, there were navy-blue uniforms: taking photographs, dusting for fingerprints, filling test tubes, scribbling notes, drawing sketches. The pathologists marked the position of the body with pins and a string. Bakharov exchanged a few words with them, before leaning over Irnik and inspecting the wounds himself.

Kosara let him usher her out of the living room into the hallway. Her stomach was tight as a fist. Irnik had died because of her shadow. Someone wanted it, and the other eleven, badly enough to *kill*. She could still smell the seer's sage in the room.

No, it couldn't be. There had to be some rational explanation. Roksana couldn't be the only person out there who smoked seer's sage. Of course, it only grew in Chernograd. . . .

Kosara realised Bakharov had asked her a question. "Sorry, what did you say?"

"I said, does the name Roksana Tatarova ring any bells?"

Kosara blinked. No, it *couldn't* be. "It does. Why?"

"Her fingerprints are all over the crime scene."

Kosara thought she might be sick right then and there, all over Bakharov's shiny shoes. She managed to swallow the bile.

"Well, what can you tell me about her?" Bakharov asked.

Kosara knew what she wanted to say, "You've made a mistake" or "Roksana can't be involved in this." But she'd read enough detective novels. Fingerprints didn't lie.

She should have known. Even Roksana wasn't reckless enough to risk crossing the Wall simply for an old friend's engagement party. The monster hunter had come here chasing the stranger and his necklace of witches' shadows. The question was, why?

When they'd met at Sevar's party, Roksana had pretended to be sympathetic to Kosara's condition. She'd acted as if she didn't know where the stranger was. And Kosara had believed her, naïve fool that she was.

What could have pushed Roksana to steal her shadow and murder a man? What could Karaivanov possibly have promised her to justify that?

Nothing, Kosara realised. Nothing could justify that.

Perhaps there was some sort of an innocent explanation. There had to be. Roksana was a hot-headed idiot, but she wasn't a murderer. Kosara had known her for years. She was *not* a murderer.

Maybe Roksana had come to see the stranger, for a nice glass of rakia and a game of cards, before someone else had barged into the room and committed the murder.

Or maybe you're being a naïve fool again, a small voice whispered in Kosara's mind.

In any case, once Kosara found her, Roksana had a lot of explaining to do. And if she was involved in this, Kosara would make her wish she'd refused Karaivanov.

Kosara blinked fast, dispelling the red curtain that had fallen in front of her eyes. She unclenched her fists. Then, she took a deep breath and told Bakharov everything she could remember about meeting Roksana at the party. She had no reason to cover for the monster hunter.

Bakharov wrote it all down in his notebook. "Thank you," he said, once she'd finished her story. "And when I told you to lie low and do nothing, how exactly did you interpret that to mean 'go straight to Irnik Ivanov's house'?"

"I'm not that familiar with the Belogradean dialect. I must have misunderstood."

She could tell Bakharov wanted to roll his eyes at her, but he kept his face professionally straight. He glanced at the crime scene, winced, and looked away again. "Did you touch anything in there?"

"No, of course not. I phoned you straight away."

"Good." Bakharov's face made it obvious he didn't believe her. "And there's nothing else you'd like to tell me? Are you sure?"

"If I knew anything, I'd tell you." Kosara raised her hands in the air. "I want this solved as badly as you do."

"I suppose you do."

"You have to interrogate that harpy from the Witch's Cauldron. I'd bet you she's involved. I saw it in her notebook, she kept trying to get her hands on the shadows—"

"Trust me," Bakharov said. *As if.* "We'll explore every possible avenue. Don't concern yourself with the investigation. As I said, lie low. Do nothing. We'll find your shadow."

"Yes," Kosara said. "Of course."

A line appeared between Bakharov's eyebrows. "I really didn't expect you to agree so easily."

"What can I say, I have full faith in the competence of the Belogradean police."

The line deepened. Perhaps she'd gone too far with that one. "Is that so. . . ."

"Detective Bakharov!" shouted one of the officers examining the scene. "You have to see this!"

"Excuse me." Bakharov rushed back into the room. He had to bend to pass under the ladder in front of the door. A copper stood atop it, scraping droplets of dried blood off the ceiling and collecting them in a test tube.

Kosara tried to follow Bakharov, but a police officer the size of a three-door wardrobe blocked her way. She stood on tiptoes to look over his broad shoulders.

"What's the problem, Lila?" Bakharov asked.

One of the officers held some kind of device towards him. It made a loud beeping noise. Electric light flashed between its two protruding wires.

"The magic interference in this room is off the charts," Lila said. The device's light reflected in her eyes. "The detector has been going wild ever since I switched it on, but look, as soon as I get closer to the victim . . ." A flash of electricity jumped between the wires, hissing.

Kosara squinted, trying to see what the device was pointed to. She made out the symbol she'd seen earlier, Karaivanov's two crossed K's, and then she saw another symbol on the floor near it. Another one was drawn on the dresser, and one on the curtain. . . . She hadn't spotted them earlier; closer up, they blended in with the gore splattered all over. From a distance, it was obvious. A magic circle covered half the living room.

Bakharov examined the device, pushing the same big red button over and over. "It might be malfunctioning."

"Maybe we should try switching it off and on again," Lila said.

"I know what it is!" Kosara shouted. The tall policeman stood straighter, trying to block her view of the scene. Too late. She waved a hand over his shoulder. "Bakharov, I know what it is."

Bakharov considered her for a second. "What is it?"

"Can I come in?"

"Obviously not. This is a crime scene. What is it?"

"It's a magic circle. Look, this symbol over here is connected to that one, right across from it. This one—to that other one over there. Do you see it?"

"Is it a trap? Is that what killed Irnik Ivanov?"

"Not a trap. The symbols scattered around the room are directions.

This one literally says 'North.'" Kosara pointed at a North arrow scribbled on the mirror frame. "And this"—she nodded at the two K's—"is the destination. It's a teleportation spell. Whoever the murderer was, they had one of Karaivanov's amulets for crossing the Wall. It teleported them straight to Chernograd."

Was this what Roksana had meant when she'd told Kosara she'd find some other way to cross the Wall again? *Christ.*

Bakharov looked down at the two K's. His lips shaped a swear word, but no sound came out.

"What does that mean?" Lila asked, the device in her hand still hissing.

Bakharov sighed. "It means they've escaped us again."

"Should I send another request for assistance to the colleagues from the Chernogradean police?"

"Yes. Send them another one. Kosara . . ." Bakharov shuffled past the policeman guarding the door. He leaned in and whispered, "Are you certain it's a teleportation spell?"

"Absolutely."

"And it leads back to Chernograd?"

"Yes."

He considered this for a second. "Darn it," he concluded. "Thank you for your help. Still, I'm going to repeat my advice: lie low. Don't get yourself in danger. We need you now, more than ever. You might be our key to untangling this mess."

"I'll keep out of trouble," Kosara said, praying Bakharov didn't notice the blood rushing to her cheeks. It always happened when she told a bald-faced lie.

"I hope you're going straight home now to pack your bag for tomorrow's quarantine."

"I'm going straight home."

"Good." Bakharov walked her to the front door. "Good."

Kosara wove through the crowd of neighbours gathered in front of the house, trying to ignore their stares. Her hands were still covered in dried blood. Bakharov's gaze was pinned on the back of her neck. He'd follow her, she could feel it.

She *was* going home. Which was why she couldn't afford to have the nosy copper trailing her.

Kosara fished for the vial in her bag. Every witch could use a bit of smoke and mirrors—but also needed to know when it was time for real magic.

She unscrewed the lid and took in the smell of moss and peppermint. Then she hesitated. The vial contained the last few drops of a potent anti-tracing potion. Kosara had prepared it last winter, in an attempt to hide from the Zmey. As it turned out, it took more than a handful of moss and a few leaves of peppermint to escape the Tsar of Monsters. It had slowed him down, but he'd sniffed her out in the end.

But the clueless Belogradean? It was more than enough to throw him off her scent.

Kosara downed the potion in one go and watched as her steps in the snow disappeared behind her.

She smiled. She was going straight home.

Straight to Chernograd.

8

Day Five

"I'm not taking you to Chernograd," Sevar said. He stood at the threshold of his house in his nightshirt, his scrawny legs poking underneath like hairy quotation marks. Judging by how quietly he spoke, Nur must have been in bed. Kosara was confused for a moment, before she remembered—they were criminals. Of course they slept during the day.

"Come on, Sevar!" she said. "You owe me as much."

"I owe you money, not my life. Why would you want to return to that hellhole, anyway?"

"That 'hellhole' is my home. And my shadow is there."

For a second, Kosara considered asking Sevar about Roksana, but then she changed her mind. If Sevar knew anything about the murder, he wouldn't tell her. Those two were obviously thick as thieves.

"You took Roksana"—*the lying bastard*—"across just the other day. It can't be that dangerous."

Sevar rolled his eyes so hard, his irises disappeared for a second. "Did she tell you how we nearly died doing that?"

"But you made it through in the end, didn't you? Besides, you smuggle wine and cigarettes all the time."

"Yes, because the Wall doesn't attack wine and cigarettes. It attacks people. I don't normally fly with them. The balloon's enchanted to drop all the merchandise in the right place."

"But when you brought Roksana over—"

"Roksana and I both know how to take care of ourselves, and we still nearly died."

"Are you suggesting I can't take care of myself?"

Sevar's gaze darted towards the ground where Kosara didn't cast a shadow. "Well . . ."

"If you get me through the Wall, I'll never mention your debt again. Consider us even."

He scratched the stubble on his chin. "I don't know, Kosara. . . ."

"You want me to go away, don't you? You don't want me here in Belograd. You don't want me to show up at your wedding. Or to your first child's christening. No one wants a witch at their first child's christening, surely you've read your fairy tales."

Sevar sighed deeply. "You won't give up, will you?"

Kosara shook her head.

"For the record, I think this is a spectacularly stupid idea." He sighed again. "Wait here."

He disappeared for a few minutes. When he returned, he wore a big fur coat which covered him from neck to ankles. A lit cigarette hung in the corner of his mouth, quickly disappearing with every long pull. "Follow me."

Kosara gave him a bright smile. He didn't return it.

She could barely contain her excitement. At last, she was going back home. Back to find her shadow.

Back to the monsters. Back to the Zmey.

The smile fell off her face. *One problem at a time, Kosara. One at a time.*

Sevar led her along the street, to a rickety shed resting against the wall of a taller building. He unlocked it and gestured to Kosara to enter.

She frowned as she took in the dusty workbenches and the tools hanging on the walls. The smell of engine oil filled her nostrils.

"Why are we in your shed?" she asked. For a second, she considered whether she ought to be scared: she was an unarmed, magic-less witch trapped inside a shed with a criminal.

Then she dismissed it. It was just Sevar, after all.

He didn't answer her question. Instead, he began moving the tools on the wall—he turned a screwdriver ninety degrees and rotated a set of pliers. Kosara narrowed her eyes, trying to see a pattern in his actions, but she couldn't spot any.

Finally, he stepped back and examined his work. A second later, with an earsplitting creak, the workbench in the middle of the shed started to turn. It sank into the floor, revealing a spiral staircase.

"Ta-da," Sevar said without any humour.

Kosara raised her eyebrows at him. His operation was obviously a lot more complex than she'd expected. The only place she'd ever encountered such secret passages were romance novels set in ancient castles.

Sevar impatiently waved at Kosara to follow him, and she did, now even more apprehensively. Being a defenceless witch in a shed was one thing; being a defenceless witch in an underground tunnel was completely different. If something happened to her, no one would find her body down there.

"Are you sure about that?" she mumbled.

"This is Belograd, Kosara. Nothing more dangerous than rats lives underground."

"That's not making me feel much better."

"Honestly, you're fine with crossing the Wall, but you're afraid of rats? Come on." He gently pushed her forwards. Before she kept walking, Kosara checked if the knife she'd hidden up her sleeve was still there.

Sevar had a lantern with him, but it was only bright enough to illuminate his own steps. Kosara rummaged through her pockets until she found her miniature flame. In its light, everything looked flat—the stairs were bands of black and white dashing beneath their feet. She didn't realise they'd reached the end of the staircase and nearly tripped on the suddenly level ground.

They walked through what seemed to be an old sewage tunnel for a while, their feet splashing in the puddles. Occasionally, small shadows darted past Kosara's feet. *Just rats,* she reminded herself. Back in Chernograd, they'd be lucky not to meet a rusalka crawling on the moist floor, or a karakonjul driven half-mad by hunger.

Finally, Sevar unlocked another door, and they were outside again.

Kosara breathed in the cold air, trying to dispel the smell of mildew stuck in her throat.

They stood in a small courtyard enclosed by the backs of four tall industrial buildings. No windows overlooked it. The hot-air balloon was tied in the middle. It was easy to spot among the snow: both its envelope and its basket were dyed dark grey, so they would be invisible in the Chernogradean sky. Without saying a word, Sevar switched on the pump to start inflating it.

Kosara turned around, chewing on her lip. The pump was making an awful lot of noise. If Bakharov had somehow managed to track her . . .

No, that was nonsense. He couldn't have possibly counteracted her anti-tracing potion. She tried to ignore the way the back of her neck prickled, as if she was being watched.

Only a few minutes later, the balloon looked ready to go, bobbing in the wind between the buildings. Kosara wondered if there was any magic involved in powering it—compared to its puny little burner, it seemed too large.

"Where did you get all that silk?" Kosara ran her hand over the balloon's envelope. "It must have cost you a fortune."

Sevar didn't reply.

"You stole it, didn't you?"

He remained silent. His gaze was fixed somewhere behind her shoulder.

Kosara spun around and swore quietly as Bakharov stepped into the courtyard. His revolver was aimed straight at Sevar's chest.

Kosara bit the inside of her cheek. She'd never had a gun pointed at her before. She was acutely aware that a twitch of Bakharov's finger could lead to disaster. Her ears buzzed.

"Stop right there!" Bakharov shouted. "Don't make another move!" And then, just when Kosara thought he'd run out of police clichés, "Keep your hands where I can see them!"

"Thanks, Kosara." Sevar slowly raised his hands. "You just had to get us arrested, didn't you? Do you know how long I've been doing this without getting caught?"

Kosara's eyes were fixed on Bakharov. The barrel of the gun kept floating in and out of focus. "Did you follow me here?"

"Actually," Bakharov said, "it's called 'shadowing' when the police does it."

That wasn't possible. He couldn't have resisted the anti-tracing potion.

Unless Kosara hadn't brewed as good a potion as she'd thought. Or maybe it had gone off in the past year. Perhaps she hadn't screwed the lid properly the last time she'd used it. That would be just her luck.

"Why did you follow me?" she asked.

"I *shadowed* you because you didn't look as if you were going home. I figured you'd take me somewhere interesting. And I was right."

Kosara scoffed. She'd call Sevar a lot of things, but "interesting" wasn't one of them.

"Please, mister policeman," Sevar said in a small voice. "I'm not interesting in the slightest. I'm a small potato. I don't deal with anything dangerous, honestly."

"Smuggling anything through the Wall is dangerous."

"But you have to admit there is a difference between selling a few bottles of wine to a homesick Chernogradean refugee, and dealing with something like human trafficking. . . ."

"Weren't you just about to smuggle this woman across the Wall?"

"I'm right here," Kosara said. What was it with Belogradeans always talking about her in the third person? "He was taking me back to Chernograd. That can't be illegal. That's where I live."

"It is," Sevar muttered. "Smuggling anything, in any direction. Completely illegal."

Bakharov moved his gun between Sevar and Kosara.

"Please, mister policeman!" Sevar cried out. "Surely we can make some kind of deal."

Kosara tutted. Bad move, Sevar. Bakharov wasn't the type of copper who made those sorts of deals. Any minute now, he'd tell Sevar how many months he'd just added to his prison sentence simply by making this suggestion—

"Hmm." Bakharov ran a hand down his chin. "Perhaps."

What the hell?

Sevar still looked as if he was about to cry, this time from happiness. "I have money!" *Do you, now?* "Just say how much."

Bakharov considered him for a few seconds. "How about you take me across the Wall?"

The courtyard fell silent as Kosara and Sevar both gaped at him.

"What?" Kosara said, and it sounded as if she had an echo. Sevar had asked the same question.

"Take me across the Wall," Bakharov repeated. "I can't exactly arrest you for smuggling if you're smuggling *me*, can I?"

"Why would you want to go to Chernograd?" Sevar asked.

"Confidential police business."

"If this is a trap—"

"I don't need to trap you. I can already arrest you."

Sevar slowly lit another cigarette. His fingers shook. "I won't bring you back. What you're buying yourself is a one-way ticket."

"Deal."

A wry smile tugged on the corner of Kosara's lips. So, this was what all the theatrics were about. Bakharov was a surprisingly good actor, though now that she thought about it, he *had* overdone it a bit with the "keep your hands where I can see them."

Somehow, she was certain this wasn't an official police operation. This was simply him, stubbornly following a dangerous criminal into an even more dangerous city.

And to think for a brief moment she'd assumed Bakharov belonged to that mythical breed of *good* coppers. That maybe the Belogradean police had their act together, unlike their Chernogradean colleagues. As it turned out, Bakharov was just as crooked as the lot of them—coming here brandishing that gun of his as if it were a toy, extorting people.

The worst part was, he looked perfectly content with himself. He probably felt justified, breaking the law as long as he did it to catch criminals.

And, truth be told, Kosara suspected he'd never get in trouble for it. If anything, he'd probably get another shiny commendation letter from the mayor once he returned to Belograd.

"You're going after Karaivanov's gang, aren't you?" she asked.

Bakharov didn't even glance at her. "I don't believe any of this concerns you, Miss Popova. You're free to go."

"Go? Go where? You have to take me with you. It's the Foul Days over there."

Bakharov patted the revolver. "I don't believe I need you."

Kosara barely suppressed her laughter. Silly Belogradean copper. "You need me. I'm a witch."

"You're a charlatan."

She clutched her chest to show him he'd dealt her a deadly blow. As far as she was concerned, she was both.

"Do you know how to counteract a samodiva's curse?" she asked.

"No, why?"

"Do you know what varkolaks are afraid of?"

"I don't."

"How to set a karakonjul trap?"

"No."

"How to kill an upir? How to render a yuda harmless? How to fight a rusalka?"

He shook his head.

"You can't go without me," she said.

"Fine."

"Honestly, Bakharov, there's no way you'll survive for five . . . Wait, did you just agree?"

"Yes. Fine. You can come. God knows I can use all the help I can get." Bakharov looked exasperated, but beneath that, Kosara could see the panic seeping in. He hadn't realised how much he didn't know about monsters.

Good. He *should* be afraid.

"Great," Sevar mumbled. "More dead weight."

He climbed into the balloon's wicker basket. Despite the cold, sweat beaded on his forehead. One of his eyelids trembled in a nervous tic.

"What are you waiting for?" He waved them over. "All aboard!"

Bakharov and Kosara sat on the bench while Sevar lit up the burner. The sweet smell of gas filled the air. Kosara's hair flew up, tickling her face and knotting itself around the rigging. The snowflakes whirled, melting when they got too close to the fire.

"I hope you know how to use that thing." Sevar nodded towards Bakharov's revolver.

Bakharov spun it around his finger. "I'm not bad."

"Show-off," Kosara muttered.

At first, they flew so low over the ground that Kosara felt as if she could reach and grab a snowball from one of the roofs. Then, slowly, they gained height. The courtyard grew smaller and smaller until it was only a white dot in the distance. The balloon was definitely powered with magic—no ordinary hot-air balloon could fly that fast. It also seemed to have some sort of a cloaking spell on, so that they wouldn't be easily spotted.

A smile spread across Kosara's face when the dark spires of Chernograd emerged out of the fog. The Wall enveloped the city like an enormous snake, its ink-black body resting in between the houses, splitting streets in half. All that was separating Kosara from it was the thin wicker floor of the basket.

Her head began to spin. She wrapped her arms around her knees, her nails digging grooves into her skin and ladders in her tights.

"Are you okay?" Sevar asked.

"I think I might be getting travel sickness."

"Great. Try not to puke all over my floor."

"Doing my best," Kosara said through gritted teeth. "I can't make any prom—"

Bakharov shushed them. His eyes darted across the sky.

Kosara turned around. They soared gently through the clouds. The horizon had grown darker, and the air smelled of an approaching storm. It was so quiet, Kosara could hear the music from Belograd's dance halls and piano bars far below.

She frowned at Bakharov. "What's your prob—"

Something slammed against the basket, sending the balloon flying. Kosara staggered, her face painfully hitting Bakharov's shoulder.

"What was that?" he shouted.

"My face," Kosara said, massaging her bruised cheekbone.

"No, I meant—"

Another hit. This time, the balloon tilted, as if blown by a strong gust of wind. From this angle, Kosara saw the Wall far below clearly.

At first, its surface was unmoving like still water. Then a tentacle shot out of it: black, almost invisible in the dusk. As it slammed against the basket, lightning flashed. In the distance, thunder rolled.

"Oh no." Kosara scrambled back, trying to get as far from the edge as possible.

Another lightning bolt illuminated the sky around them. They were surrounded by a swaying sea of tentacles, lashing at the wicker basket and wrapping around the silk envelope.

Sevar frantically pulled at the balloon's ropes, trying to correct its flight path. It did nothing. Every time a tentacle hit the balloon, it sent it flying in a different direction.

Kosara's swore quietly. This was why people spent their life savings on amulets to help them cross the Wall. They didn't simply jump into a homemade hot-air balloon with a useless smuggler, like complete, utter idiots.

You don't have your shadow anymore, she reminded herself. *You really ought to be more careful.*

The shots from Bakharov's revolver rang fast. Bullet after bullet sank into the Wall's flesh, making the tentacles stagger back, giving the balloon precious seconds to escape their grasp.

As much as Kosara hated to admit it, he hadn't been showing off: he *was* a great shot. She felt so useless without her magic as she watched him aiming and pressing the trigger, again, and again, and again. . . .

Then the revolver clicked.

"Damn it." Bakharov fell to one knee to reload.

In the corner of her eye, Kosara spotted something dark moving. One of the tentacles crawled in between the ropes and into the basket, searching.

"Oh my God," she muttered. And then, much louder, "Watch out!"

Too late. The tentacle wrapped around Bakharov's ankle. He screamed, still trying to stuff bullets into his revolver.

"Oh my God!" This time, Kosara shouted it. She pulled the knife from her boot. The tentacle caressed Bakharov's leg, slowly, almost gently, but every time it touched his skin, he convulsed as if struck by electricity. The bullets tumbled from between his fingers and rolled around the basket's floor.

Kosara staggered forwards. Just before she'd managed to strike, her fingers went numb. *Oh no, not now.* The knife fell to the floor with a clang.

The tentacle jolted. It spun towards her, drawn to the sound, leaving an inky trail on the wicker. Sevar, rather uselessly, jumped away from its path, his face ashen.

Not now! Kosara stumbled after the knife.

"Hey, hands!" she shouted. "Hey, there are two of you!"

Her fingers trembled, still not finding the knife's handle. Bakharov was looking at her, a mixture of terror, pain, and confusion on his face.

"One of you washes the other! And then both of you! Wash! The! Face!"

Her hands twitched, solidified, and closed around the knife's handle. She leaped and sank the blade deep into the tentacle's flesh.

It jerked back. Its wound began to smoke. The knife in Kosara's hand grew hotter and hotter until she dropped it. The tentacle flew backwards and disappeared back into the Wall, hissing like an angry snake.

"Oh my God," Kosara concluded. Her hand pulsated painfully where the knife had burned her. She looked down at it, red and shiny and starting to blister, and smiled a broad smile. She was so glad she could feel it.

Bakharov scrambled to collect his bullets. Kosara helped him. Warm liquid ran down her face, a sticky mixture of sweat, tears, and melting snowflakes.

"Thanks," he said when he finally managed to reload. "What was that you were singing?"

"It's kind of a chant."

"I could have sworn it was a children's song."

"No, it's definitely—" A shot interrupted her. Another tentacle hissed and disappeared into the darkness below.

"Hold on!" Sevar shouted. "Not much longer left now."

Kosara barely suppressed her urge to plant a big wet kiss on his shiny forehead. *Not much longer left.* The sweetest four words she'd heard all day.

They suffered a few more hits—one sending them flying right, and another one left. . . .

And then it all went quiet. The tentacles stayed behind, swaying after them, as if waving them goodbye. The balloon hung in the air for a moment, before slowly gliding forwards.

Kosara slumped back on the bench. A laugh escaped her throat. They'd made it! They'd crossed the Wall in a hot-air balloon. This might not have been the stupidest thing she'd ever done, but it was certainly in her top five.

She rested her head against the rigging. Cold snowflakes landed on her face. The familiar smell of Chernograd filled her nostrils: chimney smoke and burning coal, freshly baked bread and tobacco, and magic.

Home.

Bakharov let out a deep sigh before he sat next to her. His hair stuck up in all directions. His cheeks were covered in soot.

"Are you alright?" Kosara asked.

"I'm fine," he said, his voice trembling. "You?"

Kosara opened her mouth, but she didn't answer him. Instead, she spun around and vomited overboard. The taste of bile burned the roof of her mouth. Hopefully, she hadn't just ruined some random passerby's evening walk.

She turned back to face Bakharov. "I'm fine."

"Great," Sevar said. "I'm glad everyone's doing well. Now, I'll give you your parachutes."

Kosara stood up in her seat. "What parachutes?"

"I have no reason to land. The last thing I need right now is a hungry karakonjul jumping into the basket before I can get away." He pushed a bundle of soft fabric into Kosara's hands. "Put it on, and when you're about thirty steps away from the ground, you just have to pull on that cord. . . ."

"What cord?" Kosara shouted, her voice unrecognisably high in her own ears.

"This one!" Sevar reached and placed her hand on it. "What's your problem? This is the easy part."

Kosara's head spun so fast she was worried it would unscrew from her neck and float away into the night. They flew low, and she could distinguish the people in the street below, walking briskly, holding onto their coats and hats so the wind wouldn't blow them away.

"No problem," she said, squeezing her eyes shut.

"It was a pleasure having you on board," Sevar said, his voice suggesting exactly the opposite. "Thank you for travelling with us tonight." And then he slammed both his hands onto her side.

"Wait a—" she shouted, but she was already falling. The wind thumped in her ears.

The cobblestones approached fast. In her panic, she nearly forgot to pull on her parachute's cord, but in the last moment, her trembling fingers found it. Right on time. The next second, her hands turned to shadow.

She hung in the air for a heartbeat before her posterior gently landed on the wet ground. It was only then that she stopped shouting.

9

Day Five

Chernograd was quiet: the thick curtain of snow muffled every sound. The streetlamps came on one by one, illuminating the street ahead. With every hiss and flash of light Kosara flinched, expecting a monster to appear.

For a change, her luck seemed fair. They were alone in the snow-covered street. The night had just begun to fall, and the monsters still slept.

Next to her, Bakharov relaxed slightly. His hand fell away from the revolver's holster.

Still, Kosara's nails couldn't seem to stop digging into her palms. The muscles on her neck strained as she cast a quick glance over her shoulder. She was certain she spotted the Zmey's familiar figure lurking in a dark corner, until she blinked, and he was gone. *You cheating hag,* he whispered in her ear. *Did you really think you could escape me?*

Kosara squeezed her eyes shut. *Keep focused.* She'd have plenty of time to panic later. Right now, there was too much work to be done—starting with shaking off this damned copper. She had no inclination to play nanny to a clueless Belogradean.

Currently, he was turning around, trying to take in the whole street at once. Obvious tourist.

"Shut your mouth," Kosara said, "before it fills with snow."

He did. Then he whispered, "I've never seen anything like this before."

"What, the snow?"

"No. There are no colours."

At first, Kosara didn't understand him. Of course there were colours. The snow was so white it made her eyes water. The granite buildings rose high, dark with soot and dirt. Their pointed roofs pierced the grey sky.

Then she remembered the Main Street in Belograd, with its many-hued lanterns, brightly lit shop windows, and eclectically dressed people.

"You'll have to find yourself a new coat," she said. "This one's too conspicuous." In fact, his red coat was the only spot of colour around.

He raised his collar to protect his neck from the wind. "I like this one. How come it's snowing so much here? It was mild in Belograd."

"It has something to do with the world of monsters. The closer it gets to the Foul Days, the more of their weather we get. Did you know that karakonjul fur is as thick as that of an arctic fox?"

"I didn't know that, no."

Kosara started walking, the muddy snow splashing under her boots, and Bakharov rushed to catch up with her. "Where are we going?"

Somewhere I can ditch you, Kosara thought, but what she said was, "Somewhere warmer. I can barely feel my toes."

As he followed her, Bakharov kept looking around. "You know what, this isn't what I expected at all. It all seems so . . . ordinary."

Kosara knew what he meant. Other than an insomniac yuda occasionally crossing the sky high above, they'd seen no monsters. The people went about their usual business: doing their shopping, picking up their children from grandma's house, stopping at church for evening prayer.

But Kosara was a local, and she sensed the tension. The shopping baskets weren't full of groceries, but of garlic and aspen stakes. The parents walked quickly, anxious to get their children behind locked doors. There was a queue in front of every church. The only time that ever happened was during the Foul Days, when people needed to replenish their supplies of holy water.

"Believe me," Kosara said, "it'll be pandemonium soon."

Loud music and shouting came from a nearby pub. Bakharov

slowed down to gawk at it. The building was so full, the crowd had spilled outside. A waitress came out with a small barrel of wine and began filling all the empty glasses she could spot.

"What are these people doing?" Bakharov asked.

"Looks like they're having a drink."

"It's nearly nighttime! Shouldn't they be preparing?"

Kosara shrugged. "There's only so much you can do, really."

"But having fun hours before a city-wide emergency—"

"Drinking in Chernograd isn't *fun*. It's serious business."

Bakharov still seemed unconvinced. Kosara sighed. "Look, we face destruction, ruin, and tragedy every year. We have to learn how to let go sometimes, or we'll crumble under the pressure. And, believe me, we might look like a sour-faced bunch of grumps, but nobody knows how to let go like a Chernogradean."

There was a loud giggle from the pub. A large brassiere landed in the muddy snow at their feet.

"Honestly"—Kosara stepped over it—"you haven't been to a party until you go to a party in Chernograd." She pulled Bakharov by the arm, so he'd keep walking. "Come on. I have some advice for you. Maybe you should write it down. Just in case we get separated."

He raised a single eyebrow—God knows how—and pulled out the notepad from his chest pocket.

"Every monster has a weakness," Kosara said. "Upirs hate garlic, varkolaks can't stand silver. You probably know all the obvious stuff. Here are a few more handy tips from a witch. If you meet a yuda, trick her into seeing her own image in something reflective. They're terrified of it. If you encounter a samodiva, sing."

"Sing?"

"Yes, they love music. They won't hurt you until you stop singing. Same goes for varkolaks, actually. If you spot a karakonjul, ask it a riddle, and it will freeze until it can answer it. If you happen upon the Zmey . . ." Kosara paused. "Um, run."

"I thought you said they all have their weaknesses. What's its weakness?"

I suspect it might be me, Kosara thought, but she didn't say it.

Instead, she waved a hand dismissively. "I wouldn't worry too much about the Zmey. He won't bother you if you stay out of his way."

"Why's that?"

"Because you aren't a young woman."

Bakharov wrinkled his nose in disgust. "Sounds like a charmer. You seem to know a lot about him."

Kosara cleared her throat. "Anyway, one last point, and this one is particularly important." She waited until he looked down at his notebook again, and then she took a step sideways and slipped into the doorway of a block of flats. She pressed herself against the damp wall, behind a row of post boxes.

"Kosara?" Bakharov called. "Kosara?" This one sounded closer. He'd probably poked his head in the doorway. "Oh, for God's sake." He tutted. The snow crunched under his feet as he continued down the street.

Kosara allowed herself to exhale, but she didn't dare move yet. He'd already tricked her once today when he'd followed her to Sevar's house.

A few minutes later, she peeled herself off the wall and looked up and down the street. Bakharov was gone, she was fairly sure. He'd be difficult to miss in that ridiculous coat of his. Perhaps he was just as glad to be rid of her as she was to be rid of him.

Kosara breathed in deeply. She was finally alone, finally free, and finally *home*. Now, she could sort this whole mess out.

She buried her hands deep in her pockets, and her nose deep in her scarf, and walked towards Bayan's pub on the Main Square. Roksana would be there, just like she always was during the Foul Days. Kosara would get her to explain precisely what she'd been doing in Irnik Ivanov's house.

Washing lines intersected above Kosara's head, and the frozen clothes clattered in the wind. Occasionally, men and women strode past, their breaths coming out in plumes. Kosara let their voices envelop her like a warm blanket. It was good to be back home.

As she passed by the pharmacy, she spotted a young witch shooting fireballs after a startled karakonjul. Kosara deliberately hid her face in her scarf and walked faster. She recognised the girl: Siyana, who'd joined the Witch and Warlock Association last winter. She and Kosara had been sent out together to secure the church on the Main Square from monster attacks. Young Siyana had looked at Kosara as if she had all the answers. Kosara simply couldn't face her now—shadowless and helpless.

The pub was the only bright spot in the dark square. Its windows shone, sending trails of light across the freshly fallen snow. Its chimney spat out clouds of black smoke. Kosara hesitated a step away from the door, her hand in the air, ready to knock. Roksana wouldn't dare do anything to her in a pub full of witnesses, but Kosara still wasn't sure if she was ready to face her.

"Who is it?" came Bayan's gruff voice from the other side. He must have spotted her through the window.

"It's me. Kosara."

"Go away!"

Kosara sighed. She hadn't exactly expected a warm welcome. "Bayan, my old friend, no need to—"

"Don't you 'old friend' me! How dare you bring the Zmey to my pub?"

Kosara caught herself turning around in a panic, checking behind her shoulder, as if the Zmey might be right behind her.

"I didn't bring him," she said. "He found me."

"Well then, you'd better bugger right off before he finds you again."

"Come on, Bayan, you know I can handle him. I'm sorry about the other day. I panicked. I hadn't seen him this angry in a while—"

"No, you can't."

"Sorry, what?"

"You can't handle the Zmey. You can't handle him now, just like you couldn't handle him all those years ago when old Vila had to save your pimply arse from him. Now, go the fuck away."

Kosara wanted to argue, but realised she had nothing to say. He was absolutely right. If she could handle the Zmey, she wouldn't have traded her magic to escape him.

"Alright, alright," she said. "I'll go away. I just need to see Roksana. I think she—"

On the other side of the door, Bayan cocked his rifle. "Do you now? I should have known you two were in it together. Dodgy bastards, the pair of you."

"Together in what? Bayan, please, I'll go away as soon as I ask Roksana a few questions—"

"Your pal isn't here."

No way. Roksana always spent the Foul Days at Bayan's. "She's not? Where is she?"

"Fuck knows! If you see her, tell her to never show her face here again, if she doesn't want to eat lead."

"Why? What did she do?"

"Ask poor Malamir what she's done!"

"Where's Malamir?"

"Wouldn't you just love to finish the job Roksana started! Well, I'm not telling. Would you kindly fuck off now?"

Kosara had no choice but to leave. There was no use arguing with Bayan when he was this angry, and especially when he was armed. She stumbled away through the snowdrifts, swearing under her breath. *Christ, Roksana, what have you done now?*

She walked fast, trying to keep warm, but without a clear direction in mind. The next logical location to check would be Roksana's house— but something, some automatic and well-trained self-preservation instinct, told her going there alone and unprepared wasn't the smartest idea. If she still had her magic, she would have barged in without hesitation. As it was, with Roksana quickly proving to be someone more dangerous than she'd ever suspected, it seemed like too big a risk.

Kosara couldn't believe how quickly her trust in Roksana had evaporated.

As she turned into a dark alleyway, footsteps sounded behind her, muffled by the snow but still audible in the quiet. With the corner of her eye, she spotted someone appearing at her side.

For a second, she was too afraid to look. What if the Zmey had already found her?

However, the figure wasn't as large as the Zmey's. It didn't smell like him either: that familiar otherworldly cocktail of foreign seas, smoke, fire, and magic. No, this figure wore expensive perfume and stepped in the snowdrifts carefully, desperately trying to keep her elegant shoes dry.

"Sofiya," Kosara muttered under her breath.

"Kosara," said Sofiya. When Kosara turned to look at her, the other woman stared back. Sofiya was impeccably dressed, as always, in imported silks and cashmere. Her dark hair fell in luscious waves down her back and her skin glowed with a brightness which could only be bought with the best potions in town. Overall, she appeared a lot healthier and less exhausted than any witch ought to have during the Foul Days.

At her feet stepped two shadows: one was Sofiya's own, and the other she'd inherited from her godmother. Kosara's eyes quickly moved away from them. It made her so uncomfortable—Sofiya's godmother had gone to such lengths to make sure her shadow survived her death. It wasn't an easy feat, even for the strongest witch. And what was Sofiya doing with it? Completely wasting its potential.

"What do you want?" Kosara asked, a tad sharper than she'd intended.

"So, you've returned," Sofiya said conversationally, ignoring Kosara's question. "How curious. I thought you'd run away to Belograd and never look back."

"Well, I'm here. What do you want?"

"Why would you possibly come back? If I were you, I'd have been grateful for the chance to escape."

"I'm sure you can afford to pay some smuggler—"

"Oh, I'm not going anywhere. I'm happy here. You, however? With the Zmey on your heels? You're a braver woman than I."

Kosara took a deep breath and repeated, slowly, "What do you want?"

"I just wanted to say 'hi.' We're colleagues, after all."

Kosara scoffed. She and Sofiya were both witches, that much was true, but she hardly considered the other woman a "colleague." A "colleague" would have been out there, in the days before the Foul Days started, with Kosara and the rest of the Witch and Warlock Association, freezing to the bone in the snow, drawing protective circles around as many doors and windows as they could. A "colleague" wouldn't have hidden inside her swanky salon on the main street, cheerfully using the opportunity to relieve rich fools of their fortunes.

That was what Sofiya's whole schtick was: she made most of her money during the Foul Days, when the boundary between the human world and the world of monsters and spirits was thinnest. She organised seances—exclusive and eye-wateringly expensive, but people paid, since no other witch had the time for such trifles during the busiest time of year. Sofiya offered them a rare opportunity to converse with the ghosts of their loved ones.

"Well, you've said 'hi,'" Kosara spat out. "Listen, I'm in no mood for idle chatter. If you have something to say—"

"Two things. One, I know where Malamir is."

Kosara raised her eyebrows. "Where?"

"Hospital St. Marina."

"Christ. What's wrong with him?"

"I heard he got in a fight with Roksana."

Kosara shuddered. Roksana could easily put a man twice Malamir's size in hospital. "And the second thing?" she asked, keen to get rid of the other witch so she could rush to visit Malamir.

Sofiya leaned in, as if she was about to impart some great wisdom. Her cloying perfume surrounded Kosara. "You should have stayed far away. I met the Zmey the other day, and he's furious with you. I've always been impressed how you've managed to string him along for so long, but it seems he's finally had enough. Why are you back?"

Kosara didn't answer. She owed the other witch no explanations. In any case, she could waste no more time on this conversation. Sofiya had, uncharacteristically, given her a nugget of useful information. Without bothering to say goodbye, Kosara turned around and rushed to the hospital.

"You can't come in outside of visiting hours," the hospital receptionist repeated over and over again. Behind her, the phones incessantly rang. "Go home."

"But my wife just gave birth—" the man in front of Kosara kept arguing. She could only see his large back and his hairy neck peeking beneath his fur hat.

A group of young upirs had gathered outside the hospital entrance, drawn by the smell of blood. Their decomposing bodies slammed against the door. Their tongues scraped the thick glass, leaving trails of venomous saliva. Their moans grew louder and louder as they burned themselves on the wards carved around the entrance.

"Congratulations," the receptionist said. "Now go home. You can't come in outside of visiting hours."

"But—"

Kosara fidgeted behind him. Soon, he'd give up, and it would be her turn to try to argue her way in. She wasn't entirely sure what she'd say: the truth would probably get her kicked out. The receptionist's stern eyes pierced right through the man, her bright-red lips pressed into a thin line.

"But—" the man tried again.

"Go home, mister!"

"For crying out loud!" came a shout from the hallway. A messy-haired doctor flew past the reception desk, her white coat billowing behind her. "Would somebody answer the damned phone?"

The receptionist rolled her eyes and turned around in her chair. She lifted the receiver. "What?" she barked. "No, of course you can't come in if you've been bitten by a varkolak! You have to follow the established quarantine protocols."

Kosara knew she wouldn't get a better chance. She looked around. The hallways brimmed with people, but no one paid any attention to her. The doctors and nurses were too busy caring for their patients, and the patients were too busy not bleeding to death.

"What do you mean, you have no cage in the basement?" the receptionist shouted down the phone. "What do you mean, you have no basement?"

Kosara took one careful step back, then another one, and then she slipped into the hallway. She stood straighter and walked confidently forwards. She'd been a witch for a while—she had her "of course I'm supposed to be here" stride honed to perfection.

No one seemed to notice her as she tried to sneak glances in every room. Doctors and nurses rushed past her, pushing gurneys and stretchers, shouting requests for dosages of different medicines. A few medics bandaged wounds and performed CPR right there on the floor. All the beds were full of moaning, bleeding bodies.

A group of relatives huddled around what seemed to be a wounded granny or grandpa, judging by the tuft of white hair poking from under the blanket. A woman held a crying child, and kept whispering, "Please, be quiet. Be quiet, please. If you're not quiet, I'll call old Vila to come and take you away *and eat you!*"

Kosara rolled her eyes and kept walking. Simply unbelievable. Outside the building, hungry upirs crawled up the walls, varkolaks howled in the distance, and yudas flew high above, foretelling death. And yet, the scariest thing that mother could come up with was *Vila.*

Kosara never figured out how all the rumours about Vila had even started, but she knew there was no truth to any of them. That one about her luring children into houses made of gingerbread so she could eat them, for example? Utter nonsense. Vila was a terrible baker. Her gingerbread always crumbled.

"Hey, you!"

The shout made Kosara jump. She sped up. Perhaps he wasn't talking to her.

"You, witch lady! You're from the Association, aren't you?"

Damn it.

She turned around on her heel, an affable smile plastered across her face. A young doctor marched towards her. His stethoscope bounced with every step, and dry gore was smeared all over the front of his white coat.

"Hi there, Doctor . . ." Kosara threw a quick look at his name badge, "Krustev. Perhaps you're wondering what I'm doing here."

He frowned, his thick eyebrows meeting above his nose like kissing caterpillars. "Aren't you here to fix the leaky ward in the trauma centre?"

"Of course. That's exactly what I'm here for."

"Well, come on then!" He grabbed her by the upper arm and pulled her down the hallway. Kosara was so stunned he'd dared touch a witch, she didn't try to fight him. "We've been waiting for you all afternoon. I've called twice!"

"You know what it's like." Kosara struggled to keep up with his long steps. "It's madness during the Foul Days."

His bloodshot eyes met hers. "Oh, I know."

As they walked deeper into the hospital, the upirs' moans grew more distant, but the yudas' screams got louder. Kosara saw them through the windows, perched on the hospital's gutters like gargoyles. There were so many of them, their shrieks were unintelligible, which was perhaps for the best: the last thing the patients needed was to hear a yuda call their name.

As Krustev dragged her along another hallway, Kosara spotted Malamir in one of the rooms. His pale face peeked over his woolly blanket. Only his leg stuck out, tied over the bed in a cast.

He saw her, too. Confusion flashed in his eyes. His hand rose slowly to wave at her. She couldn't wave back. Doctor Krustev kept pushing her forwards.

"Here it is!" Finally, Krustev stopped in front of a series of symbols, hastily scribbled on the wall above the toilets. Kosara could barely read the wonky handwriting, but it appeared to be a ward protecting against upirs. One of the runes was so badly drawn, it had obviously stopped working.

"It started leaking yesterday," Krustev said. "We've had five resurrections since."

"What do you mean, five?" Kosara heard herself say. She couldn't help but be angry at such obvious carelessness. "Are you not following the Association's guidance? You need to place two silver coins over the eyes of the deceased, and—"

"No one has time for coins, spells, and incantations right now, lady! That's why we ordered the wards."

"The wards are meant as a last precaution. They're not a cure-all."

"Don't you tell me about cure-alls. Get on with it." He huffed, then he turned around and rushed back up the hallway.

Kosara looked at the mess of a ward someone had inflicted upon the poor wall. It wasn't entirely their fault, of course. Crafting wards was a painstakingly slow, skilful job. This was the work of an overworked, underpaid witch, with not nearly enough experience to take on a project like protecting the hospital against upir resurrections.

Kosara couldn't do anything to fix it—not without her shadow. She made sure Doctor Krustev was gone and tiptoed back to Malamir's room.

"Kosara!" Malamir struggled to lift himself up on his elbows. "What are you doing here?" He had to shout, so she'd hear him over the snoring of the man on the next bed over.

"I came to see you." She sat down on his bed. "You look awful."

He beamed at her, displaying a mouth with several missing teeth. One of his eyes was swollen shut, coloured in hues of vibrant purple flowing down into navy blue and olive green.

"I make a pretty picture, don't I?" He laughed through puffy lips. "I don't think I'll be making my glorious return to the stage any time soon. You'll never guess who did it."

Kosara waited for the snoring man to fall silent for a moment. "Roksana."

Malamir finally managed to prop himself up on the bed. "No way! How did you guess?" He blinked a few times, as if trying to focus. "What are you doing here, anyway? I thought you were on the other side of the Wall."

"I'm looking for my shadow."

"Oh." He carefully avoided glancing at the floor. Tactful as always. "Why did you ever give it away, honestly? I can't even begin to—"

Kosara raised her gloved hands in the air. "I know, I know. You don't have to tell me. It was the stupidest thing I've ever done. I panicked."

"You really need to get over that whole thing with the Zmey, doll. It will always come back to haunt you."

Get over it? As if it was that easy. Kosara had tried again and again. The Zmey always came back.

"Tell me what happened with Roksana," she said.

Malamir rolled his one functioning eye. "Believe me, I'd love to know myself. It happened shortly after you left. She snuck up on me as I came out the toilet. I've never seen her like that. She seemed absolutely furious. She pinned me to the wall and barked at me to give her my hypnotising watch. At first, I thought she'd simply had a bit too much to drink, you know what she can be like. I realised she was very serious once I lost a tooth or two." Malamir chuckled. "Good thing Bayan showed up and dragged her away from me, otherwise . . . It honestly beats me what she needs my watch for."

Kosara could venture a guess. Roksana had probably hoped to use it to talk Irnik into giving her the witches' shadows without a fight. Judging by the gory scene in Irnik's living room, she hadn't been successful.

"Did you know she's working for Karaivanov's gang again?" Kosara asked.

Malamir sighed. "I'd heard rumours. Maybe she never stopped working for him. When I left the gang, Roksana promised she'd leave too, but honestly? I wouldn't be surprised if she lied. I thought I knew the gal, but . . ." Malamir raised only his left shoulder, since the right one was trapped in a cast. Kosara flinched when she noticed the tattoo on his chest peeking through the flimsy fabric of his hospital gown. Two interlocking K's. An ugly reminder of a terrible decision he'd made in his youth. "Obviously, I don't know her all that well."

"Yeah." Kosara looked at her hands in her lap. She could feel them, trembling and disappearing every few seconds. She willed them to stop. "Me, too. There's the whole business with the stranger from New Year's. . . ."

Kosara trailed off. Until the very last moment, there'd been a small, embarrassing part of her that had hoped she was wrong. That Roksana wasn't responsible for Irnik's death. Now, looking at poor Malamir, she had to face facts.

Roksana was a violent, dangerous person. She was a murderer. And she'd sold Kosara's shadow to Konstantin Karaivanov.

It felt like a punch in the gut.

"The stranger?" Malamir asked. "The one who took your shadow?"

"Yes." she said. "I think Roksana might have murdered him. Irnik. His name was Irnik."

"No way! Murdered? Why?"

"Because of the witches' shadows. Karaivanov must have sent her for them. Apparently, they found Roksana's fingerprints all over the scene."

Malamir swore. "I'm sorry, doll. That's terrible."

Kosara shrugged. At this point, why was she even surprised? That's what everyone she'd ever trusted did: they failed her. Sevar by stealing her money and running off to Belograd. The Zmey by being the Zmey. Nevena by goddamned *dying*.

Roksana was just another name in a long string of disappointments.

Malamir shook his head. He looked more sad than angry. "Honestly, what kind of money could Karaivanov have possibly—"

"Shush," Kosara said. Something wasn't right. The hairs on the back of her neck rose. Nothing moved. The room was quiet.

The room was *quiet*. The large man on the next bed over wasn't snoring. The ward in the hallway was leaky. . . .

Damn it. She'd let herself get distracted. She couldn't afford to get distracted.

Kosara jumped up from the bed and turned around, just in time to see the man's eyes opening. They were a bright, bloodshot red.

The upir darted towards her. She was halfway through a defensive spell, before remembering she'd lost her magic and finishing it with a loud curse.

Moist fingers sank into her upper arms. Something wet touched her cheek—a tongue? She blinked, and he was on top of her, pressing her to the wall. His breath stank of rot.

"Oh my God!" Malamir screamed. "Help! Somebody help!"

Kosara tried to push the upir away, but her hands couldn't get a grip on his clammy skin. His bones were sharp under the decaying flesh, like iron rods encased in jelly. His weight was suffocating.

She had an aspen stake in her coat pocket, she was sure, if only she could reach it. . . .

"Help!" Malamir kept shouting. "Help!"

Kosara managed to wriggle one arm from under the upir. She reached for her pocket. Her fingers found the stake.

It wouldn't budge. Kosara kept pulling on it in a panic, ignoring the stinging of splinters piercing her palm. It must have got caught in the lining.

Teeth, sharp as needles, brushed against her neck. She wanted to scream, but she couldn't take in a breath.

"Will somebody please help!" Malamir choked out.

This is how I die. This whole time, Kosara had thought it would be the Zmey who got her in the end—but no, it was going to be a newly resurrected, middle-aged upir with bad sleep apnoea and even worse breath. *Oh, dear God, this is how I—*

There was a loud bang. At first, Kosara thought it had been the cracking of her rib cage as it snapped beneath the upir's bulbous torso. But then, he backed off her, confusion in his eyes.

Air! Kosara inhaled deeply, hot tears running down her cheeks. *Oh my God, air!*

What had given her this reprieve? It didn't matter. She had to move fast.

She pulled on the aspen stake in her pocket sharply. The lining finally tore, releasing it. The stake sank deep into the upir's chest, until Kosara's hand was coated in thick, black blood. The upir crashed on his back, a wet sound echoing as his flesh hit the linoleum.

Kosara blinked, her vision finally coming back into focus. The upir convulsed once on the floor like a crushed worm, before falling still. His teeth were bared, a few drops of bright-red blood glistening on their pointed ends. *Her* blood.

A hole smoked in his temple. Another hole gaped in his chest, dripping black liquid, the stake still protruding from it.

Kosara scrambled backwards to get away from him. A pair of hands grabbed her shoulders. She screamed.

"It's alright, it's me," said a familiar voice. She looked up and saw Bakharov's worried face. Honestly, this man was like a tick—impossible to shake off.

"Are you okay?" he asked.

"For God's sake, Bakharov!" Kosara pressed her hand to her heart, trying to keep it from escaping her rib cage. "I thought I was going to jump out of my skin there."

"That was so cool!" Malamir shouted from the bed. He aimed a finger gun at the upir. "Pow-pow! You should have seen it, Kosara!"

"I'm sorry, I was too busy suffocating under a frenzied bloodsucker." Kosara massaged her bruised arms. The hole in the upir's temple kept smoking. "How did you manage to wound it so badly?"

"I rubbed garlic juice on the bullets," Bakharov replied.

Clever, Kosara had to admit to herself, but she'd never say it out loud.

After only a few hours, Chernograd had taken its toll on the carefully turned-out Detective Bakharov. His perfectly pressed white shirt wasn't so perfectly pressed or so white anymore. His sleeve was rolled up, and a dirty bandage was hastily wrapped around his forearm. It wasn't tight enough.

"Did you shadow me here?" Kosara asked.

"No," Bakharov said. "We seem to be following a similar trail of investigation. Aren't you glad I showed up, though?"

Oh, dear God, yes. "Actually, I was seconds away from stabbing the upir myself. What are you doing here?"

"I need to ask your friend a few questions."

We're more acquaintances, really, Kosara thought, but then she realised that wasn't the important part. There had been a sudden change in Bakharov's voice: a steely note she hadn't heard before.

"You're not suspecting he's involved as well, are you?" she asked.

"I—"

"Unbelievable!" Kosara waved a hand towards Malamir. "I mean, look at him! What do you think he did? Dragged himself to Irnik's house on his stomach and talked him to death?"

"I didn't mean—"

"It's because he's from Chernograd, isn't it? Because you in Belograd are all nice and polite and smell like spring flowers, and we Chernogradeans are the same monsters as . . . well, the monsters."

"No," Bakharov raised his voice, which was unusual enough to make Kosara shut up. "I need him to explain how his fingerprints ended up at the crime scene."

"What?" Kosara said.

"What?" came Malamir's quiet voice.

That wasn't possible. Kosara could accept she'd been wrong to trust Roksana. But Malamir, too? No way. Once, he'd cried because he'd stepped on a slug.

"Well, Mr. Petrosyan, do you have any explanation for how this happened?" Bakharov asked.

"I, um, no," Malamir mumbled. His face had turned ashen. "No, I don't. I've never even been to Belograd, I swear. I mean, look at me! How would I get anywhere like this?"

"We checked the timing. You got admitted to the hospital forty minutes after the victim's approximate time of death. That's plenty of time for you to leave the pub—"

"My leg was broken, for crying out loud! I'm sorry I took a while getting here."

Kosara chewed on the inside of her cheek. Something wasn't adding up. "Wait a minute. Where did you find the fingerprints?"

Bakharov threw a glance towards her, then back at Malamir. "I'm afraid I can't tell you that."

"Malamir, think." Kosara leaned closer to him. "Did you touch anything belonging to the stranger? Anything he could have taken back with him to Belograd?"

Malamir bit his bruised lip and made a pained face. "I honestly can't rem—wait! I know! I asked if I could try on his reading glasses. I've been meaning to get a pair of tortoiseshell ones."

Kosara turned to Bakharov with her eyebrows raised.

"We might have found the fingerprints on the victim's glasses," Bakharov admitted, though he looked as if he didn't want to. Kosara gave him a triumphant smile. *Who's the detective now, Bakharov?*

Malamir let out a loud sigh. "Thank God! You almost had me there. I'd have had to call in the nurse to change my underpants."

"Mr. Petrosyan," Bakharov said sternly, "I still need to ask you a few questions. Could you please describe, in as much detail as you can remember, the events from New Year's Eve and the following days?"

Malamir repeated what he'd told Kosara. Bakharov wrote it all down in his notepad, occasionally frowning.

As Bakharov and Malamir talked, Kosara took care of the upir. He could have been a resurrected corpse, but that didn't mean he was undeserving of post-mortal care. She dragged him to the bed and tucked him under the covers. His wounds were messy, but they were nothing some bandages wouldn't cover before his family came to pick him up. Shame there weren't any silver coins to place on his eyes—not that they would do much good at this point.

Finally, Bakharov thanked Malamir for his cooperation.

"Take care, okay?" Kosara said, squeezing Malamir's unwounded shoulder. "And let me know when you're out. I'll brew you an anaesthetic like nothing they have in the hospital."

She and Bakharov walked out of the room and continued down the busy hospital corridors. Kosara noticed he also had his "of course I'm supposed to be here" stride down pat.

"So, what happened to you?" She nodded towards his bandaged forearm.

"One of your karakonjuls attacked me."

"A karakonjul attacked you? I told you to ask them a riddle!"

"Believe it or not, it's quite difficult to think of one when you have four rows of dagger-sized fangs buried in your arm." Bakharov ran a hand through his hair. "You know what, you were right."

"Mm?"

"Don't make me say it again. I have no idea what I'm doing in Chernograd during the Foul Days. When you first left me in the street, I thought it was for the best. I prefer to work alone, and I was certain our methods would clash. I was quite glad to see the back of you. No offence."

"None taken," Kosara said. "I was the one who hid from you behind a row of post boxes."

"You did." Bakharov showed no sign that was a surprise to him. So, he *had* spotted her in her hiding place. "Anyway, only a few hours in this cursed city of yours have shown me how wrong I was. I was chased by those karakonjuls," he said it carefully, the unfamiliar word stumbling clumsily off his tongue. "Then, an enormous golden-horned deer nearly ran me over, and the rider just laughed at me. Had this been Belograd, I wouldn't have let her go without a fat fine."

Kosara shuddered, imagining Bakharov attempting to fine a samodiva.

"I'm not used to this," Bakharov admitted. "To feeling this helpless. My gun doesn't work. The only thing that works is your knowledge."

Kosara shrugged. She would have gloated if she didn't feel just as helpless as he did. If she still had her magic, she would have dispatched the upir within seconds. As it was, the only thing that had saved her was Bakharov's timely arrival.

"You're not that helpless, judging by how you took care of that upir," she said. "You saved"—she'd be damned if she said "my life"—"me a lot of work."

"I only knew how to deal with him because you told me!"

Kosara couldn't help herself anymore—she gave him a small, tight smile. "Nevertheless. Thank you."

He smiled back, though his smile was a lot more open and, though she hated to admit it, distractingly handsome. "You're welcome."

She grabbed his wrist. He tried to flinch away. She didn't let him. *For God's sake, Bakharov, I don't bite.*

She unravelled some of the bandage and grimaced. "It looks nasty."

"I'll be fine. I rubbed some iodine on it."

Kosara scoffed. It would take more than iodine to disinfect a karakonjul bite wound. They were disgusting little beasts.

"You need a yarrow, honey, and calendula poultice," she said.

"Good thing we're in a hospital."

"No way am I leaving you to those butchers. They'd probably cut it off. No, you're coming with me."

"And where exactly are we going?"

Kosara couldn't stifle her sigh. "Home."

10

Day Five

Dust covered the floor and spiderwebs enveloped the roof beams. The wind whistled in the chimney, banged on the windows, and slammed the doors. The walls moaned, the floor creaked, the roof groaned. It was as if the house was alive, but just barely.

The kitchen was dark and cold, and completely not as Kosara remembered it. Her dad wasn't busying around, whistling while he chopped vegetables. Her mum wasn't heating up a pot of yesterday's soup, stirring and swearing loudly when the hot liquid splashed her.

Bakharov looked around. "Are your parents—"

"They passed away last winter. A freak accident."

"Monster?"

"Drunk carriage driver."

"I'm sorry."

Kosara shrugged. "This is Chernograd. People die all the time."

She tried to swallow the lump forming in her throat. *This is Chernograd*, she reminded herself. She'd been lucky to have had them both, alive and healthy, for so many years. They'd seen her complete her apprenticeship and open her own workshop. They'd been there to dry her tears after every heartbreak and bandage her wounds after countless bad decisions. She'd been luckier than most.

Kosara lit up a gas lamp and placed it on the shelf above the fireplace. "What about you? Are your parents still around?"

It was only a second later she realised that was probably not as normal a question in Belograd as it was in Chernograd.

Bakharov gave her a rueful smile. "My mum is. I never knew my dad. I can't decide who I'm more terrified of finding out I'm in Chernograd: my mum or my boss."

So, Kosara had been right. He wasn't here officially. "How much trouble will you be in with the boss once you get back to Belograd?"

He gestured to about a foot above his head. "Up to here. I'm hoping she might never find out if I play my cards right. I managed to apply for annual leave just before I left."

Of course. Most people would have been in too much of a hurry to cross the Wall illegally in unauthorised pursuit of a murderer to bother with paperwork.

Not Bakharov. He'd filed for annual leave.

"With some luck," he said, "she won't ever know I'm not at the hot springs of Hisar to treat an old back injury. If that fails, I hope bringing her the murderer will pacify her."

Kosara wrinkled her nose. Just how often did the police break the law and get away without any consequences?

Way too often, that was for certain.

As they talked, she lit a matchstick and took it to the pile of newspapers and kindling in the fireplace. It hissed and went off. She lit another one. And another one.

Before she'd lost her magic, she'd click her fingers, and the fire would burn bright. She lifted her hand up in the air and rehearsed the spell, the way Vila had taught her, with a fluent movement of the wrist and precise fingers. . . .

What am I doing? She cast a quick glance towards Bakharov, to make sure he hadn't noticed her waving her hands about. He hadn't—or at least he pretended not to.

She lit another matchstick. At last, the kindling went up. The smell of burning paper filled the room. Kosara shut her eyes for a moment and let the warm air blow in her face until her nose stopped feeling like an ice cube. Then, she placed the cauldron over the fire and filled it with water for Bakharov's poultice. It came out of the tap freezing—it would take a while to boil.

"Are you hungry?" Kosara swung a cupboard door open and searched through the jars inside. Vila always said one should never brew potions on an empty stomach. "I don't know about you, but I had no chance to grab something to eat before we left. I'm starving."

Bakharov hesitated. "I don't want to intr—"

A loud bang sounded from the hallway.

Kosara looked over her shoulder. Bakharov had already pulled his pistol and taken a defensive position, pressed close to the wall next to the door frame.

"Stop it!" Kosara shouted. "You're scaring our guest!"

A faint *sorry* drifted from the hallway, quiet as a sigh, almost inaudible over the wind's howling.

Bakharov didn't put his gun away. He stared at Kosara. "What the heck was that?"

Kosara shrugged. The voice had been too quiet to recognise. But it was certainly not Nevena: kikimoras didn't apologise.

"One of the household spirits, most likely," Kosara said.

Bakharov kept looking around, his pistol swinging back and forth. "What?"

"Household spirits. Will you please put that thing away?"

Bakharov looked down at his revolver as if he hadn't noticed it before. Finally, he returned it to its holster. "When you say 'spirits,' do you mean you have ghosts in your house?"

"Yeah, I suppose, in a way. Don't worry, you'll meet them soon enough."

"I will?"

"They'll probably come out to say hello. Don't be rude, they can be very touchy, but they're not dangerous. If you don't see them, don't panic, not everyone can. My mother never could. Well, hungry or not?"

Bakharov didn't reply. His eyes still darted around, probably searching the dark corners of the house for ghosts.

"Come on," Kosara said. "Don't insult my hospitality."

He sighed. "I suppose I could eat something."

Kosara selected a few jars from last winter's preserves and pickles. Roast pepper spread and pickled gherkins, green tomatoes and turshiya, aubergine relish and sour cabbage. Her mouth watered. Finally, some proper food.

Bakharov studied the selection carefully. "Is there any food in all of Chernograd that isn't pickled or fermented?"

Kosara rolled her eyes. If she was getting fed for free, she wouldn't have been that picky.

"Not in this house." She opened the jar of roasted peppers and took in their smoky scent. It seemed to be in perfect condition, even a year later. The kitchen spirit had done a great job preserving it. "Most of our food is imported from Belograd. It costs an arm and a leg to get it over the Wall. We can't afford anything fancy all that often."

"What about coffee or tobacco?"

"Those are necessities. We get coffee, alcohol, and tobacco first. Everything else is optional, if there's space. Can you imagine what would happen if Chernograd was left without tobacco? There would be riots!"

"Everything you just listed is terribly unhealthy."

"The average life expectancy in Chernograd is fifty-seven years. Might as well enjoy them."

"Maybe it would be higher if you led a healthier lifestyle."

"Or maybe it wouldn't. You never know when the monsters will get you. *Carpet diem.*"

"*Carpe.*"

"Whatever."

Bakharov considered this for a moment, a piece of gherkin hanging off his fork. He winced every time he lifted the fork to his mouth with his wounded arm. "What do you export in return?" he asked.

Kosara was surprised he hadn't figured it out, given his job. Then again, the Belogradean government liked to pretend Chernograd didn't exist. They didn't advertise the trade between the two cities.

She swallowed her bite of smoky pepper relish. "Magic. Amulets, talismans, potions and poisons, enchanted cosmetics, and extra potent herbs."

"Ah," Bakharov said. "Makes sense."

Once the water had finally boiled, Kosara prepared the poultice for Bakharov's wound. She selected the correct herbs and weighed them precisely, throwing them in the cauldron bubbling over the fire at exactly the right time. Honey to prevent an infection, yarrow to slow down the bleeding, lard to close the wound, marigold to help it heal faster.

Each new addition sent clouds of steam up in the air. The smell of herbs filled the kitchen. The flames leaped up around the cauldron, heating up the metal until it shone red, sending flickering shadows across the walls.

This was the one element of witchcraft she still had. Magic wasn't necessary for brewing cures and healing potions—she only needed skill and knowledge. She still had plenty of that. And she'd brew the best damned poultice in all of damned Chernograd, damn it.

Bakharov didn't utter a word as she furiously stirred the cauldron. Once the herbs had finished simmering, Kosara took them off the fire. She unravelled Bakharov's old bandage and inhaled sharply through her teeth.

"That bad?" he asked.

"Not great."

The wound looked even worse after she cleaned it: the karakonjul's curved teeth had sunk deep into his flesh, almost to the bone. She'd have to keep a close eye on it in case it got infected. Which meant that she was stuck with Bakharov for the time being.

"How did you manage to fight the karakonjul off?" she asked as she spread a thick layer of the herb poultice over the wound.

"I shot it," Bakharov said.

Kosara resisted the urge to roll her eyes. There was something disconcerting about the ease with which Bakharov shot things. Typical copper, thinking bullets solved any problem.

She knew she had no right to complain, though. His gun had saved her from an upir.

"Did it help?" she asked.

"Not at all. So, I ran. Thankfully, I have longer legs than it."

"That was lucky. They're very fast."

Kosara tied a new bandage around his arm, then took a step back to inspect her work. "There, that's better."

Bakharov moved his arm. "It feels much better already. The pain's completely gone. How did you do that?"

"I'm a witch, remember?"

He kept prodding at the bandage with his finger, as if expecting it to start hurting again any second. "Thank you. It's my shooting arm, you know, I might need it tomorrow."

Kosara smiled tensely. She'd been trying not to focus on the next morning when they'd have to surprise Roksana at her house. Nevertheless, the thought gnawed at her, always in the back of her mind.

"Hopefully you don't need it." She had no doubt he would. Roksana would never go down without a fight.

Bakharov considered her for a second. "Are you sure you're ready to see her?"

Not in the slightest.

Kosara still couldn't wrap her head around any of it. Roksana had stolen her shadow. Did she know that by doing that, she had doomed Kosara to a slow death?

Of course she did. Did she even care?

Apparently, murder was something she had no qualms about. Kosara had no idea why she expected her life might weigh heavier on the monster hunter's consciousness than Irnik Ivanov's.

Perhaps it was because Roksana had managed to expertly hide her true nature all these years. Kosara had been so foolish to trust her. After all, she knew very well that not all murderers looked like monsters. Kosara was living proof of that herself.

"I'm ready," she said. "I need to get my shadow back as soon as possible. When should we go? First thing in the morning?"

"We?" The corners of Bakharov's mouth twitched. "You mean you won't try to ditch me again?"

"Well, I considered it carefully, and I decided you can be pretty useful." She avoided meeting his eyes. "Especially in an upir attack."

"So"—he extended a hand towards her—"team?"

Kosara didn't shake it. "I really wouldn't go that far."

She stood up and collected her dirty plate. "I'll head to bed. You can sleep in my parents' room—it's the one next to the bathroom. There are extra blankets in the wardrobe. Just, please, don't go into the bedroom with the red door."

"What's wrong with that bedroom?"

That's Nevena's room.

"Just a leaky ceiling." Kosara walked away before he asked any more questions.

He'd seemed so worried when she'd told him about the household spirits. He'd probably sleep better if he didn't know about Nevena. She'd *definitely* sleep better if he didn't know about Nevena.

Kosara curled up in bed under the woolly blanket. A theatre poster hung on the wall opposite—Orhan Demirbash, the famous actor, playing an upir. He held onto the waist of a girl in a white dress with a deep neckline. His fake teeth were sunk in her throat.

Below the poster, on the vanity, rested a pile of cheap jewellery: spiderweb earrings and batwing pendants, skull bracelets and moonstone rings, and more charged quartz crystals than anyone could ever need. Kosara had regularly worn them as a teenager. Nowadays, she didn't feel the need to advertise her witchiness quite as loudly. Still, she didn't have it in her to throw these things away.

A few strands of horse-hair wigs peeked from a half-open drawer, blond and red and bright blue. They were from the time just after she'd escaped the Zmey the first time around, when her hair had been burned so badly, she'd had to shave it all off. Those, she'd meant to throw away, but she'd never got around to it.

The sound of running water drifted in from the bathroom. Asen must have decided to take a bath before bed.

She'd just started to fall asleep when his shout woke her up: "Kosara!"

She sighed. "What?"

"There's an old man in the bathroom!"

"What old man?"

"Tall, lanky, with a long white moustache and a beard. Naked."

"You can see him!"

"He can see me too!" A pause, and then, "I'm naked as well!"

"That's the bathroom spirit. Don't worry, he's friendly."

"The bathroom spirit?"

"He lives in the bathroom. He likes the warmth."

"Does he have to look at me like that?"

"You can try asking him to give you some privacy."

Silence. Kosara waited for a couple of seconds before she asked, "Did it work?"

"It worked!"

She shut her eyes again.

"Kosara!"

She opened her eyes. "What?"

"There's an old woman in the kitchen. She's got a very big rolling pin." He paused. "Is this a kitchen spirit?"

"Yes."

"What should I do with her?"

"Leave a few jars open for her. The sour cabbage is her favourite."

"What about the man in the fireplace?"

"What do you think?"

"A fireplace spirit?"

"Yes."

"Should I feed him kindling?"

Kosara had to give it to Asen, he was a fast learner. "Good idea." She shut her eyes again.

"Kosara!"

What now?

"Is there a toilet spirit?"

She pretended to be asleep.

A polite cough woke up Kosara. When she peeled her eyes open, the fireplace spirit stood next to her bed, wringing his furry hands. He wore a thick leather coat, black and yellow like a salamander's skin. His beard was fiery red, and his eyes were black as coals.

"Mistress Kosara," he said, "you've come home at last!"

Kosara rubbed the sleep off her eyes. "Hello, Uncle," she greeted him, somewhat formally, like a distant relative she hadn't seen in a while.

Just like a relative, he pinched her cheek. "You've grown so tall!"

Kosara hadn't, in fact, grown any taller since the last time she'd seen him. Nevertheless, compared to his height of roughly two hand spans, maybe two and a half, she was practically a giant.

"We've all missed you," the spirit said. "The house has been very quiet those last few days since we awoke. Of course, Mistress Nevena is still here, but she's not . . . hmm, what she used to be."

"No." Kosara sighed deeply. "No, she's not."

The spirit fished out a long-stemmed pipe from his pocket and lit it, inhaling deeply. The room filled with the smell of burning: not tobacco, but wood, covered in moss and thick with resin.

"I've been wondering," the spirit said, "you've always had excellent taste . . ." He lifted two neckties in the air. One was purple, with large, orange sunflowers, and the other—bright red, with golden stars.

Kosara recognised both of them as having belonged to her father. She hesitated. "Well, the purple one is nice, but the red one is so festive. . . ."

"The red one," the spirit said. "You're right. The red one."

"What's the occasion?"

"The feast, of course!" And then he disappeared in a puff of smoke that smelled like burning pine.

The feast. Kosara shuddered. She'd forgotten all about it—buried it deep in her mind, like an ugly dress shoved in the back of the wardrobe. Three days of drinking, eating, dancing, and more drinking at the Zmey's palace. The monsters' annual last hurrah before the break of dawn on Saint Yordan's Day.

Now, Kosara remembered it clearly, as if it hadn't been seven years. The too-tight dress she'd squeezed herself in, pinching at her waist. The heavy perfumes, the candles dripping wax, the strong alcohol the Zmey had kept pushing in her hands. His voice whispering in her ear—back then, it had been sweet promises, not threats.

Just thinking about the feast sent shivers down her spine. If it wasn't for Vila, she would have never left it.

Kosara shut her eyes hard and tried to sleep, but the house was too noisy. The spirits knocked things over, clanked with pots and pans, splashed in the bathroom puddles. The branches of the nearby horse chestnut tree lashed at the windows, sending conkers tumbling down onto the pavement.

Her bedroom door opened again. This time, the kitchen spirit stood at the threshold. Colourful stains covered her apron: the rusty red of tomato puree, the bright pink of strawberry juice, the dark yellow of mustard. Her hair fell down almost to the floor, tied in a thick braid, golden brown like ripe wheat.

"The cabbage," she said seriously.

It took Kosara a second to realise it had been a question. "It was wonderful, Aunty. Very sour."

"I've been keeping it good for you all year. We had a warm summer, remember, it wasn't easy. Some truly nasty bacteria from the canal were trying to contaminate the basement, I fought them day and night."

Kosara imagined the kitchen spirit, a rolling pin in one hand and a chopping board in the other, bravely defending the basement against the hordes of bad bacteria and wild yeast. Her mouth twitched, but she didn't dare smile. Spirits could be terribly touchy. If they thought she was making fun of them, they'd cause all sorts of inconveniences: her keys would start disappearing when she was running late, or her food would burn as soon as she stopped watching it, or one sock from every pair would vanish without a trace.

"Thank you," Kosara said. "The cabbage was wonderful and so was the pickled green tomato. I've been telling all of Belograd about our pickled tomatoes."

The spirit beamed, her cheeks gleaming red. "I've been told you have excellent taste. . . ." She produced two hats from behind her back. One wide-brimmed and elaborate, covered in wax grapes and cherries, and the other—a simple bonnet, with a single rose embroidered on the side.

So, they'd also raided her mum's closet.

"Definitely the wide-brimmed one," Kosara said. "The grapes bring out your eyes."

The kitchen spirit nodded. "That's what I thought, too."

"Are you getting ready for the feast as well?"

"Of course! I wouldn't miss it for the world." And then she disappeared in a puff of smoke that smelled of freshly baked bread.

Kosara closed her eyes again. *Splash splash,* splashed the bathroom spirit, *bang bang,* banged the chestnut tree on the windows, *thud thud thud,* thudded Asen up and down the hallway.

Splash, splash. This time the sound was in her bedroom.

She opened her eyes and found the bathroom spirit standing above the bed. Curly white hairs coated his body, and his skin was wrinkled after hours in the moist bathroom. He had two of her father's old swimming costumes in his hands: one was bright yellow, and the other had blue-and-white stripes.

"Let me guess," Kosara said. "You're here for fashion advice."

"It's for the feast."

"I'm thinking stripes. They'll make you look like a sailor."

The spirit considered this. "I like sailors. Back in my day, we used to get them from all over the world. The parties were magnificent." He sighed, his eyes growing unfocused. "Is your friend a sailor?"

"Asen? No, he's a copper. And he's not my friend."

"I don't mind coppers, either. I think it's the uniform that does it for me. Are you two . . ." The spirit wiggled his bushy eyebrows and winked at her.

"Ew, no." Honestly, they were *just* like embarrassing old relatives.

"Oh well, I'm glad you're back, anyway. It's nice to have people around. My pipes were starting to get rusty." And then he disappeared in a puff that smelled like homemade soap.

Kosara pulled the blanket over her head. The spirits had to let her sleep now, after all of them had visited her.

Well, all except for one. But she couldn't imagine Nevena coming to her for fashion advice. What would she ask, which blood-soaked gown to put on?

Kosara was just drifting off when she heard the screams.

She was out of bed and halfway down the hallway before she truly woke up. The skirt of her nightgown shushed against the floor. The tiles were freezing cold beneath her bare feet. The red door at the end of the hallway was ajar.

Asen sat on the bed, breathing hard. Drops of sweat glistened on his forehead. His undershirt was soaked, clinging to the muscles on his chest in a way that would have been distracting if Kosara wasn't so angry with him.

"What the hell are you doing in Nevena's room?" she shouted before she'd thought better of it. She forced herself to speak calmly. "I told you not to go into the bedroom with the red door."

"You told me the ceiling was leaky. You said nothing about ghosts."

"I didn't want to panic you. What happened?"

"I had a nightmare. When I woke up, I couldn't move."

Kosara knew the answer, but she asked the question nonetheless, hoping she was wrong. "Why?"

"There was a girl. A teenager. She was sitting on top of my chest, and she was getting heavier and heavier until I couldn't breathe, and she was staring at me with those huge, black eyes. . . ."

"Her name is Nevena. She's a kikimora. And her eyes are brown." Kosara hadn't intended to say that last sentence out loud. Why did it matter what colour her eyes were?

This is not Nevena, she reminded herself once again, just like she'd done for years. *This is Nevena's fear personified. This is Nevena's anger. This is not your sister.*

"What did she look like?" she heard herself asking. "Did she look all right?"

Asen blinked. "What do you mean? There was a stab wound in her chest and blood running all down her hair." He looked at the sheets. He'd gathered them into a ball when he'd been twisting and turning. "There's no blood. I'm sure she had blood running down her hair."

"It wasn't real blood. I told you, Nevena is a kikimora."

"What's a kikimora?"

Kosara pulled at the skin around her nails, watching it change from flesh to shadow between her fingertips. "A type of spirit. Of a murdered person. They rise from the pool of spilled blood."

"Why didn't you warn me?"

"I did. I told you not to come into this room. This is Nevena's room."
The colour began to return to Asen's face. "Can you get rid of her?"
Kosara hesitated. "The only way to send away a kikimora is to bring justice to her murderer."

"I see. Who killed her?"

I did. Dear God, I killed her. I can tell you what it sounded like when the knife sank into her chest. My hands are still sticky with her blood.

"You know what," Kosara kept her tone light, "I haven't got a clue."

"You never thought to find out?"

"We're not all detectives, Bakharov. Come on, get out of here and go to my parents' room like I told you to."

"I can't. The bed's broken. The mattress is completely destroyed."

Kosara suspected the household spirits had been throwing parties while she'd been away. "Fine. You can sleep in my room."

She built a barricade of pillows in the middle of the bed, so that it was completely obvious: this half was hers, and the other one was his.

She pointedly ignored him as he walked in, clutching his pillow. She definitely didn't pay any attention to how short the boxer shorts he slept in were, or how tight that undershirt was. No attention whatsoever.

"I hope you don't snore," she mumbled. Then, she turned around and didn't hear Asen's response because she was already asleep.

11

Day Six

Kosara dreamed of Nevena, tears filling her brown eyes.

"Just kill me, alright?" Nevena kept repeating. "Just kill me."

When Kosara woke up, the room was blurry. She wiped her eyes with the sleeve of her nightgown.

Asen was already downstairs, lighting up the range in the kitchen, the clanking of its metal grate reverberating through the house. The smell of coffee drifted into the bedroom.

Kosara looked at the mirror above the vanity. Crusted salty streaks ran down her face, sinking into the three scrapes on her cheek. Her eyes were red, but they could pass for still being puffy with sleep.

If only she could make the tears stop.

Murderer, whispered the Zmey in her head. *It was all your fault, and you know it.*

Kosara squeezed her eyes shut. *Go away.*

You can't be trusted to be on your own. You need me.

"It wasn't your fault," she whispered to herself in the mirror. "It was self-defence. Not. Your. Fault."

Her parents had never blamed her. Why did she find it so hard to stop blaming herself?

Kosara took several deep breaths. She washed her face in the bathroom, letting the cool water soothe her puffy eyelids. Before she climbed down the stairs to the kitchen, she slammed the red door shut. If only that stupid copper hadn't opened it. . . .

The kitchen was dark, the only light coming from the smouldering coals in the fireplace.

"Good morning!" Asen said when he spotted her. He wore her mum's apron, a triumphant smile on his face. "How many eggs?"

Kosara blinked. Her eyelids were still heavy and sticky with tears. "What?"

"Eggs," he said. "How many?"

"Um, two?"

He placed a plate of poached eggs in front of her with the flourish of a magician producing a rabbit out of a hat. They were swimming in a pool of thick yogurt, and melted butter was poured all over them.

"Where did you get all that from?" Kosara asked.

"Your neighbour Svilen. I exchanged a jar of pickled tomatoes for them."

"Why?"

"I refuse to eat vinegar for breakfast. And . . ." Asen pushed a steaming cup towards her. "He'd just finished brewing his morning coffee."

Kosara's heart skipped a beat. A real Chernogradean coffee! She'd been drinking the sickly sweet sugar-laden concoction which passed for coffee in Belograd for five long, painful days.

"Are you sure you're not a warlock?" she asked. He laughed. "What did you exchange for that?"

"I promised to get him the recipe for the tomatoes."

"That's a family secret!"

"Do you want the coffee or not?"

Kosara wrapped her fingers tightly around her cup. "I want it." She took a long drink. It tasted like the best she'd ever had, even though it was too watery and a bit gritty.

She prodded the egg with her fork. "What's this?"

"A poached egg."

"No, I mean the powdery stuff on top."

"Oh, that's cayenne pepper."

"Cay-what?"

"It's a spice. Try it."

"Do you always carry spices about?"

"Only the essentials. Cardamom, bay leaf, cinnamon, nutmeg, cloves . . ."

Kosara took a careful bite. It burned her lips and left a fiery trail down her throat. It wasn't bad, she had to admit. In fact, it was lovely.

"It's nice," she said.

"Glad you like it." Asen sat across from her, cup in hand. "Well, are you ready to catch a murderer?"

Not in the slightest. "Always."

As soon as they approached Roksana's house, it became obvious no one was home. The windows were dark, and no smoke came out the chimney. The roof was an onion dome of snow.

A bizarre cocktail of relief and desperation stirred in Kosara's stomach. On the one hand, she wouldn't have to face Roksana yet. On the other, the shadow disease now reached all the way up her arm, creeping towards her chest. She was quickly running out of time.

Asen knocked on the door three times, waited a second, and knocked again. It wasn't the friendly "knock knock, is anyone home?" of a worried neighbour or a travelling salesperson. It was an assured policeman's knock. There was no reply.

"Damn it," Kosara concluded.

"Do you know where else she might have gone?"

Kosara shook her head. Roksana knew Chernograd better than anyone. She'd explored every dark corner of the city, searching for the most exotic monsters she could get her hands on. She could have holed up anywhere.

Asen shielded his eyes against the sun as he looked up at the house. "That's almost a mansion."

"Roksana makes good money."

"Surely, she could afford wards. Why was she in the pub for New Year's Eve?"

"Oh, you'll see. Once we get in." Kosara produced a key ring from her bag. She unlocked the first lock, and then the second, but when she got to the third, the key wouldn't turn. She tried several times before swearing and shoving the key ring back in her bag. "The bastard's changed the lock. Why would she change the lock?"

"Because she knew you'd want to prod around her house?" Asen sighed deeply. "Stand closer."

"What?"

He inspected the lock. Something metallic glinted in his clenched fist. A lock pick.

Kosara caught herself in the last moment before her jaw hit the ground. He'd arrest anyone else who as much as thought about maybe purchasing a lock pick. Yet here he was, with a full set, trying them one after the other to check which size best fit the lock.

"What are you doing?" she asked.

Stupid question. It was obvious what he was doing.

"You wanted to get in, didn't you? Stand closer," Asen repeated. "Please."

Kosara stood next to him, hiding him from curious eyes—especially those that might peek out the windows of the nearby police station. She had no doubt the station was stuffed to the brim with coppers: they rarely showed their noses outside during the Foul Days. Kosara remembered one time, several years ago, when they'd promoted a new, unusually keen sergeant who'd very bravely declared his boys and girls would be patrolling the city every evening to make sure all citizens got home safe. He'd been ousted from the force by lunchtime.

"Does everyone from Belograd know how to pick locks?" she asked.

"I wouldn't think so," Asen said. "Otherwise my job would become very difficult."

"Is this a standard part of the police training?"

"It's not."

"How did you learn it then?"

"I grew up in the Docks."

Kosara gaped at him. She'd heard of the Belogradean Docks, most often in the context of, "never go to the Belogradean Docks." Not a place for a respectable lady or gentleman, she'd been told. All she'd find there were shady characters, seedy pubs, and suspect street food.

"How come you don't speak like you're from the Docks?" she asked.

"What do you mean?"

Kosara hesitated, realising a second too late she'd said something stupid. She'd hated it when the Belogradeans told her she was *so* well spoken for a Chernogradean. As if she was a circus animal who'd performed an impressive flip.

"I'd have expected you to have a stronger accent," she said carefully.

"My mum says if you speak with a strong accent, people think you're stupid."

"Wise woman."

Kosara watched, equally disappointed and fascinated, as his hands moved fast, the lock pick glinting between his fingers. It was clearly not his first time, but the lock was proving tricky. The fine line between his eyebrows deepened. Kosara even caught him mouthing a swear once or twice. She shifted from one foot to the other, casting nervous glances towards the police station.

To distract herself, she started talking. "I knew a guy who once got so drunk he broke into his own house, then reported himself to the police the next morning."

"He didn't."

"He did! He was walking home one night after the pub, completely off his head, and he saw a house that'd been left unlocked. So, he snuck in, found the secret stash under the mattress, and went to buy more booze. The next morning, he woke up, realised he'd been burgled, went to the police station, and reported it."

"Was he from Chernograd?"

"Why? Because people from Chernograd are all thieves and drunks, and you Belogradeans are all squeaky-clean, law-abiding Goody Two-shoes?"

"I didn't mean—"

"Yeah, he was from Chernograd."

Kosara froze as the door of the police station opened. A young officer came out, tightly wrapped in a navy-blue coat, an unlit cigarette hanging between his gritted teeth. He tried to light it, cupping it with his hand against the wind.

"Damn it," Kosara whispered. "The police." Then she thought about it and added, "The Chernogradean police. Hurry up."

"I'm doing my best."

The police officer clicked his lighter again, then shook his head and looked around. His gaze fell on Kosara. He walked towards her.

"He's coming," Kosara said. She glimpsed the lock pick for a split second when Asen slid it in his pocket. The next moment, he casually leaned on the door frame with a lit cigarette in his hand. It was like a magic trick.

"Excuse me," the young policeman said. "Do you have a light?"

Asen handed him a box of matches.

"Thanks. Cold morning, isn't it?" The implication in his voice was clear: *What are you two doing out here?*

"They always are," Kosara said, "this time of year."

"I bet you can't wait to get inside and put the fire on."

Kosara laughed. "You have no idea. Just having a cigarette before going in. My landlady doesn't like it when he smokes inside." She pointed at Asen with her thumb. He did an excellent impression of a Chernogradean man, all silent and brooding. He'd have looked like a local, if only it wasn't for his stupid coat.

"Been away?" The policeman nodded towards the snow on the roof.

"Visiting family," Kosara said, praying he didn't mention the lack of bags. "My mum always makes way too much food for the holidays. She insisted we stay over until we'd at least finished the baklava."

The police officer considered them for a second. "My da's the same. I remember, last New Year's Eve, I had the flu so I told him I couldn't see him, and he threatened to barge into my house with the big tray of banitsa. And I told him, 'Da,' I said, 'that would be breaking and entering. I'd have to arrest you!'"

Kosara swallowed hard. The young policeman's smile had acquired a sharp edge.

"What did he say?" Kosara asked.

"He said, 'Won't the banitsa be a good enough reason for you to look away, son?' Ha-ha! It was. His phyllo pastry is the best in Chernograd."

"Ha-ha," Kosara mumbled. She elbowed Asen in the side.

"Ouch!" Asen said. "What?"

"You've got money?" she whispered through clenched teeth, the smile never leaving her face.

"What? Why?"

Kosara elbowed him again.

"Ouch! Why do you keep—oh! I see. I haven't got much on me. . . ." Asen rummaged through his wallet and produced a shiny new banknote.

When the policeman saw the number gleaming on it in golden ink, his eyes widened.

"A donation from a concerned citizen to the brave Chernogradean police," Kosara said. "I'm sure you boys and girls have been working very hard."

"Oh, thank you for your kindness." The policeman pocketed the banknote. "Have a good evening."

"You, too."

Kosara watched him walk back to the station. Only once he'd disappeared inside, did she let herself exhale.

"Hurry up," she said, "or they'll bankrupt us."

"That was unbelievable!" Asen stomped his cigarette out on the pavement, before collecting the butt and placing it in a box in his pocket. "Asking for a bribe so blatantly? Disgusting."

"Says the copper who's currently picking a lock."

The lock pick in Asen's hand quietly chimed as it hit the lock.

"I suppose you're right," he said. "I don't even want to imagine what the boss would have said if I'd got arrested in Chernograd for attempted breaking and entering."

The lock finally clicked. Asen opened the door. His face stayed serious, despite the corners of his mouth twitching. He'd enjoyed breaking that lock, Kosara could tell.

As soon as she stepped inside, a familiar smell tickled her nostrils. Magic. The house was saturated with it: from the fluffy rugs on the floor to the chiming chandeliers on the ceiling.

She peeked into the rooms on both sides of the hallway. It was obvious Roksana had been home recently. The loaf of bread on the kitchen counter had only just started to grow mouldy. The cezve was half-filled with cold coffee, and a few eggshells rested next to a greasy frying pan.

The deeper into the house they went, the stronger the smell of magic got. When they reached the door to the bedroom at the end of the hallway, it grew so intense it made Kosara's head spin.

She pushed the door open with one finger and jumped back. Her hand instinctively curled up in a protective spell. Nothing happened.

Kosara walked into the bedroom and cast an apologetic glance over her shoulder at Asen. He put his revolver back in its holster. When he stepped over the threshold, his eyes grew larger.

"That's why Roksana spends the Foul Days in the pub," Kosara said.

The entire wall facing the bed was covered in stuffed monster heads. The karakonjul ones were less unsettling, their small toothy faces decidedly not human, but the rest of them . . .

"Why?" Asen asked.

"She likes to take a trophy from every monster she kills." Kosara shivered, imagining Irnik's face staring at her between the monsters. "I think she sees them as decoration most of the time. It's only during the Foul Days that they prevent her from sleeping."

"And you're surprised this woman's capable of murder?"

Kosara shrugged. "They're just monsters."

Except that some of them could have been Uncle Dimitar, who grew a bit hairier during the full moon, and Aunty Kalina, who'd died fifty years ago. . . .

Kosara sighed. The monsters were monsters. You killed them, or they killed you. She was a witch—she had no right to judge. She'd brewed plenty of toothache cures using upir teeth. She'd happily ground many a karakonjul ear in her mortar and pestle to make a potion for manly vigour.

She tried to ignore the monsters' accusing eyes following her as she walked around the room. The sound of her soles on the tiled floor suddenly sounded an awful lot like the flapping of a yuda's wings. The rustling of leaves outside reminded her of a samodiva's laughter.

Asen kneeled to look under the bed, then checked the cupboard. Kosara lifted the book on the bedside table.

"I've read this one! She stopped reading just before it got interesting, when it turns out thirteen of the passengers took turns to—Wait!"

Asen froze, his hand on the handle of the wardrobe. "What?"

"That must be where the smell of magic is coming from." There was nothing else in the room that seemed even remotely magical.

"What smell?"

"Step back." She rolled up her sleeves.

Asen drew his revolver. *Yeah, good luck shooting a fireball, Mister Policeman.* Then she looked at her own hands. *And good luck counteracting a spell, Miss Witch-Without-a-Shadow.*

Kosara opened the wardrobe with one sharp movement. Her heart thumped once, twice, three times, before calming down again. It was just a wardrobe. Piles of dark clothes rested inside it. Two bunches of herbs swung from the rail: one of lavender, to dispel the moths, and a second of valerian, basil, and wormwood, to keep away the monsters. Roksana's monster-hunting uniform hung next to it, its fur old and worn and its many brass bells covered in patina.

The smell was residual, Kosara realised. There had been some kind of strong magic in this room, but it was now gone.

She swore under her breath. They were too late.

Asen shook his head and walked to the window. Kosara wasn't sure what he hoped to see outside. A neat trail of footprints in the freshly fallen snow, leading straight to where Roksana was hiding? If only they had that kind of luck. . . .

She spotted two stark white stains on Asen's knees, contrasting against the dark fabric of his trousers.

"You've got something . . ." She gestured towards him.

He patted his knees, sending white clouds up in the air. "Chalk."

"Chalk," Kosara repeated, brows furrowed. She kneeled down and ran a finger over the floorboards. It came back covered in fine chalk dust. She lifted the rug.

Most of the magic circle was gone, as if someone had quickly smeared it with their foot once they were finished with it. Only a couple of symbols remained visible in the corner.

It was enough for Kosara. She'd recognise this handwriting anywhere.

"What's that?" Asen asked.

Kosara touched one of the symbols, then wiped the chalk off on her coat. "Teleportation spell."

"Like the one in Irnik's house?"

"Oh no. This one used no amulet. Just pure magic."

"Really? I thought that was very difficult."

"It is. Terribly difficult. The human body has an awful lot of organs to keep track of. You should consider yourself lucky to find one of these without a leftover body part just sitting in it in a puddle of blood."

"How come this one worked then?"

"It was drawn by someone who knew exactly what they were doing. Besides, it's slightly more manageable over a short distance. This one, for example, is for less than ten minutes' walk away."

Asen looked down at the circle. "How can you tell?"

"I know who drew it."

It was obvious. Who else would cast a difficult and dangerous spell, rather than simply walk for ten minutes?

"Come on," Kosara said. "We have to go."

"Where?"

"To see Vila."

This wasn't a good sign. If old Vila was involved in this, it was entirely possible Kosara had bitten off more than she could chew. Far, far more.

12

Day Six

The Botanic Gardens glistened white in the winter sun. The benches hid beneath snow mounds, and frozen flowers decorated the windows of the greenhouses. Notice boards with plant names peeked out, half-buried in the snowdrifts.

"Is Vila a botanist?" Asen asked as he and Kosara walked through an enclosure of blooming rose shrubs. Every gust of wind sent red petals flying in the air, like droplets of blood against the snow.

"She's a witch," Kosara said. "An old-fashioned one. She'd live in a hut in the woods if there were any woods around here."

"I see. And why are you so nervous about meeting her?"

Nervous? Kosara realised she'd been biting her lower lip and forced herself to stop. "I'm not nervous."

Asen raised his eyebrows.

Kosara sighed. "Vila's my old teacher."

"You're worried she'll be disappointed with you for losing your shadow?"

"Maybe a bit."

Truth was, he'd hit the nail on the head. Kosara *was* worried Vila would be disappointed with her: for losing her shadow, for getting involved with the Zmey, for once again needing to be saved.

"Surely, you're not her only student who's fallen on hard times. She'd understand."

"I suspect I am," Kosara mumbled.

"Sorry?"

"I'd bet you I'm her only student who's lost their magic. She doesn't accept new students easily. In fact, I don't think she ever took anyone new after me."

"How did you convince her to take you?"

"I had a gift for fire magic, and Vila knew it."

What Kosara didn't tell him was that Vila had been the only witch in the entire city who'd agreed to teach her. Young witches caused an awful lot of accidents, some more than others. Kosara had been a walking disaster.

"You kept causing fires?" Asen asked. He was starting to figure it out.

"My mum didn't like the idea that her daughter might become a witch. She tried to get me to learn a proper trade, suitable for a young lady. At first, she sent me to the milliner's. It burned down within the week. Then I was going to be a clockmaker. It took three days before the workshop caught on fire. The baker's only lasted a day."

"Why?"

"I kept getting hurt and frustrated. Pricking my fingers with the needles, stabbing my hands with the tiny screwdrivers, burning myself on the ovens. When I got frustrated, things caught on fire."

"It does sound dangerous."

"That's what Vila said. She convinced my mum I needed to be trained before I burned down the entire city. So, that summer I began learning how to be a witch. I'd train all morning with Vila, and then in the afternoon, I'd go and help the milliner, the clockmaker, and the baker rebuild their workshops. They weren't too upset with me, thank God. Things often catch fire in Chernograd, so they had excellent insurance policies."

"Because of all the young fire witches?"

"Fire witches are quite rare, actually. No, it's because of the Zmey."

Kosara could tell Asen was about to ask something else, so she hurried forwards, leaving him to catch up with her. In front of the gardenia enclosure, an enormous black cat waited for them, his yellow eyes gleaming, his paws impatiently tapping on the cobblestones.

"Hi, Moth," Kosara said. "How are you?"

The cat yawned to show her he had no time for pleasantries.

"The cat's called Moth?" Asen asked.

"Short for Behemoth." Kosara turned back to the cat. "Could you please lead us to your mistress?"

Moth walked between the trees, his fluffy tail raised up high in the air. From time to time, he turned around and pierced them with his eyes, as if telling them to hurry up.

"I thought you knew where Vila lives," Asen said.

"I know she's around here somewhere, I just don't know where exactly. Her house moves."

"Like a caravan?"

"Something like that. It's got legs."

"Legs? You're pulling my—"

"I'm not, I swear. You'll see."

The lake was frozen solid, surrounded by a wall of snow-covered ferns and reeds. Vila's house sat on a rocky outcrop in the middle. Two hen's legs rested on both sides of it, as if the house was an enormous sleepy chicken.

"You weren't joking," Asen said. "The house has legs."

"It certainly does. Vila says she got it from her ex-wife in the divorce proceedings."

Moth was obviously tired of waiting for the two clumsy humans. He darted across the lake. His nails left white scratches on the ice and clicked against the wall as he climbed up the house, diving into the chimney.

Kosara tried the surface of the lake with her toe. It didn't crack. She took a careful step forwards, then another one. Asen followed her, his shoes sliding and making him wobble.

Finally, they reached the house. Kosara raised her hand to knock on the door, but before she could, it opened with a loud creak. Vila stood in the frame with her hands on her hips. She must have been waiting for them.

Asen blinked in confusion, frowning, and Kosara suppressed the urge to elbow him in the ribs. What had he been expecting? Some decrepit old hag?

Vila had always looked as if she wasn't a day older than thirty. She was the best herbalist in all of Chernograd, and youth potions were her speciality. The only thing that advertised her true age was her long braid, white as freshly fallen snow.

"Hi, Vila," Kosara mumbled.

"Kosara! What a surprise." Vila did not sound the slightest bit surprised. "Come on in."

She led them inside, her braid swinging like a pendulum behind her. Her rubber boots left wet marks on the floor. Her hands were coated in mud—she'd probably been out picking herbs.

Kosara stepped over the threshold, and it was as if she'd travelled back in time. Nothing in the house had changed. The shelves along the walls were covered in jars and bottles: some were full of pickled gherkins and sour cabbage. In others, eyes blinked, teeth chattered, and tentacles twitched. Bunches of herbs and strings of tiny smoked fish hung from the ceiling beams, interspersed with dried varkolak ears and yuda tongues. Asen couldn't walk standing straight without them tickling the crown of his head.

The fire blazed in the fireplace, and a cast-iron cauldron bubbled over it. *A potion?* As Kosara walked deeper into the house, she smelled it— lemons, fresh mussels and mackerel heads, parsley, mint, and thyme. Fish soup. It made her eyes water.

Vila sat on the armchair next to the fire. Moth jumped into her lap. She ran her dark fingers over his fur, making him purr about as quietly as a circular saw. Kosara and Asen were left standing, like badly behaved children in front of the schoolmistress.

"Who's your friend?" Vila asked.

"This is Asen. He's not my friend, he's a police officer."

Vila clapped her hands, as if Kosara had presented her with the best macaroni necklace in the whole kindergarten class. "A police officer! Isn't this a surprise."

Of course it isn't, you old hag, Kosara thought. *You're the best seer in the city. You've seen us coming from hours away.*

What she said instead was, "I'm full of surprises today."

Vila gestured to Asen to approach her and grabbed his hand in between hers. She wrinkled her large nose. "I smell a Belogradean smell."

"He's from Belograd." Kosara could tell where this was going. Maybe she should have warned Asen about Vila.

"Are you going to stay for dinner, my boy?"

"Um," Asen said, "what's for dinner?"

"Well, I was going to have fish soup, but I'm starting to crave something a bit more exotic." She sniffed his hand again, and for a split second, in between two blinks of an eye, she changed: her hair grew thinner, hanging in front of her face in greasy streaks; her eyes turned milky white and rolled inside her skull; her skin drooped like a fast-melting candle. Asen sharply pulled his hand back.

Vila, now young again, cackled. She turned to Kosara. "Do you think he'll fit in the cauldron?"

"Very funny," Kosara said. "We can't stay for dinner. We're in a bit of a hurry."

"Is that so? And here I was, thinking you've decided to pay your old teacher a visit because you missed me. What do you want?"

"We're looking for Roksana."

"And what makes you think I can help you?"

"I found one of your chalk circles on her bedroom floor."

"Ah. Yes, I went to pay her a visit, but she'd left already. To tell you the truth, I'd like to speak to her myself."

"Why?"

"I heard some very strange rumours about that girl. Had a few peculiar visions, too. I'd hoped she'd give me a rational explanation."

Kosara shook her head. So had she.

"Unfortunately," Vila said, "what I found only confirms my suspicions. She's got herself involved with someone very dangerous."

"I know. Konstantin Karaivanov."

Vila clicked her tongue. "No." She paused. For a long moment, the only sound was the fire crackling in the fireplace. "The Zmey."

Kosara's blood rushed to her ears. It couldn't be. She must have misheard.

"What?" she said, almost inaudibly.

"Roksana is collecting witches' shadows for the Zmey."

Kosara's ears buzzed. It *couldn't* be. Vila must have been mistaken. The old woman had got herself mixed up, that had to be it. Roksana would never betray Kosara to the Zmey. Never.

Just like she'd never have stayed friends with Sevar. Just like she'd never have committed a murder. Just like she'd never have stolen Kosara's shadow.

But what about Konstantin's symbol scribbled on Irnik's floor? Had Roksana drawn it simply to throw Kosara—and the coppers—off her scent? Or had she lied to Karaivanov in order to get one of his amulets for crossing the Wall? Roksana wouldn't be so foolish as to risk angering Karaivanov. Would she?

Then again, she'd been foolish enough to agree to work for the Zmey....

"Are you certain?" Kosara asked.

"Absolutely," Vila replied.

Kosara swore under her breath. Now that she thought about it, it made perfect sense. The Zmey had always wanted a witch's shadow. He had a magic of his own: raw, wild, uncontrollable. What he'd wanted was magic he could control.

What he'd wanted was *her* magic. The only thing that gave her strength. The only thing that prevented her—in his mind—from running back to him.

He'd tried to buy it from her when she was younger. He'd offered her palaces built in one night, and caves filled with gold, and mountains of pearls and precious stones. She'd refused, as difficult as telling him "no" was.

So, he'd found another way to get what he wanted. As usual.

But it wasn't only her shadow he'd managed to steal, was it? He'd gotten Irnik Ivanov's whole necklace. What would the Zmey do with that much magic power? Kosara shuddered just thinking about it.

And what had he promised Roksana to persuade her to work with him? Roksana, who'd been there on the night Kosara had come back from the Zmey's palace. Roksana, who'd helped her bandage her burnt hands.

The floor swayed beneath Kosara's feet.

Roksana, *who'd helped her bandage her burnt hands.*

They'd never been close before that. How come as soon as Kosara had escaped the Zmey, Roksana was suddenly always around, offering her broad shoulders for Kosara to cry on?

Roksana had attached herself to Kosara like a leech. At first, Kosara had kept the monster hunter at an arm's distance. But then Nevena had died, and she'd just needed *someone,* no matter who—someone to get blackout drunk with; someone who wouldn't question all her questionable decisions.

This time, Kosara swore out loud. How could she have been so *stupid.*

Of course Roksana worked for the Zmey. It had been right in front of Kosara, all these years. How else did the Zmey always find her, no matter how hard she tried to hide from him? He always seemed to know little details about her life she'd never told him—

"Kosara," Vila's voice came as if from very far away. Kosara's ears felt like they were stuffed with cotton wool. "Kosara!"

Kosara shut her eyes and took a deep breath.

Roksana had turned out to be a snake. So what? Kosara had always known it: having friends when you lived on this side of the Wall was a very bad idea. They only made you vulnerable.

"Sorry," she said. "I was miles away. What were you saying?"

"Asen here asked me how I know where Roksana is. I know because of this."

Vila clapped her hands, and when she pulled them back apart, something caught the light in between her palms. It took Kosara a few seconds to focus on it.

A thread. Hair-thin and gleaming faintly, like a solitary moonbeam.

Kosara inhaled so sharply the room spun. "Moon yarn."

"Moon yarn," Vila said. "I found it tied to a bedpost in her house."

"You can't expect me to believe that. Once tied, moon yarn can't be untied, everyone knows that."

Vila snorted. She tied a knot in the yarn and untied it again, her fingers moving fast.

"Oh," Kosara said. "How?"

"I might teach you one day."

"I'm sorry," Asen said. "What's moon yarn?"

Kosara scratched the scar on her cheek. "The Zmey's palace, it exists beyond . . ." She made a helpless gesture with her hand. "Beyond . . ."

"Time-space," Vila said.

"Time-space. You might be able to get there, but you can't find your way back, unless you've got a ball of moon yarn. You tie one end to something here, in the human world, and you unravel it as you walk. Then, when you want to come back, you simply follow it."

There was a thud and a hiss as Moth reached for the yarn and got smacked on the paw.

"Not for you!" Vila shook a finger at him. He meowed, jumped from her lap onto the floor, and disappeared up the chimney. She followed him with her eyes. "He won't talk to me for days now."

"Why did you take the yarn?" Asen asked, every bit the policeman. He was getting dangerously close to informing Vila what sentence she'd get for theft. "Doesn't that mean that when Roksana tries to get back, she'll just end up here?"

"That's exactly what it means. And the two of us are going to have a nice, long talk."

The flames in the fireplace grew larger, elongating Vila's features, making the fine lines on her face deeper. Her shadow danced on the wall behind her. Kosara suspected that Vila's talk with Roksana would be long, but it certainly wouldn't be nice.

She still hoped to get to Roksana before the old witch.

Vila clapped her knees with her hands, rather dispelling the effect the flames had created. "Right, now who'd like a nice, hot cup of tea?"

Kosara only ever drank tea when she was sick. She tried to say as much, but Vila insisted it would calm her nerves while shoving a cup in her hands. And she was right. Kosara didn't dare ask what was in the tea—all she could smell was camomile—but after only a sip, her heart finally stopped racing.

"How is it?" Vila asked.

"It's nice," Kosara admitted. "A bit sour."

"Oh dear!" Vila slapped her forehead loudly. "I forgot the honey! Listen, my boy"—she turned to Asen—"do you mind grabbing some from the cupboard upstairs? My old knees aren't what they used to be, and I can't handle the ladder . . ."

Kosara rolled her eyes. She'd bet there was nothing wrong with Vila's knees.

Asen, however, looked genuinely concerned. "Of course."

Vila waited until he'd disappeared up the stairs.

"What?" Kosara asked.

Vila leaned in and whispered dramatically, hiding her mouth behind her hand, "Your friend isn't too hard on the eyes, is he?"

"I can't say I've noticed," Kosara lied. "And he's not my friend."

"Well, don't let his pretty face fool you. He stinks of magic."

Kosara frowned. "No, he doesn't."

Vila tapped the side of her nose with her index finger. "Oh yes, this old honker doesn't lie. *Reeks*, I tell you. And you'd better find out why."

Kosara sighed. This was the last thing she was worried about right now. "He probably uses Chernogradean cosmetics. They've got tons of them in Belograd."

"Well, then he wouldn't mind telling you about it. But make sure to find out. It could be dangerous."

Asen's footsteps sounded on the stairs. Vila shushed Kosara, as if they hadn't already both stopped talking.

Once she'd spooned half a beehive's worth of honey into her tea, Vila drank it in silence for a few minutes. Kosara didn't dare enjoy this rare respite from the old witch's questions. She knew it wouldn't last long.

It didn't. Vila wasn't even halfway through her cup when she asked, "Where's your shadow?"

Kosara nearly spat out her tea at the sudden change of topic. She'd been expecting the question, but she nevertheless found herself at a loss for words. Vila watched her, her dark eyes unblinking.

"It doesn't matter," Kosara mumbled, her gaze drawn towards the floor. Hopefully, if she stared at it hard enough, it might take pity on her and swallow her. "It's nothing."

"What do you mean, nothing? Your shadow's gone."

"It's not that big a deal. I barely notice the difference."

Vila snorted.

"You know that I've always been a mediocre witch," Kosara said.

"No. You've always been an impatient, impulsive, often outright stupid witch. Never mediocre. I don't take mediocre students."

"My spells never worked properly."

"Because you lack patience. You can't try a spell once or twice and give up when it doesn't work."

Kosara kept inspecting her boots. She felt as if she was ten again, with wrists cramping from waving her hands about, fingers numb from weaving spells, and eyes full of tears.

Vila used to make her repeat the same spell over and over again, for days or weeks or months, until it worked. It was most often months.

"I know exactly what happened," Vila said. "I've been waiting for you to turn up at my doorstep. I bet you just gave it to him when he asked, didn't you? You didn't even try to fight him."

"I couldn't fight the Zmey!" Kosara heard her voice reverberating through the room and forced herself to speak quieter. "You know what he's like when he's angry."

"Yes, I know very well. As you remember, I have faced his anger before. And I fought him."

Kosara looked down at her hands. Shadow, flesh, shadow, flesh. She was too distracted to make them stop. "I'm not you. I'm not nearly as powerful as you."

"Stupid witch. It has nothing to do with power. The Zmey feeds on fear and insecurity. The only way to defeat him is to face that little, horrible voice in your head telling you that you're not good enough and force it to *shut the fuck up*."

Kosara rolled her eyes. It was easy for Vila. The Zmey actually feared her.

"So, what are you going to do?" Vila asked. "Are you going to sit here and wait to turn into a shadow, or—"

"How do I find the Zmey's palace?" Kosara forced the question out. That was the last place she wanted to go.

"You tell me," Vila said. "You've been."

"I don't think I can use the same mode of transport as the last time."

"What was that?" Asen asked.

He seemed completely calm. Kosara would have expected the talk of visiting the Zmey's palace to have rattled him—but then again, he was a Belogradean. He probably had no idea how dangerous that trip was.

Or maybe it was something else. Kosara had seen Asen in several dangerous situations now, and it seemed the man was just that hard to rattle. He'd strolled into Chernograd during the Foul Days as if it was nothing. Granted, he'd nearly lost his arm to a hungry karakonjul only several hours later, but nevertheless, Kosara couldn't help but be a little impressed.

She pretended she hadn't heard his question. She couldn't tell him the truth: that she'd flown on the Zmey's back.

"No, of course you can't do that," Vila said. "But think. What did you see?"

Kosara shut her eyes and tried to think back to that night, seven years ago. She'd gotten terrible travel sickness. Bile burned the back of her throat and her hands shook. Hot and cold waves ran through her body.

But there was also something else. The smell of brine and seaweed. She'd dared to open one eye for a brief second, and all she'd seen were rolling waves stretching into the distance.

Of course. Most royalty would be satisfied with a simple moat to protect their castles. Not the Zmey. He had to have an entire sea.

"We had to cross the sea." Kosara opened her eyes and met Vila's gaze. "I remember now."

"Wait," Asen said. "You have a sea in here?"

"Only during the Foul Days. The rest of the year, it's a small lake in the wilder end of the park. The Zmey told me it's enchanted, brought straight from his realm"—Kosara turned back to Vila—"and no human could ever cross it uninvited. How the hell did you cross it?"

Vila laughed. "The old fool would like to think his sea can't be crossed! All you need is Blackbeard's compass. You know Blackbeard, the sea captain?"

"Unfortunately."

A few years back, Blackbeard had asked every witch in the city to help him look for his magic compass. He'd offered Kosara enough money she put up with his terrible attitude all evening, trying every object-locating spell, amulet, or talisman she could think of.

There was no sign of the compass. As if it had vanished into thin air—or as if it were hidden by a witch powerful enough to erase any trace of it.

"Do you still have it?" Kosara asked.

"Oh no, I got rid of it years ago. I hate holding onto useless knick-knacks, you know that."

Kosara looked around the cramped room, full of a large variety of useless knickknacks. "What did you do with it?"

"Well . . ." Vila examined her soil-caked nails. If Kosara didn't know better, she would have thought the old witch was embarrassed. "Have I ever told you how Blackbeard married one of my old students, Algara? And he wouldn't let her practice? The fool was terrified of witchcraft. Why the hell would you marry a witch if you're so scared of magic?"

"You have told me," Kosara said. "Repeatedly."

"Anyway, Algara died a few years back. So, I thought it would make for great poetic justice to bury the bastard's compass with her. You know, the thing he treasured above all else, buried with the one treasure he never learned how to appreciate."

Kosara swore internally. The compass was in a *grave*. The graveyard came right after the Zmey's palace in her list of places she'd least like to visit during the Foul Days. The last time she'd been there still gave her nightmares.

"You're expecting me to go and dig it out?" she asked.

"Oh, don't look at me like that," Vila said. "I thought we'd left that whole thing with the Zmey behind us. How was I supposed to know you might need the compass again?"

Maybe by using those notorious seer powers you've got?

"Listen, how about I make it up to you?" Vila began rummaging through her many pockets, and suddenly, all her air of mysticism disappeared as she pulled out dirty hankies, old wrappers, and long-forgotten boiled sweets.

Finally, she drew a ball of moon yarn. The silver light illuminated her face and made the whites of her eyes glint.

"You can have my moon yarn," she said. "It's not like I plan on using it. Truth be told, I'm getting way too old for a trek to the palace. Though I hope you realise that means I can't come and save your arse if you mess up again."

Then, without warning, she threw it. Kosara was so startled she almost let it hit her in the face, but at the last second, she managed to jerk her hands up to catch it.

It didn't feel as Kosara had imagined it would. She thought it would be silky soft but substantial, like nice cashmere. Instead, it felt like nothing. She saw it resting in between her opened palms, but all she touched was air.

"Thank you," she said. The ball of moon yarn bounced slightly at the sound of her voice, as if urging her forwards: "Come on, time to go, time to see the Zmey."

The yarn and Vila seemed to be in agreement. "You'd better be on your way. You have no time to lose."

My little Kosara, the Zmey's voice whispered in Kosara's ear. He sounded so real, she found it hard not to look over her shoulder. *Finally coming back to me again. I knew you would return.*

Kosara buttoned up her coat. It took her forever, with her fingertips switching between shadow and flesh every few seconds. She hated for

Vila to see her like this, but she simply couldn't find the focus to make them stop.

Before she'd managed to say anything else, Vila was already pushing them towards the door.

"You're a witch," Vila said, as if reading her thoughts. "You've been taught by the best. Go and get your shadow back."

A weak witch. A useless witch. You're nothing without me, Kosara.

Could she really do this? Could she return to the Zmey's palace?

Did she have a choice?

"Yes," Kosara said. "I will."

Vila grasped her elbow and leaned close to Kosara's ear. "And remember to check why your Belogradean stinks of magic."

Then she slammed the door shut.

13

Day Six

The house was unusually quiet. The only sounds were the creaking of the floorboards and the wind whistling in the chimney. The spirits had finally fallen asleep after banging about all night. Kosara put the copper cezve on the stove and waited for the coffee to come to a boil.

It was getting late, and her eyes were closing on their own, but she couldn't waste time sleeping now. She had monsters to catch.

She cast a quick glance towards Asen over her shoulder. He sat next to the hearth, carving aspen stakes and whistling. Now that she knew what she was looking for, she had to admit Vila had been right. He smelled of Belograd—of spices and fruits and the sea—but under it lingered a familiar smell. Magic. It was barely there, expertly hidden, but once Vila had pointed it out, it was unmistakable.

"Do you carry an amulet?" Kosara asked, busying around the stove, completely casual.

"Excuse me?"

"An amulet. Or a talisman. Something like that?"

"I don't, as far as I'm aware."

"What about a potion? An elixir? A tincture of some sort?"

"I have some lip balm in my pocket if that's what you're after."

"Not unless it contains magic."

"I'm fairly certain it's one hundred percent beeswax. Why?"

"Just curious."

There had to be some innocent explanation for this. He'd probably bought an enchanted baldness cure, or a magical pimple concealer, and was too embarrassed to admit it. Belograd was full of magic, even if they didn't create any of it. Vila was being dramatic about it, as usual.

What were the chances he'd acquired a dangerous spell back in Belograd? After all, he was just a clueless copper.

A clueless copper who'd looked like he had no problem accompanying her to the palace of Chernograd's most powerful monster. . . .

"Listen," she said, "are you sure you want to come on this trip? It's a suicide mission."

"And yet, you're going."

I have no choice. Kosara's shadow sickness now gripped her shoulder, its dark tentacles stretching towards her chest. Once her heart turned to shadow . . .

Actually, she had no idea what would happen. Shadow sickness was taboo and, as such, not that well researched. It was considered a fitting punishment for being stupid enough to give your shadow away. As stupid as Kosara had been.

Would a shadow heart attempt to pump shadow blood through veins made of flesh? Kosara winced. She'd rather not find out.

"That's different," she said. "I have to get my shadow back."

"And I have to catch a murderer."

"It will be dangerous."

"Please, I crossed the Wall illegally, defying the explicit orders of my boss. I thrive on danger."

Kosara measured him with her eyes. "Do you really?"

"Of course not. I've never done anything so foolish before."

Interesting. Kosara had started to assume Asen disobeyed the rules as a matter of habit. He'd been so casual about crossing the Wall and breaking into Roksana's house. And now, he was willing to risk his life to catch a murderer.

"What is it about this murder?" she asked. "How come you're suddenly happy to break all the rules?"

"I'm not *happy* about it," he said, which didn't answer her question.

"What is it about Karaivanov's gang?" she pressed.

"Nothing. I'm just doing my job."

Yeah, right. No one was that pure-hearted. There was something about this particular case that was personal to Asen. Something which was perhaps related to the magic Vila had sniffed on him. After all, Karaivanov was most famous for smuggling magic objects across the Wall.

Asen isn't as clueless as he looks, Kosara reminded herself. She was starting to fall for his friendly copper act again. She couldn't allow herself to let her guard down.

As long as their goals matched, she'd keep him around. He *could* be useful. But the moment his quest—whatever it was—got in the way of her getting her shadow back, she wouldn't hesitate. She'd drop him like a bad habit.

"In any case," Asen continued, "that Zmey of yours can't be any scarier than my boss."

That Zmey of yours. Kosara knew he was only joking, but all he did was remind her of Sevar. *You're still hung up on that Zmey of yours. . . .*

Kosara turned around and took the coffee off the fire a second before it had boiled over. She placed a cup in front of Asen and poured one for herself.

Coffee grounds had gathered at the bottom of the pot. Kosara deliberately avoided looking at them, too afraid their portentous shapes would show her something she didn't want to see of her future.

"With any luck, you won't even get to see just how scary the Zmey is," she said. "His palace is large. He'll be too busy entertaining his guests to even notice us. We'll sneak in, get my shadow and your murderer, and sneak back out. Easy-peasy."

Asen didn't seem convinced. He gave her a sideways smile. "So, are we going to the graveyard?"

Kosara ran her fingers through her hair, to cover up the fact they were trembling. "Not right now. It's almost time for the upirs to begin waking up. We'll have to wait until the morning. Then, we'll get Blackbeard to give us a lift across the sea in exchange for his compass."

"You'll give him the compass back? Vila won't like that."

"Oh, she'll hate it. But we don't have a choice unless you're hiding a ship in a pocket somewhere."

"And, of course, we need to figure out how to sneak inside the palace."

Kosara shook her head. She didn't need to figure it out: she already knew how to sneak in. There were only three days every year when the doors to the palace opened. "We'll go to the Zmey's feast. He throws one every year for all his monsters."

"We don't exactly look like the Zmey's monsters."

"I was thinking we can pretend to be household spirits."

Asen considered this for a moment. "What kind?"

"I'll be the spirit of the fireplace," Kosara said. She'd thought about it before, about where she'd settle, if she had to stay in this world after she died. "I like smoke, warmth, and the smell of fire."

"What about me?"

"I don't know. Is there a place that makes you happy? Somewhere you feel at home?"

Asen took a careful sip of his coffee, made a face, and added another sugar cube to it. "I'll have to think about it."

"Of course, we'll also need to get an invitation."

"Are you suggesting we steal one?"

"I'm suggesting we ask one of the monsters nicely for theirs."

Asen looked at her as if he couldn't decide whether she was joking.

She wasn't. She'd spent some time considering it, trying to remember all the gossip she'd heard about the Zmey's court. The varkolaks couldn't stand the upirs. The upirs hated the karakonjuls. The yudas didn't like anyone, and no one liked the rusalkas.

The samodivas used to live in the Zmey's palace, but they'd had a big falling out with him years ago, and they'd moved out.

"Who are we going to ask?" Asen said. "Your household spirits?"

"Oh no. They'd be in huge trouble if we get caught. I'll ask the samodivas."

He coughed on his coffee. "What?"

"The samodivas. They don't need their invites. The Zmey invites them every year, and they never go."

"You think they'll just give one to you?"

"Well, no, obviously not. I suspect they'll take some convincing."

"So, what's the plan?"

The plan? Silly Belogradean. As if you could plan your encounters with terrifying creatures from another dimension.

Kosara bit her lip. It tasted bitter, like coffee. "Just like witches' magic is in our shadows, the samodivas' magic is in their veils. If you take their veil off, they're helpless."

"And how do you do that?"

Good question. Kosara had never taken a samodiva's veil before. She knew what to do in theory: Vila had taught her all about hunting monsters, cutting yudas' feathers, collecting upir venom, trimming karakonjul ear hair, and shearing varkolaks. The old witch considered it a matter of professional pride that she gathered all her potion ingredients herself.

Kosara, on the other hand, had no qualms about buying hers from the pharmacy. They came already dried, clearly labelled, and distilled to the correct strength.

"Samodivas have one weakness," she said, remembering Vila's lessons. "They love music. They're known for capturing musicians and forcing them to play until they drop dead from exhaustion."

"And that's a weakness?"

"Yes, because while the music plays, the samodivas will dance. They'll be distracted, and I can snatch one of their veils."

Concern flashed across Asen's face. "I can only play the accordion. Not very well, mind you, but it might do."

"Sorry?"

"I can maybe manage a few chords on the tamboura, but I'm not that great at it."

"Oh," Kosara said. "Don't worry, you're not coming."

"Then who's going to distract the samodivas while you're trying to steal their veils?"

Kosara smiled. "In the war against the monsters"—she walked towards the large cupboard in the corner—"our greatest ally is modern technology."

She opened it to reveal a dusty gramophone. Her father had ordered it from Belograd as a name-day present for her years ago. Kosara didn't even want to know how much he'd paid for it.

"That's actually quite clever." Asen, annoyingly, seemed surprised. "What record will we play?"

"It doesn't matter what I play," Kosara said, emphasising the *I*, hoping he'd finally get the message. "They'll dance to anything."

Asen kneeled down next to the gramophone and went through her selection of records. He pulled one out of its sleeve and lifted it to the light, revealing a black-and-blue photograph of a rib cage. "Is this album etched onto an X-ray?"

"Yeah," Kosara said. "It's cheaper than vinyl."

"*You're My Blood Type* by the Rotting Upirs?"

"That one's a classic."

"*Bites in the Night* by the Filthy Animals?"

"Great band."

"*Gurgle Gurgle Gurgle* by the Drowning Rusalkas?"

"Excellent album."

"The Mystery of the Chernogradean Voices?"

"Oh, this one's my mum's. It's one of those folk affairs, with flutes and drums and gadulki and gaidi. So boring."

Asen pulled it out and studied the cover. Several women in traditional dress posed in front of a blooming cherry tree, while a red-faced man blew the flute.

"Looks pretty good to me," he said.

"Of course it does."

"I think we should choose this one."

Here was that *we* again. "I told you, you're not coming."

"What if something goes wrong? You need me to cover your back."

"You'll just get in the way."

"Excuse me?"

Kosara grasped for words to explain it to him. She'd seen plenty of men, and quite a few women, enchanted by samodivas. Their relatives brought them to her in the middle of the night, half-dead from exhaustion, covered in bruises, their eyes wild and their mouths foaming. They didn't want water or food or sleep. They only wanted the samodivas.

"The samodivas' magic is very strong," she said.

"You think they'll enchant me, but not you?"

"That's exactly what I think."

"Why?"

Kosara considered him. "Are you attracted to women?"

"What does that have to do with anything?" he asked, slightly flustered.

"It's the way their magic works. Vila told me all about it. It's nothing to do with you as a person, it's to do with their pharaoh's moans."

"Their what?"

"The way they smell or something."

"You have nothing to worry about. Magic doesn't work on me."

"What do you mean, it doesn't?"

"It just doesn't. You know how my job is arresting witches and warlocks? You have no idea the number of curses I've accumulated over the years. 'May you turn into a toad,' 'May your nose fall off,' 'May you grow a big ugly wart on your behind . . .' Did I grow a big ugly wart on my behind?"

"How am I supposed to know?"

"No, I didn't."

Kosara narrowed her eyes at him. He looked infuriatingly sure of himself, especially for someone who stank of magic. Little did he know, that wart on his behind could still be coming.

"Look," she said. "This isn't some silly old warlock's half-baked curse we're talking about. This is proper magic. It works on everyone."

"Not on me."

"Listen to me, you silly foreigner. I know my monsters. Their magic is like nothing you've ever seen before—"

"Which is exactly why I won't leave you to face them alone. I need your help to catch my murderer, and I can't let you get yourself killed. I'm coming."

I can't let you? Since when did he expect her to ask him permission?

Kosara sighed with exasperation. "You know what, fine. But it's at your own risk."

Stupid, stubborn copper. He'd get enchanted, and she wouldn't waste time trying to save him. She'd leave him there to be a slave to the samodivas, and it would be his own damned fault.

And, if he insisted on coming, he could at least be useful. "Can you dance?" she asked.

"I've been told I'm not bad."

"You'd have to be pretty good to keep up with them. They're very fast."

"I'm sure I'll manage."

"There are some rules. Make sure you remember them. Following them might be the only thing that can save you."

"What rules?"

Kosara made her voice a tad more sinister, just to telegraph the seriousness of the situation. She realised she sounded a lot like Vila. "There are three things you should never do when you meet the samodivas, if there's to be any hope for you to escape their magic. Firstly, whatever you do, never look them in the eyes."

"Seems simple enough."

"Secondly, no matter what, never tell them your name."

"That one's easy."

"Thirdly, and this one is the most important, never drink from their wine."

"All right, no problem."

He still looked completely calm. Stupid, stubborn foreigner.

Kosara chose one of the big kitchen knives hanging on the wall and tucked it in her boot. If only she had a silver-handled dagger or an ivory sword—something a tad more dramatic than her dad's carving knife, thinned from years of sharpening. Not that it wouldn't do the job.

"Come on," Kosara said. "Time to go dancing."

14

Day Six

As Kosara and Asen approached the samodivas' square, the street changed. In place of the grey cobblestones grew grass: tall, dark green, heavy with dew. Ivy enveloped the city chambers, hiding the building's severe granite and sharp edges. Tall oaks rose instead of streetlights. Here and there, a moonbeam broke through their canopy and fell at an acute angle, like a spotlight.

The air grew suffocatingly warm, but Kosara refused to take off her coat. It wasn't really warm—it was simply part of the illusion. Another one of the samodivas' tricks. Except knowing that didn't stop her body from sweating or her skin from growing red.

Asen still shivered in his coat. Perhaps he'd been right, and magic didn't work on him. Or perhaps he was being a soft Belogradean. After all, they never saw a proper winter on the other side of the Wall.

The samodivas' pale figures floated out of the mist. One of them had pulled the moon down, as if with an invisible rope. A second held it in place with both her hands. A third milked it, squeezing pieces of it in between her long fingers. They collected the glistening moonlight into a large demijohn.

They wore simple dresses, white and made of linen, hanging loosely from their shoulders. Semi-sheer veils hid their faces. They'd pass for people, if it weren't for their bright, impossibly white skin, and their gleaming hair the colour of moonlight.

When they heard Kosara and Asen approach, they looked up. Something wild glinted in their eyes, like predators who'd smelled prey.

They let the moon go. It flew up to its place in the sky as if it were a large balloon.

Kosara walked past the samodivas and placed the gramophone in the middle of the square. As soon as she dropped the needle, the sound of quick drums and flutes filled the silence. A multitude of female voices rose, some low and throaty, some shrill, harmonizing about their husbands' death at war, or death at sea, or death in the mines.

Kosara rolled her eyes. *Folk music.*

Asen had been right, though. The samodivas loved it. Their feet already tapped in rhythm in the tall grass.

"How considerate," one of them said, "you've brought us a gift."

"I thought you might be bored without music."

"I didn't mean the music." The samodiva extended one long, lean arm towards Asen. "Will you dance with us?"

He caught her hand, then lifted his gaze and met hers. A stupid smile lit his face. "Of course."

Damn it. Kosara had warned him not to look them in the eyes.

The samodivas grabbed both his hands and dragged him into their dance. They danced wildly: their hair slashed the air like whips, their dresses billowed like ship's sails, their feet pounded the earth like war drums. Asen did surprisingly well keeping up with them, his steps careful and his breathing measured, but occasionally he fell behind, and they pulled at his arms sharply.

"What's your name?" one of them asked.

"Asen!" he shouted.

"Asen," the samodiva repeated.

Kosara felt their magic tightening its grip around him. She swore internally. Had he not listened to a single word she'd said? Stupid, stubborn copper.

The wind grew stronger. The oak leaves rustled, tearing away from their branches and landing heavy on the ground. The grass swayed like a stormy sea. The dew splashed beneath the samodivas' feet.

Kosara could tell Asen was getting tired. His steps grew heavier and his breathing, shallower. He'd taken his coat off and his T-shirt was soaked in sweat, sticking to his chest. One of the samodivas handed him the demijohn, and he drank, the moonlight running down his chin and landing on his shirt in large, gleaming drops.

Kosara swore again, this time out loud. She couldn't quite decide who she was angrier with: Asen, for not listening to her; herself, for letting him convince her this was a good idea; or the samodivas, simply for existing.

"Bakharov!" she shouted.

Look at me, she willed him in her mind. *Look at me!*

After a long while, he managed to tear his gaze off the samodivas. Kosara exhaled sharply. His eyes were still his—not the glassy, wild stare of an enchanted person. She still had time to help him escape their magic.

Frankly, she shouldn't have bothered. She'd told him not to come, and he'd insisted. How would he ever learn his lesson if she saved him from every otherworldly creature who threatened to make him dance to his death?

Kosara sighed. Of course she was going to save him. She was a witch. It was her job to save idiots from monsters. She angled her knife so it caught the moonlight and aimed it at Asen's eyes.

He blinked. She glowered at him. *If you've got the tiniest little bit of sense left . . .*

Asen caught one of the samodivas by the waist. He leaned closer to her neck, inhaled the scent of spring flowers radiating from her skin . . .

And dragged her across the square, past the trees, to a nearby side street.

Kosara ran after them. She could still hear the music there. The grass began to disappear, only showing in patches between the cobblestones.

Asen held onto the samodiva tightly. They danced so quickly they were two blurs: him—red and black; and her—white and silver.

Kosara kneeled in the grass. Her fingers squeezed the knife's handle, white with pressure. The cold dew seeped in through her trousers. Asen and the samodiva's shadows ran past her so quickly she felt dizzy.

"Now!" she shouted.

Nothing happened. They kept dancing, clinging to each other. Kosara bit the inside of her cheek until she tasted blood. Was she too late after all?

"Now!" she repeated.

He paid no attention to her.

"For God's sake, Bakharov! Now!"

Finally, his eyes caught hers. He stopped in his tracks. The samodiva staggered and held onto his shoulder.

With one sharp movement, he took her veil off and threw it towards Kosara.

The samodiva shrieked, leaping after it. Too late. Kosara pierced the veil with her knife, pinning it to the ground.

The samodiva crumpled to her knees. The shine seeped out of her skin. Her hair dulled, as if covered with patina. On the ground, her veil turned and twisted like a silky snake. Kosara held the knife's handle in place with both hands.

Asen leaned on one of the trees, breathing heavily.

"Are you okay?" Kosara asked.

He opened his mouth to reply but began coughing. Instead, he lifted a thumb up in the air.

"Are you sure?"

This time, he lifted both thumbs.

Kosara looked at the samodiva she'd caught, trying to avoid her dark gaze. It wasn't easy, since their eyes were at the same level as they both kneeled. The monster seemed strangely small in the tall grass.

"Let me go, you little gremlin!" the samodiva said. "Why are you torturing me?"

Really, what was Kosara doing? Why was she causing distress to such a beautiful creature?

Kosara caught herself starting to pull the knife out of the ground. She shook her head to dispel the samodiva's magic and sank it deeper into the damp earth.

"I'll let you go," Kosara said, "if you do me a favour."

"What do you want?"

"I need your invitation to the Zmey's feast."

The samodiva threw her head back and laughed loudly, her white teeth glinting in the moonlight.

Kosara didn't think she'd said anything particularly funny. "What?"

"Why do you want to go to the Zmey's stupid party? It's so dreary!"

"That's none of your business."

"Honestly, he's turned into such a bore in his old age. He doesn't even dance anymore."

"Well, in that case, can I have your invitation?"

"Why are you asking me? I'm sure he'll give you one if you ask nicely. Getting in the palace would be easy for you—it's the getting out you have to worry about."

Kosara glared at the samodiva. That was the point.

"Listen, I understand," the samodiva said. "You're avoiding him. I don't blame you, I've been as well. To be honest with you, my funny little dwarf"—the samodiva leaned forwards, as if sharing a great secret—"he hasn't been the same, ever since his sister disappeared."

"What sister?"

"He blames himself, and he blames us, and it's not our fault in the slightest, since we were out dancing when it all happened. Maybe she's fine, you know? Maybe she simply wanted to get some space from him—you know very well how overbearing he can be. . . . Well, will you let me go now?"

Kosara's left hand reached for the knife's handle. She caught her wrist with her right hand and pressed it close to her body. "What sister?" she asked again. "What are you talking about?"

"Oh dear, I always forget how short your little human lives are. For you this must be ancient history."

Kosara let out an exasperated sigh. Was it that difficult to have a frank, honest conversation with a samodiva without her starting to misdirect and evade your questions, and tell you stories from hundreds of years ago?

No, of course not.

"Can I have your invitation?" Kosara said again.

The samodiva stared at her, her eyes black and shiny like beetles. "Maybe. I'll think about it. It's not like I need it. I'm not going to set my foot back in his palace until he apologises. Mark my words, my little troll, mark my words."

Kosara casually leaned her hand on the knife's handle, making it sink even deeper into the ground. The samodiva screamed.

"Fine, alright, you nasty goblin." The samodiva clicked her fingers. A thin silver disc materialised in her hand. She sighed a quiet sigh, like the wind rustling through the trees, and handed the disc to Kosara.

It was hard but brittle, like quartz—though Kosara suspected whatever material it was made from didn't come from this world. She couldn't see any writing on it. When she ran her finger over it, it felt completely smooth.

"That's it?" she asked.

"Yes," the samodiva said.

"If you're trying to trick me—"

"You know I can't lie to you while you've got my veil, my dear half-witted hobgoblin. Lift it to the moonlight."

Kosara did and gasped. A series of symbols appeared on the disc, gleaming like bright stars. It didn't look like any language she'd ever seen before. It was so elaborate, it seemed almost impractical. As if its main purpose was looking beautiful.

"See?" the samodiva said. "Can I go now?"

Kosara knew she couldn't keep the samodiva captive for much longer. The ground around the veil had started steaming. The knife's wooden handle had turned black, and soon the blade would begin to melt.

Besides, Kosara had got what she'd come for. She pulled the knife out of the ground.

The samodiva inhaled deeply, as if she'd been suffocating. Her veil leaped into the air, and she caught it, draping it over her face. She stood up and towered over Asen and Kosara, her skin shining, her hair cascading down her back in silver waves. She didn't look terrified anymore, she looked terrifying.

"It's time for me to return to my sisters. Are you coming?" The samodiva extended a hand towards Asen. Her fingers hung in the air, white and long like a statue's. Her eyes were black mirrors.

Even if he'd somehow managed to resist the samodiva's magic before, there was no chance he'd manage it now. It was so strong even Kosara felt it, drawing her towards the monster like a magnet.

"He's not going anywhere." Kosara's fingers grew pale around the knife's handle. She was surprised by how angry she felt.

You're not getting attached to the damned copper, are you? This was just like that time her dad had brought a bunny home to fatten it up before taking it to the butcher, and Kosara had made the silly mistake to name it.

"Are you coming?" the samodiva repeated, her magic growing even stronger, fogging up Kosara's mind.

"He's not going anywhere," Kosara repeated through gritted teeth. She could imagine sinking the knife deep into the samodiva's snow-white chest. Not that it would do much: it took a lot more to kill a samodiva. If anything, it would only make the monster angrier.

The samodiva made a gesture at Kosara's face as if swatting a fly.

"Are you coming?" she said for the third time. Her magic was now so powerful, it saturated the air, making Kosara's ears ring. She could almost taste it on her tongue.

Kosara gripped the knife. She had to do it. Otherwise, Asen's death would be another damned thing to haunt her. She'd have to fight the samodiva without any magic of her own. She took a deep breath, preparing to strike—

"No, thanks," Asen said, "I'm rather tired."

"What?" The word tumbled out of Kosara's mouth before she could stop it. She wasn't sure who looked more surprised—she or the samodiva.

The samodiva recovered first. "Are you sure?"

"Pretty sure."

"Very well." She turned on her heel and walked back towards the square. Just before she'd disappeared between the trees, she looked over her shoulder at him, confusion in her eyes.

"Did we get what we needed?" Asen asked.

Kosara placed a hand on his forehead. It wasn't warm. His eyes were normal. He'd formed a coherent sentence. None of this seemed right.

"Are you alright?" she asked. "You're not feeling dizzy or anything?"

"Just tired. You weren't joking when you said they're very fast."

"But you looked them in the eyes, and you told them your name, and you drank from their wine—"

"You didn't believe me that magic doesn't work on me. I thought I'd show you."

"But you looked enchanted!"

"Well, they were supposed to think I was, weren't they?"

Kosara exhaled, all the pressure finally leaving her body. He was fine. He wasn't enchanted.

He smiled at her, and she smiled back, wide and excited. They'd got the invitation to the Zmey's feast. It had all been so easy.

Surprisingly easy. Worryingly easy. Kosara's smile faltered. In her experience, such rare moments of good luck were simply the universe giving her a breather before the next disaster struck.

She replayed the events of the evening, trying to find where the catch was. As far as she could see, it had all gone according to plan. They'd got the invite. Asen had danced with the samodivas, and he wasn't enchanted. . . .

Kosara swore under her breath. Asen had danced with the samodivas—he'd looked them in the eyes and told them his name and drunk from their wine—*and he wasn't enchanted.*

This wasn't good luck, this was terrible, dreadful luck. There was only one explanation for how that could be possible, and it wasn't one she liked. At all.

He couldn't be enchanted by the samodivas because he was already enchanted by someone else. Someone whose magic was stronger than that of the samodivas. There couldn't be more than a handful of such people in all of Chernograd.

That was just Kosara's luck. As if visiting the Tsar of Monsters wasn't dangerous enough already, the copper she was bringing along to help her was under a spell.

Kosara lifted the samodiva's invitation to the kitchen window and let the moonlight illuminate the symbols. She'd gone through several of her books, searching for anything that looked similar. No luck. It seemed that whatever alphabet the monsters used, no witch had ever noted it down.

To distract herself from her more pressing problems, Kosara did. She copied the symbols carefully onto an empty page of a thick tome.

Asen sat across from her at the table, cleaning his revolver and whistling one of the songs from the folk record. He looked as if he'd had a refreshing workout, not as if he'd fought a terrifying monster from another dimension.

While she worked, Kosara kept throwing secret looks at him. How did he end up enchanted? Where did he even meet a witch or warlock stronger than the samodivas?

"Why do you keep looking at me?" he asked.

Evidently, Kosara's looks hadn't been that secret. "Do you remember when magic stopped working on you?"

"Shortly after I joined the police. I think it's because I started encountering more witches and warlocks, and I finally saw them for what they really are."

"Criminals?"

"People."

"Did anything unusual happen around that time? Did you meet a particularly strong witch or warlock?"

"Not that I remember. Why?"

"I'm worried you might be enchanted."

He laughed. "I really don't think so. Surely, I would have noticed."

"You might not have. Sometimes enchantments can be insidious and lie dormant for many years before activating."

"Right. And what would activate them?"

"Stress. Adrenaline. Strong emotions. You never know."

"I'll try to stay calm, then."

Kosara sighed. He wasn't getting how serious this could be.

Given his job, it was likely the enchantment he was under wasn't anything pleasant. In fact, Kosara would bet on it being a curse. A curse that could compel him to do something terrible, at any given moment, and she wouldn't be able to stop him. Not without her magic.

He could have been cursed without him even realising. Witches and warlocks were experts at hiding curses in otherwise innocent-looking talismans and amulets. Kosara had once met a man who thought he'd bought a love potion from a witch, except instead of making the beautiful woman he liked fall in love with him, it made him fall in love with the witch.

Asen yawned. "Maybe I'll go to bed. I can't believe how tired I am."

"I can't believe you're still able to stand after you danced with the samodivas."

"That's nothing. I'll take you to one of my family's weddings one day, they last for three days."

If Kosara wasn't so worried, she'd have been more surprised he'd just invited her to a wedding. Most people wouldn't consider bringing a witch to a family gathering.

Asen disappeared up the stairs. Kosara waited until she heard his snoring, then walked to the living room where an old mirror gathered dust on a high shelf. Vila had given it to Kosara back when she'd still been her apprentice. Kosara was supposed to only use it in emergencies. After a brief hesitation, she decided this counted.

She wiped the dust off the mirror's surface with her sleeve, then tapped on the glass.

"Um, hello?"

"Kosara?" Vila's irritated face floated in the mirror. She was in her nightgown, her white hair falling over her shoulders as she peered down into the bowl of water she used to communicate. "Do you know what time it is?"

Kosara checked the clock over the sofa. Three A.M. "Sorry."

"I'm an old woman, Kosara. I need my sleep."

"Sorry," Kosara repeated. "But I need an expert opinion. Asen and I just got back from dancing with the samodivas but—"

"You did what? Why would you take him with you?"

"Let me finish. Their magic didn't work on him."

A second of silence, before Vila swore.

"What do you think?" Kosara asked, although she knew the answer.

"He's been enchanted already. Do you know who's done it?"

"Not a clue."

"Does he know?"

"I don't think so. It's most likely someone he'd tried to arrest."

Vila kept clicking her tongue, like she always did when she was thinking.

"This could be dangerous," she said at last. "Are you sure the curse isn't active? What if he's currently acting under the spell?"

"I don't think he is. He doesn't act enchanted. His eyes—"

A loud tut interrupted her. "Forget about his eyes. Have you smelled his breath?"

Kosara hesitated. "It doesn't smell of magic. I don't think it does."

Another tut. "This could be dangerous," Vila said again.

"I know."

"Where does he sleep?"

"In my room."

"And you?"

"In my room as well, but it's not what it sounds like—"

"Don't give me that nonsense. How many years have I known you? When was the last time you let a strange man in your house?"

"I don't know, I—"

"You need to kick him out and lock the door. Not just out of the room. Out of the house. You have no idea when the curse will take hold and what it will make him do. He's a ticking time bomb. Find out who cursed him. And kick him out." And then she hung up. The mirror grew dim.

Kosara stared at the dark surface, massaging her temples.

Kick Asen out? Only a day ago, she wouldn't have hesitated. But now, after they'd fought monsters together, it felt difficult to treat him like a stranger.

She was going to sleep on the couch tonight, perhaps with a knife under her pillow, but she wouldn't kick him out. She couldn't. It was the middle of the Foul Days. It would be too dangerous for him out there on his own.

With some luck, the curse would stay dormant until she got her shadow back, just like it had done for years. Then, she could deal with it.

Kosara pointedly avoided thinking about how her luck had fared so far.

She got ready for bed and snuggled on the couch. It was a bit too short for her and her legs stuck out over the armrest. The knife under her pillow poked the back of her neck. Still, she was so tired, she fell asleep almost immediately.

Asen's screams woke her up.

Vila's warning rang clearly in her mind: *you never know when the curse will activate.* Kosara grabbed the knife from under the pillow and rushed towards the bedroom.

It took her a second before her eyes got used to the darkness, and she saw him. He'd wrapped himself in a cocoon of bedsheets. He breathed fast, his brows furrowed. He didn't seem as if he was under a spell—just having a nightmare. Kosara exhaled with relief.

"Boryana!" he shouted. "Boryana, don't!"

Who the hell is Boryana? Was she the witch who'd cursed him? Kosara shook him by the shoulder until he stopped screaming.

"What?" he muttered.

"You were having a nightmare. Are you alright?"

"I'm fine." He didn't look fine.

"Who's Boryana?" she asked.

Asen stared at her, wide-eyed. "Just someone I used to know."

It didn't seem as if he'd elaborate. His breathing was still ragged. Kosara considered reaching for him and squeezing his hand, or maybe giving him an encouraging pat on the shoulder.

She decided against it. He was a ticking time bomb.

"Why are you holding a knife?" he asked. His eyes must have got used to the dark, too.

"Oh," she looked down, as if noticing it for the first time. "Just in case."

"In case of what?"

Kosara shrugged. "Try to get some sleep. It'll be a long day tomorrow."

She returned to the sofa. The room had grown colder as the fire in the hearth was reduced to a few smouldering coals. No matter how many blankets Kosara piled on herself, her toes remained freezing.

There was another scream. She got up with a sigh and walked back to the bedroom.

Asen's hands were clenched into fists. He shouted at Boryana again, begging her not to do something. Not to curse him?

Kosara shushed him. It did nothing.

"Asen!"

He didn't wake up. She reached for him and held his hand in hers. His fist unclenched, and he squeezed her tightly. Finally, he stopped shouting.

After a few minutes, once he seemed to be sound asleep, Kosara tried to shake him off. He wouldn't let go.

She sighed deeply and lay down on her side of the bed, her arm extended over the barricade of pillows. One of her hands squeezed the knife, and the other held Asen's.

When she woke up in the morning, she was still holding his hand, but she was also snuggled against him, her head on his shoulder, his other arm draped across her.

For a second, she simply lay there: both because she didn't want to risk waking him and making the situation awkward, and because— she had to admit—he was warm and comfortable.

Then slowly, carefully, she untangled herself and tiptoed out of the room.

Good job keeping yourself away from the cursed copper, she scolded herself. *Really amazing job.*

15

Day Seven

The morning was bitterly cold. The wind whipped at Kosara's face, making her eyes run and freezing the tears onto her lashes. The pale sun reflected in the snowdrifts, blinding her.

Asen walked next to her, his teeth clicking audibly. He'd said nothing about last night: about his nightmares, or about Boryana, or even about the knife he'd found on the floor next to Kosara's side of the bed.

Kosara, in turn, didn't mention his curse again. They had to focus on the problem at hand—finding the compass in Algara's grave.

"Is the graveyard far?" Asen asked. He kept blowing on his hands, trying to warm them.

"Just a few minutes away," Kosara said. "We need to get the key from Malamir first, though. They lock the graveyard during the Foul Days. Not that it stops the upirs from getting out." *Or the stupid teenagers from sneaking in.*

"Why would Malamir have a key? I thought he worked at the theatre."

"He does, but he also helps with funerals when he needs some extra cash. He does the makeup."

"What makeup?"

"The dead's makeup. Before they're buried."

Asen wrinkled his nose, as if he found the mere mention of the dead distasteful.

"Is something wrong?" Kosara asked.

He hesitated. His fingers played with the brass buttons on the cuffs of his coat. "Talking about the dead reminded me we're about to dig up a body, and I just . . . I really don't like the idea of becoming a grave robber."

Kosara had suspected that was the case. The Belogradeans seemed to have a peculiar aversion to disturbing the dead—probably because their dead didn't tend to disturb the living.

"Don't you sometimes have to dig up graves as the police?" she asked. "What if someone was murdered, but you didn't know about it until after they'd been buried, and you need to get the body out to check for evidence?"

"We do exhume bodies occasionally," Asen admitted. "Very occasionally. And only with a court order. We haven't got one of those."

"Just imagine we've got one."

"I can't just imagine court orders. That's a slippery slope to becoming a—" he lowered his voice, "—crooked cop."

"Says the man who's breaking the law just being on this side of the Wall."

"Nevertheless, digging a grave . . ."

"Listen, I'm sure Algara wouldn't mind."

"How can you be so sure?"

"She's a witch. I'm a witch. I'd be glad if someone dug me up from time to time after I die. You know, she'd probably appreciate the fresh air, the change of view, our nice company . . ."

"She's dead, Kosara."

"Dead, alive, over here in Chernograd, they're two sides of the same coin."

"I don't know about that. . . ."

"Just trust me on this one. We'll dig her up, we'll get the compass, and then we'll put her right back where we found her. No one will even notice."

Asen sighed again before nodding. Kosara gave him a bright smile. She'd never admit it out loud, but she was glad she wouldn't have to go to the graveyard alone.

Finally, they reached Malamir's house: a low, shabby building with tiles missing from the roof and paint missing from the walls. A few of the upper-floor windows were boarded up to keep the heat in.

Malamir's mum opened the door. She wore a sunflower-patterned nightgown, its skirts flapping in the wind. The clay mask on her face cracked when she frowned. Her milky-white eyes looked straight through Kosara. Her walking cane tapped on the ground in front of Kosara's feet.

"Who is it?" she asked.

"It's Kosara, Mrs. Petrosyan," Kosara said. "Is Malamir home?"

"Kosara, what time is it? Malamir's still in bed. . . ."

"Could you wake him up? It's urgent."

Mrs. Petrosyan sighed deeply and disappeared back inside, muttering something about today's youth, the rollers in her hair clanking. Kosara noticed she moved slower than usual and accompanied every step with a soft moan.

A few minutes later, Malamir came to the door, blinking against the pale sunlight. His eyes were still blue and swollen, and his body hung loosely between his crutches, but he seemed to be in good spirits.

"Kosara!" He gave her a wide smile. "How nice of you to visit."

"Are you feeling better?"

"Much better, thanks. Doctor Krustev says I'm making amazing progress. I've even been going for short walks."

"What about your mum? She seems a bit unwell."

Malamir waved his hand. "She's fine. She's been up for hours scrubbing the house clean. You know what she's like."

"If she needs a potion . . ."

"I'll let you know, doll."

Kosara nodded, then stood there, unsure how to steer the conversation in the right direction.

Thankfully, Malamir did it for her. "So, Mother says you need me urgently."

"We do. Do you still have your graveyard keys?"

Malamir's mouth became a thin, pale line. "You're not planning on going to the graveyard during the Foul Days, are you?"

"Well, yeah, but only during the day." Kosara laughed, as if the utter horror that flashed in his eyes wasn't perfectly understandable. "Come on, Malamir, don't look at me like that. It'll be fine."

"Will it?"

"Of course. I know what I'm doing."

"But the last time—"

"Pfft, the last time." Kosara waved a hand dismissively. "That was years ago. I'm much older and wiser now." *I'm older, in any case.*

"Well . . . If you're sure it's safe . . ."

"Of course I'm sure. I wouldn't even dream of going there if I wasn't sure."

Malamir considered her for a few seconds. "Give me a minute."

The rhythmic clicking of his crutches faded as he disappeared into the dark hallway. Soon, he returned, carrying a shiny key ring shaped like a bedazzled articulated skeleton.

"Isn't it wonderfully tacky?" Malamir asked when he saw her face.

Kosara opened her mouth to confirm that it was, in fact, awful, but she was interrupted by a loud thud inside the house. A growl sounded.

"Malamir!" Mrs. Petrosyan screamed. "You've let that beast out of your room again! I told you to keep your door shut!"

Malamir swore quietly. "Sorry, Mum!" he shouted over his shoulder. "I'll get him in a second!"

"It's going to ruin my crochet sofa throws, Malamir!"

"I'll be there in a second, Mum!" He turned back to Kosara and hesitated, the keys dangling between his bandaged fingers. "Listen, I have to go. Will you promise me to be careful?"

Kosara snatched the keys. "I promise. What the hell is 'the beast'?"

"Oh, I got a new dog. Mum's being *so* dramatic about it. Truth be told, I'd be glad if he eats the crochet sofa throws, they're dreadful."

Kosara frowned. That growl hadn't sounded much like a dog.

"Malamir!" Mrs. Petrosyan shouted again. "Now it's chewing on the carpet!"

"Just a second, Mum!" Malamir grabbed Kosara's hand and squeezed it. "I have to run. You two be careful, alright?"

"I told you, I know what I'm doing."

She could tell by Malamir's face he had his doubts about that. "I'll wait for you here. If you aren't back by sundown—"

"We'll be out of there by lunchtime. Don't worry."

"Malamir!"

"I'm coming, Mum!" He considered Kosara for a long moment. "See you soon. I hope." And then, he closed the door.

"Is it really that dangerous?" Asen asked quietly. His face had grown ashen, only the tips of his nose and ears glowing red in the cold wind.

"Nah," Kosara said, trying to sound casual. "Malamir is worrying over nothing. The upirs sleep during the day. We'll dig up the grave, get the compass, and we'll be out of there in time for lunch. Easy-peasy."

"Are you sure? You look terribly nervous."

Kosara's fingers gripping the keys trembled so badly, the bedazzled skeleton chimed. Her shadow sickness tickled her collarbones. Every time she shut her eyes, she saw Nevena's face.

The last time she'd visited the graveyard during the Foul Days had been the last time she'd seen her sister alive and healthy. It had all gone downhill from there.

Kosara gave Asen an encouraging smile. "I'm certain. It will be fine."

The graveyard gate loomed tall over Asen and Kosara. From behind wafted the smells of an awakening Chernograd: freshly brewed coffee, warm pastries, and just-lit fireplaces. Ahead, the graveyard had a different scent—wild, green, of moss and centuries-old pines, and magic.

It was cold, but not like the cold in the city which made you crave hot chocolate and turned your cheeks rosy. The cold here was alive. It tore at Kosara's throat with sharp claws, slithered down her spine like a snake, curled up inside her lungs as if in a burrow.

Kosara pushed the metal door open. Several of its poles were bent where a frenzied upir had tried to walk straight through it. Teeth marks covered the hinges. Kosara gripped one of the silver coins in her pocket so hard, it probably left an impression on her skin.

"So, what's the plan?" Asen asked.

"No plan," Kosara said. "We get in, we dig out the compass, we get back out."

"But what if there's trouble?"

"We run."

"I truly believe we should come up with a plan of action. Who's going to keep watch, who's going to protect the flank . . ."

"You do that. Personally, I'm going to run."

Fresh snow covered the graves, as if the dead slept under white blankets. Here and there, deep holes gaped in the ground. All but the laziest upirs had long ago left their graves.

In between the cracked, moss-covered headstones, one glinted, new and shiny. A bouquet of red roses lay in front of it. Kosara bent down to read the inscription: *Damyan Petrov, heart surgeon, his loving wife is heartbroken—*

The ground cracked. A blackened hand shot up, reaching for Kosara's ankle.

Kosara jumped back. "Oh!" She kicked the hand. "You scared the hell out of me!"

The hand hesitated, its fingers waving about, as if asking a question. Kosara dug her heel into its flesh. There was the loud crack of broken bone. The hand quickly limped back under the snow on four fingers.

"Heal that fracture!" Kosara shouted after it.

"He's a heart surgeon," Asen said.

"So?"

"He doesn't heal fractures. You're looking for an orthopaedist."

"He'll be looking for an orthopaedist if he doesn't stay underground!" she said loudly, to make sure the upir would hear her.

"You said they'd be asleep during the day."

"They are. This one must've just reanimated. Which is pretty lucky, actually."

"Why?"

"He's young and inexperienced. He didn't try to trick us."

"Trick us? How?"

"Who knows? He could've pretended to be a child stuck under the snow. Or he could've impersonated someone we know. 'Asen, my old friend, I haven't seen you in ages, could you give me a hand to climb out of this grave, old chum?' They're great at probing at your mind. This here, however, is a real embarrassment."

"What is?"

"This!" Kosara pointed at the hand which had started crawling back out. "A doctor's wife, most likely well-to-do and educated, but she didn't bother to bury her husband with the appropriate rituals to protect him from resurrecting! No aspen branches in sight, no church candles burning on the grave, no incense, and, I'd bet you, no silver coins on his eyes. It's frankly shocking. They don't take care of their dead, and then they run to us. 'Help, my husband died and now he's trying to suck the cat's blood!' Well, of course he is, if you didn't bury him properly! There's so much information out there nowadays, the Witch and Warlock Association releases a pamphlet every year, it's a shame no one ever bothers to read it!"

Kosara angrily pulled out the garlic bulb, peeled a clove and dabbed it behind her ears. She passed it to Asen. He took it from her carefully, as if he was worried she might bite his hand off.

She'd perhaps gotten a tad too passionate discussing the drawbacks of not laying your dead to rest properly—but she simply couldn't believe how ignorant some people were. Chernograd would have been a much safer city, if only it listened to its witches.

They advanced through the graveyard carefully, keeping to the snow-covered path. Every so often, Kosara stopped and listened, making sure they hadn't awoken any more upirs. Asen kept turning around, as if looking for something. Perhaps he also imagined hungry upirs lurking behind every gravestone.

They found Algara's grave easily, following Vila's directions. It was deep within the graveyard, only a few minutes' walk from the church. The headstone was so overgrown with shrubs, their bare branches completely enveloped it. Her name was barely visible underneath: *Algara Yalanjieva, witch.*

"Unbelievable," Kosara said. "Blackbeard hasn't even bothered tidying up her grave. I'm glad she didn't resurrect—she'd probably have died from embarrassment." Kosara dusted her hands. "Well, ready to get digging?"

Judging by Asen's face, he wasn't. He crossed himself before he nodded.

They borrowed tools from a rickety shed leaning against the church wall. The gravediggers wouldn't need them anyway, as there were no funerals during the Foul Days.

It soon became obvious Kosara had underestimated how long digging a grave took. The earth was frozen solid. Asen chipped at it with a mattock, and loud ringing sounded every time he hit the ground. Kosara shovelled, the lumps of soil hard and heavy like river stones.

They worked all day, stopping only for a painfully short lunch: a couple of sheep's cheese pastries and a warm cup of coffee from the nearby bakery. They ate them standing outside in the snow, too afraid that if they sat down, they wouldn't have it in them to get back up.

Just after lunch, Asen disappeared for half an hour or so, claiming he had important business to attend to. Kosara spotted him walking towards a large marble monument.

She didn't want to pry, but she couldn't help but wonder what business a Belogradean copper could possibly have at the Chernogradean graveyard. She kept working, sweat rolling down her forehead. She kind of wished she'd followed him.

You're being silly. He probably just needed the toilet. The two of them weren't tied together, after all. He was allowed to do things without her.

When Asen returned, it was already starting to get dark. In the distance, the streetlamps lit up with a hiss. The winter days were short in Chernograd, which was a problem since the long nights were full of monsters.

"We need to hurry up," Kosara said. "We can't stay in the graveyard after dark." Then she had a proper look at him. "Have you been crying?"

He frowned, wiping his red eyes with his sleeve. "It's the wind."

"Right." Kosara narrowed her eyes at him. She knew it—she should have followed him earlier.

"How much time do we have?" he asked, grabbing the mattock.

"No more than an hour. But we should be almost there."

They *had* to be almost there. Kosara's muscles ached and her hands smarted. She'd taken off her coat, and her top was drenched in sweat. It turned freezing cold whenever she stopped working.

A howl sounded in the distance, chilling her even further.

"Varkolaks?" Asen asked.

"Yes."

"Should we go?"

Probably.

"We can't give up now," she said.

"We can come back tomorrow."

"What if someone finds out about us digging around and gets it before us? Malamir is a lovely boy, but he can't keep his mouth shut."

"And what if the upirs get *us*?"

Kosara licked her lips. Bad move, in this weather. It only made them drier.

"Another five minutes," she said. "Then we'll go."

She didn't think she had it in her, but somehow, she shovelled even faster. Every movement cut straight through her aching back. Each lump of soil felt heavier than the last.

"Found it!" Asen shouted at last. He scraped another layer of soil with the mattock, revealing the dark wood of the coffin's lid.

"Oh, thank God."

It was so dark now Kosara could barely make out Asen's features as he fell to his knees and pulled on the lid. She joined him. The rotting wood crumbled away in her hands. The iron hinges were bright orange, corrosion bleeding out of them in large drops. Instead of opening, the lid snapped in half, cracking loudly in the quiet graveyard.

For a second, Kosara was too afraid to look in the grave. She was a witch—she'd seen plenty of dead people, sometimes many years after their funerals when they crawled out of their graves. It was the surprise of opening a coffin that always got her. She never knew what she'd find inside it, like the world's worst name-day present.

Thankfully, not much was left of Algara. Most of her clothes had rotted away, and only her ivory buttons and golden jewellery remained. Her skull poked from above her many pendants, a gaping bullet hole in her forehead. A fat earthworm wriggled in one of her eye sockets.

Asen turned away, leaning against the headstone. Kosara couldn't blame him. The stench of the grave was nauseating—of damp, mildew, and rot.

Algara's hands were clutched in front of her chest, and in between them, something golden glinted. Kosara muttered an apology, just in case Algara's ghost still lingered, before she removed the compass from between her bony fingers.

Kosara weighed the compass in her hand. It was still bright and shiny, as if it had been buried yesterday. The arrow pointing North trembled like a butterfly wing. A name was engraved on the lid: Blackbeard.

Kosara grinned as she dropped the compass in her coat's inside pocket, buttoning it shut. After gripping the shovel all day, her fingers were red and painfully swollen. Her palms stung. Nevertheless, it had all been worth it—they had Blackbeard's compass. The one thing he loved above all else. There was no way he'd refuse to help them now.

"Let's get out of here," she said. "Before the upirs arrive."

"Not to alarm you, but I'm afraid we might be too late. Listen."

Kosara listened, and she heard them: the scraping of their fingers on the frozen ground, the shuffling of their feet in the snow, the gurgling sound as they inhaled through the remnants of their nasal cartilage.

A second later, she saw their white figures creeping among the gravestones. Their teeth glistened in the moonlight.

Kosara had been too distracted by the compass to notice them earlier. A rookie mistake. Always keep vigilant when you're in the graveyard during the Foul Days, every witch knew that.

Asen drew his revolver. "Should we maybe—"

"Run!"

Kosara climbed out of the grave, her fingers sinking into the soil, her feet sliding down the damp earth. She ran up the path towards the exit. Her shoes were heavy with clay from Algara's grave. It stuck to her and pulled her down like an anchor.

More and more pale figures appeared between the headstones. Kosara could feel them probing at her mind, like burrowing worms. She pressed her temples with both her palms, as if that would help.

"Can you feel them?" she asked.

"Feel what?"

Thank God. She'd been worried Asen's curse wouldn't protect him against the upirs' magic. This was terrible news in the long run, of course. He'd been enchanted by someone stronger than the samodivas *and* the upirs. But it was exactly what they needed right now.

A song rose in the distance, loud and out of tune. Kosara recognised her voice immediately. Nevena had always been a terrible singer.

Oh, dear God, not this, not now. Out of all her memories, the upirs had to dig out this one.

Then again, it hadn't taken much digging. It had been at the back of Kosara's mind all day—the last time she'd come to the graveyard during the Foul Days. It had been seven years ago, it had been a complete disaster, and it had been all Kosara's fault.

"Listen," she turned to Asen, realising a second too late she was shouting in order to drown a song only she could hear. She lowered her voice. "You have to keep me from going to them. It doesn't matter what I tell you, it doesn't matter how much I plead, you can't let me go to them."

"I won't," Asen said sincerely. "Don't worry. I won't."

They ran through the snowdrifts. The graveyard's tall doorway rose ahead, with its cast-iron gargoyles perched on top, and beyond it flickered the lights of the city.

They were nearly there. Nearly back to safety.

Kosara stopped in her tracks. A large group of upirs congregated in front of the doorway, like an impenetrable wall of pale, rotting flesh.

Goddamn it.

"There's no way we'll get past them," she said. "We have to turn back."

Asen waved his revolver about, as if unsure which enemy to focus on. "And go where?"

Kosara could see only one option. "The church."

"Is it safe there?"

"It's safer than out here."

She was already running up the path, retracing their footsteps in the snow. From time to time, Asen turned back and aimed his revolver at something, but he never pressed the trigger.

The church was dark against the snow. No light came from the painted windows. Only a single lantern flickered, way up in the bell tower, under the patina-covered dome. Perhaps a thoughtful priest had left it out, to guide lost souls towards the church—or lost fools who'd got themselves trapped in the graveyard during the Foul Days.

Kosara opened the door and its creak echoed in the empty nave. The sharp smell of incense hit her: the priests must have burnt it for protection against evil spirits. Hopefully, it would help.

Pictures of saints hung on the walls, with long beards and elaborate robes, their faces dark within their golden halos. They stared at Kosara sternly, almost disapprovingly, as if they knew the church wasn't a place for a witch. The flickering of the candlelight made it seem as if their eyes followed her through the nave, as she and Asen piled up church furniture in front of the door: wooden chairs, large candleholders, an enormous carving of a cross. Even if the saints hadn't minded Kosara's presence earlier, they definitely did now. She'd completely ruined their interior design.

Asen placed one last chair in front of the door, then stepped back and inspected their work. "It's not the best, but it should hold for a bit."

Kosara couldn't hear him over the singing in her head, but she managed to read his lips. "How long?" she asked.

"Depends on how many upirs are out there. Should we go up and have a look?" He pointed towards the bell tower staircase with his thumb.

The staircase was so narrow, their shoulders touched the walls as they climbed up. The steps creaked, each in a different tone, like a badly tuned piano.

Once they were up on the balcony, Nevena's song grew louder. Kosara pressed her ears with her palms to try to quiet it. It was no use.

A cold wind rose and brought the smell of death. Kosara shivered, despite her many layers of woollen undergarments. Down below, pale shadows moved among the fog.

"Get ready to shoot," Kosara said. "The bullets won't kill them, but they'll slow them down."

It was getting difficult to form coherent sentences. She felt as if her head was stuffed with cotton candy. The wind grew stronger, dispersing the fog, and a familiar silhouette stepped out. Tall, lanky, wobbly on her high heels. Nevena.

She was so bright and real. Her cheeks were rosy from the cold and her hair was messy after a night of dancing. Her lips were painted in her favourite lipstick: deep red, like heavy wine. The wind carried her smell, of jasmine, and roses, and tobacco smoke.

Kosara knew this memory. Nevena had looked like that on the night they'd snuck into the graveyard, seven years ago. They were walking home after some obscure local band's gig. Nevena had gotten one of their songs stuck in her head and kept singing it all night.

Kosara clearly remembered Nevena's warm hand in hers, the flask of cheap rakia they'd hidden in a rucksack, and the cigarette they'd shared—neither of them could smoke a whole one without getting dizzy. And then, there was the memory of what came next: the pack of wolves and their leader.

A shot fired. Nevena staggered back, her hand on her forehead, panic in her eyes. Her fingers came away red.

"Nev!" Kosara stepped towards the balcony's railing, but someone pulled her back.

She turned around, expecting to meet the pack leader's grin. Instead, she saw the worried face of a man. He looked vaguely familiar, but she couldn't quite place him. His fingers were like pliers around her upper arms.

She squirmed. The man didn't let go. *Oh my God.* Someone was shooting at her sister, and Kosara had been taken hostage. *Oh my God!*

Nevena had been right. They shouldn't have come into the graveyard. It had been a stupid idea. Kosara's stupid idea.

Nevena shook her head. Droplets of blood scattered in the snow. She kept walking towards the church. Towards Kosara.

"Take cover, Nev!" Kosara shouted. "Leave me and take cover!"

Another shot. Nevena stumbled on her high heels. A steaming wound gaped in her left knee. She shook her leg, as if to check whether it still worked, and continued walking.

Kosara tried to wriggle from the man's grasp, but he held her tightly. She elbowed him in the stomach. He bent in half, gasping softly. She twisted and finally escaped him, stumbling towards the edge of the balcony.

The railing was freezing cold under her palms. She had to jump. It wasn't even that high. She'd probably sprain her ankle, or even break her legs, but there was no other way. Nevena needed her. They had to get out of the graveyard before the wolves came.

Another shot. Nevena fell face-first in the snow. A red puddle began forming under her body.

Oh my God, no, not again. I can't lose her again.

Kosara tried to climb over the railing, but the man got a hold of her again. He pulled her back with his left hand. In his right, he clutched a revolver. Kosara's sluggish mind finally realised who'd been shooting.

"Monster!" she wanted to shout, but only a wild roar came out. She swung at him. He didn't move, and her hand slammed into his face. Her nails dug deep into his skin. He kept squeezing her.

"Oh my God, Nev, please run! Get help!"

Nevena jerked and looked up. She didn't run. She pulled herself forwards on her stomach, leaving a red trail in the snow. Her eyes never left Kosara's. They gleamed through the curtain of blood covering her face: just as warm and brown as they'd always been.

So much blood. Too much. She's going to die again.

And it's all my fault.

"Nev!" Kosara reached for her sister again, grasping at the railing.

"Time for a strategic retreat," the strange man said.

Before Kosara could react, he lifted her off the floor and threw her over his shoulder. She slammed her fists against his back, kicked and shouted, but he didn't let her go.

She turned to Nevena. In the last moment before her sister disappeared out of sight, Kosara spotted the dark shadow of the wolves creeping in the fog behind her. A man walked among them, a toothy grin splitting his face. The man they'd been so afraid of. The pack leader.

His eyes glinted in the darkness, blue like candle flames, and his hair fell down his shoulders like molten gold.

Kosara tried to scream, but no sound came out. Only sobs.

A door creaked. The smell of incense burned her nostrils. From the walls peered grumpy old men in golden dresses. As she watched them, they began moving. One of them winked at her.

Someone hit her on the head. It all went dark.

16

Day Seven

Kosara opened her eyes. High up above her, chubby winged babies played the harp.

She blinked. The smell of incense and melting wax. The candles. The saints on the walls. She remembered where she was: in big trouble.

"Are you alright?" Asen's body language suggested he was shouting, but she could barely hear him over the ringing in her ears. He'd stopped in the middle of the church, a tall candleholder in his hand.

Kosara got up on her elbows. She was lying on the floor, on top of Asen's coat. A small puddle of saliva had formed beneath her cheek. She tried to wipe it with her sleeve without him noticing and smiled apologetically when he caught her.

Sharp pain pulsated at the back of her head. She felt it with her fingers. A lump had begun to form.

"Why did you hit me?" she asked.

"I didn't. You knocked your head on the wall when you were tossing about." He carefully placed the candleholder in one of the few empty spaces in front of the door, in between several carved wooden chairs.

Outside, someone moaned. Something heavy slammed against the door. The pile of church furniture creaked.

"And thank God for that," Asen added and, realising where he was, quickly crossed himself. "I wasn't going to manage to hold you for much longer."

"Why? What was I doing?"

"You were trying to jump off the bell tower! You were shouting

something unintelligible and climbing onto the railing, and those upirs downstairs were salivating."

The blood rushed to Kosara's cheeks. She recalled the events from
the graveyard with disturbing clarity: the upirs, the singing, Nevena.
Her clawing at Asen's face as he held her.

In the dim light of the candles, the scratches were barely visible.
Good thing she kept her nails short.

"I'm sorry." She gestured at his face.

"It's fine. You weren't yourself. Those upirs were obviously messing
with your head."

"You saw them?"

"Of course I saw them. Decomposing corpses. Grey-skinned, their
hair falling out in clumps. Completely disgusting."

Kosara nodded. *Completely disgusting.*

"Thank you for not letting me go to them."

Asen smiled. "Don't mention it. It's what friends are for."

Kosara almost smiled back, before hesitating. *Friends?* Did he really think that's what they were?

No, of course he didn't. He was just being polite after she'd nearly
clawed his eyes out.

She turned back towards the door. At least the upirs had given up
on the singing. Only moans and gurgling came from outside. They
must have been loud, if she could hear them clearly over the ringing
in her ears.

The upirs slammed against the door again. One carved wooden
chair came tumbling down and crashed on the floor.

"It's not going to last much longer," Asen said. "We'll have to come
up with a different plan."

Kosara nodded and immediately regretted it when the painful pulsating in her head sped up.

Asen ran a hand through his hair, making it stick up. "Here's what I
suggest," he said. "I'll go first and try to render as many of them helpless as I can. You'll follow me, taking care of anyone who's still showing signs of . . ." he hesitated. "I mean, anyone who's still moving."

"Too risky. If they manage to enchant me again, I'll stab you before you've realised what's happening. If they enchant you, you'll shoot me."

He opened his mouth to argue.

"I know, I know," Kosara said. "They won't enchant you. My point still stands."

"Do you have any better ideas?"

She didn't. They were stuck. She'd got them trapped in the church. Would she ever learn her lesson? Never go to the graveyard during the Foul Days. What kind of a stupid, stubborn idiot made the same stupid, stubborn mistake twice?

Asen wasn't going to say it, but she knew he was thinking it, too. She hated that look in his eyes, even though she was starting to become painfully familiar with it: *I told you this was a bad idea.*

Kosara squeezed her eyes shut. There was no time to panic. She had to think.

They couldn't fight the upirs while she was susceptible to their magic. And she couldn't protect herself from their magic without her shadow. Unless . . .

"How much garlic do you have left?" she asked.

"A few heads. Why?"

"Give them to me."

Kosara sat on the floor and began peeling the garlic bulbs, leaving nail marks in their soft flesh in her hurry. Their paper-like skin stuck to her trembling fingers.

"What are you doing?" Asen asked.

"I'm going to eat them." To demonstrate, she took a handful and stuffed them in her mouth. Her eyes filled with tears as the garlic burned her tongue.

Asen watched her, his head slightly tilted. "Why?"

"To make myself as unappetizing as possible. They can't enchant you, and I'm trying to make it so they won't *want* to enchant me. I'm turning myself into a walking upir repellent. The first ingredient is garlic."

"I see." Asen sat next to her and helped her peel the rest of the cloves. "How much garlic will it take?"

Kosara shrugged. She kept dropping the garlic to the floor whenever her fingers turned to shadow. *Hey, hands,* she thought at them sternly. *Hey, the two of you, one of you washes the other. . . .*

Finally, she was left with a pile of peeled garlic. She chewed, tears streaming down her cheeks. Her tongue went numb. She'd taste nothing but garlic for days.

"Do you think it will work?" Asen asked.

Kosara shrugged again, unable to talk with her mouth full. *Who knows?*

"What's next?" Asen said. "What's your second ingredient?"

Kosara still couldn't reply, so she gestured towards the elaborate holy water fountain near the entrance. It was large enough to fit her if she crouched down. Its purpose was something of a mystery to Kosara, though she suspected it involved a lot of chanting and reciting passages from the Holy Book. Everything in the church seemed to.

"I tried moving it to block the door." Asen slammed his hand against it, the clap echoing in the nave. "Too heavy. I think it's solid marble."

"I'm not asking you to move it." Kosara stood up and dusted her knees. She ran her tongue across her teeth, trying to dislodge the pieces of garlic stuck between them. "I'm asking you to help me climb into it."

Asen considered this. "Are you sure you won't burst into flames? Being a witch and all that. . . ."

"Ha-ha," Kosara said without humour. "Come on, give me a hand."

She flung her arms over Asen's shoulders, her face turned to the side to save him from her breath. He boosted her up until she kneeled on the marble edge of the fountain. The holy water beneath her was inky black in the dim light, candle flames reflecting in its depths. A few chubby cherubs glared back at Kosara, disapproval in their marble eyes.

What if she *did* burst into flames?

She carefully dipped a finger into the fountain. The cold water slid off her skin, making her shiver. There were no flames. Kosara took a deep breath and submerged her whole body in the water.

Cold. So goddamned *cold*. Could it be cold enough to freeze her brain? It certainly felt like it.

She held her breath for as long as she could. Her hair floated around her—she couldn't see it in the dark, but she felt it tickling her face. Her teeth chattered, cold water filling her mouth.

A few seconds later, she emerged and inhaled deeply. Her nose and ears were filled with holy water. Her eyes smarted, from the mixture of water and mascara running down her face.

"Are you feeling reborn?" Asen asked.

"I'm feeling cold, mostly."

"Now what?"

Kosara bit her lip. What else could she do to deter the upirs? Fashion herself a suit of armour from the pictures of saints in the walls? Learn a few passages from the Holy Book to chant? Would they even work, when recited by a nonbeliever?

The pile of church furniture swayed, dangerously close to collapsing. They didn't have much time left. And, Kosara suspected, if they stayed here much longer, even if the upirs didn't get her, the hypothermia would.

Holy water ran down her hair, collecting in a puddle at her feet. Her whole body shook. Her skin felt like nothing but goose bumps.

Kosara grabbed a large silver cross from the pile in front of the door and squeezed it with both her trembling hands like a two-handed sword. Asen caught her eyes and drew out his revolver.

He gently pulled on the leg of one of the chairs in front of the door. The pile of furniture swayed again. Kosara could see how, once the chair was removed, the rest of it would collapse like a card tower.

"Are you ready?" Asen asked, his hand still on the chair.

Kosara nodded. Her teeth were chattering so loudly, the sound echoed around her.

Asen said, "On one . . . two . . . th—"

"Wait!"

There was something wrong. Kosara could feel it with her every goose bump. The moans outside had grown quieter. The upirs' breathing quickened—the damp, gurgling noise getting faster, like boiling water.

"I think . . ." Kosara hesitated.

The upirs' feet shuffled in the snow, and then there were thumps, as if they bumped into each other in their hurry to escape.

"I think they might be running away," she said.

Asen listened for a few seconds. "They seem to be. But why?"

Kosara met his gaze. Could she have done such a great job of turning herself into an upir repellent, they could smell her through the door? Surely not. She was missing half the right ingredients. "I have no—"

A growl sounded. For some reason, Kosara recognised it. She'd heard this low, rumbling noise before, she was certain.

And then, a rhythmic sound drifted in, like wood clicking against frozen ground. *Click-click-click,* closer and closer.

What the hell . . .

Something much stronger than an upir slammed against the door. That was the last straw for the pile of church furniture. It swayed, backwards and forwards, and collapsed. Carved wood inlaid with silver and gold rained down, crashing onto the floor around Kosara and sending splinters flying up in the air.

The door banged open. A dead upir lay in the snow at the threshold, his glassy eyes staring at the sky. A karakonjul the size of a large dog leaned over it, pieces of decaying flesh dangling between four rows of fangs. Snowflakes glistened in its brown fur and gathered in the grooves of its curved horns. Its donkey-like ears pointed straight up, the hairs sticking out of them blowing in the wind. Its muzzle was black with upir blood.

Its horned head turned to look up at Kosara. Hunger flashed in its yellow eyes. Its growl grew louder.

Goddamnit. Out of the frying pan and straight into the karakonjul. Kosara scrambled to find the aspen stake in her pocket. It wouldn't help much against a karakonjul, but it might slow it down. If only she hadn't spent the last half an hour turning herself into a weapon against *upirs* . . .

She searched through her mind in a panic, desperately trying to remember a riddle. Asen had been right. It wasn't easy once you were faced with eyes like lanterns and the mouth full of endless teeth.

What walks on one leg in the spring, and on two legs in the winter? Was that a riddle? Or was it just nonsense?

The beast opened its mouth, spitting out the upir's rotten arm. It looked ready for something much fresher and witch-flavoured. Kosara froze, hypnotized by its eyes. The taste of blood filled her mouth.

Asen aimed his revolver, but he didn't pull the trigger. In his eyes Kosara saw the same panic she felt. He'd already been attacked by a karakonjul once, and he knew the bullets wouldn't stop it.

The beast's shoulders tensed, the muscles tightening beneath its thick hide. It was going to jump. Kosara swore quietly, gripping the useless aspen stake with both hands.

"Down, boy!" a familiar voice drifted from outside.

Yeah, good luck with that. As if you could command a bloodthirsty beast from another dimension.

The karakonjul blinked. Its talons screeched against the floor. And then, it took a step back and sat on its hind legs. Its tail flapped against the ground like a happy puppy's.

Kosara gaped at it. *No way.*

A messy-haired Malamir emerged from the fog behind the beast, leaning on wooden crutches. *Click, click, click,* they clicked against the frozen ground as he walked. His breathing was ragged, but a smile tugged on his lips.

"Good boy!" Malamir shouted and threw the karakonjul a piece of pale meat. Chicken? Kosara surely hoped it was that and not more upir. It disappeared into the beast's gaping mouth before she could have a good look at it. "Give me a paw!"

The creature laid its furry paw into Malamir's extended hand. *No. Way.*

"Don't ever rush in front of me like that, do you hear me?" Malamir shook a finger at the karakonjul. "Or I won't let you off the leash anymore."

Kosara swore quietly. *The leash?* Was she hearing what she thought she was hearing?

"Dear God, Kosara!" Malamir turned to her. "You stink of garlic. Why is your hair soaking wet?"

"Malamir . . ." Kosara said in her best schoolteacher's voice. It came out stuttered since her teeth were chattering. "Malamir," she repeated, "this is a karakonjul."

"I know. Don't worry, he's been trained."

"Malamir," Kosara said, slowly. Patiently. "You can't train karakonjuls."

Malamir lifted his eyebrows. He whistled. The karakonjul had started to wander off, but it immediately circled back to him. Its muzzle was still black, and saliva bubbled in the corner of its mouth. It was only then that Kosara noticed the karakonjul wore a collar, with the name "Button" hanging off it on a golden disc. *Button!*

Malamir ruffled the karakonjul's head. "Who's a good boy! Go say hello to Aunty Kosara."

The beast trotted to Kosara. She did her best to suppress her instincts screaming at her to run, wondering the entire time if she was making a mistake and should, in fact, run. The karakonjul placed two large paws on her knees and looked up at her. The upir's blood dripped from its mouth and landed on the toes of her boots.

"Um, good boy." Kosara carefully patted its head. Its fur was surprisingly soft and smelled like daisies. Malamir must have shampooed it.

"How did you train him?" Kosara asked.

"With lots of patience and treats. We had a rocky start, I have to admit." Malamir pulled up his sleeve to show her a red bite impression, now healing. "But I think we're finally on the right track. Right, Button?"

The karakonjul gave out a short bark.

Kosara took a step away from it. "How did you find us?"

"I heard the screams."

"From your house?"

"No. Button and I just happened to be passing by."

Kosara was left speechless for a second. "You followed us? What kind of idiot goes into the graveyard in the middle of the Foul Days?"

"Well . . ." Asen said.

"We didn't have a choice."

Malamir shrugged. "You were taking your time in here, and I thought you might need a hand." He giggled, lifting one hand in the air. Half his fingers were still bound, the bandages now soaked in sticky upir blood. That couldn't be sanitary.

"Why are you looking at me like that, doll?" Malamir asked. "I just saved you from a bunch of hungry upirs."

Kosara fidgeted. Perhaps she was coming across as a bit ungrateful. At the same time, she couldn't believe she'd just been saved by a man who could barely stand up and his pet *karakonjul*.

"Well," she said, "thank you. But I assure you I had the situation under control. You should be in bed."

And that karakonjul should be in a cage, she thought, but she didn't say it out loud. She was worried the beast could understand her. Its teeth were dangerously close to her calves.

"I've been in bed long enough. I'm bored out of my mind."

"Then read a book! Honestly, Malamir, you're not in a condition to be hunting upirs."

Malamir stumbled, leaning heavily on his crutches. "Perhaps you're right, doll."

"Of course I'm right!" Kosara said. "Come on. We need to get you home."

Kosara let him lean on her and led him towards the door. The karakonjul followed them, wagging its tail.

They made their way back to the graveyard gate without meeting any more upirs. Kosara hated to admit it, but she strongly suspected she had Button to thank for that.

A pet karakonjul. Utter nonsense.

Later that evening, once she'd managed to peel herself out of the bath and had brushed her teeth approximately ten thousand times, Kosara opened a bottle of wine to celebrate their success. It was one of her dad's vintages: cabernet sauvignon with a touch of whatever fruit was cheapest at the market that day. Asen refused to drink it, and Kosara didn't blame him—the smell alone was strong enough to make her eyes water. She poured him a glass of lemonade.

"Thanks." He stopped scrubbing his coat to take it. The scent of lemon juice enveloped the kitchen. In the sink, the baking soda foamed and hissed. He'd got some upir blood on his coat back in the church.

Kosara leaned on the counter and sipped her wine. She coughed, then lifted the bottle and read the label, just to make sure. Yes, it definitely read "cabernet sauvignon," not "wine vinegar."

"Why are you so upset?" Asen asked. Kosara looked up and realised he'd been watching her for a while.

"I'm not upset!"

"You've bitten your lip so hard I can see the teeth impressions. What's wrong?"

"Nothing's wrong. Everything's great. We found the compass. We got out of the graveyard alive."

"What did you see in that graveyard?"

I saw Nevena.

Kosara started to bite her lip again but stopped herself. She couldn't tell him. They were temporary allies, not friends. They were *not* friends. If anything, the upirs using her memories of Nevena had cemented it further in her mind: friends made you vulnerable.

"In the graveyard?" she asked, casually. "I can't remember. I must have hit my head too hard."

"What then? Are you nervous about tomorrow?"

"About what?"

"Visiting the lair of Chernograd's most dangerous monster?"

"Nervous? No, not at all. We'll be fine. I told you, the Zmey won't even know we're there. We'll sneak in, catch Roksana, get my shadow, and sneak back out. Easy-peasy."

A quiet pop sounded. Something warm tickled the back of Kosara's hand. She looked down: her cup was broken. Tiny pieces of glass glistened all over the floor. Her fingers were red with wine and—she noticed a shard sticking out of her palm—blood.

She must have squeezed her glass too hard. It didn't hurt yet, but she knew it would start soon.

"Oh," she muttered.

Asen looked up at her. The blood drained out of his face. "Oh my God." He dropped his coat back in the sink with a splash. The next second, he leaned over her, inspecting her bloody hand. "Where do you keep your bandages?"

"The big cupboard in the living room. The second drawer from the top."

He had another look at her hand. "What about tweezers?"

"The vanity in my bedroom," she said. And then, remembering a particularly steamy romance novel she kept there, quickly added, "The left drawer. Not the right one."

Asen disappeared up the hallway and soon returned with a box of bandages and a pair of tweezers. He began pulling out shards of glass from her hand, collecting them in a bloody, glistening pile on the table. Kosara sucked in air through her teeth. She was feeling the pain now.

He worked slowly, his fingers turning her hand to locate the shards. His touch was light, as if she was something delicate that might shatter if he pressed too hard. Kosara wasn't used to being held this gently. Her rough, scarred hands had been through much worse than a few shards of glass.

His brows furrowed in concentration. In the light of the fire, his eyes were a deep, dark brown. Several-day-old stubble covered his chin. It suited him. He lifted his gaze, catching her looking at him, and smiled. Now, he looked even more handsome. He was so close, Kosara saw the fine lines crinkling in the corners of his eyes.

He was so close, she smelled the magic on him. There was a small lump under his T-shirt, near his neck, as if he wore a pendant. Immediately, she was certain: this was where the magic came from. It had to be. Even without her shadow, she could recognise a talisman this powerful.

She instinctively reached for it. He jumped back, his smile faltering, panic in his eyes.

"What are you doing?" he asked. His fingers grasped the pendant through his T-shirt. He caught himself and let it go, smoothing the fabric over it.

"Sorry," she said, realising how inappropriate she'd been. "I was curious about your talisman."

"What talisman?"

"Your pendant. Can I see it?"

"No. You can't."

Kosara's hand still bled in her lap, and she pressed it against the fabric of her trousers, making the glass shards sink deeper. She winced. "Sorry," she repeated. "I was curious."

"It's just a pendant."

It's definitely not just a pendant. So, he either didn't know his pendant was magical, or he didn't want *her* to know. Maybe it wasn't a curse, after all. Maybe it was something embarrassing, like a nice-breath potion or a spell to make his eyelashes longer.

On the other hand, no one made a nice-breath potion strong enough to defeat a samodiva's enchantment. . . .

"Who gave it to you?" she asked.

"That doesn't concern you."

"I'm worried it might be cursed."

"I don't think so."

"Are you sure? It could be dangerous."

"It's nothing. Forget about it. Give me your hand. Please."

She did, and he continued picking out pieces of glass with the tweezers, perhaps a tad faster than before. Once he'd gathered them all, he unwrapped the bandage.

"I can do it myself," Kosara said. She could tell he was upset. He'd stopped talking. He didn't even look at her.

"With one hand? Don't be silly."

Asen bandaged her with fast, precise movements, like someone who'd aced the police first aid course. He did a much better job than she would have managed, she had to admit.

"I think I'll sleep on the couch tonight," he said finally. "It's my turn."

"Are you joking? It's too small for me. You'll have to fold in half to fit."

"I'll be fine. I've slept in worse places." He got up and took his wet coat out of the sink to hang it in the bathroom. "Good night."

He moved fast, obviously eager to leave.

"Listen," Kosara said, "about that pendant—"

"Good night," he repeated, and all but ran out the door.

He knew the pendant was enchanted. No one acted this shifty over a regular pendant. He'd jumped about a foot up in the air when she'd tried touching it.

At the same time, he seemed certain it wasn't dangerous. Perhaps she ought to drop it. It was obviously private, and besides, he'd given her no reasons to doubt him. Other than him being a copper, of course, which made him inherently untrustworthy.

Kosara poured herself another glass of wine. Her wounded hand throbbed painfully. Her other hand shook as she lifted the glass to her lips.

She wasn't going to drop it. She had to find out what kind of talisman it was.

Not because she cared about him. Not at all. She cared about her own skin, and about what an enchanted Asen might do when she was least prepared. In the middle of the night when she was fast asleep. When that pillow barricade had been breached again and she woke up in his arms, but this time, he wasn't himself anymore—he was something cursed and dangerous.

She worried the inside of her cheek. *Fine,* she admitted. Maybe she cared about him a little bit.

Kosara downed the wine in one go. *Perhaps,* a sensible, used-to-being-ignored voice said in her head, *perhaps you should respect other people's right to keep secrets. You have your secrets. He has his.*

What secrets? Kosara snapped.

The voice grew even smaller. *Well, you know, Nevena . . .*

That was completely different. Asen couldn't find out what had happened to Nevena and keep seeing Kosara the same way. He already thought of witches as criminals.

What would he think if he discovered he'd been helping a murderer?

17

Day Eight

Kosara had seen the sea in Belograd: blue, flat as a mirror, with white sailboats bobbing lazily across the surface, and scantily clad women sunbathing on the beach.

The Zmey's Sea was different. Its waves rose high, edged with snow-white froth, slamming against the rocks with a deafening crash. Its wind brought the smell of brine and rotting seaweed, but also of something otherworldly. Something that made Kosara's hair stand on end.

The pale bodies of rusalkas drifted in the dark waters. Their hair floated behind them, green like moss, brown like kelp, black like sea urchins. Their scaly tails glistened in the pale sun. Occasionally, they reached a bony hand out towards a low-flying seagull, grabbing it and dragging it under.

Some had lights hanging from their foreheads like lantern fish, flickering far in the distance. Kosara would have thought them lost fishing boats if she didn't know better.

"Help!" The crashing of the waves couldn't drown their screams. "Help me!"

She walked down the beach, holding onto her coat with both hands to prevent the wind from snatching it. Asen followed carefully, his soles sliding over the smooth rocks. The moon yarn unravelled behind them, barely visible in the fog. Blackbeard's lighthouse shone up ahead.

"Please help me!" A shout sounded, loud and throaty. "They've got me! Oh my God, they've got me!"

"Is that a child?" Asen stopped in his tracks. His panicked eyes searched the waves.

"It's not a child," Kosara said. "It's a rusalka. They'll do anything to lure you into the water. And please try to speak quietly if you're within arm's reach of the sea. They can steal your voice."

"My voice?"

"Hush! Yes, your voice. That's what you're hearing. Stolen voices."

"Please help me!" It sounded like a young girl, terrified, barely managing to keep her head above the water. It would have been convincing, if it weren't for the dozen other voices, just as realistic as hers.

"But what if it's really a child?" Asen asked.

"It isn't."

"Do the rusalkas ever manage to catch children?"

"They do sometimes." Kosara tried hard not to think of the many worried parents she'd had to console back in the day. They'd come to her workshop, their faces wet with tears, begging her to help them look for their children. The dads usually shouted and waved their fists about, while the mums tried to explain, as if Kosara was blaming them: *I only let little Nadya out of my sight for a second, I swear. She must have wandered off. She loves collecting shells on the beach—*

"So, how would we know if they've got a real child?" Asen asked.

"We wouldn't. That's why it's important to never go anywhere near the water—if the rusalkas catch you, no one would answer your cries for help. Don't fall for their tricks, no matter how much they beg and plead, no matter their heart-rending words—"

"You daft bastards!" came a voice. "Fucking hell!"

Kosara and Asen shared a look.

"That didn't sound much like heart-rending words," Asen said.

"What the actual fuck! Do you have a death wish?"

Kosara looked around. The shore was empty.

"Step away from the water, you idiots! Step! Away!"

Kosara finally looked up. Blackbeard stood on his lighthouse's balcony, his silhouette dark against the bright lantern room.

Any other time of year, the lighthouse looked bizarre, perched on the side of the lake. During the Foul Days, it seemed out of place, too: a perfectly ordinary building on this foreign shore the Zmey had transported to Chernograd. Its peeling white walls contrasted against the dark sand.

"Blackbeard, my old friend!" Kosara shouted. "I haven't seen you in ages!"

"Who the hell are you?" Blackbeard replied. "You know what, I don't care! Soon you'll be rusalka feed if you don't step away from the water!"

"We're miles away from the water!"

"That's what you think. Rusalkas have an arm span of up to three times their height, did you know that?"

"I did, actually. Listen, we need to speak to you. Do you mind coming down?"

"Sorry, too busy! I have to wash my beard."

Kosara fished for the compass in her pocket and pulled it out, swinging it by its long chain. "Look what we found!"

Blackbeard disappeared. What seemed like an impossibly short time later, the lighthouse door opened.

His beard wasn't black anymore: it was grey and thick like chimney smoke. He wore it in tiny braids with amber beads glinting among them. His eyes were full of ruptured blood vessels and irritation.

Blackbeard grabbed at the compass. Kosara was faster. She'd known exactly what to expect from the old scoundrel. She snatched it away and hid it in her pocket again.

"You have to give it back," Blackbeard barked. "It's mine."

"Do you have any proof?" Kosara asked.

"My name is etched on it."

Kosara swore internally. She'd forgotten all about that little detail. "Well, you don't get to claim everything you've written your name on."

"Give it back!" His words boomed among the rocks like cannon shots. "Or I'll call the police!"

Kosara snorted. No way would he ever risk bringing the police to his lighthouse full of stolen goods.

"I think you'll find"—Asen pulled the badge from his pocket— "that I am the police."

The unpleasant sound of bone rubbing against bone echoed between the stones. It took Kosara a second to realise where it came from—Blackbeard was grinding his teeth.

"I should have guessed," he said. "Extortionists, the lot of you. What do you want?"

"We want you to take us to the Zmey's palace," Kosara replied.

Blackbeard laughed, making the beads in his beard chime. "So, you *are* suicidal."

"You've done it before."

"When I was young and stupid! Believe me, you'll find nothing of any real worth in the Zmey's palace. What did all the gold I stole from him bring me?" Blackbeard waved his hand to encompass the rocky shore, the sea, and the lighthouse. "It's all cursed! You gamble with it— you always lose. You splash out on drink—it tastes like vinegar. You spend it on wenches—they bring you nothing but misery!"

Kosara suspected it was Blackbeard's terrible attitude that spoiled his fun, not the Zmey's cursed gold.

"We're not interested in the Zmey's gold," Asen said. "We're investigating a homicide."

"Yeah?" Blackbeard asked. "Good luck arresting the Zmey!"

"He isn't the suspect. I suppose he's a witness."

"You're going to try to *interrogate* the Zmey?"

"Well, no, most likely not—"

"It doesn't matter why we're going to the palace," Kosara said. "What matters is: do you want your compass back or not?"

Blackbeard's eyebrows were two rain clouds hanging low on the horizon. "I'll take you to the palace if you give me my compass now."

He must have been taking them for idiots.

"No way," Kosara said. "You'll take us there, *and* you'll bring us back, *and then* I'll give you the compass."

"Extortionists. The lot of you. Come back tomorrow—"

And give you enough time to prepare a trap for us? "We have no time to lose," Kosara said. "We have to go now."

"Are you joking? In this weather?"

Kosara looked up at the pale sky. She thought she felt a drop of rain on her face, but it could just as well have been sea water. It seemed like a mild winter day, for Chernograd. The old rascal was obviously stalling.

"Do you want your compass back, or should I try to find another sea captain to give us a lift? I'm sure plenty would be happy to get their hands on the compass. . . ."

Blackbeard harrumphed. "I should have let the rusalkas eat you. Wait here."

He turned around and disappeared into the lighthouse. A minute later, he returned, garbed entirely in yellow oilskins, with a wide-brimmed hat hanging low over his eyes. He led them around the lighthouse, down to a stone jetty where his ship was moored.

It wasn't some kind of pleasure yacht or a simple fishing vessel. It was a proper ship. Two tall masts stretched towards the sky, their sails flapping in the wind like overexcited ghosts. The figurehead depicted a bare-chested rusalka: her golden scales caught the light of the winter sun, and emeralds shone in her hair. Her face was human and her eyes were fixed somewhere in the distance.

"All aboard!" Blackbeard shouted. There was nothing left of the tired old man now—his eyes gleamed like rusalkas' lanterns. He grinned from ear to ear, flashing a set of teeth plated in gold and precious stones.

"Shush!" Kosara said, her gaze darting to the pale bodies floating behind the stern. "The rusalkas."

Blackbeard rolled his eyes. "Do you think I'm stupid? They can't get you while you're on my ship."

"Oh," Kosara said. She had, in fact, thought he might be stupid—or losing it in his old age.

She looked around. The ship seemed empty—only the fog floated above the deck, thick and white as milk. However, as soon as Kosara and Asen climbed up, the sails dropped sharply. The wind grew stronger, whistling between the rigging. The ship glided across the water.

"Where's North?" Blackbeard asked.

Kosara pulled out the compass and pointed towards the horizon where dark clouds gathered.

"*Safina,*" Blackbeard shouted to no one in particular, "right standard rudder, heave ho!"

The ship began to turn. Up on the quarterdeck, the wheel spun on its own. A flock of seagulls cawed, hovering behind the stern.

As the ship moved through the bay, it cut its way through a group of rusalkas. One of them reached a hand out. There was a scream. A seagull disappeared.

A minute later, the waves spat out a small assortment of bird bones, picked clean. Kosara shivered.

"*Safina,*" Blackbeard shouted again, "ease your rudder left ten degrees, old salt, ten degrees!"

The wheel turned again. For a moment, as the wind dispersed the fog slightly, Kosara could swear she glimpsed the dark silhouette of a woman behind it. She blinked, and the woman vanished.

"*Safina,* steady as she goes!"

It took them a few hours to clear the bay. The waves grew higher, smashing into the hull of the ship, making the wood creak and groan. The deeper into the sea they sailed, the more the sky changed. The stars grew brighter, flickering and shifting around, rearranging themselves in constellations Kosara had never seen before. The sun set and the moon rose enormous, hanging low over the horizon like a rusalka's lantern.

Blackbeard changed as well. After a few swigs from his hip flask, he got chatty. He told them stories about his past voyages, the strange islands he'd found, and the sea monsters he'd slain. Kosara listened politely, though she wished they'd go inside and warm up. If only Blackbeard was willing to share whatever was in his hip flask. . . .

Finally, he must have heard her teeth chattering. He led them down to the hold, through a maze of barrels and boxes. The smells of salted fish and pickled gherkins competed with each other, hitting Kosara in waves.

"The two cabins at the end are free. You can sleep there." Blackbeard gestured down the hallway. Kosara didn't dare ask who lived in the other cabins. "Make yourselves at home et cetera, et cetera. Personally, I think I'll have a nightcap, if you'd care to join me."

"Thanks for the offer, but I'll head to bed," Asen said. "I'm very tired."

Kosara was tired too, but she was also curious: why had Blackbeard suddenly decided to play the perfect host?

"Come on," Blackbeard said, sensing her hesitation. "Just one. It will help you sleep."

"All right, just one."

Asen gave her a long look, as if to say, "Be careful." Kosara tried to reply with a look that said, "Don't worry, he's just a grumpy old bastard, but he's not dangerous." It was a lot of meaning to try to stuff into a look, but Asen must have more or less understood her, because he nodded and walked away.

Blackbeard led her to his cabin. The lampshade swung with the waves and the sea left salty marks on the windows. He sat behind his desk with his feet up and lit his pipe. A large wooden globe served as his ashtray. It was all painted blue, and here and there, someone had added handwritten notes and drawn sea monsters. The cabin filled with thick smoke, tickling Kosara's nostrils.

"Wine?" Blackbeard asked.

"Sure."

He pulled a dusty bottle and two glasses from a desk drawer. Kosara accepted her glass, pretending not to notice the greasy marks on it.

"Cheers!" He downed his in one gulp. Kosara took a swig from hers. The wine was dark red, almost black, and sour like Chernogradean lemonade. She tried not to make a face.

"You play dice?" Blackbeard asked.

"I've been trying not to gamble recently," Kosara said, but he'd already taken out three bone dice.

"Come on, it'll be fun."

"I don't have any money."

"I don't need money! What would I do with money?"

"What do you want to play for, then?"

He grinned. A few drops of wine ran down his moustache, colouring it red. "Stories."

"What stories?"

"Interesting, preferably."

Kosara smiled back at him. So, this was why he'd invited her over. There was nothing sinister about Blackbeard's sudden politeness. He was just a lonely old man who wanted to hear a good story. And no wonder—he'd been stuck in that lighthouse, completely alone, ever since Algara's murder.

Kosara threw the dice once, as a test run. Three sixes. Her luck obviously worked tonight.

"How about this?" Blackbeard said. "We'll throw three times. The winner can ask the loser for one of their stories. The catch is, you have to tell the truth."

"And how exactly would you know if I'm telling the truth?"

Blackbeard lifted his index finger in the air and wiggled his eyebrows, before he drew a dusty vial from the drawer. A few drops of bright pink liquid splashed at the bottom. Kosara would recognise the way it bubbled and climbed up the walls of the vial anywhere. Truth serum.

"That's illegal," she said.

"So?"

Kosara shrugged. "Nothing." Why had she even mentioned it? She'd obviously spent too much time with Asen.

Blackbeard poured two thimble-sized glasses of truth serum and left them in the middle of the table, next to the dice.

"How about we play best of three?" Blackbeard said.

Kosara grabbed the dice and threw first. A two, a three, and a five. Completely useless. She wished she hadn't wasted her three sixes for the test run. Blackbeard won with two fives and a four.

Kosara threw the dice again. She got a weak combination once more. Luckily, Blackbeard's dice were even weaker.

"One-one," he said, as if she wasn't paying attention.

Before she threw the dice again, Kosara rubbed them in between her hands and blew on them for good luck. It didn't help. Three ones. It couldn't get any worse than that.

Blackbeard also rubbed the dice between his large palms and blew on them, his moustache twitching as he tried to cover his smirk.

He threw three sixes. Unbelievable.

"You win," she said with a sigh. This was why she had to stop gambling.

Instead of replying, he pushed the glass of truth serum towards her.

She downed it in one go. It slid down her throat, thick as syrup, and sat heavy in her stomach.

For a long moment, Blackbeard stared at her. Droplets of wine caught in his moustache, rolling down his beard, glistening just as bright as the golden beads.

"Tell me"—his eyes flashed—"how you lost your shadow."

Kosara tried not to let the surprise show on her face. "So, you noticed."

"You don't get to grow as old as I am in Chernograd if you don't have a very sharp eye. Well?"

Kosara started talking. She couldn't stop. Her tongue shaped the words on its own, her lips moved against her will. She told him everything: about the game of Kral and Irnik, and the teleport brogues, and the Zmey. . . . That last part was particularly embarrassing.

Perhaps this had been a mistake. She should have gone to bed like Asen rather than sit here, spilling her guts in front of a stranger. The one thing that made her feel better was the fact that after all this was over, she'd probably never see Blackbeard again.

Towards the end, she felt the serum's hold over her weakening. Just to make sure, she sneaked in a few small lies. It wasn't easy. Her tongue fought against her as she struggled to form the words, but she won in the end.

"And that's how I saved the prince-regent of Belograd from drowning," she concluded.

Blackbeard ran a hand over his beard, making the beads clang. "I didn't know you could take a witch's shadow."

"You can't. It needs to be given willfully."

"And once you've given it away . . ."

"I have no power over it."

"I've heard they don't come cheap."

"They are expensive," Kosara said, before she managed to stop herself, finally. She'd been trying for a while. She didn't like where his line of questioning was going. "But that's a different story."

Blackbeard gave her a knowing smile. He finished his drink in one long gulp.

"One more game?" Kosara asked. That was her problem with gambling. Once she started . . .

Blackbeard took the dice. He won the first round, but Kosara beat him the second. The third time, he threw the dice at the table with such gusto, two of them rolled off the surface and landed on the floor, immediately disqualifying him.

"Oops." He laughed. "You win."

He didn't seem to mind losing—from what Kosara had seen of him earlier, he enjoyed telling stories.

The glass of truth serum glinted in the lamplight as he raised it in the air. "Cheers!" He downed it in one go and shook his head rapidly, as if to dispel an unpleasant taste. "Ask."

"The compass," Kosara said, feeling its weight in her pocket. She'd had a while to think about her question. "Where did you get it from?"

"Great choice." Blackbeard flashed a smile. "That's an interesting story."

He poured himself another glass of wine and took a big drink before he started talking. "I'm a born sailor. Just like some people are born witches, and others are great singers or painters. I can find the Polar Star on a cloudy night. I can smell a wind change hours before it happens. I can get you through a storm without you ever feeling it. I started working on my da's ship as soon as I could walk and got made captain at thirteen. I sailed around the world when I was fourteen. Everyone knew my name in both Chernograd and Belograd. Back then, before the Wall, they were like the same city."

Kosara lifted her eyebrows but didn't interrupt him. She hadn't realised he was old enough to remember Chernograd before the Wall. He certainly didn't look it. Was he even fully human?

"One evening," Blackbeard continued, "years and years ago, there was a knock on my door. I open and what do I see? Three old farts, dressed in fancy suits, speaking all posh. Obviously from Belograd. 'We're from the Royal Council,' they say, 'and we require your assistance on matters of national security.' They *required*, they didn't ask. You didn't argue with the Royal Council back in those days, if you didn't want to end up accidentally stabbing yourself in the back half a dozen times. They wanted me to sail them across the Zmey's Sea. I told them no way. I'd tried sailing it, and it was impossible to navigate. The stars are different, and compasses don't work. That's when one of them handed me the compass. 'You can keep it,' he says, 'if you manage to get us there and back safe.'"

"Did they give you the ship as well?" Kosara couldn't help but ask. She felt as if she was a child again, sitting on her granny's lap, listening to bedtime stories.

"Oh no, the ship's mine. It was my da's, and his da's before him. But that's a different story. Anyway, me and the three farts sailed across the sea and reached the Zmey's palace. I didn't dare get off the ship that first time. 'Wait here,' one of them says, 'we'll be back in a jiffy.' Truth be told, I was scared stiff. 'What if the Zmey catches me?' I asked. 'What if he decides to pop out of his feast for a smoke, and there's little old me, just sitting here?' One of them just winked at me. 'Maybe the hunter will become the hunted tonight,' he told me. The hell was that supposed to mean?

"It turns out, I'd been worrying about the wrong monster. The farts returned, leading on a leash—as if it was a bloody puppy—the most terrifying monster I've ever seen. Three heads on three long necks, tossing like a rabid dog's, stirring up a wind strong enough to lift you off your feet. Its every step sent the ground shaking. Its horns pierced the clouds, making thunder and lightning come out. Honest to God! Thunder and lightning! Its three mouths were full of teeth the size of swords, and in between them, fire squeezed out! Fire! My ship's made of wood! I told the old farts, I said, 'No way, you're not taking this thing on my ship,' and they said, 'Not to worry, we've sedated her, she's just about to fall asleep.' And the damned thing did. It dropped on the deck like a beached whale. It slept like a baby until we reached Chernograd."

Kosara's sixth sense tingled. Suddenly, she was aware this wasn't simply a bedtime story. A few drops of the truth serum glistened bright pink on Blackbeard's moustache. This had all truly happened.

And there was something about it that seemed terribly familiar. Blackbeard had said those men were from the Royal Council. . . .

"What did they do with the monster?" she asked, afraid she already knew the answer.

"Who knows? I can only tell you this—I sailed them back to Chernograd safely. I went to bed, and when I woke up, there was a Wall around my city."

Kosara gasped quietly as the last piece of the puzzle fell into place.

She'd wondered about it before: how did the Royal Council manage to cast a spell strong enough to last all these years? Now, the answer seemed obvious. The best way to ensure the longevity of any structure was to embed someone in it. It was old, black magic. It truly worked.

They'd embedded the monster in the Wall. It was a good idea, in theory—the magic of monsters was stronger than that of people. They'd make for better guards. The only problem was, embedding them wouldn't kill them. Monsters could only be killed with silver bullets and aspen stakes, holy water, and mirrors.

The monster in the Wall was still alive. This was why it thrashed and flailed and slammed its body against the dark surface. This was why sometimes, on a quiet night, people claimed they heard the Wall scream.

Kosara swore under her breath. That conversation she'd had with Roksana at Sevar's engagement party floated to the forefront of her mind.

Roksana had asked about a three-headed monster, right before she'd started prodding Kosara about embedding magic. She'd even given Kosara a name: *Lamia*.

Roksana had *known*. She'd practically revealed it all, and Kosara had been too distracted to pay attention. And then Roksana had said that like every monster, the Wall could be defeated.

Was this why she and the Zmey were collecting witches' shadows? Were they going to *fight* the Wall?

No way. It took a lot more than raw power to undo magic this old and this strong. Destroying a spell took just as much skill and knowledge as casting it in the first place, like unravelling an expertly knit jumper.

"One more game?" Blackbeard asked.

Kosara shook her head. "It's getting late."

Truth was, she couldn't concentrate on the game. Her mind raced.

She stood up and swayed on her feet—from the waves or from the wine, she couldn't quite tell. Through the window outside, the stars shifted and changed.

If the Zmey attempted to destroy the Wall, Kosara had no doubt the whole thing would only end in flames and devastation. He lacked the precision to do it. His magic was like a wildfire, not an accurately aimed bullet.

And the worst part was, Kosara didn't think he'd care. If destroying the Wall took half of Chernograd with it, that was no skin off his back. After all, he'd have the whole world to terrorise once the Wall fell. Who cared about Chernograd?

He'd let his monsters wreak havoc on the other side. And while a small, rather unpleasant part of Kosara felt that perhaps the Belogradeans deserved it, she was sure the Zmey wouldn't stop there. That was just the sort of man—no, *monster*—he was. Once he got that first taste of blood, he'd find it difficult to rein himself in.

She shuddered. She *had* to get her shadow back.

18

Day Eight

Kosara curled up on the hard berth in her cabin. The ship creaked and moaned, the waves crashed against the hull, the seagulls cawed. It had been a long day, and she should have been tired to death, but she couldn't stop thinking: about the monster trapped in the Wall, about the Zmey, and about how with every minute, they got closer to his palace.

Was she wrong to follow Roksana there? Perhaps she ought to have prepared better. Given enough time, she could have come up with some brilliant, foolproof plan.

Except she didn't have time. In three days, the gates to the palace would shut again until next year. And next year, she would be a shadow.

Kosara squeezed her eyes shut and turned on her back. Then she turned on her stomach. On her back again.

And then, there was Asen. Asen with his enchanted pendant, and the panic in his eyes when she'd tried to touch it. Asen, who was obviously hiding something. Was she making a mistake trusting him?

It wouldn't be the first time she'd placed her trust in the wrong person. Or the first time she'd ignored the obvious signs that someone only pretended to like her, just because she wanted it to be true.

Kosara turned to her side again. There had to be *someone* out there who deserved her trust. Someone she could let close without them betraying her.

But was Asen that person? Or was he just another Roksana?

Kosara threw the covers to the side. Her bare feet touched the cold floorboards, sending a shiver up her spine.

She crossed the hallway to Blackbeard's cabin. He snored with the covers pulled over his head, his hairy legs and woolly socks sticking out below. Kosara tiptoed in, quietly cursing every squeaky floorboard.

Blackbeard hadn't tidied up after she'd left. The truth serum was still on the table, and so were the half-finished bottle of wine and the two glasses. She grabbed them all.

"Hey, hands," she kept forming with her lips as she walked back out, just in case. "Hey, the two of you . . ."

Once back out in the hallway, she poured the serum into the wine and shook the bottle to mix them.

Then, she paused. Was she really going to do this? Truth serum was illegal. Much worse, it was immoral.

He's a ticking time bomb. He needs to be defused.

Kosara knew very well that being morally right wasn't her job. She was a witch—her job was being *right*. After only a moment's hesitation, she knocked on Asen's door.

He opened, messy-haired and bleary-eyed. Since she was well-mannered, Kosara looked him in the eyes, though she couldn't help but notice he wasn't wearing trousers. His briefs were striped blue and white. Interesting, had he chosen them specially for going sailing?

"Kosara?" he asked. "What's wrong?"

"I can't sleep," she said.

He stepped to the side and let her in. She left the bottle and the glasses on the bedside table and sat on the berth. He moved his meticulously folded clothes from the chair and spun it to face her.

"What's the matter?" he asked.

"Nightmares. Wine?" Without waiting for a response, she poured two glasses.

"Because of what happened in the graveyard?"

"Yes." Kosara pushed one of the glasses towards him and lifted hers. "Cheers!" She pretended to take a sip.

"What did you see?" He didn't touch his glass.

"When?"

"In the graveyard."

At first, Kosara thought it was mere curiosity fuelling the question, or maybe his professional obsession with finding out the truth. But then she saw the genuine worry in his eyes.

Guilt prickled at her skin. He was worried for her, and she was about to attempt to sneak truth serum into his drink. She licked her lips.

A familiar taste filled her mouth, sickly-sweet. Something thick and syrupy slid down her throat. Kosara froze. *Oh no.*

She felt her tongue loosen.

Oh no. She looked down at her glass of wine—untouched, except for a drop of red, smeared on the rim. She hadn't noticed it when she'd pretended to be taking a drink.

Good job, Kosara. You were supposed to drug him, not yourself.

She couldn't linger on the thought any longer. Her lips were already shaping the words. "I saw Nevena."

Goddamnit.

"What happened to her?"

Kosara took a deep breath. And the words poured out of her, as if they'd been waiting to come out for years. As hard as she tried, she couldn't stop them. "It was the Foul Days. We were sixteen. We were walking home after a gig at some seedy bar—they wouldn't serve us alcohol in the classy ones—and I thought it was just the best idea ever to go into the graveyard. I was going to be a witch, and she was going to be the best monster hunter in all of Chernograd. Nothing could go wrong, right?" Kosara laughed, too loud and throaty. "We jumped over the fence. We started walking around, reading the tombstones, laughing at the tacky statues and the old-fashioned names. We were very quiet and careful at first, but then we got sloppy. The flask of homebrewed rakia we gulped surely didn't help. We must have got too loud. A pack of wolves found us. Varkolaks."

"Oh no," Asen said.

"It gets worse. I'd trained as a witch for a while at that point. I knew we could calm them down with singing. So, I told Nevena to just keep singing that awful song the band had played earlier. I honestly thought we'd get away. . . ."

Kosara paused. This was where her memory had faded for years.

She'd always wondered what had happened for things to end the way they did.

She prepared to say as much, but her tongue had a mind of its own. "The Zmey was there."

"What?" Asen asked.

What? Kosara echoed him in her thoughts. Of course the Zmey hadn't been there. What was she saying?

But then she remembered what she'd seen the previous day in the graveyard, when the upirs had dragged her memories out of her mind against her will. The pack leader, with his golden hair and blue eyes. The same hair she'd run her fingers through countless times. The same eyes that still haunted her nightmares.

For years, she'd inserted some other, vague face in his place. She'd imagined a nondescript Chernogradean man, with the sort of face you couldn't pick out in a crowd—because, she realised now, it didn't exist.

The pack leader had been the Zmey.

"Yes," she said, slightly giddy. Even though she knew it was the se-rum talking, she was still relieved to finally be sharing the story with someone. "The Zmey arrived. I'd completely forgotten about that, can you believe it? The Zmey was there."

"Oh no," Asen repeated.

"He was pissed off with me for escaping him. . . . Actually, no, he was furious. I've never seen him that angry—until this New Year's Eve, that is."

Kosara inhaled deeply. How could she have ever forgotten this part? Had the Zmey enchanted her somehow? Had her own mind erased it, in some botched attempt to protect her psyche?

"He set his varkolaks on us," she continued. "I remember it so clearly now. I managed to run away, God knows how, but Nevena . . . In the last moment, as we were climbing the fence, one of them bit her ankle."

"And she turned into a varkolak? Did she attack you?"

"That's not how it works. You remain human until the next full moon. I hoped right until that point that she wasn't infected. That the bite wasn't deep enough. She begged me to just kill her if she ever turned. I told her she was being stupid. I was a witch. I'd been trained to deal with situations like that. We never told our parents so they wouldn't worry, which I now realise was a mistake. Instead, once the next full moon came, I convinced them to go visit my dad's cousin for a few days on the other end of town. I locked Nevena in the basement with a couple of tins of boiled pork and enough water. She should have survived the three days."

"But?"

"But it turned out varkolaks are stronger than I thought. She broke down the door. I woke up with something wet and hot dripping on my face. When I opened my eyes, I saw her looming over me, with her mouth open and saliva running down. Her breath smelled like a wet dog. She slapped me across the face." Kosara ran her fingers down the scar on her cheek. Three raised scrapes. "I stabbed her right before she bit me. I'd been smart enough to hide a knife under my pillow. And you know the worst part? Her eyes were still hers: brown and warm. I'll never forget the pain in them as my knife pierced her chest."

Kosara blinked quickly to chase away her tears. It didn't help. They rolled down her cheeks, landing heavy on her chest. She didn't want to look up at Asen and see the accusation in his eyes. If only she'd managed to keep her big mouth shut. . . .

Asen's hand landed on hers, and Kosara jumped. What was he going to do? Arrest her?

Instead, he squeezed her hand. "You didn't have a choice," he said, his voice gentle. "It wasn't your fault."

He's lying, whispered the Zmey in her head. *You're a murderer. You know it. And now he knows it, too. It's all your fault.*

Kosara squeezed her eyes shut. *Shut. Up.* She furiously wiped the tears with her sleeve.

"Kosara, look at me," Asen said. There was no accusation in his eyes, only compassion. "It wasn't your fault."

"Whose damned fault was it then?" she said, her voice cracking. She couldn't stand him being this nice to her after she'd admitted to *murder.* Was it that hard to meet one goddamned copper who knew how to do his job? "Whose stupid fault could it possibly be? I asked her to go to the graveyard. I was reckless. I was so relieved to finally be free of the Zmey, so eager to make up for all the damned time I'd lost in his damned palace, I made stupid decision after stupid decision, and it all culminated in an absolutely *idiotic* decision, and Nevena died. Because of me."

Saying that last sentence out loud was a struggle. Her tongue fought against her, just like when she'd told Blackbeard lies about her trip to Belograd. The effect of the serum was growing weaker.

Except the fact she'd killed Nevena wasn't a lie. Was it?

Asen looked at her strangely for a moment, and Kosara realised she'd never told him about her and the Zmey before. But he didn't ask her any questions. He squeezed her hand tighter. "You were sixteen. Of course you made stupid decisions."

There, I told you he agrees. Murderer. It's your fault. It's all your fault for making me angry.

"But what happened isn't your fault," Asen continued. "The Zmey murdered your sister. He didn't do it because of you. He did it simply because he could. Because he's a monster."

Kosara stared at Asen, his face doubling and tripling through the tears in her eyes. "I led her there," she said, but her resolve was starting to weaken. "The Zmey is a monster. He can't be held responsible for doing what monsters do."

"Why the hell not?"

Kosara opened her mouth and then shut it again. *Why the hell not?*

Because you're too afraid, little Kosara. Because admitting I murdered your sister means you'll have to do something about it. Because it's easier to fight with yourself over it than to fight me.

Because you know you're too weak to face my fire.

Kosara was full-on sobbing now, loud and ugly. She couldn't stop. Asen watched her with those big, worried eyes of his, obviously unsure what to do, his hand occasionally squeezing hers.

For a moment, he looked as if he wanted to do more. Gently wipe her tears with his hand. Get up from his seat and embrace her in a tight hug.

But he didn't. Something stopped him. His expression was still worried, but for a moment, something else flickered across his face—guilt. Guilt that he was touching her at all.

If Kosara wasn't so busy wiping at her face with her sleeve and letting out loud, throaty sobs with every gulp of air, she would have paid more attention to it. Even if something stopped Asen from getting any closer to her, she'd bared herself completely, and she found it hard to pull back now.

She hadn't cried like this in years.

Get a hold of yourself, for God's sake!

Another loud gulp. And another, but this one slightly shallower.

Nothing had changed tonight. Absolutely nothing. Deep down, Kosara had always known who'd murdered Nevena. If she hadn't, she'd have done something long ago to finally bring her poor ghost peace.

Yes, you, my little Kosara. You murdered her.

No, she said, surprising herself. "No," she repeated out loud, and her tongue didn't fight against her, because it was the truth. Suddenly, she found it easier to stand up to him, even if it was only in her head. *Not me. You did.*

"What was that?" Asen asked.

"Nothing. It was nothing." Kosara took several deep breaths, forcing the tears to stop, pushing it all to the back of her mind. It shouldn't have been this difficult. After all, she had years of practice.

Only this time, she wasn't going to forget. She was going to take all her fear and hurt, calcified and hard after all those years, and she was going to use them as a weapon.

Once she got her shadow back, she'd make the Zmey pay for what he did. Even if it took her years of training to become strong enough to defeat him. Even if she died in the process.

She was done running.

"Honestly, Kosara," Asen said. "Why would you focus on a reckless decision you made seven years ago, when you have such a wide array of reckless decisions we're making right now to choose from?"

Kosara half-sniffed, half-snorted. She wiped her tears again. "Thank you," she said. "I think I needed to talk about it with someone. Sorry I woke you up."

"Don't worry about it, I was awake anyway."

"Nightmares again?"

Asen nodded. He didn't look as if he'd say anything else.

"Come on," Kosara said, her eyes still burning. "I told you my deepest, darkest secret. Your turn."

Asen laughed, as if she'd been joking. She hadn't.

"Maybe some other time," he said.

He let go of her hand and reached for his wine glass. Instead of drinking from it, he swung it between his fingers, from his left hand to the right and back.

Once again, Kosara hesitated. She could still stop him from drinking the truth serum. After experiencing its effects twice, she was hesitant to inflict it on someone else. It was so distressing, being unable to control your own tongue. She could come clean and explain herself, and he'd probably understand and forgive her, the nice person that he was.

No, she thought. This was how Sevar had tricked her: by acting as if he cared. This was how Roksana had tricked her, too.

She wasn't going to be tricked again.

Kosara lifted the glass to her lips once more, pretending to take a sip, this time taking extra care not to let her lips touch the glass.

"The wine's not bad, by the way," she said.

Asen looked down, as if only now realising he was holding the glass. "Actually, I don't drink. Haven't I told you before? Sorry, I should have said something before you poured me a glass."

"But it's just wine! It's made from grapes. Perfectly natural. It's full of vitamins."

He shrugged. "Nevertheless."

Kosara swore internally. This was just her luck. If only she'd kept the serum, she could have tried mixing it with his breakfast tea the next day. Instead, she'd wasted it pouring it into the wine. Just her luck.

Kosara put down her glass. She had to think. There had to be some other way to trick him into revealing what his talisman was.

She raised her hand, pretending to be fixing her hair, her fingers tangling in the knots. Her elbow slammed against her wine glass. It rocked on its stool, and then it tumbled over. The wine flew out, painting a wide arch in the air, landing with a splash on Asen's T-shirt.

"Oh my God!" Kosara said. "I'm so sorry!"

Asen looked down at his top. He laughed. "Don't worry about it. Red is my favourite colour, anyway."

He didn't make to take it off. He simply sat there, completely unfazed, while the stains on his T-shirt grew larger as the wine sank in deeper.

All right. Fine. Time for a new plan.

A large candleholder stood on the shelf above his head. All the candles were lit. If Kosara managed to knock it over, she might set his stupid T-shirt on fire. . . .

Or maybe she'd burn his hair, or his face. Or the ship would catch on fire. Blackbeard would throw them both straight into the sea, to swim with the rusalkas.

Kosara sighed deeply. There was no other way. She stood up. After only a moment's hesitation, she walked around the table, grabbed the collar of his T-shirt, pulled him closer, and kissed him.

For a moment, his lips were firm under hers, and she thought he'd push her away. She must have looked terrible, with her messy hair, her red face, and her eyes puffy from crying. Hardly a seductress.

Then, his lips softened. He breathed out, as if he'd been waiting for her to do this, and buried his face in her hair. His nose tickled her neck. His breath was hot on her collarbone. He smiled in between kissing her.

It felt nice, she had to admit, as his fingers caressed her skin. His touch was gentle but persistent, forming circles on her lower back.

She ran her hand down his spine to the hem of his T-shirt and paused. What she did next would ruin this—whatever *this* was.

But she had to do it. She had to know.

Her hand crept up, her fingers dancing over the tense muscles of his stomach and chest, to the pendant hanging around his neck. It was just as warm as his skin, made of some kind of soft metal, and shaped like . . . a ring?

Asen's hand shot up and caught her wrist. He pulled away from her, his eyes wide with raw, genuine hurt.

He didn't look like a traitor whose inevitable betrayal she'd just thwarted. On the contrary—he looked betrayed.

Kosara stared back, her lips still warm from his, unsure what to say. A half-formed explanation was on her tongue, but it didn't seem to make any sense, so she swallowed it.

Her actions from the past hour shifted in her mind: only a moment ago, they'd seemed completely logical, just like most stupid decisions did in the middle of the night. Now, she saw the gaps in the story she'd spun for herself. The gaps she'd filled with some sort of sinister intent on Asen's part.

The truth was, he'd shown her no reason to suspect him. He'd done nothing wrong, other than wear a talisman he didn't want to tell her about.

"Sorry, I . . ." She trailed off. *You what, Kosara, you stupid idiot? You what?*

"Please leave," Asen said, his voice level. Only one throbbing vein of his temple suggested how angry he was.

"I'm sorry."

"Get out."

He opened the door, waited for her to go out, and closed it after her. Kosara stood in the hallway alone, hot from embarrassment and furious. At herself. A tear tickled her cheek as it rolled down.

She wasn't crying. She was *not* crying.

What kind of pathetic loser cried twice in the same night?

Not Kosara, that was for sure. Her eyes were simply burning because of the salty air. Her tears were because of the cold.

She'd ruined everything. Her fragile friendship with Asen. Their plan to sneak into the palace. Asen would have every right to return to Chernograd, leaving her to face the Zmey alone.

She couldn't do it alone.

Kosara raised her hand to knock on the door. She could try to explain: *Listen, I asked you who enchanted you, but you didn't tell me, and I was worried. . . .*

Then she lowered her hand again. It was way too late for that now.

19

Day Nine

When Kosara finally fell asleep, she dreamed of the Zmey. His eyes changed from blue to completely black—like a samodiva's—to being mounted onto a ring, staring at her and never blinking.

A door creaked. He was here. He'd finally found her.

She peeled her tear-crusted eyes open. A dark silhouette rummaged through her coat's pockets. He was bulkier than the Zmey. His hair fell in greasy streaks down his large back, draped in bright yellow oilskins.

Kosara swore internally. When she'd suspected there was someone on the ship she shouldn't have trusted, she'd been right. Except, it wasn't Asen. Of course it wasn't Asen.

She tried to stay quiet, but Blackbeard must have heard the change in her breathing. He spun towards her. For a moment, they stared at each other. Then he rushed to her and pinned her down to the berth.

"Where's my compass?" His breath stank of alcohol, brine, and something rotten, like seaweed washed up on the beach. He slammed her into the berth. "Where is it?"

Kosara kneed him between the legs. Blackbeard gasped. She pushed him back and ran.

"Bakharov!" She hoped Asen hadn't gone to sleep yet. And that he wouldn't simply ignore her—even if she deserved it.

The thudding of Blackbeard's steps echoed behind her. The rusalkas screamed. Kosara's heartbeat grew louder and louder until it drowned everything else.

She climbed to the deck. Waves were slapping the side of the ship, sending it swaying, spraying salty water in her face. Her wet night-gown stuck to her body, freezing cold. Her feet slid on the floorboards.

She reached the stern and turned, her back pressed against the metal railing. Her eyes darted around in panic.

Blackbeard moved towards her, deliberately slowly. He didn't need to hurry. She was trapped.

"What do you want?" Kosara shouted over the crashing of the waves. She was simply trying to win time. She knew very well what he wanted.

"You know very well what I want." There, he agreed.

"We had a deal. I'll give it back once you take us to the Zmey's palace."

"No. You'll give it back now, and I might not throw you in the sea."

Kosara's gaze slid past Blackbeard to the dark waters behind, where several pale bodies drifted. The compass pressed hard against her chest. She wasn't sure why she'd thought to hide it in her bra. Some kind of sixth sense.

Similarly, she wasn't sure how she knew that even if Blackbeard got his compass back, he'd still throw her in the sea. Sixth sense, again.

Kosara had said too much when they'd played dice, she realised. That glint in his eyes when he'd asked about the witches' shadows: it wasn't the polite interest of a lonely old man; it was the excitement of a retired rogue who smelled easy money.

"You intend to go to the Zmey's palace alone, don't you?" Kosara asked, pushing her wet hair off her face with her palm.

Blackbeard stopped a few steps away from her and watched her without replying.

"You think you can steal the witches' shadows," she continued. "But that can't happen."

"Why?"

"Because you don't know where the Zmey's hidden them."

"Where?"

"Well . . ." Suddenly, she remembered an old fairy tale her mum used to read to her. "He's hidden them in his triple-locked iron chest."

"What?"

Come on, Asen. He couldn't have slept through the commotion—he was too restless a sleeper. And no matter how much she'd hurt him, he wouldn't simply leave her in Blackbeard's hands. He couldn't.

"Oh, yes," Kosara said, "the Zmey's legendary iron chest."

"What chest?"

"Hidden inside a needle, which is in an egg, which is in a duck, which is in a hare . . ."

"What the fuck are you on about?"

Asen, come on!

"Which is in an iron chest, which is buried under a green oak tree, which is on the island of Buyan in the ocean."

Blackbeard's hand was so fast, it was almost invisible. He caught Kosara by the collar and pushed her backwards. The small of her back hit the railing, sending a wave of pain up her spine.

"Mad hag." Flecks of Blackbeard's warm spit landed on her face.

Kosara tried kicking him, but he'd learned his lesson. He evaded her and kept pushing. The upper half of her body hung over the water.

Her hands scratched at his face, leaving red marks on his grimy skin, until she couldn't feel them anymore. Her shadow sickness tickled her fingertips.

"Wait!" she shouted, but Blackbeard didn't let go. His eyes glinted beneath his hat's brim. His fingers dug into the soft underside of her arms. Kosara's ears hummed as more and more blood rushed to her head. "Oh my God, wait!"

She couldn't push him away. Her hands were completely swallowed by her shadow sickness. She couldn't make him let her go, either—he was too strong. Unless . . .

"Wait, you idiot!" she shouted again.

Blackbeard hesitated for a second, and she seized the opportunity. "You have to know how to make the shadows *yours*. You can't take them otherwise."

He must have felt some sincerity in her voice, since he loosened his grip. "How?"

"You need to say the magic words."

"And what are the magic words?"

"Go fuck yourself."

Kosara forcefully pushed her shadow sickness up her arms, towards where Blackbeard's fingers sank into her skin, leaving him grasping nothing but shadows.

While he turned around, confused, she slid away from him and kicked him in the shin. He staggered forwards, crashing into the railing. His hands searched for something to hold onto.

Blackbeard was a tall man, and the railing was low. He bent in half over the water. His eyes grew wider. His nails clawed at the railing, in vain.

There was a split second in which Kosara could grab him and drag him back on deck. His terrified eyes looked at her, pleading. His hands reached for her.

But then Kosara saw it: he wasn't trying to hold onto her so he'd stay on board. He wanted to drag her down with him.

She slammed her hands into his body. His feet lost all purchase. The last thing Kosara saw before he tumbled overboard were his eyes, wide with horror.

A splash sounded, followed by a throaty scream. "Get me out of here! Please get me out!" Another splash. "Man overboard, man over—"

In the sea below, the rusalkas shrieked. Then there was silence.

Kosara grasped the railing with both hands. Her head spun. Her eyes searched the dark water, her breath escaping in fast, choked gasps.

All that was left of Blackbeard was his wide-brimmed hat, floating on the waves. His bones would soon rise up, white with salt and picked clean.

Kosara wasn't sure how long she stood there, staring at the sea, waiting. She caught a movement out of the corner of her eye. Something red emerged from the thick fog surrounding the ship. Then, Asen put his hand on her shoulder.

"Kosara." He was trying to keep his tone neutral, she could tell, but his eyes were full of concern. "I heard you shouting. What's wrong? You look like you've seen a ghost."

Kosara turned back towards the waves. Where was Blackbeard? His bones should have surfaced already. She tried to chase away the image of the rusalkas holding him underwater, their talons tearing his flesh, their bubbling laughter echoing around him.

"Where's Blackbeard?" Asen asked.

Kosara nodded towards the hat floating in the waves. "He wanted his compass." Her voice was hoarse after all the screaming. "He fell." She thought about it. "I pushed him."

"It sounds like self-defence to me."

Kosara let out a throaty laugh. Where had she heard that one before?

Everywhere she went, she left a trail of ghosts behind her.

Asen considered her for a long moment, before his police training kicked in. He draped his coat over her shoulders. At first, she tried to push him away—she didn't deserve him being this nice after what she'd done—but then she changed her mind. The coat was soft and warm, and blessedly dry. It smelled like him. She wrapped herself tightly in it until her teeth stopped clicking.

"Come on." Asen gently led her down the stairwell. "We'll catch a cold if we stay out here."

Blackbeard was dead. They drifted through a sea full of monsters on an unmanned ship. And Asen was worried about colds!

"Come on." He kept his hand on her shoulder until they reached below deck. Kosara's feet left wet marks on the carpet.

"Do you know how to control the ship?" Asen asked.

Kosara blinked. "What?"

"Do you have any idea if we're going in the right direction? Since Blackbeard fell overboard . . ."

"You mean, since I threw him."

"Since he *fell*."

Kosara looked around. She had no idea where to even begin. Of course, she'd read plenty of romance novels taking place on pirate ships. She knew the wheel was something like a bicycle's handlebar, which could be used to change directions. The masts were the long poles on which the sails hung, and the hold was the place where the young captain often found himself shirtless while the heroine's loins burned.

Kosara fished the compass out of her bra, ignoring the way Asen quickly averted his eyes. She opened the lid. As far as she could tell, they still moved in the right direction.

"*Safina,*" she shouted, just as she'd heard Blackbeard do, "steady as she goes!"

Nothing changed.

"Will it work?" Asen asked.

"With a bit of luck."

Asen said nothing, but it was written on his face what he thought about their luck so far. They stood there for a long moment, the silence stretching between them.

"Listen, about earlier—" Kosara started.

Asen waved a hand. "I don't want to talk about it right now. We have enough problems as it is."

Kosara didn't dare hope, but she'd noticed that "we." "You mean you won't abandon me and go back to Chernograd?"

"What? No. A bit too late for that, don't you think?"

Kosara stifled her sigh of relief. But then, the doubts started to surface again. How come he still wanted to go to the palace? What exactly did he hope to find there?

Not now, she told herself sternly. She'd pushed him enough for one night. Now, all that was left for her to do was apologise. Easy. No problem. She could say she was sorry. She'd apologised before, surely, and she'd survived. She took a deep breath. "I just wanted to say—"

"Tomorrow," he said. "Go to bed, Kosara. You look like death."

She gave him a pointed look, her hair dripping salty water on the carpet.

"I mean, you look exhausted," he said. "Goodnight."

He turned around and left her there, soaking wet, shivering under his coat.

She walked back to her cabin and hid under the blankets. The nightmares lurked in the dark corners of her mind, ready to pounce as soon as she fell asleep. She was simply too tired to stay awake.

Blackbeard's face floated behind her shut eyelids, pale and swollen, seaweed rotting in his hair. "Where's my compass?" he shouted over and over again. "Where's my compass?"

He splashed among the waves, fighting to stay afloat, and around him, the sea spat out corpse after corpse: Irnik, Algara, Nevena in her blood-splattered nightgown . . .

Kosara woke up early the next morning, tangled in the sheets. Her face was wet with tears and cold sweat. She could still hear Blackbeard.

"Where's my compass? Where is it?"

One of the rusalkas must have stolen his voice. Kosara's skin crawled. She knew she couldn't listen to his raspy screams and stay sane for much longer.

Thankfully, Blackbeard's screams weren't the only thing she heard. The sound of waves crashing against the shore echoed in the distance. Through the open window, the breeze brought the smell of brine and seaweed, but there was something else, too. A smell which sent a shiver down Kosara's spine. Magic.

The Zmey's palace was close.

When Kosara emerged from her cabin in her mother's fiery-red gown, with her eyelids painted in flame-bright orange and her lips the red of smouldering coals, Asen was waiting for her. He leaned on the wall, watching the sea through a tiny circular window.

He wore one of her dad's old suits. It didn't fit him quite right, pulling at his shoulders. It was also about a decade behind the current trends—its lapels too wide, its buttons too large—but Kosara had the feeling monsters weren't keeping up with the cutting edge of fashion, anyway.

He heard her approaching and turned around to face her. His eyes widened in surprise. She could swear she heard him inhale sharply. It was a bit of an overreaction to an old gown and some makeup, but it still felt good. She supposed he'd never seen her dressed up before: the last few days, she'd barely had the time to brush her hair.

She smiled at him. He didn't smile back.

The smile fell from her face. She opened her mouth to say something, but he raised his hand.

"Don't," he said. "Please don't apologise. Give me a bit of space."

Kosara shut her mouth. With a sigh, she climbed to the helm. She still had to try to control the damned ship.

They approached the island from the opposite side of the Zmey's palace, so he wouldn't spot them docking. It took Kosara a while to convince the ship to change direction, probably because she didn't know the right sailing lingo.

It took her just as long to figure out how to actually dock. In the end, the ship did it for her. The anchor tumbled overboard, as if pushed by a pair of invisible hands. The ship gently glided to the beach.

The palace was just visible far in the distance, floating in and out of sight atop its rocky outcrop, thick fog curling up its towers. Since they'd docked so far away, it would take them most of the day to reach it.

Kosara felt absolutely ridiculous traipsing through the dusty rocks in a gown. She was glad she'd decided not to bother with heels, though she had to admit her dirty boots somewhat ruined the ensemble. If her makeup hadn't been enchanted by the best herbalist in all of Chernograd, it would have melted down her face hours ago.

Asen walked a few steps ahead of her without turning back, never uttering a word. She tried to keep up with him, but the slope grew steeper. She searched for tufts of grass to hold on to. Asen ran forwards like a mountain goat.

Kosara wasn't entirely sure what he expected her to do at this point. Now, in the light of the day, the whole thing seemed so silly. What was all the drama about, anyway? A kiss. Big deal!

People kissed for all sorts of reasons, including to wring information out of someone. When she was little, Kosara used to kiss the boys on the playground in exchange for sweets. She hadn't even considered she was doing something immoral, until her mum caught her with pockets full of honey and walnut biscuits and screamed at her for being an "underage lady of the night."

It wasn't a big deal, she told herself forcefully, though there was an undeniable gnawing at the pit of her stomach. If she stopped to examine it, she suspected it would feel a lot like guilt.

Which was why she was determined not to examine it.

Because deep down, she knew that if she took a moment to unravel her feelings, she'd find two things: one, she'd crossed a line, and a witch could never admit that. Two, the reason she felt so terrible about it was because she'd grown to care about Asen, and Kosara could never admit *that*.

The sun had started to set when they reached a wall of white marble and an arch overgrown with ivy. Asen hesitated, finally casting a glance back at Kosara.

"The Gardens of the Zmey," she said. She'd heard rumours about them—about how smelling the flowers could poison you, and how the trees were alive, their leaves sharp as daggers. "Be careful."

Asen nodded gravely and bent to walk under the arch. Kosara followed him.

She couldn't help but gasp. The rocks behind them were bare, except for where the occasional wind-gnarled tree had sunk its roots in the dust collected between the cracks. Here, large oaks rose, their leaves gleaming gold and ringing like bells. Blades of grass bent in the wind like thin strands of real metal. Wildflowers peeked out among them, their scent making Kosara's head spin. The air was heavy with magic.

Kosara felt a prickling at the back of her neck. She looked up at the palace looming far above, half-expecting to see a dark silhouette in a window, or the glint of binoculars on the balcony. No one was there.

Nevertheless, she couldn't shake the feeling that someone was watching her.

They'd reached deep into the garden when a whooshing sounded above their heads. The crowns of the trees almost touched, like old gossips leaning to whisper in each other's ears, and in the thin line of sky between them, something flashed and then disappeared. The branches shook. A couple of leaves fell heavy at Kosara's feet.

"Wait," she said. Asen raised his eyebrows but asked nothing.

Kosara held onto a low-hanging branch and pulled herself up through the thick crown of leaves. The wood beneath her fingers was smooth and cold, more metal than bark.

She reached the top and popped her head out. The evening air was cool on her face, and the smell of flowers grew less suffocating. Hundreds of lights dashed across the sky. They all came from Chernograd and flew towards the palace, the thin threads of moon yarns extending behind them.

Kosara ducked inside the tree's canopy so one of the lights wouldn't crash into her. It turned out to be a lantern, hanging from the handle of a flying broom. Three old women rode it, their skirts fluttering in the wind and revealing their striped socks. Golden leaves glinted in their messy hair. Their giggles echoed in the distance.

Kosara followed them with her eyes until they disappeared into the palace gate.

"What was that?" Asen finally broke his silence.

"A flying broom," Kosara replied.

"Sorry, what?"

"A broom that flies."

The lanterns kept whizzing past. From time to time, Kosara could make out what they were attached to: more flying brooms than she could count, but also flying rugs, pots and pans, chairs, stools, and sofas, and in one case, a four-poster bed with its curtain stretched like a sail.

"What's happening?" Asen called out again.

"I think the guests have started to arrive for the Zmey's feast."

Kosara squinted, searching the night for familiar faces, until she found her household spirits. The bathroom spirit sat in her granny's old cast-iron bathtub. The kitchen spirit flew in an enormous copper cauldron for brewing rakia. The fireplace spirit rode upon a poker, his purple tie flapping in the wind.

Kosara waved at them. The kitchen spirit spotted her first, and her eyes grew larger. She looked an awful lot like Kosara's mum when she'd caught teenaged Kosara smoking in the toilet. The spirit opened her mouth, but before she'd managed to say anything else, the cauldron carried her away.

Kosara started to climb down. "It looks like we got here right on time," she shouted. "I mean, we wouldn't want to be late for the Zmey's f—"

A loud crack. The branch she stood on snapped beneath her. Her feet lost purchase. Instinctively, she grasped the branch above it while the broken one tumbled to the ground.

She swore loudly. Her arms strained to support her full weight. Her muscles burned.

"Let go," Asen appeared underneath her, his arms outstretched. "I'll catch you."

Kosara hesitated. Just how upset was he with her? Enough to let her crash onto the ground and break her neck?

"Let go!" he said again.

It wasn't as if she had a choice. She tried to pull herself up to the next branch, but her lower body was too heavy. She was left hanging there like an overripe fruit. The shadow sickness tickled her fingers.

She took a deep breath and, a second before her fingers turned to shadow, she let go. Asen caught her before she hit the ground.

"Thanks," she said breathlessly. For a second, they stared at each other, his arms still wrapped around her, her hand on his shoulder.

Then he quickly put her down and stepped away from her. "I couldn't let you break your leg now, could I?" He obviously tried to sound facetious, but it came out forced.

"No, that would have been unfortunate." Kosara straightened her dress.

There was a long, awkward pause. The only sound was the chiming of the grass at their feet.

"Listen, about yesterday . . ." she began, not entirely sure how she'd continue. Was she going to confess about the truth serum?

No, that would be a bad idea. He'd overreact, just like he overreacted about the kiss.

She didn't have to say anything else, because he was quick to interrupt her. "Let's not talk about it. It was obviously a momentary lapse of judgement. On both our parts."

Kosara let out an internal sigh of relief. That worked for her. It was a good thing he wanted to talk about his feelings just as much as she did.

They continued making their way through the gardens in silence, but it was a less tense silence than before. Asen didn't rush ahead of her. They walked shoulder to shoulder. It was nice, Kosara had to admit, to have him act somewhat normal again, even if she knew he was still upset.

She kicked the grass as she walked, making the strands chime. The closer she got to the palace, the louder the Zmey's voice in her head grew. From time to time, she heard him so clearly, she had to look over her shoulder to make sure he wasn't standing there.

Crawling back to me, little Kosara? You knew you could never truly leave.

It was as if returning to the palace sent her back in time. Back seven years ago, to when the Zmey had first brought her here. Back to when she'd been stupid enough to let him.

She caught Asen casting worried glances at her and forced a smile. *Stupid witch,* the Zmey kept repeating in her head. *Weak witch. Useless witch.*

The Zmey's palace perched on the rocks, vulture-like. Its domes glistened golden, green, and purple, as if covered in scales. The windows gleamed, unblinking, and the gate gaped open like a hungry mouth. Kosara's skin crawled, pierced by hundreds of tiny needles.

She was back. Seven years later. Even more powerless than the last time. She was either very brave, or very foolish.

Oh, who was she kidding? Very foolish. Definitely very foolish.

The feast's din echoed between the trees—the yudas' shouts, the rusalkas' shrieks, the laughter of the samodivas, and howls.

"Dogs?" Asen asked, hopeful.

Kosara shook her head. "Wolves."

Along the staircase leading to the palace door, two rows of varkolaks waited. Silver cuffs gleamed around their ankles, and thin silver chains tied them to the railing.

Kosara held Asen by the crook of his elbow. His muscles tightened for a moment under her touch, before relaxing. They walked forwards confidently: two household spirits, here to pay tribute to their Tsar.

As soon as they stepped on the staircase, the varkolaks on both sides stood up, pulling on their chains and making them clatter. Under Kosara's hand, Asen's arm twitched. He must have been itching to draw his revolver.

The varkolaks growled and bared their teeth. A whiff of wet fur and bad breath hit Kosara. The image of Nevena's face on the night of her death kept trying to float to the front of Kosara's mind—she kept pushing it away.

She looked over her shoulder, back towards the garden, where the moon yarn gleamed in the darkness. If things went wrong, there would be no point in running. The wolves were faster.

One approached Kosara and sniffed her, touching her ankle with his damp nose. His growls subsided. Then, one by one, the varkolaks relaxed. Some of them curled up on the floor, like sleepy dogs.

Kosara finally exhaled. As she climbed the stairs, the wolves greeted her, wagging their tails. One licked the back of her hand with his rough tongue. They couldn't smell the difference between a witch and a household spirit. *Thank God.*

Kosara could see, however, that she and Asen had another obstacle to overcome, and this one didn't have an IQ smaller than his shoe size. In front of the gate, at the top of the stairs, stood an ancient upir. He wasn't like the upirs from the graveyard, with minds clouded by bloodthirst and bodies weak with malnutrition. This one had recently fed: his bloated belly strained the buttons of his shirt. His hair fell down his shoulders, delicate as cobweb.

When he noticed Kosara and Asen, he extended his hand. His elbow creaked like an old hinge. "Your invitation?"

Kosara handed him the silver disc.

"Hmm." He looked Kosara up and down, and then down and up. She tried hard not to shrink under his gaze. "You aren't a samodiva. What are you?"

Damn it.

"Me?" Kosara let out a laugh. It sounded terribly fake. "Of course not! Little old me—a samodiva? Ha-ha. Ha. I'm but a simple household spirit."

"This is an invitation for a samodiva."

"Is it? I never bother reading these things anymore. Oh well, there must have been some sort of mix-up. You'd better let the big boss know. Now, if you'll excuse me . . ."

Kosara tried to squeeze past the upir, but he stood his ground. He exhaled loudly through his nostrils. "What kind of spirits are you, anyway?"

"Household," Kosara said.

"Specifically?"

"I am the fireplace spirit from Seventeen Kokiche Street. And he is . . ." She gave Asen a pleading look.

"The spirit of the police station," he said.

Kosara blinked. What had she told him? *Pick a place that feels like home.* Oh dear.

"Hmm." The upir looked unconvinced. "You stink."

Kosara followed his gaze to her bag. *The garlic!*

"What is it?" the upir asked, his nose wrinkled.

She gave him a tense smile. "I've got a new perfume."

"It smells awful."

"You know how it is, it all depends on your body chemistry. For example, I love the smell of jasmine flowers, but on me, they stink of cat piss."

"Hmm."

The varkolaks on both sides of the stairs grew restless again. Their growls rose like a wave.

Asen leaned his hand on his revolver's handle. Kosara reached inside her bag and grabbed the aspen stake. How long would the two of them last against all these monsters? Not very long, no matter how good a shot Asen was.

At least Kosara could make sure that when she died, she took this ancient abomination with her. She gripped the stake in her fist.

"Aaa—" A scream sounded. Something whizzed past Kosara, making her stagger.

"—aaa—" There was a loud bang. The cauldron for brewing rakia crashed to the ground. It zoomed forwards, screeching against the stones, sparks flying behind it. The upir's eyes grew wider.

"—aaa—" The cauldron finally came to a halt. Two legs clad in colourful stockings stuck out of it and kicked in the air.

"—aah!" the kitchen spirit concluded. "Will no one help an old lady up?"

The varkolaks rose on their hind legs and growled, but they didn't attack. Their eyes searched for their master. He was nowhere to be seen. Only the pointy toes of his shoes peeked out from under the cauldron.

Kosara rushed to help the kitchen spirit. The spirit fixed her puffy hair, adjusted her numerous underskirts, and finally, she looked down at the upir.

"Oh, deary me! I'm so sorry!"

"Mfffhhh," said the upir from under the cauldron.

"I tested the brakes before I left, I swear." She slammed her fist against the cauldron. "But they stopped working just as I started to descend. They don't make them like they used to, am I right?"

"Mfffhhhhh!"

"Look, don't worry, these strong young lads and lassies here"—she waved towards the varkolaks—"will help me move it, alright?"

The varkolaks looked around, as if they weren't quite sure who she was talking to. One of them whined helplessly.

"Come on!" the kitchen spirit shouted. "A few of you go over on the other side and push, and the rest of us here will pull . . ."

The spirit threw a quick glance at Kosara, the question clear in her eyes: *What are you two still doing here?*

"Thank you," Kosara shaped with her lips. It had been an enormous risk for the kitchen spirit to help her like that, and she suspected no amount of sour cabbage and pickled green tomatoes would ever repay her debt. She grabbed Asen by the arm, and they slipped through the palace gates.

20

Day Nine

Outside, in the dark, the palace had looked stark white, like marble. Kosara knew that was an illusion. It was built of melted bone. Columns of skulls supported arches of ribs, fingers intertwined on the walls, and rows of teeth framed the windows. Some of the bones had belonged to monsters, and here and there, crooked horns and spikes jutted out. Varkolak incisors and upir fangs decorated the ceiling. The chandeliers were delicate yuda wings, covered in dripping wax.

Yet others were human, and they made Kosara's stomach turn. From the pillar opposite her, the empty eye sockets of a skull stared back at her. It looked so ordinary in between the elongated, deformed heads of the monsters.

Kosara could easily imagine her own skeleton becoming a part of the furniture if she wasn't careful tonight. She had a small gap between her front teeth, so they'd probably be hidden in a corner. Her hip bones would nicely fill a hole somewhere. Her skull would fit perfectly in the centre of the archway above the entrance, to silently warn all visitors: never cheat the Zmey at cards, especially if you intend to sneak into his palace afterwards.

Her fingertips twitched. She watched as the shadow sickness swallowed them, crawling up her arms, reaching for her neck. Her breathing grew faster.

Kosara shut her eyes and forced herself to inhale and exhale slowly. There was no time for this. She could panic later on, when she'd got her shadow back, and they'd escaped the palace.

"Are you okay?" Asen asked.

Kosara nodded. "Let's get this over with."

The macabre décor obviously didn't faze the guests. The spirits spun in a wild dance: their feet slammed against the floor and their hands clapped in rhythm. Some of them led karakonjuls on long leashes, occasionally losing control of the beasts and letting them climb all over the piles of food on the tables. Here and there, upirs slowly swayed and moaned. A few varkolaks joined the dancing, as far as their chains allowed them.

Kosara couldn't shake the feeling of déjà vu. She almost expected to spot her younger self running through the crowd, and the Zmey chasing her, both of them giggling.

She clearly remembered the dress she'd worn that night seven years ago. The Zmey had given it to her. It was bright pink and frilly, and absolutely not her. The running around was also not her. The giggling? Not her in the slightest.

You're nothing without me, the Zmey hissed in her mind.

Perhaps, but I was never myself with you.

She'd only spent a night at the Zmey's palace back then, but it had felt as if it had lasted months. She'd drunk nothing but moon wine and eaten nothing but the fruits the Zmey had given her, until she could barely remember her friends or family. She could barely remember herself.

She knew now she shouldn't touch any of the overflowing platters scattered around the bone halls. Every time a monster tried to hand her a glass of moon wine, she shook her head and pushed it away.

She and Asen walked from one hall to the next, their soles clicking against the calcified floor. High above them, the chandeliers clattered. Music echoed between the columns, its source impossible to trace.

Each hall was larger than the last: more monsters caught up in the dance, more tables covered in glistening goblets of moon wine, and fruits so large and plump they looked as if they were made of wax. The ceiling was so tall, it disappeared in the darkness high above. The music got louder.

Kosara walked faster and faster, her breath catching in her throat.

How long had they been here for? Somehow, it simultaneously felt like five minutes and five years. Or fifty. Kosara looked down at her hands, half-expecting to find them wrinkly and frail.

They weren't. They were still her hands, switching between flesh and shadow.

"We're walking in circles," Asen said finally.

Kosara leaned her back against a column, trying to catch her breath. "Impossible. I know the palace."

"We've been in this hall before. I'm certain we have."

"Impo—" Kosara began, but then she spotted the human skull at the centre of the arch, right above the entrance. They'd gone full circle.

She let herself slide down to the floor, holding her head between her hands. "We've been here for ages!"

Around her, the bright lights of the feast spun in a blur. The music grew even louder, the beat pulsating in time with her heart.

Her mouth was so dry, her tongue felt like sandpaper. If only she could reach and grab a glass of wine from the table—

Asen pushed her hand away. "Here." He handed her a bottle of water from his bag.

Kosara drank, letting the icy liquid run down her chin. Then, she poured some on her palms and used it to wash her face, pressing the balls of her thumbs onto her eyes. The colourful spots that danced in front of her vision looked just like the feast's bright lights.

But her dizziness started to subside. Her head stopped spinning.

Kosara opened her eyes. Then, she fished for Blackbeard's compass in her bag. "I think I'm ready to try again. You?"

Asen nodded. This time, Kosara let the compass guide them further and further North, deep into the Zmey's palace. The air grew hotter. The stench of the Zmey's magic made Kosara's heart race.

They walked under a tall arch and entered an unfamiliar hall. A band played on a low stage in one corner: three terrified guitarists, one scared flautist, a petrified bagpiper, and a nervous drummer. Humans. Kosara couldn't begin to guess how much the Zmey had paid them to play at this particular feast.

"Why did we have to pretend to be spirits?" Asen whispered in Kosara's ear. "If there are people here."

"I can guarantee you that everyone knows these people. The Zmey must have warned his subjects that if any harm comes to the band, they'll have to answer to him. Until the feast is over, at least."

The song ended, and applause filled the hall. The bagpiper timidly waved at the crowd. The elderly spirit standing next to Kosara leaned on her shoulder.

"A great tune, huh?" he gasped out.

Finally, the applause faded until only the slow clapping of a single pair of hands remained.

"Bravo!" said a voice that sent a chill up Kosara's spine. "Bravo!"

She looked up. High above her, on a platform of skulls just below the tooth ceiling, the Zmey sat on his throne of bone. Even from afar, she saw his wide grin. A young woman in a white dress sat in his lap. Her face was hidden behind a veil. Kosara shivered, waves of disgust and terror and anger washing over her.

Had she looked this young herself? Most likely. She'd only been sixteen. She'd been a child.

Murderer, whispered a voice in her head. For a change, it was her own.

On another platform, this one slightly lower, lounged the Zmey's favourite subjects. Two samodivas had answered his invitation, after all, undoubtedly without telling the rest of their sisters. A few yudas pecked at a plate of fruit, fighting over the ripest berries. An elderly rusalka soaked in a small hot tub, her scaly body hidden under the water and her white hair floating just above the surface.

Kosara's heart climbed to her throat when her eyes fell on the last member of the Zmey's company. She sat next to one of the yudas, her arm wrapped around the yuda's waist, her mouth pressed to the monster's ear. Her hair was gathered in two thick braids—the golden thread she'd tied them with glistened as the yuda grabbed them and pulled her in for a kiss.

Roksana.

Kosara's throat closed up on itself. She realised with surprise that, right until this moment, there had been some small part of her that hoped she'd got it all wrong. That Roksana's involvement with the

Zmey wasn't as deep as it seemed. Perhaps she'd needed to see it with her own eyes to fully believe the extent of the betrayal.

Roksana didn't even have the decency to look guilty. On the contrary, she seemed to be having fun.

Kosara touched Asen's arm and pointed upwards.

"Is that her?" Asen asked.

"It is."

Kosara took a deep breath to calm her heartbeat. Roksana was so close. And if she was close, so was Kosara's shadow.

"We need to get up there," Kosara said.

"Are you sure this is a good idea? The Zmey might spot us. We can wait until the feast ends and corner Roksana on the way out."

"I can't wait if I want to get my shadow back."

Kosara couldn't see if Roksana still wore the witches' shadows around her neck, or if she'd sold them to the Zmey already. Chances were, the Zmey had left the negotiations for after the party was over, and the monster hunter was too drunk on moon wine to bargain.

Kosara had expected Asen to argue—to tell her that he was here to catch a murderer, and her shadow wasn't his problem.

"How will we get there?" he asked instead.

Kosara smiled at him, despite the guilt coiling in her stomach. This was the man she'd suspected of trying to trick her just last night. Yet here he was, ready to risk getting captured because of her shadow. It turned out her mistrust in people was just as badly judged as her trust.

She looked up, shielding her eyes from the bright light of the chandeliers. As far as she could tell, the only way to reach the platform was to fly. "We'll have to find someone to give us a lift."

"What about your household spirits? I'm sure we can all fit in that massive cauldron."

"I can't ask them to do this. Household spirits are strictly forbidden from getting close to their humans. The kitchen spirit took a huge risk getting us in here. Besides"—she pointed up towards the platform—"do you see any household spirits up there? It seems obvious: this celebration down here is for the low-class, native monsters. The one up there is for the monsters the Zmey brings with him."

"All right," Asen said. "Let's assume we can find one of the Zmey's entourage to give us a lift. What will we do exactly? Snatch Roksana mid-flight and sweep her away into the night, right under the Zmey's nose?"

"Perhaps. The Zmey seems distracted."

He and the girl in his lap were locked in heated conversation. She gestured wildly, and he threw his head back and laughed. Then, he reached over, lifted her veil, and kissed her deeply. She didn't pull away from him; on the contrary, she pressed herself harder against his chest. Acid burned in the back of Kosara's throat.

"What's this feast for, exactly?" Asen asked, suspicion in his voice.

Kosara struggled to keep her tone neutral. "It's for the Zmey's wedding."

"You told me it takes place every year."

"It does."

He paused. "This girl is human."

"Yes."

"Did he kidnap her?"

"No, they go to him voluntarily."

Asen paused again. "Why?"

Kosara scratched the scar on her cheek. Excellent question. One she'd been asking herself for years. "He's very charming."

"But he murders them every year!"

"Technically, it's not him who murders them. Listen, you know how karakonjuls eat human flesh, upirs drink blood, and yudas feed on carrion? The Zmey consumes love. Every year he comes to Chernograd to hunt, and he catches himself a new bride."

"How?"

"Well, look at him—powerful, intelligent, handsome . . ."

Asen looked up again, clearly unimpressed. "His teeth aren't great."

"Come on, imagine you're a young girl and the Tsar of Monsters himself is paying attention to you. He treats you nice—only you, no one else—and it makes you feel special. Wouldn't you fall for him?"

"But they know his past partners are all dead."

"Some of them know, but they think they'll be different. That this is true love, not like the others. That it will conquer all. That maybe they can fix him." It felt dishonest to be speaking in third person, rather than first. That was what she'd thought, too. It was easy now with the distance of time and the knowledge of what had happened after, to imagine she'd been smarter than that. She hadn't.

He'd tricked her. She'd let him trick her. He'd told her what she wanted to hear—praising her mind and her powers, swearing his never-ending love. He'd pretended she was different. He'd pretended *he* was different when he was with her. *Only you can change me, Kosara. . . .*

She had no doubt he'd said the exact same words to that poor girl in his lap. And the one before. And the one before. . . .

The humiliation twisted in her stomach.

"And then he eats them?" Asen asked.

"No, I told you. He eats their love. In the beginning, they act like the typical happy newlyweds. He's nice, gentle, thoughtful. The girls write to their parents occasionally; they even go out to see friends. Then, little by little, he devours their love of their family and friends, and then everything else, everything that brings them joy, until he's the only thing left. And then he takes that away, too. First, they stop going out, then they stop getting out of bed, and then they stop eating. At the end, they stop breathing."

Asen swore quietly. An actual swear word. Kosara wasn't used to such strong language coming from him. His hand inched danger-ously close to his revolver.

"You aren't going to do anything reckless, are you?" she asked.

Please don't try to arrest the Tsar of Monsters!

"We have to help her escape," Asen said.

"We can't." Kosara was trying to convince herself as well as him. They couldn't help the girl. She'd got herself into this mess. "I told you. No one is forcing her to be here. She wants it. Do you suggest we kidnap her?"

"For God's sake, yes! She can't be older than eighteen, Kosara!"

Kosara looked up at the girl again. He was right. She was a child.

But it didn't matter. The girl wouldn't want her help. Kosara knew because she had been that girl.

Are you afraid, little Kosara? the Zmey's voice whispered in her head. He sounded so real, she had to check to make sure he was still on his platform.

"We can't just leave her here," Asen said. "We need to bring her back to her family."

Are you just going to leave her here because you're too scared to make me angry?

"Her parents must be worried sick, Kosara," Asen said.

"All right!" Kosara shouted over both of them. "Fine. Once I get my shadow back, we'll figure it out. I'll try talking to her. We can bring her to her parents, but don't blame me if she makes her way back here. Now, could we concentrate on the problem at hand, *please*?"

Asen looked up at the Zmey again and wrinkled his nose, as if he'd smelled something rotten. "How come you know so much about him?"

Kosara took another deep breath. There was no avoiding the question. She had to tell him, sooner or later. She waved a hand, completely casual. "Oh, we used to date."

Saying it out loud made her stomach turn. They hadn't *dated*. He'd tricked her, played her, taken advantage of her. There had been nothing mutual about it. There had never been "we," only him.

"I'm sorry, you what?" Asen said.

"I was exactly his type when I was sixteen. Young and stupid."

Asen looked at her as if she'd just uncovered the source of the rotten smell, and had presented it to him, proclaiming it a great delicacy. "What happened?"

"My mum forbade me from seeing him."

"And you listened to her?"

"Of course not. Not at first, anyway. But then the Zmey started letting his mask slip. At the start, he'd been the perfect fiancé. He pretended he was human. But soon, I began catching glimpses of the monster beneath. I realised I had to walk on eggshells around him or else risk his anger. He was sweet as honey when I obeyed him, but when I dared to speak my mind . . ." She shook her head. "And then after he'd hurt me, he'd apologise, and shower me with affection. It was a constant, exhausting cycle, until finally, I realised I needed to get out or he might kill me. Trouble was, by that time, I was trapped here in the palace. With him."

"But you managed to run away in the end?"

"Only because Vila found me. My mum got desperate and went to her for help. Vila showed up and snuck me out."

"Thank God," Asen muttered.

Kosara avoided meeting his eyes, too scared to see the pity in them. Instead, she watched the monsters dancing around her, occasionally pushing against her with their bodies. "Thank God. He didn't like it, though. He's never forgiven me."

"What, did he expect you to wait around to die?"

"I suppose. He's the Tsar of Monsters. He's not used to being denied." She finally looked at Asen and saw no pity. Instead, there was something that seemed a lot like anger. *Please,* please *don't try to arrest the Tsar of Monsters!*

She cleared her throat. "We'd better find someone to give us a lift."

They were surrounded by monsters, but none of them appeared as if they belonged on the Zmey's platform. A few kitchen spirits held hands and spun in a circle, kicking up clouds of flour. A fireplace spirit stomped, flames bursting beneath his feet. A bathroom spirit grabbed a water spirit of some sort—of a river or a lake—and the two of them drifted through the hall, leaving puddles behind them.

The drummer finished a particularly complex solo, then stumbled and fell on the stage. Kosara automatically took a step towards him before she remembered: she was a household spirit. She didn't care about mere humans. The other guests didn't even look at the exhausted musician. The flautist kneeled next to him and helped him to a drink of water.

In the silence, Kosara heard two familiar words. "All in."

She followed the voice and saw three of the yudas from the platform, sitting on one of the bone benches and playing cards with a moustached fireplace spirit. The spirit swore loudly, threw a handful of tokens in the face of the tallest yuda, and marched away.

They must have come down for a game of Kral. And Asen claimed Kosara never had good luck.

"Look," she whispered.

Asen followed her eyes. "Are you sure this is a good idea? I thought you got into this whole mess because of a game of Kral."

"I got into this mess because I trusted people I shouldn't have."

"But maybe if you just stop for a second and think, instead of throwing yourself into danger—"

"I'm not throwing myself into danger. In fact, I was considering throwing you into danger."

Asen's mouth hung open for a second, before a sound came out. "What?"

"Well, I've seen you dance. You're pretty good."

"I'm excellent."

"So, I was planning on betting you. I'll tell them that if I lose, they can have a dance with you."

Asen considered this, his dark brows furrowed. "How come the only time you ever have a plan, I'm the sacrificial lamb?"

Kosara smiled brightly. "What do you say?"

Asen looked up at the platform where Roksana was downing a glass of moon wine the size of a salad bowl. "Fine."

"Really? I expected to have to convince you."

"I don't want her getting away again. Do what you must."

Kosara turned away from him so he wouldn't see her rolling her eyes. *Do what you must?* She'd asked him to dance with a yuda—not to marry one.

"Girls!" Kosara shouted when she got near them. "How about a game?"

The yudas turned their gleaming gazes towards Kosara. Their faces were pale and distractingly human, surrounded by a crown of waxy feathers. Their wings were folded around them, shifting from black to purple to dark blue and glistening as if slathered in oil. They loomed over Kosara as they perched in their seats, their taloned feet grasping the bone bench.

"Maybe," one of them said. Her voice was loud and hoarse, like a hawk's scream. "Depends on what we're going to play for."

"If I win, you'll take us up to that platform over there, so we can capture a dangerous criminal."

"Who?"

"You know Roksana?"

One of the yudas shoved the other with her wing. "Some of us know her better than others, right, Sokol?"

"We're just talking," said Sokol, without even looking at her friend. Her bright, yellow eyes were focused on Kosara. "What if you lose?"

"If you win," Kosara said, "you'll get a dance with my date."

Asen harrumphed behind her back. He was leaning on one of the columns with his arms crossed, looking like a martyr.

"He's an excellent dancer," she added.

One of the yudas opened her beak and produced a loud, throaty sound. It took Kosara a second to realise she was laughing. "I'm sure Sokol will like that."

"Shut up, Orel," Sokol mumbled.

The yudas made room for Kosara to sit between them on the bench. Their smell enveloped her: of pine needles and ozone, as if they'd just flown through a rain cloud.

"Well, girls, who's going to deal?" she asked.

They played a variant of Kral that Kosara wasn't familiar with, but she quickly figured it out—or at least, she hoped she did. Orel dealt her two cards and began placing cards face up on the table. Kosara was fairly certain she had to make up her hand from a combination of all available cards.

She raised the bet a few times before she lost. Just like she'd planned. Let them think they'd beat her easily.

Orel dealt again. This time Kosara bet high, despite having a bad hand. The yudas didn't call her bluff. One-one.

"So, Sokol," Kosara said, while Orel shuffled. "How long have you known Roksana?"

"Since last year," Sokol said. "We're just talking!"

"I wasn't suggesting anything else."

"What has she done?" the third yuda said—the one whose name Kosara didn't know.

"She's murdered someone." Kosara quickly remembered herself and added, "One of my spirit friends. She's a monster hunter."

"I knew it." Orel spat the words out. "I knew she couldn't be trusted. The Zmey acts as if she pisses gold, your Roksana—"

"She's not mine!" Sokol shrieked, her talons gripping her seat tighter. "And she only hunts dangerous monsters. Your friend must have been a wraith."

"He wasn't."

Sokol shrugged. "Who cares about spirits, anyway? You're nothing but humans without any of the tasty parts. No offense."

No offence? How come people always added that right after saying something deeply offensive?

"In any case," Sokol continued, "your friend must have been asking for it."

Sokol really liked Roksana, Kosara realised. Not enough that she'd do something to protect her, but enough to flirt with her in front of the other monsters and suffer their jokes. How could you justify falling for someone you wanted to eat?

Kosara barely managed to stop her nose from wrinkling.

"How about we use my deck for the third round?" Sokol pulled a new deck of cards from underneath her wing. "It's my lucky deck," she said in reply to Kosara's raised eyebrows.

"As long as it's not been doctored. . . ."

Orel's laugh was so high-pitched, Kosara felt it scraping her bones. "It's not. Don't worry, we wouldn't let her cheat."

Kosara smiled tensely. Behind Sokol's back, Asen gave her a worried look, and she shrugged her shoulders slightly in response. She didn't like this, not at all, but there was nothing she could do. She couldn't risk angering the yudas and having them give up on the game altogether. If only she'd kept her mouth shut about Roksana. . . .

First, Orel placed a few cards face up on the table. At the beginning, they all seemed familiar—a five, a six, an ace . . . And then came the last card.

What the hell?

The picture in the middle of this card showed a monster Kosara had never seen before: three-headed, sharp-toothed, curved-horned. Steam rolled out from its large nostrils. Lightning flashed above its head.

Kosara hadn't seen it, but she'd heard of it. *Lamia.* The monster the Council had kidnapped from the Zmey's palace. The one they'd embedded in the Wall.

"What the hell's that?" Kosara blurted out before she thought better of it.

"This?" Orel tapped the card with her long talon. "It's a queen of hearts, of course."

"No, I mean, what's that monster?"

"Oh, you mean *who's* that?"

Good job, Kosara. I'm sure the yudas appreciate a bit of casual speciesism.

"Yes, of course that's what I mean," Kosara said. "Who's that?"

"She's the Zmey's sister, Lamia. She's been gone for a while now. Disappeared without a trace. We've never managed to figure out how, since she'd been explicitly forbidden to leave the palace during the Foul Days, what with her anger issues—"

Kosara couldn't hear the rest of the sentence through the sound of blood thumping in her ears. The Zmey's sister. The monster trapped in the Wall was *the Zmey's sister.* How come he'd never mentioned her before, not even once?

"Were they close?" Kosara asked.

Sokol barely lifted her gaze from her cards. "Mm?"

"The Zmey and his sister."

"Oh, they bickered like any siblings, but I think he truly loved her. He's not been the same ever since she disappeared."

So that was why he'd never mentioned her. He was still grieving.

Could the Zmey grieve? It felt surreal, knowing he had been capable of actually loving someone at some point in the past. Perhaps, if Kosara had met him before all this had happened, things would have been different. . . .

She shook her head. She was falling into that old, familiar trap again, making excuses for him. *Oh, he's not truly evil, he's just misunderstood.* It was a slippery slope. You showed the Zmey even the slightest bit of empathy, and he took your whole hand.

Kosara forced herself to return to the game. She kept her face neutral as Sokol handed her two cards. The first was an upir crawling out of his grave, blood dripping out of his gaping mouth. The second depicted a winged monster covered in golden scales, breathing fire. The Zmey. He had to be a king. And if Kosara knew the Zmey as well as she thought she did, he was the king of hearts.

She suppressed a smirk. A king of hearts in her hand and a queen of hearts on the table. Her chances weren't looking bad, not at all. She raised the bet.

The nameless yuda folded and revealed her cards. She held two monsters, too: a varkolak howling at the moon, and a trio of rusalkas covered in seaweed. Only the yuda's frustrated face indicated her hand wasn't strong enough.

Kosara and Sokol kept betting until the showdown. The yuda's face was unreadable. Her feathery eyebrows were furrowed just like they'd been throughout the game. The corners of her mouth occasionally twitched, but whether she suppressed a frown or a smile, Kosara couldn't tell.

Finally, they placed their last bets. Sokol let the smile spread across her face. She didn't make to show her hand, waiting for Kosara to reveal hers first.

Kosara turned her cards around. Orel sucked in a breath through her teeth. That had to be a good sign.

Except, Sokol's smile didn't falter. The yuda slowly revealed her cards: first a six of clubs, and then a monster card. It showed a yuda, her wings raised high, framing the full moon.

"I win," Sokol said.

It took Kosara a few seconds to make sense of the yuda's words. She'd lost. She held two great cards, judging by Orel's reaction, and she'd lost against a six and a yuda.

"How come?" Kosara asked.

"Yudas beat all other cards," Sokol said, as if she was talking to a child.

"That doesn't sound very fair."

Sokol shrugged. A surprisingly human gesture if you ignored the way her feathers rustled. "When you play with yudas, you play by their rules."

Kosara couldn't believe it. She'd lost. "Three games out of five?"

Sokol laughed her high-pitched laugh. Then, she jumped from her seat and extended a hand towards Asen. He didn't try to protest. He didn't even let the disappointment show on his face. A true gentleman.

Kosara wanted to warn him—be careful, don't get too close to her, make sure she doesn't smell your fear—but before she could do anything, the two of them disappeared in the crowd.

Kosara was left standing among the monsters, biting her lips, trying to come up with a new idea. The varkolaks were getting tired: some of them had fallen asleep standing, with their tails between their legs. The upirs swayed about, their movements slower and slower. Most of the spirits sat on the floor, drinking honey mead, smoking herbs, and telling stories.

Occasionally, Kosara spotted Asen and the yuda in the crowd. The dance floor slowly emptied around them, as more and more monsters stopped to watch. The spirits stood up, circling the couple, and clapping in tune with the music. He really was a good dancer.

Too good, perhaps. The more attention he drew to himself, the more likely it was they'd get discovered. Kosara waited, her nails sinking deeper into her palms, her heart beating faster and faster.

At last, the song ended. Asen bowed to Sokol. She nodded her head. Kosara sighed with relief, but it immediately turned into a gasp, as the yuda drew Asen into a hug.

Sokol froze. Her eyes grew larger. Her nose twitched, buried in his hair. Her face twisted.

Oh no, no, no.

Kosara rushed towards them, grabbed Asen's arm, and tried to pull him away from Sokol. Too late.

"I smell human flesh!" Sokol shrieked.

The circle of spirits tightened around them. There was nowhere to run. All around them, the spirits whispered. Kosara couldn't understand a word, but she felt their disapproval. Their eyes prickled at her skin.

"Human? Him?" Kosara's smile was so tense, she was afraid her jaw might lock. Her voice shook. "You must be mistaken."

Sokol slashed at Asen's cheek with her talon. A second passed, and then blood began to trickle, ruby red. Human blood.

The varkolaks awoke and rose to their feet, their low growls filling the suddenly quiet hall. The upirs startled out of their trances. They moved towards Asen, as if summoned by the call of his blood. They were fast now—faster than Kosara thought possible. She blinked, and one of them was right in front of her, grasping at Asen's face with bony fingers.

Asen swore and hit the upir with the handle of his revolver.

"Stand back!" Kosara shouted. "We are guests of the Zmey!"

"We don't know you," said Sokol. The crowd picked up her words, *don't know you, don't know you . . .*

Kosara took a step back and bumped into the large, moist body of a bathroom spirit. A kitchen spirit swung his rolling pin at her head, and she managed to duck a second before it slammed into her skull.

A group of karakonjuls surrounded Asen. One clacked its teeth towards his ankle.

He waved his revolver in the air, unsure where to aim it. There were monsters everywhere. More and more of them crawled out of dark corners, slid out of the hallways, and descended from the platforms above. Everywhere Kosara turned, she saw sharp talons and bared teeth.

She pulled the aspen stake out and clenched it in her fist. She wouldn't go down without a fight.

Asen had been right. This had been a terrible idea. No, this had been a series of terrible ideas. The only silver lining was that the Zmey hadn't sniffed her out yet. The monsters—they'd give her a quick death. They were too impatient to taste her blood. Too excited to tear up her flesh.

The Zmey would have toyed with her. He would have mocked her and revelled in the fact he'd caught her again.

My little Kosara, did you really think you could ever escape me?

His voice made the hairs on the back of her neck stand up. It sounded as if it had an echo outside of her head, in the hall.

Oh no, please no . . .

"Welcome, my little Kosara." He spoke quietly, but his words reverberated through the hall.

The monsters fell silent. The Zmey had descended from his platform. As he walked among them, they stepped back to make a path for him, bowing.

"I've been waiting for you." The Zmey's voice dripped with honey. "You have no idea how glad I am to see you."

21

Day Nine

The Zmey stepped under the light of the bone chandeliers. Kosara's heart sank to her stomach.

He looked exactly like she remembered him. His blue eyes were fixed on her. He'd left the last few buttons of his embroidered shirt undone and his chest hair glinted golden beneath. Kosara still remembered what it felt like under her fingertips with stomach-churning clarity. His coat shushed against the floor as he walked, flowing from deep purple to bright green like snakeskin.

There was, however, a significant difference. He didn't have one shadow. He had twelve.

They followed at his feet, all of them different: short and tall, skinny and plump, long-and short-haired. . . . But, disturbingly, Kosara recognised young women in all of them. She also spotted herself. There was no mistaking her, with her puffy hair, and the way she stood, slouching slightly.

They were too late.

Kosara looked up at the platform, just in time to see Roksana hopping on Sokol's back. The two of them flew out an arched window and disappeared into the night. Kosara's nails dug into her palms. *Goddamnit.*

"I see you've spotted my newest acquisitions," the Zmey said. "Twelve witches' shadows. Aren't they magnificent?"

He snapped his fingers, and they danced at his feet, twirling and twisting like snowflakes in the wind. Kosara's eyes followed her shadow, its coat billowing, its hair tossing wildly. It turned to face the Zmey as it passed beneath the soles of his boots, and it stuck its tongue out at him.

Kosara's eyes widened. She herself was too frozen in fear to move. She wished she had her shadow's nerve.

The Zmey's fire couldn't hurt her shadow, but it could hurt her. It would run up her skin, gentle at first like a lover's touch. Then it would grow hotter. It would sink deeper and deeper until she felt as if her bones were on fire. All she'd smell would be burning hair and searing flesh and melting bone. Throbbing blisters would encrust her skin, bubbling to the surface and bursting, again and again, until it hurt to move. It hurt to scream. It hurt to *breathe*.

Kosara shuddered violently. How could she feel so cold and so hot at the same time?

"Why aren't you talking to me?" the Zmey said. "Why do you look so scared?"

He watched her, worry and confusion in his eyes. As if he didn't know. As if he hadn't been the one laughing while he burned her seven years ago. She could still hear it, his cackling rolling over her, sweet and sticky, suffocating her.

Why couldn't he just get this over with? What was the point of all this idle chatter, when they both knew how this would end? *Just burn me already,* she willed him with her mind. *Just burn me.*

"How about a dance?" the Zmey said.

"A what?" The words barely squeezed past the lump stuck in Kosara's throat.

The Zmey extended a hand towards her, his fingers waiting, like a dead spider lying on its back. "Dance with me. You can't deny me at my own wedding."

Of course he wouldn't simply burn her. Where would be the fun in that?

All around Kosara, the monsters glared and whispered. Asen tensed next to her, his fingers inching towards the revolver's trigger. She couldn't let him get involved in this. If there was any hope for him to make it out of this alive, she couldn't let him fight the Zmey. This was her fight.

Kosara placed her hand in the Zmey's, trying not to flinch at his touch. Her lips twisted in a smile. "Of course I'll dance with you."

She let the Zmey lead her towards the empty space at the centre of the hall. As they walked, she looked over her shoulder at Asen. She only shaped the word with her lips: *Run.*

The music began to play. The monsters tightened their circle around her and the Zmey, and she lost sight of Asen. She could only hope he listened. She could only hope that when she'd pinned him for just another selfish, ruthless copper way back when they'd met in Belograd, she'd been right.

She had the sinking feeling she'd been wrong.

"You seem distracted," the Zmey whispered in her ear, barely concealing the irritation in his voice. How dare she not make him the centre of her attention at all times?

His hand tightened around her waist, clawing at her side. The music was slow, and at first, Kosara was grateful: the last thing she needed right now was to have to follow the Zmey in some wild dance. She was a terrible dancer, especially when she had an audience. The monsters' hungry eyes followed her every move.

Now, she realised the slow dance was a great excuse for the Zmey to keep her close. She felt every disgustingly familiar contour of his body pressed against hers. Whenever the exposed skin of her arms touched his, it burned and itched like stinging nettles. The bile stirred in her stomach.

She forced herself to keep smiling. "I was just thinking about how much tonight reminds me of the first time I visited your palace."

"Were you, now? I can only hope you've learned your lesson. This time, I won't let you get away."

Kosara's smile never faltered, but the shadow sickness crept up her face, making dark spots dance in front of her vision as it passed over her eyes. An obvious sign of her fear.

"What if I don't want to get away?" she asked.

His hand moved down her side to her hips. She fought with herself not to slap it away.

"Oh?" he asked.

"Maybe I've realised I made a mistake when I left you. We were always a great team. Remember that time I helped you catch one of your varkolaks gone rogue?"

"I remember. We burned him."

You burned him. Kosara avoided looking around the room, searching for his calcified bones in the walls of the great hall.

Her eyes fell on the Zmey's bride in the crowd, watching them dance, her face slowly curdling like spoiled milk. *You don't have to be scared I'll take him away from you, silly. You have to be scared I won't.*

"Did you think I simply stumbled my way here by accident?" Kosara said. "I wanted to come back. We could be great together."

The Zmey spun her, sending her flying away from him and then drawing her close again. His nails dug at her hip. "Do you really think I'm that stupid?" His breath tickled her ear. "You're here for your shadow."

Kosara's sickness blinded her for one terrifying second. Once it cleared, the Zmey was staring back at her, his teeth bared.

She shrugged one shoulder, completely casual. "Can you blame me for trying?"

The Zmey laughed. His eyes, however, remained devoid of all humour. "I can't. That's why I've always liked you, Kosara, you never admit defeat."

"Do you like me enough to give me my shadow back?"

The Zmey lifted his hand, and she flinched, expecting him to strike her. *Too mouthy, Kosara, way too mouthy. . . .*

He pushed her shoulder playfully. "Perhaps. When I said I was happy to see you earlier, it was the truth. I'm wondering if you can help me."

Kosara frowned. Was he being serious? Or was this another trick? Was he going to exclaim, "You can help me by dying!" before leaping forth to pierce her heart with a dagger concealed up his sleeve, like a villain in a romance novel?

"Help you?" she asked.

"Yes, help me. I need your help. I bet you like that, little hag, don't you?"

Yes. Yes, she did in fact like it. Provided this wasn't just another of his games.

Kosara allowed herself to relax just a little. Her sickness still crept up her face, its shadowy tentacles tickling her cheeks, but a tiny bit of the breath she'd been holding escaped her lips. Maybe not all was lost. Maybe there was a chance—no matter how minuscule—to get out of this.

"What do you want?" she said.

"I want you to teach me embedding magic."

And there was her chance of getting away evaporating into thin air. Out of all the things he could ask her, it had to be this.

Kosara wanted to deny him, but the words wouldn't come out. She couldn't deny the Zmey. At the same time, she couldn't agree to teach him. Embedding magic was dead for a reason.

She'd once heard about a school of witches who danced on hot coals to chase away evil spirits. They had to be fast, placing their feet just right, never stopping. That was how Kosara felt right now. One wrong step could drop her into a fiery inferno.

"Who are you going to embed?" Kosara asked, but then she thought about it. It was obvious: the Zmey's sister had been embedded in the Wall. He wasn't trying to perform the spell. He wanted to undo it.

He laughed. "I won't embed anyone, Kosara. You know me—I'd never commit such a vile act. I'm going to destroy the Wall." His eyes flashed. His teeth glistened, white and sharp. "Why do you look so surprised? I know you want it gone just as much as I do. All of Chernograd does. Imagine if the Wall fell!"

Kosara squeezed her eyes shut. She imagined herself walking from Chernograd's grey streets straight onto Belograd's white cobbles. She'd wake up in her bedroom in Chernograd, only to nip over to Belograd for a hot chocolate and a piece of baklava. Chernogradean merchants would load carts full of amulets and talismans to trade at distant overseas markets. Chernogradean girls and boys would go to the famous science schools of Phanarion and the music academies of Odesos.

But to get there, they had to free the Zmey's sister. Kosara imagined that too: the screams when Lamia's dark shadow flew over Belograd. The flames enveloping the red rooftops. The blood running down the white cobblestones.

"I can imagine," Kosara said.

The Zmey smiled at her. It made her shudder. His smile was hungry, predatory. "Will you help me, Kosara?"

The music abruptly stopped. The Zmey let her go and she stumbled away from him. He stared at her, waiting for her answer. The monsters watched her without blinking.

Kosara bit her lip until she tasted blood. The Zmey wanted to release one of the most dangerous monsters Chernograd had ever seen. With that, he'd free Chernograd from the Wall. Was there a right answer here? She felt as if there wasn't.

"I can't teach you embedding magic," she heard herself saying.

The monsters' whispers rose like a wave, only to fade away again when the Zmey drew in a sharp breath. "You can't?"

"I promised Vila I would never teach anyone but an apprentice."

It was the truth. It was also the wrong thing to say.

"Don't ever mention that old hag's name in front of me again," the Zmey hissed. "Do you understand?"

Kosara had made a wrong step. Her heels were on fire. She squeezed her eyes shut and awaited the inferno.

For a long time, the only sounds were the Zmey's sharp, angry inhales and Kosara's own gasping breaths. *Any minute now . . .*

"You will teach me embedding magic," he said at last. "Whether you want to or not. You can do it voluntarily, or you can do it grovelling at my feet, begging for your life, drowning in my fire. I also remember that night seven years ago, Kosara. You looked so pathetic."

Kosara's face grew numb as all the blood drained from it. Her lips trembled. *The only pathetic thing was that I ever trusted you.*

"You have one night to think it over," the Zmey said. "Take her away."

Kosara's eyes flew open. She couldn't believe it. There was no smell of sulphur, no burning hair, no searing flesh. She wasn't surrounded by flames. She was alive. She'd denied the Zmey and *lived*. Again. At least until tomorrow.

He really, truly needed her.

"What about him?" one of the yudas asked.

Kosara's moment of triumph quickly fizzled away when she saw who the yuda was holding. One of her long, curved talons was pressed against his neck. A trickle of blood dripped down his skin. His dark eyes were wide with panic. Asen.

You stubborn idiot, Kosara thought loud enough that he might hear her. *When I tell you to run, you run!*

And yet, she couldn't help but let a small, bitter smile cross her lips. Asen was still here. He hadn't left her.

"Him?" the Zmey asked. "Who's he?"

"Nobody," Kosara said quickly. "Just an acquaintance. He's not important."

"He stinks of magic."

"He . . ." Kosara scrambled for an explanation. "He, um . . ."

"I want it," said the Zmey. "Give it to me."

Asen opened his mouth, shut it, opened it again. Through his T-shirt, his fingers gripped the talisman he wore around his neck.

"Give it to me," the Zmey repeated, stepping towards Asen.

Dear God, please, just give it to him. Don't make him angry with you.

Asen didn't move. His mouth still hung open, but no words came out.

The yuda snatched the talisman, gripping it between her talons. Asen reached to stop her. Too late. The yuda threw the talisman towards the Zmey, its long metal chain flying behind it.

The Zmey caught it in his fist and let it dangle while he inspected it. It looked like a simple ring band. As far as Kosara could see, it had no writing on it: no magic symbols and no runes.

"What the hell is that?" she said, not really expecting an answer.

Asen didn't look at her. His eyes were fixed on the talisman. "It's my wedding ring."

"You're married?" Kosara had to shout, so he'd hear her over the wind howling through the cage's bars and the screams of the yudas hovering outside. Their prison was located at the top of the palace's tallest tower. Everywhere she looked, Kosara saw dark sky and flickering stars.

"Kosara, please," Asen said. "I don't want to talk about it right now."

He looked terrible. The bags under his eyes had acquired an unpleasant purple tinge. He kept running his fingers through his hair, over and over, making it stick up in all directions. As if the Zmey had taken a lot more than a simple ring.

"Really?" Kosara said. "And when would you like to talk about it, exactly? You could have mentioned it at any time at all. For example, you could have told me before you stuck your tongue down my throat!"

"I never did that. I don't remember any tongue."

"That's not the point!"

"Kosara, please."

Kosara rolled her eyes and moved as far from him as she could, which wasn't all that far in the cage. She slid down to the floor. The metal bars were freezing against her back.

Far below, the gardens shifted and blurred, their paths tangling together and separating again. The grass rustled softly, and the leaves chimed like tiny bells. Beyond them stretched the dark expanse of the sea. The sound of the waves crashing against the rocky shore echoed in the night.

And beyond that, was Chernograd. Its lights seemed so close, Kosara felt as if she could reach out and hold them in her palm like fireflies. Yet, she knew that they were very, very far away. A labyrinthine garden, an uncrossable sea, and a palace full of monsters away.

The Zmey had taken her moon yarn. Without its guidance, Kosara would never find her way out of here. Frankly, she struggled to see how the situation could get any more dire.

"Kosara?" Asen said after a while.

Finally, an apology! It had taken him long enough.

"What?" she asked.

He wasn't looking at her. Had he looked at her at all since the Zmey took his wedding ring away?

"Kosara, I . . ." He cleared his throat. "I need a second opinion. How much blood can someone lose before they die?"

"I'll think about it," Kosara said, and then she realised he hadn't asked for forgiveness. "Wait, what?"

"How much blood?"

"It depends on how fast you're losing it," Kosara said carefully. It was starting to sound like their situation had indeed managed to get even more dire. "Why?"

Asen sighed and rolled up his trouser leg. A fresh bite mark bloomed red on his calf. Four rows of long, crooked fangs. Karakonjul teeth.

Kosara inhaled sharply. "When did that happen?"

"When the monsters had us surrounded. Before the Zmey turned up. Don't worry about it, it's not deep. It's just a scratch really, I'm sure it will heal just fi—"

His head drooped, hitting the metal bar behind him with a thud. His body slumped to the floor.

"Asen!" Kosara rushed towards him. The wound definitely wasn't just a scratch. It was deep and messy, soaking his trouser leg in blood. "Asen! Goddamnit!"

Kosara tore off a piece of her skirt and pressed it against the wound. She looked around in a panic, at the dark sky and the yudas circling the cage. Their shouts penetrated the night. Kosara struggled not to imagine them calling Asen's name.

"Help!" she shouted. "Can someone hear me? Help! Heeelp! Heeeee—"

"Oh, will you be quiet?" said a high-pitched voice.

Kosara turned around and saw Sokol, hovering a step away from the cage, her wings flapping every few seconds. Her feathery face was unreadable, but Kosara knew she liked people. Otherwise, she would have ignored Kosara's screams, just like the rest of the yudas.

"Sokol!" Kosara smiled as if she'd met a long-lost friend. "Just the woman I need. Could you do me a favour?"

"What do you want?"

"My . . ." Kosara hesitated. What was he to her exactly? "This man is wounded. Karakonjul bite."

"Nasty."

"Could you bring me something to disinfect it? And some bandages?"

Sokol considered her for a few uncomfortably long seconds with those large, gleaming eyes of hers. Then, without saying a word, she turned around and flew into the night.

Kosara could only hope Sokol would bring her what she'd asked for. Karakonjul bites were a nasty business. If she didn't take care of the wound, it would become infected, and that was the last thing they needed when they were stuck in a cage on the tallest tower of the Tsar of Monsters' palace. It wasn't the most hygienic environment for an amputation, for starters.

A sudden thought struck Kosara that perhaps she was fretting over the wrong thing. Asen's wound wouldn't matter if they both died here.

No, she decided. She was fretting over the only thing she could control.

She'd been right to trust Sokol. The yuda soon returned, carrying a roll of bandages and a bottle of cheap grape rakia.

"Thanks," Kosara said. Her arm barely fit through the cage's bars as she reached for them. "Where did you get them?"

"Some ill-fated adventurer tried to scale the palace's walls last winter. He fell, of course. I found them in his rucksack."

"Thanks," Kosara repeated since she didn't know what else to say. She couldn't exactly continue making small talk. What would she ask next? *Oh, what did he taste like?*

"No problem." Sokol nodded towards Asen. "He's a very good dancer. It would be a shame if he goes to waste."

"I would have thought you were looking forward to our demise." Kosara realised a second too late that it wasn't the most tactful remark.

Sokol wrinkled her nose. "I don't eat people I've spoken to."

And then, before Kosara could ask something silly, like "Is this the yuda version of vegetarianism?," Sokol was gone. She flapped her wings and joined her sisters in their tireless circling around the tower. Kosara tried to spot her in the mass of waxy feathers, wondering vacantly if it was any fun flying around the cage again and again, night after night. It was probably more fun than being stuck inside.

Kosara sighed and opened the bottle of rakia. The sharp alcoholic smell made her eyes water.

She washed the wound, slowly and carefully. Only occasionally, when her heartbeat got too fast and her hands started to shake, did she stop to take a swig from the bottle. Not too much, though. She'd need it for keeping the wound clean.

Once she finished bandaging his leg, she left Asen to sleep. He stirred, sweat beading on his forehead. His skin had an unhealthy, yellowish tint. Kosara lifted the bottle once more, missing her mouth slightly. The burning liquid poured down her chin.

Asen snored quietly. His eyelids fluttered like butterfly wings. He smelled strongly of sickness, sweat, smoke, and . . . Kosara moved closer to make sure. Magic.

This was impossible. He had given his talisman to the Zmey.

Kosara breathed in again. It was definitely magic. Strong magic.

Slowly, she reached out and touched the collar of his shirt. Asen inhaled sharply. Kosara pulled away. He muttered something under his breath, turned to his side, and fell quiet once more.

Kosara carefully leaned in again to move his collar aside. His stubble scratched the back of her hand. His shirt was wet with sweat. Under it, his chest rose and fell in quick, uneven gasps. The corner of something black was just visible near his right collarbone, contrasting against his ashen skin. A tattoo? Strange, he didn't seem like the type.

Kosara moved his shirt a little further. She jumped back, as if his skin had burned her.

It wasn't a tattoo. It was a brand. Two interlocking K's.

The sign of Konstantin Karaivanov.

22

Day Ten

"How much did you drink, exactly?" Asen's voice woke Kosara up. She'd fallen asleep on the cage's floor. The rain quietly drummed on the ground around her, soaking her clothes through. Her neck was stiff, her back hurt, and the hangover was just starting to creep on her. The bottle of rakia rested next to her, empty.

"Only a glass," she muttered.

"You should really slow down on the drinking. You're going to cause irreparable damage to your liver."

"Forget about my liver. Why is your chest branded with the sign of Konstantin Karaivanov?"

Asen looked as if she'd slapped him. His eyes darted across the cage. If he was looking for his revolver, he wouldn't find it. Kosara had it.

He tugged at the rags she'd used to tie his wrists to the bars of the cage, as if he'd only just noticed them. Then he raised his upper body to look at his tied ankles. Finally, his gaze fell on the raggedy edge of Kosara's shirt.

"Is this really necessary?" he asked.

"Was it necessary for you to hide you're one of Konstantin's men?"

"I'm not his man. I haven't seen him in years."

"What about the brand? And the enchanted wedding ring? Who are you? Because you certainly don't look like a naïve Belogradean copper right now."

"I am a naïve Belogradean copper. I swear."

Kosara raised her knife in the air and ran her finger over the blade, in what she'd imagined would be an intimidating gesture: *start talking now, or else . . .*

She immediately regretted it because she cut herself.

"Kosara, you have to believe me," Asen said. "Why would I be trying so hard to solve this murder if I worked for Konstantin?"

Kosara had considered this and had come up with a theory somewhere between her fifth and sixth glass of rakia. "Maybe you're not trying to solve the murder at all. Maybe you're just pretending to be so you can follow me here and steal my shadow."

"Right. I put my life in danger countless times so I could steal your shadow."

Kosara shrugged. It didn't seem that far-fetched. People had done stupider things for a witch's shadow.

"What is it then?" she asked. "Why are you branded with Konstantin's sign?"

Asen let out a sigh. Then he started speaking without looking Kosara in the eyes. "I was working undercover. My first assignment when I joined the police was to infiltrate Karaivanov's gang. They gave me the case because I was a boy from the Docks and Karaivanov would never have suspected me. He instantly liked me, since I could string two sentences together, unlike most of his recruits. I had to agree to the brand when he insisted, you have to understand—"

"You know that this brand binds you to him forever? That it's like an oath that you will always be loyal to him—only it's even more powerful than an oath, because it's actually imprinted on your stupid chest?"

"I know."

"And you expect me to believe you agreed to something like that just so you wouldn't break your cover? You're either even more naïve than I thought, or you're lying to me."

"Believe what you want. It's the truth."

He tried to get up on his elbows so he could look her in the eyes, but she'd tied him too tightly. Finally, he gave up and lay back down.

"The reason," he said, "I agreed to be branded is that spells don't work on me. You know this. You've seen it. For me, this isn't a powerful magic symbol—it's just an ugly tattoo."

"So, you already knew you were immune to magic when you started working for him?"

"I discovered it shortly after, when one of Karaivanov's cronies tried to kill me with water magic. He was jealous that the boss liked me better. He was going to fill my lungs with water, and then, once he was sure I was dead, throw me into the river. It would have looked like I'd drowned. No one would have questioned it, given the amount of drugs and alcohol Karaivanov was burying me in."

Asen stopped talking when Kosara began sucking on her wounded finger.

"Continue," she said. "The spell didn't work?"

"It didn't work. I thought I must be unique. That there must be something in my genes that protects me from magic. I didn't figure it out until recently, when you started asking questions. Magic stopped working on me right after I got married."

"And when did that happen?" Kosara asked, trying not to sound bitter.

"Not long after I began working for Konstantin. I wasn't completely honest with you earlier. The first reason he liked me so much was because I was useful. The second reason was that I'm his son-in-law."

Kosara realised she was staring at him, her mouth hanging open. She forced it shut. "You're married to Konstantin Karaivanov's daughter? How? Why?"

"We met when I started working for her father. We did a few heists together, one bank robbery, several smuggling operations. We fell in love. We got married. I didn't know she was a witch."

"What exactly did you expect Konstantin Karaivanov's daughter to be? A joiner?"

"Actually, she wanted to study architecture. At some point in the future. Once we'd saved enough money."

"By robbing banks."

"By robbing banks. She didn't want to live in her father's shadow. That must have been why she hid from me that she was a witch."

Was a witch, not *is* a witch. Oh dear.

"But she enchanted your wedding ring to protect you from magic," Kosara said.

"Obviously."

Kosara chewed on the inside of her cheek. She'd never heard of magic this powerful before, and her instincts told her two things: one, there was no way it worked without any limitations; and two, Karaivanov's daughter couldn't have used her own magic to power it. She simply couldn't have survived a power drain this massive, even if she'd been the strongest witch in all of Chernograd.

"Do you know how many spells the ring can absorb?" she asked.

Asen frowned. "No. Why?"

"Because I suspect our little trip to the Zmey's palace has pushed it to its limits. And I suppose you have no idea how your wife made it?"

Asen's gaze drifted to the floor. He mumbled something.

"What was that?"

He sighed. "I'm not a witch, and I don't really know how these things work, but . . . I think she might have embedded her shadow in it."

Kosara shuddered. "Why do you think that?"

"You'll think I'm mad."

"I promise I won't."

"I see her sometimes. In the corner of my eye. I thought I was going insane at first, that the grief had got to me. But now . . . I think she's still here. With me."

Kosara swore internally. Karaivanov's daughter had most likely been an inexperienced, self-taught witch. Her attempt to seal her shadow inside the ring could have ended in disaster. And who was to say it wouldn't have effects for Asen, given that he'd held onto his wedding ring. It could end in disaster still, once the ring finally broke under the strain of all the curses it had soaked up. Embedding a shadow could be as dangerous as embedding a monster.

Kosara looked around the cage, in case she could spot the shadow of Asen's wife hiding in the corner. She wasn't there.

"You should have told me earlier," she said. Asen didn't answer.

Even if the ring was as volatile as Kosara suspected, it could have proven useful if she'd known about it. If only Asen hadn't kept it a secret. Kosara sighed. It seemed that she wasn't the only one with ghosts in her past.

"What did your boss say when she learned you married Karaivanov's daughter?" Kosara asked.

"She didn't say anything because she never learned. Boryana and I married secretly. I thought that things would work out, eventually. That I'd arrest Konstantin, and she'd understand and forgive me. We'd go to see him in prison sometimes. Once we had children, we'd take them to meet Grandpa. . . ." He shook his head. "I was young and foolish."

I'll say. "What happened?"

Asen took a deep breath. It sounded hoarse, as if there was something stuck in his throat. "Konstantin killed her."

He fell silent. The rain kept on falling. The raindrops drummed on the floor, measuring the seconds of uncomfortable silence: tap, tap, tap . . .

Kosara scrambled for something to say that wouldn't sound insensitive or hollow. "I'm sorry to hear that," she said finally. *Good job, Kosara, you managed to sound both insensitive and hollow.* "How did it happen?"

"I was getting close to catching him. We'd set a trap for him one night at the docks when he was expecting a large shipment of smuggled objects. But then, he found out I was with the police. Don't ask me how, I still haven't figured it out. So, he told me I had to let him go, or he'd detonate the bomb he'd hidden under our bed. Boryana was there, I'd . . ." He took another deep breath. "I'd asked her to stay home. She'd normally be helping her father, but I was so scared she'd get caught in the crossfire, I . . ."

He stopped talking. Kosara didn't look at his face to check if he was crying. She could hear it in his voice.

"He hid a bomb under his own daughter's bed?" she asked.

"I don't think he truly meant to hurt her," Asen said. "I think he was just trying to scare me, but he got the timing of the bomb wrong. No one is that much of a monster."

Kosara stayed silent. She'd met plenty of monsters that bad, and worse.

"The worst part is he buried her in Chernograd, just to spite me. I mean, she left Chernograd when she was four, why would he bury her there, other than to prevent me from visiting the grave?" Asen took a deep, uneven breath. "And you know what I keep thinking about? What if it's my fault?"

"It's not your fault," Kosara said. She heard the echo of her own thoughts in that last question. She'd asked herself the same every day, ever since Nevena died.

She almost felt like untying him now. Almost.

Asen took another deep breath. "But what if it is? What if he killed Boryana because he suspected she'd been feeding me information?"

"You mean she wasn't? You were married."

"I never told her I was with the police. For all she knew, I was a petty criminal from the Docks, and I never intended—"

"Wait." Kosara interrupted him, waiting for his words to start making sense. "Wait a minute." Still waiting. Surely, she must have misheard him. "What do you mean, she never knew?"

"I couldn't tell her while the operation was still ongoing. I was working undercover."

"You couldn't . . ." Kosara repeated, rolling the words around in her mouth, as if saying them herself would somehow make them sound reasonable. "You couldn't tell her because you were working undercover." Nope, still made zero sense. "You were married, Bakharov!"

"I was undercover. Revealing myself to her would have put the whole operation and all my colleagues in jeopardy."

"You were married!" Kosara said, this time even louder. She was surprised she couldn't hear the yudas outside calling his name, because she was so angry, she could kill him. "You swore an oath to that woman, and she swore an oath to you, and the entire time, you were lying to her."

"I had no choice. I couldn't tell her the truth. For her own good, as well as mine."

"Oh no, no, no. Don't you dare act all high and mighty now. You didn't tell her because you knew she'd leave you if she discovered the truth."

Asen finally managed to push himself up and looked at Kosara. He was such a sorry sight with his tired eyes and his messy hair, and the tears rolling down his cheeks mixing with the rain. Kosara would have felt pity for him if she wasn't furious.

He'd lied to his wife. Worse, he'd lied to a witch.

"I tried to protect her," he said quietly.

"No, you tried to protect your precious sense of self-righteousness. You think you're pure as the driven snow, don't you?" He opened his mouth to say something, but she didn't let him. "Well, you're not. There's a difference between being technically right and morally right, and you'd choose technically right every single time. Even if it means letting people die because of it."

Kosara stopped talking, realising only a second too late she'd maybe gone too far. Hurt flashed across Asen's face. Who was she to talk about "right"?

"Who are you to talk about 'right'?" he snapped. Honestly, could he read thoughts? "You cheat and trick and manipulate people. The moment I start to think that maybe you deserve even the tiniest crumb of my trust, you do something to make me change my mind."

Oh, was he really going to bring that up again? "Listen," she said patiently. "As I said, I'm sorry about the serum and the kiss, but that's in no way comparable to—"

"What serum?"

Kosara stared at him, caught like a karakonjul in the fireball light. He didn't know about the serum. *Goddamnit it.* Would she ever learn to think before she spoke?

"Oh," she said quickly, "it's an old Chernogradean saying. *A serum and a kiss.* It comes from a sea shanty, I believe."

Asen kept staring at her. She had to admit it had been a clumsy attempt at a cover-up.

She sighed. "I put a drop of truth serum in the wine the other night."

"You spiked my drink?"

"It sounds awful when you put it like that. . . ."

"How else would I put it?"

"I encouraged you to open up to me using a perfectly safe, already tested substance?"

He said nothing. His glare drilled a hole in Kosara's forehead.

"You don't understand," she said. "I was worried for you, as well as for myself. Wearing a random talisman, you'd got from who knows where, was putting us both in great danger."

"I know exactly where my talisman came from, thank you very much."

"Then why didn't you tell me about it when I first asked? If you'd said your wife—"

"Because it's none of your business." He sounded dangerously close to yelling. He shut his eyes and took several deep breaths. "I don't know you. You don't know me. We're not friends."

Kosara inhaled sharply.

"Why do you look so hurt?" Asen asked. "Friends don't try to trick each other. Friends don't put strange, illegal substances into each other's drinks!"

Kosara hesitated. What could she possibly say to that? *I'm sorry?* Was she even sorry she'd done it, or was she only sorry she got caught?

Did it even matter? He was right. They weren't friends.

"I told you I have no unsafe magic on me," Asen said. "Why can't you just trust me?"

Because trust is dangerous. Kosara had trusted the Zmey. She'd trusted Sevar. She'd trusted Roksana.

Truth was, most people didn't deserve to be trusted. Asen had just proven it to her, too. She would bet his wife had trusted him.

Kosara turned around and walked back to her end of the cage. She lay down on the cold floor, shivering under her soaking wet coat, and tried to sleep.

Asen was quiet for a while, and then the screaming started. She didn't get up to calm him down. Let him scream his throat raw. He deserved it.

She didn't need *friends*. Friends made you vulnerable. Friends made you weak, and ashamed, and scared for their lives, not just your own. Just like she felt now.

The moon crept up the sky, then slid back down. The horizon grew brighter. The stars disappeared, one by one, like streetlamps getting extinguished.

Kosara drifted in and out of sleep. Every time she woke up, she expected to find herself in her own bed. All of this was obviously a bad dream. She'd never be stupid enough to attempt to sneak into the Zmey's palace. Would she?

Finally, she sat up and rubbed the sleep off her eyes. The yudas were flying away now, tired of circling the tower, their wings gleaming pink and orange and yellow in the rising sun. Kosara had got so used to their shrieks, it was suddenly very quiet. Quiet enough she could hear her thoughts. She didn't like it.

This was going to be her life, she realised. The Zmey would never let her out unless she gave him what he wanted. And she couldn't do that. Embedding magic was dead for a reason.

Besides, even if she taught him, what was stopping him from killing her afterwards?

She'd spend the rest of her days in this cage. How long did she have? A few weeks at most. The sickness would slowly take over until nothing remained but shadow. Asen wouldn't survive much longer without her to take care of his wounds.

Kosara would be trapped here, with the yudas screaming outside and that damned liar's bones in the corner. She'd haunt this place forever, adding one more layer of terror to the nightmare that was the Zmey's dungeon.

And it was all her goddamned fault for being stupid enough to have come here in the first place. What was she thinking—that she'd simply convince Roksana to give her shadow back? And then what? She'd confront the Zmey?

Nonsense. She was a mediocre witch. She could never fight the Zmey. She would never get her shadow back.

She buried her face in her hands. *Stupid witch,* said the Zmey in her head, and she couldn't find the energy to make him go away. *Useless witch. Weak witch.*

"Shut up," she whispered. He didn't shut up. He kept repeating the words over and over and over again. *Stupid witch. Useless witch. Weak witch. Stupid witch. Useless witch. Weak witch. Stupid—*

"Kosara?" said a familiar voice. Kosara ignored it. There was only space for so many voices in her head. *Stupid witch. Useless witch. Weak witch.*

"Hello—Kosara?" the voice insisted. "Kosara!"

Kosara finally looked up. She blinked several times to make sure she wasn't seeing things. Perhaps she'd managed to fall asleep after all and was dreaming. Perhaps the yudas' shrieks had already driven her mad.

"Roksana?" she said.

Roksana sat on Sokol's back, holding tight onto her feathers. The yuda's face was just as unreadable as always. If anything, she seemed bored.

"What are you doing here?" Kosara asked.

Roksana laughed. Her two braids blew in the wind. "What does it look like?"

Asen stirred on the floor. He opened one swollen, crusty eye. "What's going on?"

"I'm bloody saving you, that's what," Roksana said. "Well, are you two lovebirds ready to go, or do you need a minute to finish wallowing in self-pity?"

Kosara hesitated. This could very well be another trap. No, this was *almost certainly* another trap.

Still, what were her choices? Stay in this cage forever or leave with a murderer and a traitor.

She got up. Whatever she did, she didn't want to risk giving Roksana the impression that her actions were in any way acceptable. Or forgiven.

"Roksana," she said. "If I wasn't so glad to see you, I would kill you."

Roksana grinned. "My dear Sokol here assured me she sees no imminent death in my future. I checked. Now"—she produced a key from her pocket—"would you like to hop on?"

23

Day Ten

People weren't meant to fly. Kosara felt it in every one of her dense, heavy bones. She gripped tight to Sokol's greasy feathers until the yuda shrieked at her to let go. Far below, the tall grass swayed like a field of daggers.

She'd watched Sokol take Roksana down first, then Asen, and the two of them seemed to still be in one piece. Kosara spotted them waiting for her down in the garden. Of course it would be just her luck that, on the third trip, something would go horribly wrong. Kosara would lose balance and tumble down. Or Sokol would decide she'd had enough, after all, and shake off the clumsy human. Kosara couldn't blame her. Without realising, she'd grabbed the yuda's feathers again.

Finally, Sokol began to descend. They couldn't have spent that long in the air—the palace still loomed over them, and the din of the feast echoed between the trees. Kosara stumbled off Sokol's back and fell to her knees in the grass. Her stomach twisted painfully, last night's rakia climbing up her throat.

"Thank you," she said.

Sokol only looked at her for a few seconds before flapping her wings and flying away.

"How did you convince her to help?" Kosara turned to Roksana, who watched after Sokol, a smile tugging at the corners of her lips. Kosara fought the strong urge to smack it away.

"What can I say, I'm very persuasive. Come on, we need to get you out of here." And then she tried to grab Kosara by the hand. The nerve! Kosara shook her off. For all she knew, Roksana was leading her straight into a trap. That would be just the Zmey's style: letting Kosara briefly taste freedom, only to snatch it away again.

"Come on," Roksana said. "We have to go before the Zmey realises you've escaped. I'm so sorry, I never knew he intended to imprison you. He should have known you'd rather die than work with him."

Sorry? That was all she had to say after what she'd done? She was *sorry?*

Kosara dug her heels into the ground. "I'm not going anywhere with you. How could you do this?"

"For fuck's sake, Kosara. Now's not the time."

How come people kept using that excuse on her? "You stole my shadow." Kosara tried not to raise her voice. She failed. "You tricked me. You sold me to the Zmey!"

"I only borrowed your shadow temporarily. The Zmey promised to give it back once he sets Lamia free. I told you, I never expected you to come after me. I thought I'd bring it back to you in a few days' time, no harm done."

"*No harm done?* Do you have any idea what I've been through these past few days?" Kosara moved her collar to show the tendrils of her shadow sickness crawling up her neck.

Disgust flashed across Roksana's face, as if she'd seen an open wound. "I'm sorry. I didn't mean for it to go like that. Everything I did, I did for Chernograd. I've had enough, Kosara. Enough of watching our city grow darker and poorer and more afraid every year."

"So, you thought the best person to solve that problem for you was the Tsar of Monsters."

"It's the Wall that's the true monster and you know it. The Wall is slowly suffocating us. The Belogradeans who built it are the true villains, and it's high time they paid the price. I can't wait for them to get what they deserve. Can't wait. Everything I do, I do for Chernograd."

Kosara had no time for philosophical debates with a murderer. "Did poor Irnik also have to die for Chernograd?"

Roksana's smile finally faltered. "That was a bloody accident."

Bloody accident indeed. "You minced his face with your fists by accident?"

"No, I . . ." Roksana shot a glance towards Asen, who was trying to sneakily draw out his revolver. Once he realised he'd been caught, he shrugged and aimed it at her.

"I didn't do it." Roksana slowly raised her hands in the air, as if the gesture came to her automatically. Kosara supposed she had plenty of practise. "For fuck's sake, you can't truly believe I did it! You know me, Kosara."

"Excuse me if I don't believe a word you say."

"I *liked* Irnik. Did you know why he came to Chernograd in the first place? Academic research. He was collecting folktales, for crying out loud! That's how he solved the spell for those shoes of his. That's how I got him to help: I promised to show him all my trophies, tell him all my stories of glorious monster battles so he could write them down. . . . He didn't deserve what happened to him."

"And what was that, exactly?"

Roksana threw a quick glance over her shoulder, as if she expected to find the Zmey standing there. Then she whispered, "The Zmey came up with the plan to take your shadow. He already had eleven. He knew he needed twelve. He insisted on taking yours—beats me why but, you know, he's the boss. I'm so sorry, Kosara. I feel like such an arse. I did it for Chernograd, I swear."

"Wait." Kosara stopped her before she spouted any more patriotic nonsense. "Let me see if I understand you correctly. You met a random Belogradean wandering about collecting folktales, and you decided he was *just* the person you needed to complete your mad plan."

"I wouldn't say 'random.' Irnik and I had been exchanging letters for a while. He wrote to me to ask about the monsters. I only realised later he'd been treating them as semi-mythical beings, not as . . . well, monsters. He was the one who pointed me to the Devil's Bridge story."

"So, you bring him to Chernograd, and you ask him to play cards with me until I gamble away my shadow. Meanwhile, you deal him just the right cards to beat me—"

"Except you wouldn't do it. I knew you wouldn't do it. That's when we moved onto plan B."

"The Zmey," Kosara said, and Roksana nodded. "I still can't believe you trusted some near stranger with twelve witches' shadows."

Roksana sighed. "What would you have me do? He refused to share the spell for the teleportation brogues with anyone. Besides, it was only ever meant to be temporary. The shadows weren't meant to ever leave my sight. He was never supposed to bring them with him to Belograd. He double-crossed me, and I—"

"And you killed him."

"I didn't bloody kill him! I told you, I never laid a hand on the man."

Kosara was getting really tired of her stalling. "What happened to Irnik?"

"Fucking Malamir is what happened!" Roksana raised her voice so suddenly, it made Kosara jump. "I shouldn't have shown the witches' shadows to that greedy bastard. He immediately ran off and told his boss."

"His boss?"

"Konstantin-fucking-Karaivanov."

Kosara shook her head. Really, really tired of her stalling. "What actually happened?"

Roksana twisted the end of her braid between her fingers. "Irnik was obviously upset with me for not telling him the full story about the monsters. So, he refused to give me the shadows back, like we'd bloody agreed. I followed him to Belograd to talk some sense into him. And then, just when he was finally coming around, guess who turns up? Fucking Malamir. With that goddamned karakonjul of his."

Kosara's mouth gaped open. "He brought Button to Belograd?"

"Button? No, I'm sure its name was Pickle."

Dear God, just how many karakonjuls did Malamir keep?

"Anyway," Roksana continued, "Malamir demands we give him the shadows. Konstantin wants them, he says. Does he, now? Well, it turns out Malamir can't control that beast as well as he thought. A few strong words were exchanged, I might have said something un-savoury about his mum and clobbered him on the head. . . . And then, that karakonjul of his goes *bloody mental*. I'm not proud of this, but once it got its fangs into Irnik's face, I scrammed. I don't know what happened to Malamir."

"He had to go to the hospital," Kosara said distantly.

"No wonder. That karakonjul was in a bloody frenzy. I don't think it liked having been kept on a leash."

Kosara chewed on the inside of her cheek. Did Roksana's story make any sense? At the start, Kosara had thought Roksana was simply spinning tales, trying to distract her. Now, she realised what the monster hunter claimed to have happened was possible. Even likely. It explained the broken mirrors in Irnik's living room, and—acid climbed up Kosara's throat—the wounds. . . .

"Were the wounds on Irnik's body consistent with a karakonjul attack?" Asen asked. His train of thought had obviously gone in a similar direction. He was talking to Kosara, but his eyes didn't leave Roksana.

"Yes," Kosara said. "Yes, they were. A particularly vicious one."

Kosara had assumed Irnik had been killed with a curved knife or a dagger. The idea that a karakonjul could have somehow crossed the Wall hadn't even occurred to her. Now that she thought about it, it was obvious. It hadn't been a knife—it had been curved talons, and teeth the size of daggers.

Malamir, you absolute idiot!

A karakonjul couldn't be trained. Monsters weren't pets.

Still, Kosara felt as if Roksana wasn't telling her the whole story. She hadn't mentioned trying to steal Malamir's watch. Or the fact that some of Malamir's injuries hadn't been caused by a karakonjul.

"What happened to the karakonjul?" Kosara asked.

Roksana shrugged. "Fuck knows. Malamir must have managed to calm it down eventually and taken it back through the Wall."

"How? He was badly injured."

"He had one of Karaivanov's amulets for crossing the Wall with him. Maybe he managed to trick the beast to step inside the teleportation circle. For fuck's sake, Kosara, I don't know, I'm only guessing. You'll have to ask him."

Asen considered Roksana for a long moment, before putting his revolver back in its holster.

"You believe her?" Kosara asked.

"I do. When I said we found Malamir's fingerprints on the crime scene, I wasn't only talking about the glasses. There was also a partial print on the victim's throat."

"And you didn't tell me?"

"I couldn't tell you. It's classified information."

Kosara let out a loud swear. Her hands were clenched in painfully tight fists, and the only thing saving Asen and Roksana was that she couldn't quite decide who she wanted to punch more.

That, and the fact she'd never punched anyone, and she was afraid she might break her knuckles in her anger.

"Kosara," Roksana said. "You have to go. Before the Zmey catches you."

Kosara barely heard her through the sound of blood rushing to her head. So, Roksana was telling the truth. Which meant that Malamir was a smuggler and a criminal, and Roksana was a traitor and a shadow-stealer. Neither of them was a murderer, at least not on purpose. Kosara let out a throaty laugh. That was the most positive thing she could say about either of them right now.

And then there was Asen, who still hid things from her after everything they'd been through. Was it any wonder, really? He'd hidden that he was a copper from his own *wife*.

Roksana shook her by the shoulder, and Kosara cringed under her touch. "Kosara! Please go."

"Roksana's right, you know," Asen said. Good job, siding with the traitor. "We should go."

Go? Go where? The Zmey still had her shadow. Leaving would mean certain death. Staying here would also mean certain death.

Kosara looked at the path weaving through the Zmey's gardens. Beyond them, a dead man's ship waited for her. Another senseless death she'd inadvertently caused. So much death. So many ghosts. . . .

The garden around her grew restless. The smell of flowers was nauseatingly strong, filling Kosara's nostrils and dimming her mind. The trees rustled, their branches slashing at the sky, their leaves cutting through the air like throwing stars. Their roots crawled beneath the damp earth, shooting out and reaching for Kosara, trying to wrap around her ankles. She kicked one of them until it retreated back underground.

It was as if the gardens knew she shouldn't have been there. As if they sensed the Zmey's anger.

"Kosara," came Asen's worried voice. His eyes searched the dark spaces between the trees. "We have to leave."

"Please go," Roksana insisted. "You need to go *now*."

She heard both of them as if from very far away. The wind ruffled her hair and made tears fill her eyes.

"Really? So soon?" Now, this voice shook Kosara right out of her thoughts. It slithered down her spine, tightening around her core and squeezing. She looked over her shoulder, certain she'd imagined it. That he was only in her head again.

She hadn't imagined it. The Zmey stood behind her. His coat billowed in the wind, changing from silver to purple to green, like spilled oil. His twelve shadows danced at his feet. His face was unreadable, a porcelain mask.

"Your radiance," Roksana said, bowing deeply. Kosara cringed from secondhand embarrassment. She couldn't quite believe this was the same Roksana she'd known for years. It was truly a magical transformation: Roksana had suddenly turned into a spineless, cowering fool.

"It's not what it looks like, your radiance." Roksana never lifted her eyes from the ground. "I was simply trying to convince her to help us, your radiance."

The Zmey didn't look at her. His eyes were fixed on Kosara.

"And where exactly would you go, my little Kosara?"

"Never call me that," Kosara said, simply to check if she could still speak. The shadow sickness crept up her face and tickled her lips.

The Zmey's laugh made her stomach churn. Again, she remembered that night seven years ago, when he'd chased her through the crowd, laughing. When she'd hoped he'd catch her.

"Look at yourself," the Zmey said. "You're wasting away without me. Let me help you."

"Kosara, please," Roksana said. "You know it's the sensible thing to do."

"I'll give you your shadow back," the Zmey said, "if you help me free my sister."

Kosara clenched her jaw so hard, her teeth hurt. He had the audacity to ask for her help? After everything he'd done to her? After what he'd done to Nevena?

And he expected her to simply trust him. To believe he'd give her shadow back if she helped him.

No way. He'd never return her shadow. The Zmey never gave anything. He only took.

Kosara looked him in the eyes. "No."

"I'm sorry?" The edge to the Zmey's voice was razor-sharp.

"I said, no."

That was it. She'd gone too far. His last remnants of self-control evaporated, leaving behind only fire. His face twisted. Kosara was always surprised by how he could look so handsome one second, and so ugly the next.

It suddenly struck her: he'd seemed so grown-up back when she'd been sixteen. An ancient, mystical being from another dimension.

Now, she realised why he chased young women who didn't know any better. He had the emotional maturity of a teenager. Too bad he *did* have the magical power of an ancient, mystical being from another dimension.

"What's going on?" Asen whispered.

"I've made him angry."

"But what's happening to him?"

The Zmey's chest rose as he inhaled sharply, and with every breath, it grew bigger. His skin bubbled. Scales sliced cleanly through, glistening golden. First, they covered his face, then his neck, then they disappeared under his shirt, but only for a second—his chest rose again and his clothes tore, falling to the ground.

He was so tall now his curved horns poked above the treetops. The flapping of his wings sent leaves flying through the air.

"Don't ever," the Zmey's voice thumped in Kosara's ears, "*ever* defy me again."

He grinned, revealing a mouth full of scimitar teeth. His nostrils flared and steam poured out of them.

Kosara was frozen. She'd never seen him this angry. Not at the feast seven years ago. Not last New Year's Eve.

She wanted to run. She *had* to run. She couldn't move.

Then she felt a warm hand in hers. Asen dragged her after him. She stumbled before managing to catch up with his long steps. The smell of sulphur burned her nostrils.

"Watch out!" Asen pulled her after him as he dove to the ground.

Just in time. A wave of fire rolled above them, brushing the backs of their necks. Kosara gagged at the smell of burning hair. The air grew so hot it rippled. The tree trunks glowed red. The grass caught fire, now a sea of flames.

Kosara's eyes burned from the smoke, tears rolling down her cheeks. She ran, stumbling through the grass, unsure of which direction she was going. She'd lost Asen's hand in her panic, but she heard his voice calling her, further and further away.

This was why you never made the Zmey angry. What was she thinking? Her mind was stuck on the familiar refrain: *I'm going to die, I'm going to die, I'm going to die—*

Kosara bumped headfirst into something hard. She raised her hand and—oh dear God—she felt the Zmey's scales beneath her fingertips. Smooth and scorching hot. Her vision cleared enough that she saw him through the tears. His teeth were bared. Flames reflected in his eyes.

"Got you!" he said, playful, as if this was a game to him. He grabbed her, his talons sinking into her upper arms. "Haven't you learned by now you can never escape me?"

His every word was like a needle piercing her skin. She wanted to cry but, this close to his heat, her eyes were dry as parchment. So, she fought, slamming her fists into him until her knuckles were raw and bloody. He wouldn't budge.

Her skin sizzled and blistered in his fire. Every breath seared her lungs. She tried to scream but her tongue had turned to shadow.

I'm going to die, I'm going to die, I'm going to—

And then, some desperate survival instinct kicked in. Her mind cleared, as if she'd wiped the mist off a window.

He was right. She could never escape him. Not while his monsters descended on her city every year. Not while he could bribe her people with promises of a better future.

There was only one way out of this. The question was, would she be strong enough?

"Fine," her voice came out hoarse, barely audible.

"Sorry?" the Zmey said. "I didn't quite hear you."

Kosara took a deep breath. It tasted bitter, like smoke. "I'll help you."

Kosara's hands were in the Zmey's again. This time, his touch was gentle. Soothing. It still made her flinch.

He'd flown her to one of the palace's many balconies. Through the arched windows behind them came the bright lights and the clamour of the feast. Far below in the garden, Kosara could just make out the dark shadows of Roksana and Asen, standing a few steps away from each other, waiting.

The Zmey had changed back into his human form. His clothes were human, too, impeccably tailored, and clinging to his every muscle. He'd put them on deliberately slowly, as if he thought the sight of him naked might stir something long forgotten in her. It hadn't.

He whispered a spell and ran his fingers over Kosara's scorched skin, again and again. The blood clotted. The wounds closed up. At first, even the gentle breeze made her blisters smart. Now, only a distant stinging remained, as if her newly repaired skin was slightly too tight to fit her body.

Clumps of charred hair fell down in front of her eyes. They stank, unsurprisingly, of burned hair. It made her sick. Or perhaps it was the Zmey's touch that made her sick.

His fingers kept working the healing spell into her hands. He could be so gentle when he wanted. That's what made him so dangerous. If he'd always been an angry, violent mess, she would have never fallen for him. It was moments like this when she'd caught herself wondering if maybe, with a lot of love and care, he could be redeemed.

He couldn't, she reminded herself. *He wouldn't.*

"Are you feeling better?" He smiled at her.

It was a handsome smile. It sent shivers down Kosara's spine. He'd fooled her before when she'd been younger, but now she knew: he might play the role of human expertly, but he wasn't human. Beneath his friendly mask hid a monster. His twelve shadows twirled and twisted on the floor beneath him.

"Much." Her voice came out hoarse. She'd swallowed too much smoke.

"I'm glad. I didn't want to hurt you. Please don't make me hurt you again."

Kosara moved her eyes away from him. She thought she saw the flicker of Asen's metal pen in the garden below. And was that a notepad in his hands?

Was he *interrogating* Roksana? Right now?

"What are you thinking about?" the Zmey asked.

Kosara had committed the cardinal sin of not paying enough attention to him.

"The spell," she said, turning back to face him. "It will be difficult."

He shrugged. "You said it yourself, we make a great team."

Kosara looked down at her hands. Her newly formed burn scars were smooth and bright red. They'd fade to white soon. The Zmey wasn't going to make them disappear, she knew, even though it would only take him a few words. He'd leave them there as a reminder.

His lips curved in a smile. "Don't think I'm leaping into this without any preparation. I know the spell requires a lot of raw magic power."

"Why the hell do you need me, then? You've got plenty of that."

"It also requires a lot of skill. It will be just like the good old days when we used to cast spells together. My power and your steady hands. No one will be able to stop us."

Kosara avoided his gaze. She didn't want him to see the terror in her eyes. *Just like the good old days.* She'd be responsible for reining him in. If they failed, it would be her fault.

"I'm rather out of practice. . . ." she said.

"You're underestimating yourself, as usual. Your runes have always been exceptional. Besides, you still have time to practise—provided you're ready before the end of the Foul Days."

"That's in two days."

"You're a fast learner. Remember how you always used to cram all the studying for Vila's exams into a single night?"

"This is not an exam. It's a dangerous and powerful spell that could cost both our lives. Besides, I always cheated at exams."

"Well, cheat now. Make yourself some notes. I'm sure you'll manage."

I'm glad at least one of us is sure.

The Zmey measured her with his eyes. "I'll get the spirits to prepare one of the guest quarters for you."

Kosara felt the sharp sting of panic that always came before she dared to defy him. "No. I have to go home."

"Why?"

"I need peace and quiet."

"I'll tell the spirits you're not to be disturbed."

"I also need my books and notes."

The Zmey said nothing. His fingers stopped working their magic into her hands, and a few of her newly closed wounds slowly opened like red, painful flowers.

"You know I can't escape," she said. "Where would I go?"

The Zmey kept watching her.

"I need my shadow to survive. You're the only one who can give it back to me. I'll meet you at the Wall on the last night of the Foul Days. I promise."

The Zmey's eyes flickered, the light of the windows reflecting in them. He stared at Kosara for a few long seconds. "Tell me, Kosara, are you happy?"

She startled. "Excuse me?"

"I've been watching you. Every year when I come to see you, you're weaker. Less sure of yourself. More miserable. You could have been great, if only you'd stayed with me. We could have achieved so much together."

"I would've been dead if I'd stayed with you."

The Zmey shrugged. "Perhaps. Perhaps not. You're stronger than you give yourself credit for. My brides don't always die at the end, you know. Just ask Vila."

Kosara blinked. *No way.* He couldn't be telling the truth. He was simply trying to knock her off-kilter. Make her question herself. Vila hated him, and he hated Vila.

Then again, they say the boundary between love and hate is thin. . . .

The Zmey sighed, his hot breath tickling her skin. "You can go. I'll send Roksana with you."

"I don't need a nanny. I said I won't try to escape—"

"What if someone finds out what we're planning to do? Roksana is going with you for your own protection. End of discussion."

Kosara rolled her eyes, internally. *End of discussion?* Who did he think he was, her mum?

"No," she said. "I told you I need peace and quiet. Roksana never shuts her mouth. I'm going home and I'm not taking any of your monsters with me."

The Zmey tutted, his split tongue appearing and disappearing between his teeth. "Always so stubborn . . ." He grinned at her. "You're lucky I find it endearing."

Kosara wasn't sure "lucky" would be a word she'd use to describe herself ever again. "And in two days, you'll come alone. I don't need some pea-brained karakonjul or frenzied varkolak interrupting the spell."

"Of course. I'll come to pick you up at midnight." The Zmey squeezed her hand, letting his talons sink into her skin until they drew blood. He healed it again almost immediately, but not before he'd felt her flinch and try to pull her hand away from him. "You're mine, Kosara. You can never escape me. You know that well, don't you?"

Kosara sighed. "I know."

Kosara couldn't believe she was back in Chernograd. It felt surreal, walking the streets she thought she'd never even see again, the streetlights flashing above her head instead of flickering far in the distance. When she saw her house, she barely managed to contain her sobs of relief.

She watched as the yudas who'd escorted her and Asen back to Chernograd disappeared into the distance. She'd been worried the Zmey wouldn't keep his promise to summon them away. The last thing she needed was his monsters breathing down her neck while she tried to learn the spell.

Once they were safe inside the locked house, Kosara leaned her forehead on the cold doorframe. She was so tired and so sore. Every breath scratched her throat.

"Please tell me I've misunderstood." Asen stood behind her, his arms crossed. "Tell me you're not planning on unleashing a dangerous, angry monster on both our cities."

Kosara had no energy to argue with him. If he wanted her to share her plans with him, he shouldn't have hidden information from her. She tried to walk past him towards the bathroom. He followed her.

"I mean," he continued, "just imagine the destruction the monsters would cause in Belograd if the Wall fell! People would die."

"But it's just fine when the monsters cause destruction and death in Chernograd?"

"No, obviously not. But it's not the same. You know your monsters."

Kosara shut her eyes and didn't open them again until she stopped seeing red. "*Our* monsters?"

He kept rattling on. "Belograd doesn't know how to fight the monsters. We don't know that upirs are killed with silver bullets, and varkolaks with aspen stakes—"

"The other way around."

"What?"

"It's the other way around!" Her voice echoed in the house.

"See? We don't know that. The monsters would slaughter us."

"You'll learn," Kosara said. "Or they'll slaughter you."

"Surely you can't mean that."

Kosara pushed past him with her shoulder. Asen made an exasperated harrumph, before turning on his heel and storming out the door into the cold night. Good. Kosara didn't need his help. She didn't need anyone's help.

First, she washed the grime and soot off herself. The water ran off her in black streams between the bathroom tiles. It was freezing cold, but she didn't turn the heat up—she didn't want to irritate her newly healed wounds.

No matter how hard she scrubbed, she didn't feel any cleaner. The sticky residue of her conversation with the Zmey still clung to her.

You're mine, Kosara. You can never escape me.

She dried herself off, her teeth still clattering, and climbed the stairs to the bedroom. She was so tired, her knees shook. Her eyes burned from exhaustion, but there was no time for naps. Researching embedding magic should have taken her weeks, or even months.

She didn't have weeks or months. The Zmey had given her two days.

In that timeframe, she had to go through all her old notes on embedding. It was like trying to remember a foreign language she'd studied a long time ago but never got the chance to practise. The gaps in her theoretical knowledge grew bigger and more frustrating the deeper into her research she went. It certainly didn't help that teenaged Kosara seemed to have spent most of her time in class doodling hearts and writing the name of Orhan Demirbash, the actor, in the margins of the notebook.

The pile of books loomed tall over her. No, there was no time for naps.

24

Day Eleven

Kosara woke up slumped on the bed, with the hard edge of a book pressed into her cheek. She lifted her head and realised she'd drooled all over *Magic for the Advanced User*, making the ink run. Vila would be furious.

Her temples pulsated painfully after she'd spent hours staring at the book's tiny script. Every time she shut her eyes, magic symbols swam behind her eyelids. She badly needed a coffee.

But she'd done it. She'd figured the spell out. It seemed so obvious now that she knew how it worked. She could see its outline, as if stamped into the Wall's dark surface.

Kosara staggered out of bed. As she walked by the vanity, she caught a glimpse of herself in the mirror.

She truly was a sorry sight. The tendrils of her shadow sickness flashed across her face every few seconds, like inky veins running just beneath her skin. She'd had to chop off most of her hair, and suffice to say, if the whole witch business fell through, it wasn't likely she could make a living as a hairdresser. Her old wigs would have to make an appearance again.

Kosara stumbled down the stairs to the kitchen. The range stared back at her, cold and intimidating. She hesitated, telling herself it was because she needed a minute to fully wake up. It certainly wasn't because the mere thought of fire sent her right back to the Zmey's palace.

No, certainly not. She was a fire witch. The Zmey could never take that away.

Kosara lit a match. It illuminated the kitchen with soft, gentle light, yellow and orange and red. It looked nothing like the Zmey's cruel flames, so hot they glowed blue at their centre. She smiled watching the flame, letting it almost reach her fingertips before she threw it into the hearth.

Now, with the fire on, the kitchen was less cold, but it was just as empty. There was no one for her to share a coffee with. No one to fry her an egg and sprinkle some sort of a colourful, foreign spice all over it.

You don't need him, she reminded herself. *You don't need anyone.*

She sat by the fire, waiting for the water to come to a boil. A flicker of light ran across the wall above the fireplace. Kosara blinked, and the light disappeared. She furrowed her eyebrows, searching for its source around the room. The kitchen was dark.

She walked to the window. The curtains were wide-open, revealing the white street outside. Something metal glinted on the roof of the house opposite. The shadow of a large woman ducked behind the nearest chimney. Only the smoke of her pipe remained visible, curling in the wind.

Kosara rolled her eyes. Of course the Zmey hadn't kept his promise.

She drew the curtains shut. Once the water in the cauldron began to bubble, she didn't mix coffee in it. Instead, she chose a few bunches of herbs and stirred them in. Wisps of smoke rose from the cauldron.

Kosara poured the mixture into a flask. Then, she threw her coat on and changed her slippers for a pair of boots. She crossed the windy street, keeping her chin close to her chest, and climbed up the fire escape of the house opposite.

"Hi, Roksana," she said.

For a moment, the roof seemed empty, except for a cloud of seer-sage-scented smoke hovering in the air. Then, Roksana peeled herself away from the chimney.

Her sheepish smile made her pipe bob up. "What gave me away?"

"The binoculars." Kosara nodded towards the pair hanging around her neck. "The lenses reflected the sunlight."

"Oh. Oh well, that was a bit silly of me, wasn't it? Look, I'm only here because—"

"I know you're only here for my protection."

"You do?"

"I mean, imagine how the people would react if they learned what we're trying to do. So many have family in Belograd."

"Exactly! I'm so glad you understand. I was worried you'd be upset with me."

"I'm not upset." *I'm furious.*

"Really? I'm so bloody relieved to hear that. Listen, I know I made a complete mess of this. You can't imagine how sorry I am." Roksana shifted from one foot to the other. "I just want you to know . . . I really value you as a friend, Kosara, I really do."

"You do?"

"Of course I do! You've always been there for me. I'm so sorry. I'd do anything to make this right."

"Anything?"

"Anything."

"How about you help me steal my shadow back from the Zmey?"

Roksana let out a sharp laugh. "Very funny."

Kosara sighed internally. For a brief second, she'd let herself hope.

"The Zmey told me how you agreed to help us," Roksana said. "He told me he hadn't expected it from you, to be so reasonable. Personally, I'm relieved you saw reason. Once we bring the Wall down and you get your shadow back, everything will be just fine. You'll see."

"I hope you're right." A gust of wind ran across the rooftop, making Kosara shiver. "God, Roksana, you must be freezing sitting out here." Kosara pulled the flask from her pocket and unscrewed the lid, letting steam escape into the air. "Here, I made you some tea."

Roksana didn't take it. "What is it?" Suspicion crept into her voice.

"Just some herbs. Mostly lavender. Look." Kosara took a small sip.

Roksana relaxed and accepted the flask. She should have been more careful. In her place, Kosara would have examined the flask for markings. Roksana probably thought she was invincible—nothing could take down a woman who regularly smoked seer's sage.

What she'd failed to consider, however, was that Kosara had been trained by the best herbalist in all of Chernograd.

Roksana took a drink from the side marked with a small black dot: the side rubbed with lemon balm, valerian root, and magnolia bark. She coughed and staggered. Her eyes glared at Kosara accusingly. Then, they shut.

In the last moment before Roksana's head hit the roof, Kosara caught her under the armpits and let her slide down against the chimney.

Roksana gave out a loud snore. She looked so innocent, her eyelids flickering in a dream, a thin trickle of saliva running down her chin.

Kosara climbed back down the fire exit and knocked on the neighbours' door.

"Good morning," she said once her neighbour opened it. Kosara was certain she knew her name. It was something common, Maria or maybe Desislava? The woman furrowed her white eyebrows when she saw Kosara.

"Kosara?" she asked. "What's the matter?"

"There's a woman passed out on your roof. I can't wake her up. You might want to phone the hospital."

"Oh my God! What's wrong with her?"

I poisoned her. "Who knows? You know these youngsters nowadays, they'd put anything in their systems."

"Oh my God," the woman repeated. "I'll phone an ambulance at once."

"No hurry," Kosara said. "I reckon she'll be asleep for a while."

Kosara turned and walked back to her house, leaving the neighbour to watch after her, confused.

She could have made Roksana sleep for a hundred years—she knew how to brew that potion, too. She'd settled for a week instead. And even then, Roksana would probably wake up sooner, once they'd pumped out her stomach in the hospital. She'd have a mouth as dry as an ashtray and a headache to rival the worst hangover.

Served her right. As long as she slept until the end of the Foul Days, she wouldn't be able to get in the way.

Kosara filled up the cezve, sat next to the fireplace, and extended her freezing toes towards the fire. The smell of coffee filled the room.

Her eyes flickered towards the clock in the wall. She'd lost so much time already—she shouldn't have let herself fall asleep.

Oh, who was she kidding? Even if she spent every waking moment reading, she wouldn't be able to fully prepare for the spell on time. There was simply too much to do.

She drank her coffee in one large, long gulp. Then, she swirled the sediment around, turned the cup upside down in its saucer, and waited for the grounds to fall. As usual, it took her a moment to distinguish any shapes. Once she saw them, however, they seemed obvious: a snake, a broken heart, and a . . . dog? She squinted.

No, not a dog. A wolf.

Kosara sighed. The coffee only confirmed what she'd already known. There was no way she'd pull this off by herself. She needed someone she could trust. Someone she could ask to help her steal her shadow back, without him laughing in her face.

She needed a friend.

Kosara looked for Asen everywhere. He wasn't in the hospital, thank God. She didn't find him in the Botanic Gardens, or in the park. . . .

She walked faster and faster, kicking at the snowdrifts. It only made her fit in better with the few people still out in the streets. It would start getting dark soon. Everyone was in a hurry.

Asen had proven he could take care of himself, but Kosara still worried. What if the upirs found him by following the smell of his leg wound? What if the karakonjuls sniffed him out and came back to finish what they'd started?

Finally, just as she passed a group of schoolchildren exchanging vials of holy water for cigarettes, it hit her. Asen had told her his wife had been buried in Chernograd. *Oh no, you Belogradean idiot. . . .*

Kosara nearly ran to the graveyard, sending sprays of snow into the air, her long scarf flying behind her. She wove through the tombstones, as quietly as she could, listening for waking upirs. It was almost an hour before sundown, but she wasn't taking any risks. Her fist squeezed the aspen stake in her bag. Her skin reeked of garlic.

Soon, she found the monument, stark white against the quickly darkening sky. It was a tall, tacky thing, depicting several angels crying into their open palms, with a sappy poem carved on the slab. Nothing about this marble monstrosity suggested a witch had been buried there, let alone an aspiring architect. As far as Kosara was concerned, Karaivanov had built it to show off his wealth rather than to pay tribute to his dead daughter.

Asen kneeled at the foot of the monument: a crumpled spot of red. Kosara approached him carefully, but still made enough noise so as not to startle him. The snow crunched beneath her feet.

"Hi," she said.

He jumped. She'd startled him, after all. Before he turned to face her, he quickly wiped his eyes with the sleeve of his coat. It came away wet, the tears glinting in between the deep pile of the wool.

"Hello," he said hoarsely.

Kosara sat on the cold stone next to him. For a moment, Asen looked uncomfortable, as if he wanted to shuffle away from her. He didn't. That was a good sign.

"I'm sorry," she said quickly. Before she'd changed her mind.

He considered her for a long moment. "What are you sorry for?"

"For manipulating you. For trying to drug you."

"And?"

"And for not trusting you to know what you're doing. God knows you've shown you can take care of yourself, and, well, occasionally save my skin, too. I shouldn't have assumed I know better."

He nodded slowly. "And it won't happen again?"

"Never again. Not worth the effort. You didn't even drink the goddamned serum!"

Asen laughed and turned his bloodshot, puffy eyes towards her. "I'm sorry, too."

"What are *you* sorry for?"

"For being technically right rather than morally right?"

Kosara smiled. At least he'd been listening. Suddenly, it struck her this was the second apology she'd received today. It sounded like the only sincere one.

"I should have told you about Malamir's fingerprints," he continued. "I shouldn't have kept it a secret. We're in this together, after all."

"Why didn't you tell me?"

"In the beginning, I didn't know if I could trust you. Then I wanted to be absolutely sure before I accused your friend of murder. I saw how much learning that Roksana was involved hurt you, and, well, I didn't want to do it again. Hurt you, I mean. I'm sorry."

Kosara nodded. She extended her hand towards him. "Team?"

He smiled as he took it. "Team."

In the distance, something creaked. It was probably just the shutters of a shop window or the door to a block of flats, but Kosara's heartbeat quickened. It sounded an awful lot like the groaning of a coffin's rusty hinges.

"Asen, look—"

"I know what you're going to say. I shouldn't have come here. It's too dangerous."

Kosara stayed silent. That was exactly what she was going to say.

"I just wanted to see her." Asen ran his fingers through his hair. Kosara noticed with some degree of envy that he'd kept all of it after the fire. "So I could try to explain to her. So I can apologise. You were right, I was an absolute idiot to do what I did."

"Well, now that you've apologised to her . . ."

"No, you don't understand. I want to see her."

Kosara blinked, the meaning of his words slowly seeping in. "You hope she'll turn into an upir?"

"Not an upir. A kikimora. I checked one of your old books. It said kikimoras haunt either the place where they were killed, or where they were buried. I never saw her in our old house. It also said kikimoras tend to awaken if someone who's caused them great harm in life comes near. I caused Boryana great harm. I want to ask her to forgive me."

Kosara suppressed a juicy swear. That was such a fundamentally stupid idea, she didn't even know where to begin. "Didn't you read the part in my book which describes what kikimoras are?"

"Of course. Why?"

"Because you can't apologise to a kikimora."

"Why not?"

"Because they're not people, Bakharov! They're not like the spirits. They're . . ." She grasped for words. "They're nothing but human-shaped, angry, sizzling bubbles of negative emotion. They can't be reasoned with."

"I met Nevena. She seemed reasonable."

Kosara let out a throaty laugh, completely devoid of humour. "Nevena was one of the calmest, most level-headed people I've ever known. Her kikimora does nothing but scream and bleed on people."

"I don't think I'd ever use the word 'calm' to describe Boryana." Asen must have realised how much trouble that put them in, but he still smiled. "She was completely, infuriatingly, wonderfully hotheaded. If she'd seen me sitting here, she'd have screamed my head off."

Kosara shivered. Did she imagine it, or did the ground tremble? "Well, what are you still doing here, then?"

Asen ran a hand down the carved letters of Boryana's name. "You're right," he said. "We should go." But he still didn't make to get up.

The ground was definitely shaking now, the snow falling off the gravestones in chunks. The wind howled, growing stronger, making the branches of the scraggly trees scratch at the marble monument.

Kosara blinked, and she thought she spotted the angels move. She could swear she heard their cries.

It's just the wind, she reminded herself. *They're not really crying. It's just melting snow.*

She barely suppressed her urge to yank Asen back to his feet and drag him out of the graveyard. When was she going to learn her lesson? Never, under any circumstances, no matter what, go into the graveyard during the Foul Days.

"We really need to get out of here," she said.

"Yeah," he mumbled. Then, finally, he got up and patted the snow off his knees. "Let's go."

Kosara quickly turned on her heel, eager to leave. She had to stop so suddenly, she almost fell backwards. A figure stood in her path.

Kosara gulped down her scream. She stumbled backwards until her back hit the marble gravestone.

The kikimora hovered in the air, her black dress billowing in the wind, her bare feet dangling a step above the ground. Her hair was bright red, floating around her face like a puddle of freshly spilled blood.

"Boryana," Asen breathed, and Kosara saw how much effort it cost him not to step towards the wraith. His fingers twitched to grab hers.

"This is not Boryana," Kosara said. "This is Boryana's anger personified."

And, dear God, she was *furious*. She opened her mouth and the resulting scream rang between the tombstones. Her feet slammed against the ground. She ran towards Asen, pushing him against the marble, her hands clawing at his face.

And he let her. Blood trickled down his cheeks and collected under her long fingernails. They were painted red, like her hair. Like his coat.

"Goddamnit, Bakharov, fight!" Kosara shouted, but he was frozen. His hand limply rested on the handle of his revolver. He didn't draw it.

Kosara reached to drag him away by the hand, his trembling fingers grasping hers. That was a mistake. The kikimora spun towards her and slapped her across the face. Kosara's left cheek burned. She raised her fingers to it and felt three scrapes, mirroring the ones she already had on her right cheek.

Kosara swore. There was only one kikimora she ever let hit her. She slammed her hands into the wraith's body, sending her flying backwards.

"Come on!" Kosara shouted.

Before they'd made a step, the kikimora flew towards them again, her teeth bared. Her nails clawed at Asen's chest, slicing clean through his shirt, digging into the skin beneath.

When she spotted her father's symbol carved into him, she flung her head back and shrieked. Her hands moved faster and faster, becoming a blur of bright-red fingernails and bright-red blood.

Bile rose up Kosara's throat. She knew what would come next, but she was helpless to stop it. The kikimora would dig until she revealed his rib cage, and then she'd reach in and pull out his heart, still beating, and she'd devour it.

And the bloody fool didn't look like he'd fight her. He drew his revolver, but didn't aim, letting it hang loosely between his fingers. His big, worried eyes were fixed on his wife's ghost. As if he was about to ask her if she wanted a cup of tea, to calm her throat after all the screaming.

Kosara swore under her breath. She was running out of time. The panic turned her brain to mush. There had to be something she could use to communicate with the kikimora, anything at all, if only she could focus. . . .

Kosara's fingers found the wound on her face again. Of course. A promise made in blood couldn't be broken.

"Hey, Boryana!"

The kikimora turned towards her. Once she was certain she had the wraith's attention, Kosara ran a finger along her bleeding cheek. She dragged it across the marble gravestone, leaving a red, glistening trail.

The kikimora stopped screaming. She let Asen go and he stumbled to the ground, his fingers pressing at his wounded chest. She watched Kosara, occasionally blinking, her long lashes brushing against her cheeks.

Once Kosara was done, she looked the kikimora in the eyes. They were a bright, almost golden hazel. Painfully human. No wonder Asen had found it so difficult to fight her.

For a few long seconds, the two of them simply stared at each other. The wind died down. The graveyard grew very, very quiet.

Then, Boryana nodded. She raised her hand in something resembling a wave. Thin wisps of smoke rose from the ground where she was standing, enveloping her. Her dark shadow was barely visible, floating above the ground.

When a gust of wind blew the smoke away, Boryana was gone. All that was left of her was the impression of her bare feet in the snow and the faint smell of blood.

Kosara let out a breath and slumped to the ground. Her ears still rang. Despite the cold, sweat rolled down her face and made clumps of hair stick to her forehead. She tried to move them away, but her fingers had turned to shadow.

Asen kneeled down next to her. "Are you alright?"

"I'm fine." Her voice was barely louder than a whisper. She'd screamed too much. "How are you?"

He didn't answer. She had to admit, it had been a stupid question.

"How the hell did you do that without your shadow?" Asen asked. He pressed at his chest, blood seeping between his fingers. Another nasty wound for Kosara to worry about. Kikimora nails weren't any cleaner than karakonjul teeth.

"How did I do what?" she asked.

"That!" He nodded towards the series of bloody symbols on the gravestone. Kosara's handwriting had never been great, and in this case, it was practically undecipherable. It was a good thing Boryana had understood.

"You just drew some sort of magic circle, didn't you?" Asen said. "A spell?"

"It's not a spell. It's a promise."

"What promise?"

She looked at him through her singed remnants of hair. "The only promise that matters to a kikimora. That by the next Foul Days, I'll bring justice to her killer."

25

Day Eleven

Once they were back in the house, Kosara lit the fireplace and placed a cauldron of water over it. She chose a few jars and a bundle of herbs from the drawer.

"Will you tell me what you're planning now?" Asen asked. He sat at his usual place at the table, his pocketknife in hand. He didn't need to carve any more aspen stakes. Kosara suspected he was doing it to calm his nerves.

"What plan?" she asked.

"Well, you surely aren't going to let the Zmey's sister out. So, what's the plan?"

Kosara considered the bubbling cauldron over the fire. "I'll tell you, on two conditions. First, you'll let me bandage your wounds."

"All right. And second?"

"Second, you'll deal with mine." Kosara raised her hand to the three slashes on her cheek. They'd stopped bleeding, but she had to keep her expressions measured so they wouldn't open again. "I think I might need stitches."

Asen almost imperceptibly flinched, but he quickly covered it with a smile. "Deal."

First, Kosara cleaned the karakonjul bite. It looked much better already: the rakia had done an excellent job preventing an infection. Then, she unravelled the makeshift bandage on his chest to deal with the kikimora scratches. They were deep, but cleanly cut: the monster's nails had been razor-sharp. They'd heal nicely.

Her fingers gently spread the antiseptic, feeling the goosebumps rising on his chest. Whenever she took care of wounded customers in her workshop, she managed to disassociate from the personal nature of it. But the fact that she wasn't in her workshop, but in her kitchen, and the patient wasn't a customer, but Asen, made it much harder. The last time she'd touched his bare skin was when she'd pretended she wanted to kiss him.

Or maybe it hadn't been entirely a pretence.

Once she was certain the antiseptic had done its job, she began stitching the wounds up. There was always something distressing about stitching human flesh as if she was adding a new patch to her coat. She worked quickly, avoiding touching him as much as possible.

Christ, what was wrong with her? She was a professional witch, not some blushing teenager.

Finally, Kosara bandaged his torso and took a much-needed step back. "There, you're all set."

"Thanks." He turned around, checking the tightness of the bandage. "Your turn."

Kosara let him clean the slashes on her cheek. His touch was gentle, but she could barely conceal her pained grimaces. Her cheek felt like an open wound, and occasionally, like nothing at all when it switched to shadow. She couldn't tell which one she found more unsettling.

"So," Asen said while he worked. The wrinkle that appeared between his eyebrows when he concentrated grew deeper. "Are you going to share what you're planning now?"

Kosara hesitated. "It might not work. Making plans isn't exactly my strong point."

Asen met her eyes. She forced herself to stop chewing on her lips. They were dry and peeling already, and she only made it worse.

"Why?" he asked. "What are you afraid of?"

"I don't know. Making a terrible mess of a dangerous spell?" As she said it, she realised it wasn't the entire truth. If they were going to be a team, she had to be honest with him. "I don't want to show the Zmey he's been right all along. That I'm weak and useless. That I'm nothing without him."

"Why would a powerful being from another dimension put so

much effort into bringing you down if you were weak and useless?" As he talked, Asen spread the herbal mixture over her cheek. It burned, but Kosara gritted her teeth and made no noise. Soon, it would start working and numb that entire side of her face. "And more importantly, if you were weak and useless, how come he hasn't succeeded?"

Despite the pain, she couldn't suppress her smile.

That wasn't the only thing that bothered her, though. Kosara had been careless in the past, and it had ended in her sister dying. She needed help, but was she willing to risk Asen's life for this?

Then again, it wasn't really up to her, was it? She had to stop making decisions for him: he'd come to Chernograd for a reason. Besides, he'd shown over and over again he could take care of himself.

"It'll be dangerous," she said.

"Oh, I know."

"It might result in both of our deaths."

"Yes, I figured. Now, will you please tell me what your plan is?"

Kosara took a deep breath. "I think I've cracked it. The embedding spell." She couldn't help but let some excitement seep into her voice. It was such a brilliant piece of magic. "It took me so long because I kept thinking it didn't quite fit. Parts of the magic seem to simply dangle there, unused. It turns out, I was right. It doesn't fit."

"It doesn't?"

"No. And the reason is, when the Council went to take Lamia, it wasn't Lamia they were looking for. It was the Zmey."

Asen raised his eyebrows. "You think so?"

"Definitely. The way the spell is structured, it builds on the kinetic energy—" Asen's eyes began to glaze. Kosara waved a hand. "I won't bore you with the details. The point is, when they were designing the spell, they left a Zmey-shaped hole in it. When they had to make do with Lamia instead, it still worked, but not exactly as planned."

Asen threaded the surgical needle with practised hands. Kosara did her best not to focus on it as he lowered it to her face.

"What do you mean, 'not exactly as planned'?" he asked.

Now that the anaesthetic had started working, Kosara had to shape her words only with the right side of her mouth. They came out muffled. "It was supposed to let people cross the Wall this entire time. It was meant to only trap the monsters. How brilliant would that have been?"

Asen nodded slowly. Kosara didn't let herself continue on that tangent. It had been difficult to concentrate on the spell once she'd figured that out, instead of wasting time imagining what could have been.

"You see, the Zmey is kind of in between a human and a monster," she said. "I mean, he's a monster, definitely, but he looks human. He thinks like a human. He takes human brides."

"Right."

"Right. So, he's what the Wall needs to function properly. And the Council knew it. Except something went wrong. The Zmey wasn't home. They had to make it out of there as quickly as possible. Whatever sedative spell they had prepared was running out of power. They grabbed Lamia . . ."

"And they embedded her instead. How is that relevant to what we're about to do?"

"It's relevant because I now know how the spell was built."

"I'm sure that's fascinating from an academic point of view but—"

"Which means I know how to make it work as intended."

"Oh. I see."

Kosara knew he still wasn't completely *getting* it. He didn't need to. All he had to do was follow her lead.

"The Zmey wants us to perform the spell to release Lamia together," she said. "To do what I'm planning, I need him powerless. I can't complete the spell while he has the witches' shadows."

"So, we'll have to make him give them up."

"Yes. That's what I need your help with. I need someone who can sneak into the theatre and borrow a couple of spotlights. They lock it up during the Foul Days."

Kosara had expected Asen to ask questions. He didn't. Instead, he kept methodically stitching her wounds shut. He seemed to be fully on board with her plan, no matter what it was.

"Is that all?" he asked.

"I also need your voice recorder."

"I don't know, Kosara, this is specialised equipment issued to me by the Belogradean police . . ."

Kosara gave him a long, straight-faced look.

He exhaled through his nostrils. "I'm joking, I'm joking!" He pulled it out of his pocket with the hand that wasn't holding the needle and placed it on the table.

Kosara smiled a half smile. "Which button do you press to record?"

Kosara kept flicking through the pages of *Magic for the Advanced User*, reading the same couple of paragraphs over and over again, without absorbing a word.

She'd stayed home to catch up on her reading while Asen went to the theatre. She knew the place was shut during the Foul Days, but she was still nervous. What if the guard caught him sneaking about? What if he stumbled upon a monster hiding in a dark corner in between the stage props?

But if she was honest with herself, Asen's mission wasn't the only thing making her nervous. When she couldn't take it anymore, Kosara stood up. Slowly, she walked up the hallway and knocked on the red door. There was no response. What had she been expecting?

She pushed the door open. The room looked just like it had on that night seven years ago. Except now, a thick layer of dust coated every surface and spiders lived in the lampshade. The curtains were drawn shut, letting in only a trickle of light. The sheets were crumpled from when Asen had stayed there. His bare feet had left a trail on the dusty floor.

"Nevena?" Kosara said. She felt like an intruder, coming back here after all those years.

For a long moment, nothing happened. Then a figure appeared, only for a brief second, flickering in the corner of Kosara's eye. Kosara looked down at her own flickering form, changing between flesh and shadow.

She'd practised what to say. First, she'd apologise for never coming to visit. Then she'd tell Nevena how much she missed her. The words were stuck in her throat. Suddenly, they seemed so meaningless. What would a wraith care about any of that? There was only one thing Nevena wanted to hear.

Kosara peeled off the plaster on her cheek and scratched her wound until it started bleeding again. When she touched it, her fingers came back red, making her wince. She sat in front of the vanity and scribbled in blood on the mirror. It was the same promise she'd made Boryana: *I'll bring justice to your killer.*

And then, she thought about it, and added: *or I'll die.*

Kosara couldn't be sure, but she thought she saw Nevena smiling back at her in the mirror before her ghostly figure faded away again.

Kosara sat there for a while. The faint trace of Nevena's perfume lingered in the air, jasmine and roses. Her bag still hung on the door, her favourite lipstick peeking from the front pocket. Kosara's eyes started to water, and she furiously wiped them with her palm. Nevena would have made so much fun of her if she saw her sitting here in an empty room, bawling like a baby.

"Goodbye, Nevena," Kosara whispered, "I'll miss you."

She stood up and had one last look around the room. Then she tiptoed back out.

Instead of returning to the bedroom, Kosara threw her coat on and walked to the door. She was dying to get some sleep, but there was one more job she had to do. She had a phone call to make.

The post office was quiet. A single telephone operator sat at her desk behind a dirty glass panel, connecting the outgoing calls, jumping every time there was a loud noise outside.

Kosara walked to the cabin the operator had indicated. For a while, she stared at the telephone, rehearsing the conversation in her head. Was she making a mistake getting a dangerous criminal involved in this already messy situation? Probably. Was there any other way to fulfil her promise to Boryana? Not really. In the end, she lifted the receiver.

"It's me." What a silly thing to say. The operator had already told him who was calling.

"Hi, doll," Malamir replied, speaking fast, not letting Kosara get a word in. "I'm so glad to hear from you. I was starting to get worried. Did you get your shadow back?"

The hairs on the back of Kosara's neck stood up. She doubted it was only because of the cold outside.

"Why?" she asked. "So you can rat me out to your boss?"

Malamir was silent for a few seconds. "No," he said finally. "Because I've been worried about you. Has Roksana been filling your head with her nonsense?"

"We spoke."

"And you trust her? She's a murderer, Kosara! A murderer and a madwoman."

"And you're one of Karaivanov's cronies, despite what you've been telling me."

Silence again, and then, "It's hardly the same." He didn't deny it. "Roksana stole your shadow. Did she tell you what she's been trying to do?"

"She wants to destroy the Wall."

Malamir let out a groan. "Isn't that the stupidest idea you've ever heard?"

"Why? Because your boss would lose his income if there isn't a Wall to smuggle magical objects through?"

There was a loud, hollow noise. It took Kosara a second to realise it had been Malamir, slamming his bandaged fist against a hard surface. "No. Because the Wall protects us from Belograd's debased influence. You've been over there. You know what they're like."

Debased influence? That was a bit rich, coming from a smuggler.

"What are they like?" Kosara asked.

"Spoiled. Soft. Easy life has turned them all into cowards."

Kosara shuffled awkwardly in her seat. She'd agreed with him, back before she'd seen Belograd for herself. After spending a few days there, and a few days in Chernograd with Asen, she'd realised Belograd was a city like any city, and the people there were like any other people. They had monsters of their own. Some of them even came from Chernograd—like Konstantin Karaivanov.

"I don't see why that's a problem," Kosara said.

Malamir hesitated. "Because they hate us, you know? They really hate us. To them, we're subhuman. If the Wall falls, they'll put us in their ghettos, and they'll only remember us when the monsters attack. And even then, they won't treat us like humans. They'll take our magic as if we owe it to them. We're better off behind the Wall. It protects us from them."

Kosara was way too tired and grumpy to suffer any more nonsense. It was obvious Malamir was stalling, trying to distract her from the real problem.

"Tell me the truth," she said. "You can't expect me to believe you agreed to work for Konstantin again because of your high ideals."

Malamir mumbled something.

"I'm sorry?" Kosara said.

Malamir sighed. "It's Mother. God, she'll kill me if she finds out I told you."

"She won't find out."

"She's sick. Did you notice how much difficulty she has walking? And she simply doesn't listen to me. She should be resting, not obsessively cleaning the carpets and washing the floor . . . She needs an operation, and it costs more than our house."

"And Konstantin promised you the money?"

Malamir sighed again. "If I get him the shadows. I swear, Kosara, I didn't expect it to go the way it did. After I met Irnik in the pub, he seemed like an easy target. I thought I'd convince him to give me the shadows no problem, but . . ." Malamir trailed off.

"It was your karakonjul who murdered him, wasn't it?" Kosara asked.

"It wasn't Pickle's fault, Kosara, believe me. It was that bastard, Roksana. Me and Irnik were having a perfectly friendly conversation. In fact, he'd just agreed to sell me the witches' shadows, since they only caused him trouble. I would have given you yours back, of course. . . ."

Kosara rolled her eyes, grateful he couldn't see her. *Of course.*

"And then," Malamir continued, his voice trembling, "that big bastard barges in, swinging her fists about and swearing. Pickle was a sweetheart, honestly, but I hadn't completed his training yet. He got confused and scared, and things got a bit out of control. . . . Honestly, Kosara, it's been haunting me every day. My own conscience is my worst punishment. You can't imagine the guilt I feel about what happened. And having to put Pickle down . . ."

On the other end of the line, Malamir quietly sobbed. Truly, a touching performance. He could have convinced Kosara he was truly sorry—if, after watching his karakonjul tear a man to pieces, he hadn't adopted another one.

"You have to get rid of that karakonjul," Kosara said. "They're not pets."

"I . . ." For a second, he sounded as if he was about to argue. Then he sighed. "You're right. I know you're right. It's so hard, though, when I see their cute little faces."

Kosara threw a glance out the window to where a group of karakonjuls ran through the snow. Their curved fangs crossed in front of their crooked muzzles. Saliva dripped from their mouths in long, sticky strands, landing on the pavement in radioactive-green puddles. "Cute" wasn't the first word that came to mind.

"I'll release Button into the wild," Malamir said dreamily. "He can enjoy the last couple of the Foul Days wreaking havoc around the city with his brothers and sisters."

"Right," Kosara said, not entirely sure if that was supposed to be a good thing. She fidgeted in her seat again. "Listen, there's a reason I wanted to speak to you tonight. Remember what you told me about the Zmey? That I need to get over him?"

"I don't remember saying it, but it's the truth."

"I think I figured it out. I can't get over him while he keeps coming here every year. I have to get rid of him once and for all."

"I'm listening."

Kosara kept her tone light. "Would your boss be interested in him?"

"Interested in . . . talking to him?"

"No. Interested in him. The Zmey. Would your boss like to buy him?"

Malamir was silent for a moment, the only sound being the cracking of the phone line. "I'm not sure if I understand what you mean."

"I want the Zmey destroyed. I want those blue eyes of his gouged out and mounted onto rings. I want his teeth pulled out one by one and strung up as a necklace. I want his scales scraped off like a fish's and melted for a crown. Think about how much money you can make selling the Tsar of Monsters. I can deliver him to you."

"I . . ." Malamir swallowed loudly. "I'll have to speak to the boss."

Kosara waited, trying not to think about how much that phone call would cost. Five minutes later, someone else picked up the receiver on the other side.

"Yes?" Kosara said, expecting Malamir.

Instead, she heard the smooth voice of Konstantin Karaivanov. "Name your price."

26

Day Twelve

At exactly midnight, there was a knock. Kosara wiped her sweaty palms on her trousers and opened the door.

The Zmey stood at the threshold. Wisps of vapor rose whenever a snowflake landed on his face. His snakeskin coat billowed in the wind. His teeth were bared in a smile.

He extended an arm towards her. "Shall we?"

She didn't take it. "I need to grab a few things."

"I'll give you a hand."

Kosara swallowed in a dry throat. The Zmey had never set foot in her house before. Not even back in the day, when he'd show up in the middle of the night, hovering outside her bedroom window. She'd always had enough sense not to let a snake into her home.

Now, she had no choice. She gestured at him to follow her, trying to ignore the way her stomach lurched.

His first step inside, he took deliberately slowly, probably expecting a trap. There was no trap. The Zmey smirked as the pointed toe of his boot landed on the tiled floor.

He looked so out of place in the cramped hallway, a royal guest in a peasant's hut. His eyes ran over the faded rugs, the peeling paint on the walls, and the mildew growing in the corners.

"A nice place you've got," he said.

Kosara rolled her eyes and led him to the kitchen. On the table, she'd arranged everything they'd need for the spell: a pile of notes and books, a piece of chalk, another piece of chalk—in case the first one broke—and a tiny, thimble-sized glass of rakia. A complicated spell didn't require complicated props, but knowledge, skill, and steady hands.

"What's that for?" the Zmey nodded towards the rakia.

"To calm my nerves," Kosara said and downed it in one go. It burned her throat and made her eyes water, but at least her hands stopped shaking. She pushed the notes to the Zmey's chest. "Here, you take those."

He did. "Well." He gestured towards the door. "Lead the way."

They walked shoulder to shoulder along the snowy street. From afar, they probably looked like a couple: a handsome young man walking his girlfriend home after school, piles of notes and books in their hands. From close by, everyone recognised the Zmey. There were few people out—mostly monster hunters, pacing the streets, clutching loaded rifles and unsheathed knives. They avoided meeting Kosara's gaze.

The monsters were out too, enjoying their last night in Chernograd this year. The clop of hooves rang over the rooftops as the samodivas rode their gold-horned deer. A gang of karakonjuls ran past Kosara, their split tongues swinging out of their mouths like pendulums. One of their furry heads brushed against Kosara's arm, and she shivered, even though she knew they wouldn't bother her when she was with the Zmey.

"You're trembling," he said.

So, he'd noticed. "It's a cold night." She buried her face up to the nose in her scarf—to protect her from the cold, but also from his eyes.

He shook off his snakeskin coat and handed it to her. The perfect gentleman. "Here."

Kosara draped it across her shoulders, over her own coat. It enveloped her in shushing, shimmering fabric. It smelled like him, sickly sweet. Pleasant at first. But once Kosara had detected the stench of rot lingering beneath, she couldn't ignore it. It made the hairs on the back of her neck stand up.

"Thanks," she mumbled.

As they approached the Wall, the snow grew sparse, but the wind got stronger. It whistled through the empty streets, climbed down the cold chimneys, and made the boarded-up windows rattle. Most of the houses this close to the Wall had long been abandoned: no one wanted to wake up to its dark tentacles creeping through their bedroom window.

Kosara looked up and saw it towering over her, stretching high into the sky. Its surface rippled and swirled, as if it could sense their presence. As if it was excited.

"What now?" the Zmey asked.

Kosara nodded towards Asen's wedding ring, swinging on its long chain around the Zmey's neck. "You have to take it off."

"Why?"

"Because it's a spell suppressant. And because I say so."

The Zmey undid the chain. He threw the wedding ring at Kosara, and she pocketed it, stopping the sigh of relief a second before it escaped her lips. She was worried he'd try to argue.

"What happens next?" he asked.

She extended a hand towards him, palm up. "Give me your hand."

He quirked one perfect eyebrow. "What?"

"Your hand. I need to hold it."

"What for?"

Kosara let out an exasperated sigh. "Who's the witch here? If you want this to work, do as I say."

The Zmey held her hand. She winced as the heat from his skin reached hers. Then she felt something else: a warm sensation stirring in the pit of her stomach, running through her body, ending with a tingle at her fingertips. Her shadow sickness melted away, like a drop of ink dissolving in water.

Kosara took a deep breath. It felt like her first one after she'd been held underwater. The colours grew more vibrant. Every sound resonated in her ears.

Her magic was back.

It wasn't completely hers, of course—she shared it with the Zmey. While she held his hand, the two of them were one.

Kosara felt the magic, but she also felt *him*. A dark, sticky presence, slithering in the corners of her mind. She couldn't read his thoughts, not exactly, but she made out their distorted, vile shapes. There was nothing human about them tonight.

Kosara cleaned the snow off the ground with her boot and fell to her knees, dragging the Zmey after her. The cobbles were cold and wet, and painfully hard. She paid no attention to any of it. Her fingers gripped the chalk and she began drawing.

The symbols came to her automatically, even though she was out of practice. Kosara didn't even need to consult her cheat sheets all that often. When she did, she had to fight with the wind so it wouldn't snatch them away.

She put all her focus into drawing—she could afford no mistakes. The embedding magic tugged at her own body, hungry for a victim. If she failed to perform the spell, she'd be the one it would take as retribution. Getting imprisoned in the Wall was perhaps the only fate worse than turning into a shadow.

Ignore the Zmey's eyes following your every move. Ignore his hand in yours. Ignore the echo of his thoughts, detailing exactly what he'd like to do to you. . . .

The Zmey faded to the background, and so did the Wall, the monsters, and the rest of the dark city. All that was left was the scratching of the chalk.

Kosara bit her lip. The circle was nearly complete. As she turned to draw the next symbol, she looked up briefly, to make sure the Zmey was watching her. His hungry eyes followed every line as it appeared under the chalk.

"What does that mean?" he snapped immediately, pointing at the last symbol.

"What?" Kosara shuffled in her place, pretending to be having a closer look at it. Her hand holding the chalk fell behind her, right next to a different symbol—an intricate interlacing of lines which meant "wall."

"This rune over here." The Zmey tapped his finger next to it. His eyes narrowed down to slits. "What is it?"

"Oh?" Kosara shuffled again. The rustling of the Zmey's coat masked the screech of her chalk against the ground, as she ran it over the symbol behind her. "It's a part of the circle, of course."

"No." The Zmey squeezed her hand tighter, his talons sinking into her skin. "No, it isn't. Did you really think I wouldn't research the spell myself before asking for your help? Answer me: what is this symbol?"

Kosara gave him a sheepish smile and used the back of her hand to wipe the symbol away. Truth was, it wasn't even a real symbol. Just a squiggle. "Sorry. I must have got distracted and drawn the wrong thing."

The Zmey's smile returned to his face, the edge to it a tad sharper. "Easily done."

And then, once the Zmey had turned his attention to the newest magic symbol she was drawing, she risked throwing a quick glance over her shoulder, to the one behind her.

Perfect. An almost indistinguishable dot had appeared over the symbol for "wall"—a small white window in the otherwise busy drawing. A Zmey-sized gap.

Internally, Kosara sighed with relief, but she couldn't let herself celebrate just yet. She had to do it once again. She waited until the Zmey momentarily turned his gaze towards the Wall. A tiny, practically invisible line appeared under the symbol for "release." It now read "imprison."

That last one was risky. Given more time, she would have come up with something less obvious. All she could do now was to try to keep the rune out of sight. She shuffled again, draping the skirts of the Zmey's coat over it, careful not to smear it.

The Zmey let out a loud harrumph, making her jump.

"Are you nearly ready?" he asked.

"Nearly."

She drew the last few symbols, fast and sure. Her runes flowed flawlessly from one to the other. Her lines were precise. Every symbol stood in its place, impossible to misinterpret. It was a magic circle of which even Vila would have been proud. All that was left was to see if it would work.

Kosara put the chalk down and grabbed the Zmey's other hand. She squeezed him tight. He held onto her, his eyes searching her face.

"Is it working?" he asked.

"Shush!" Kosara began the incantation, just the way she'd written it down in that scruffy notebook years ago. Just like Vila had taught her.

The twelve shadows stirred, as if barely containing their excitement. They moved faster and faster, growing darker with every spin around the magic circle.

The Zmey's lips followed Kosara's, repeating each word, building up the spell. His magic fit so well with hers, filling in the gaps she'd left for him. His long fingers were intertwined with hers. His mind reached for hers and enveloped her in its dark, soothing presence. She'd expected to hear the familiar refrain of accusations from him again, but it didn't come. What came instead was unexpected. *Clever witch,* purred the Zmey in her mind. *Good witch. My witch.* There was no threat there anymore, only something . . .

Something that felt strangely, pleasantly familiar.

She remembered now why she used to like him so much. They made such a good team. Fire meeting fire. Together, they were strong enough to tear down the Wall and release Lamia. All it would take was for Kosara to turn around, wipe away her little modifications in the magic circle, and the Zmey's sister would be free to devastate the city that had imprisoned her. The city that had imprisoned them all.

Could anyone blame Kosara if she freed Lamia, really? Belograd deserved a taste of the monsters. It greeted every New Year's Eve as if it was a cause for celebration. It toasted the monsters' arrival. It drank to the slow death of her city.

Kosara met the Zmey's eyes. They pierced right through her. He couldn't know what she was thinking, but he sensed the shape of it. He smirked.

The spell grew stronger, making the air crackle. The streetlights flickered, elongating all shadows—all but Kosara's and the Zmey's. Their twelve shadows danced around them in a circle.

Kosara tasted her bitterness, burning at the back of her throat, encouraged by the Zmey's dark thoughts intertwining with hers. She

squeezed her eyes shut. Behind her eyelids replayed every time she'd
been betrayed. Every time someone she'd loved disappointed her. She
could burn it all and start fresh. Rise up from the ashes like the Fire-
bird.

But could she really sacrifice an entire city to Lamia? Innocent
people would die. People like Asen. People like Gizda. Good people.
And for what? Just to satiate her desire for retribution, for decisions
made by a group of dusty old bureaucrats a hundred years ago. Just to
show the Zmey she wasn't weak.

He stared at her, his eyes smouldering. He was so handsome, his
bloodthirsty grin splitting his face in half. The fire in his eyes was
beautiful.

This is the monster who killed Nevena. Keep. Focused.

Her voice grew hoarse. Her temples thumped from the effort of
reciting the spell, without letting her tongue slip and make a fatal
mistake. Over the roofs of the nearby buildings, the sky was growing
brighter.

And the Zmey was growing impatient. His eyes ran over the notes
in Kosara's hands. "How much more?"

"A few pages," Kosara said, marking how far along they'd got with
her finger. The truth was, she only had a few sentences left. She'd been
stalling for the past few minutes, dragging out the spell, waiting for
this exact moment.

"It's nearly—"

"Not much longer left."

"I don't have much longer, either. It's nearly dawn." His eyes were
fixed on the quickly brightening sky.

Kosara was about to shush him again, but she couldn't. A cockerel
crowed.

The Zmey's eyes widened. His mask cracked, revealing something
that looked a lot like terror. This was perhaps the first time Kosara had
seen him genuinely afraid.

"Oh no," he whispered. "Oh no."

"We need to finish this," Kosara said. "Or it could imprison us both.
Focus."

"I can't *focus,* you stupid hag! I'm about to be sent away!" Spittle flew out of his mouth. His fingers painfully clenched hers.

Another cockerel sounded, this time louder.

Kosara took a deep breath. It was now or never. "In that case, you have to give me the shadows."

"What?"

"There's no other way. I need to finish the spell after you're gone."

The Zmey looked down at his hands holding Kosara's, as if unsure why he hadn't started fading away yet. *Come on, come on . . .*

"Come on!" Even she heard the desperation in her voice. "You'll see Lamia next year. I need to finish the spell."

The Zmey sharply pulled his hands out of Kosara's.

She'd expected that with him, his power would also withdraw. It didn't. She still felt the magic at her fingertips. The twelve shadows circled both of them, waiting for her to complete the spell. *Thank God.*

"What are you doing?" Kosara asked. Her mind struggled to keep the threads of the spell together.

The Zmey stood up and walked towards the light.

"Where are you going?" Kosara's voice was high-pitched and frantic. This wasn't how it was supposed to go. This wasn't what she'd planned.

She ran after him, pulling on his arm, trying to slow him down. The Zmey shook her off and kept walking. He crossed the street and squeezed into the gap between two dark houses. The shadows stepped out of his way, sensing his anger.

Kosara followed him through the gap, the rough stone scraping her back. She found herself in a snowy back garden. Asen stood in the middle. A projector from the theatre rose behind him, and several more were scattered in the gardens around, shining at the sky.

In his hand, he held his voice recorder. Its red light flickered. The recording of the cockerel's crow sounded again, loud and crackling. The sky behind him was still black.

Asen stared, wide-eyed. Kosara realised her face was stuck in a similar expression.

What was she thinking? Tricking the Tsar of Monsters with a set of theatre lights and a voice recorder? It had been a stupid plan to begin with. A pathetic attempt.

The taste of blood filled her mouth. This was all her fault.

"Wait!" Kosara tried to grab the Zmey again, but he evaded her. In the corner of her eye, she saw her shadow on the ground mirror her efforts. *Interesting. . . .*

Asen fumbled to draw out his revolver. The Zmey backhanded him across the face, casual, as if brushing away a fly. Asen flew backwards. His head hit the projector's stand with a thud, and he slumped under it. He didn't move.

Kosara felt as if she'd been punched in the solar plexus. She wanted to scream, but her voice was gone. *Oh no no no.* She stepped towards Asen, but the Zmey stood in her way.

Asen's chest rose as he inhaled deeply. Kosara let out a breath. He was all right. Just unconscious.

The Zmey turned towards Asen again, as if considering whether he ought to finish the job. Kosara hung onto his arm, trying to pull him back, and dear God, it worked. He turned his full attention back to her. Dear God.

"You. Stupid. Hag."

She took a step back. Her heart performed a complicated series of loops and leaps, crashing around in her rib cage. "We need to finish the spell! Do whatever you want with me afterwards, but please—"

"I'll kill you. I swear, this time I *will* kill you."

Kosara turned around and ran towards the Wall, too afraid to look back. She didn't have to. She could hear the Zmey's short, fast breaths, and the thumping of his feet as he chased her through the snow.

She reached the Wall and stopped, her back almost touching the dark surface. The Zmey stood a step away from her, his breathing ragged.

"You lying, cheating, snake of a witch," he spat out. That was rich: getting called a snake by a man whose body was currently in the process of growing scales.

Kosara imaged how his horned head would rise above the rooftops.

How he'd open his mouth and flames would shoot out, and the stench of sulphur and burning flesh would envelop the night. . . .

"Listen, you have to calm down." She knew it was no use trying to reason with him as soon as she opened her mouth. He was too far gone.

Steam rolled out of his nostrils, melting the snowflakes between them. Beneath his feet, the snowdrifts turned to water, running in a stream between the cobbles. If they reached the circle she'd drawn and smeared the symbols, all of this would have been for nought. They'd both be trapped in the Wall.

He took a step towards her. The shadows scrambled to get as far away from him as possible, huddling together in a dark corner at the foot of the Wall. Even as shadows, they were still terrified of him. Just as terrified as Kosara was.

The Zmey's fist clenched around her forearm. Kosara screamed. Her skin sizzled under his touch. *Oh no, not again. . . .*

"Listen to me," she said again. "If you want to see your sister again, you have to calm down."

The Zmey's grip around her arm loosened ever so slightly. His eyes studied her.

"You cheating hag," he hissed. Then he grabbed her with both hands and swung her across the street. Her body crashed against the ground, pain shooting up her spine. Hot blood trickled down her arms, from the gashes where the Zmey's talons had sunk into her.

"Listen . . ." she mumbled, but she had nothing left to say.

In any case, he wouldn't hear her. He loomed over her, tall and terrifying, with the Wall rising behind him.

She felt as small as she had seven years ago. Like a frightened bunny rabbit trapped in the snake's lair. And just like a bunny rabbit, she thought her heart might simply give up. It would have been a more merciful death than whatever the Zmey had planned for her.

No, insisted a voice in her head. *You're not that terrified little creature anymore. Think.*

But there was also the other voice in her head, the one she knew so well. *I'm going to die, I'm going to die, I'm going to die, I'm—*

Think! You owe it to Nevena.

Kosara looked at her shadow, standing in front of the other eleven, protecting them with its ink-black body. She also owed it to them: the eleven other witches who'd lost their shadows to the Zmey.

The eleven other witches . . .

An idea started to take shape. A witch's shadow couldn't be taken away, it had to be given willingly. And just how willingly had those twelve been given? In her case, the Zmey had taken her shadow with treachery and tricks. She'd bet, looking at the way they acted, the Zmey had coerced the other eleven from their owners with threats. They were given away in fear. They were never truly his.

Kosara raised her hand in the air as if to protect her face from the Zmey and watched as her shadow raised hers. Through the fear and panic, she couldn't help but smile. It was like fighting monsters with an old friend again.

"Please, help me," Kosara shaped with her lips.

The Zmey's fingers clenched around her throat, blistering hot. For a long, terrifying second, everything turned black. Kosara blinked fast through the tears.

"Please," she whispered again.

The Zmey must have thought she was talking to him. He squeezed her harder. She clawed at his hand, scratching herself as well as him, warm blood trickling over her fingers. All she smelled was sulphur. Every breath burned.

Perhaps she had been wrong after all. Perhaps she would die here.

"Please," she tried to say, but no sound came out. "Help me and I will protect you."

The Zmey's face swam before her vision, coming in and out of focus, his teeth bared. The twelve shadows ran across the ground behind him, trembling in the wind. For a long moment, they simply watched her.

Then, slowly, one by one, they peeled themselves off the ground. Kosara inhaled sharply. She tried not to focus her gaze on them—not to let the Zmey notice anything was wrong.

The shadows crept up behind him. *Don't turn back, please don't turn back. . . .*

In the last moment before they enveloped him, he spun around. Too late.

The fire in his eyes died down, to be replaced by the haunted look Kosara had seen earlier: the look of utter terror. He let go, and she slumped to the ground. She gasped in the cold winter air, letting it sooth her burning throat. It tasted so good.

The Zmey took a step back, stumbling through the snow. Not fast enough. The shadows rolled over him like a wave of ink. They stuck to his pale skin and clung to his golden hair.

"Kosara!" His terrified eyes searched her face. "Kosara, please . . ." The shadows filled his mouth, twisting around his split tongue. His breathing grew fast and shallow, as if he was drowning. "Please, help me."

Kosara pushed herself up from the ground, breathing hard. She bared her teeth into a smile. No amount of begging would convince her to spare him—just like no amount of begging ever made him spare anyone.

Her heart slammed against her rib cage, once, twice, three times. The magic words were ready on her lips. The spell pulled at her mind, aching to be completed. The Wall demanded another sacrifice.

But Kosara hesitated. The Zmey's blue eyes were fixed on her, hopeful.

What the hell are you afraid of?

That once the ghosts from my past are gone, I'll be all alone.

She recognised that small voice. It sounded a lot like her younger self. The girl who'd let the Zmey take her away. The one who'd almost died for him.

Kosara knew now it was better to live alone than with monsters in your head.

"Please." The Zmey reached for her, his fingers grasping at the air. "Please, my little Kosara . . ."

"I'm not little. And I'm not yours."

Kosara uttered the last words of the spell, completing the circle. Sealing it shut. In her head, eleven other voices repeated the words after her.

The Zmey screamed. His wide-eyed face appeared and disappeared between the shadows as they dragged him to the Wall. He tried to fight, shoving them and clawing at their dark bodies, but they were too strong.

Somehow, Kosara was herself, but she was also them, the eleven other witches. She saw the Zmey through their eyes. Heard his screams with their ears. She stood in the snow, but she was also around him, grabbing him, dragging him and pushing him, taking him where he belonged.

The Wall swallowed his body hungrily, no matter how hard he thrashed. It stuck to him, sliding down his pale skin, enveloping him in a suffocating embrace. His pleading eyes never left Kosara's. His mouth never stopped screaming.

A second before he was gone, his terror turned to anger. His scream became a roar.

Kosara watched, frozen, as the flames emerged from his mouth, rolling towards her, coming to take her back to his fire.

I'm never going back.

Kosara clicked her fingers a second before the flames enveloped her. They raged around her—yellow, and orange, and bright turquoise blue, caressing her skin and sliding down her singed hair.

She felt nothing.

Her magic protected her. It was stronger than the Zmey's fire. It was stronger than it had ever been. Kosara stood there, a dark shadow between the raging flames, and watched the Zmey disappear into the Wall.

And she laughed with the voices of twelve witches.

It was eerily quiet.

The Zmey was gone. All that was left of him was residual heat and the stench of sulphur. Kosara was alone, standing in a puddle of melted snow. Soot covered the cobblestones, except for a stark white, Kosara-shaped outline.

She turned around, checking behind her shoulder, half-expecting to find him still lurking in a dark corner. *Hello, Kosara.* He'd smile his handsome smile. *Did you really think you could get rid of me that easily? How cute.*

But his voice in her head wasn't so clear anymore. It sounded like a distant memory.

Her laugh echoed in the empty street, high-pitched and slightly hysterical. She had defeated him. It had only taken seven years. The Zmey was *gone.*

Her shadow slid across the ground and stopped at her feet. Then, one by one, the rest followed, until Kosara was surrounded by shadows.

She felt bigger surrounded by them. As tall as the Zmey. And just as powerful.

Simply to try it out, she clicked her fingers and uttered a fire spell. She was at the brink of exhaustion after keeping the embedding ritual going for so long, and she wouldn't have been surprised if nothing happened.

But it did. On the tip of her thumb, a flame danced, red and so hot she felt the heat on her face. It cracked and sizzled. She smiled. Finally, she was whole.

Then, her flame twitched and grew even hotter. It changed from red to a bright, brilliant blue. The same blue as the Zmey's.

Kosara swallowed hard. She'd been expecting that would happen— her magic couldn't come back unscarred by him. She forced the smile to remain on her lips.

Her magic was scarred, just like her hands. But it was still *hers.*

The Zmey was gone.

He's gone, she could swear she heard her eleven additional shadows whispering. Celebrating, just like she was. *He's gone.*

Kosara stumbled between the houses to the back garden. The twelve shadows followed her as she staggered towards Asen. He was still slumped with his back against the projector, resting in a pile of muddy snow.

Kosara checked the back of his head. The wound was already swelling. It would grow into a nasty bump by tomorrow.

"Honestly, Bakharov," she muttered, "keep it up and I'll run out of bandages."

"Mm?" He unglued his eyes, blinking, trying to focus on her. "Kosara? What happened?"

"We won."

Asen smiled his bright smile at her. Then, without saying another word, he shut his eyes again.

Lazy bastard, Kosara thought affectionately. She grabbed him by the underarms and dragged him through the snow, huffing and puffing. Her breath escaped in plumes in the cold air.

It took her a while to get him back to the house. Through it all, she couldn't quite decide why she didn't simply ask her shadows to help her carry him. They wouldn't hurt him.

Would they?

27

Kosara clicked her fingers. The blue flames danced on her fingertips.

Her twelve shadows waited at her feet. She felt so small next to them, but at the same time, enormous. Like she filled her entire kitchen, and if she inhaled too deeply, she might cause the walls to burst.

It was difficult to keep focused. The shadows' murmur filled her head. Some of them showed her visions of the past: pale figures darting in her peripheral vision like ghosts. Others whispered of the future, and no matter how hard she tried, she couldn't convince them she didn't want to know.

Was that how it had been for the Zmey, carrying around the shadows of twelve witches? And if so, how could he bear it?

Kosara felt as if she might crack any minute. As if she'd lose her own thoughts in between the shadows' constant chatter. As if she'd lose *herself*.

And would that be so bad, after all? She could become something more than just herself. Something much stronger. A lot more dangerous.

Concentrate, she ordered herself. *You can deal with that later.*

Later, she'd have to try to locate the shadows' owners—whether she'd find them alive or dead was another matter. And if she found them alive, could she bear parting with the shadows? Now that she'd tasted power, could she give it up and go back to her ordinary self?

Later. Now, concentrate.

She opened a vial and carefully guided the blue flames inside. For a second, the fire resisted capture, trying to climb up the walls and slide back out. Kosara muttered a curse and screwed the vial shut.

Then, she wrote a simple note: *I've got him.* She tied it with a cord around the vial's neck and clicked her fingers again. The vial evaporated in a puff of smoke.

Karaivanov had wanted proof she'd captured the Zmey. Now, she'd given it to him.

Only a few minutes later, a piece of paper flew down Kosara's chimney. She dug the note out of the ashes.

She smiled as she read Karaivanov's answer: *Meet me on the stone bridge at dawn.*

It was the first morning after the Foul Days, and Chernograd was asleep. The only shadows darting over the rooftops were those of stray cats. Kosara deliberately waited until she'd heard not only the first cockerel's crow on Saint Yordan's Day but also the second, just in case the first had been a fluke.

She and Asen crossed the dark streets. His blond wig caught the light of the streetlights, and his snakeskin coat shushed against the snow-covered ground. When they got closer, he leaned against Kosara, as if badly wounded. He didn't have to pretend much, she realised, as his feet dragged in the snowdrifts. He looked much better this morning, after a few hours of sleep, but he must have still been dazed after hitting his head. The wig fell in front of his face, hiding it.

When they reached the bridge, Karaivanov was waiting for them. He sat on the stone railing, his feet dangling above the ground, cradling a cigarette between his fingers. With his round face and rosy cheeks, he looked more like a friendly uncle than a criminal mastermind. The only thing suggesting his true position were the two broad-shouldered bodyguards, dressed in black and openly carrying guns, waiting on either side of him.

Once he spotted Kosara, Karaivanov jumped off the railing. The wrinkles in the corners of his eyes deepened as he gave her a broad smile. They met in the middle of the bridge, where its stone hump arched over the river.

"You're late," Karaivanov said. His bodyguards stood behind him, eyeing Kosara and the man she'd brought with her. One of them casually rested her hand on the grip of her gun.

Kosara shrugged. "You can't rush defeating the Tsar of Monsters."

For a long moment, tense silence fell over the bridge. Then, Karaivanov laughed—a loud bark that made Kosara jump.

"Well, let's see then." He extended one finger, carefully moving aside a lock of blond hair from Asen's face.

Karaivanov jumped back as if he'd been burned.

"Hi, Konstantin." Asen stood straighter. He took off Kosara's wig, letting it fall to the ground. The Zmey's snakeskin coat glinted as Asen drew out his revolver and pointed it at Karaivanov's chest. "How have you been?"

"Hello, *son*," Karaivanov spat out. Kosara had to give it to him, he'd managed to hide his surprise quickly. "It's been a while."

Behind him, his bodyguards cocked their guns in synchrony.

"Where's the Zmey, then?" Karaivanov asked. "I heard the monsters talking. The Zmey's gone. I would have never agreed to meet you if he wasn't. Where is he?"

Kosara gave him a toothy smile. "He's with his sister."

Karaivanov swore, but it came out flippant. Almost jolly. "I should have known. That's a surprise, I have to admit, and I don't get surprised often. For instance, you, my boy, rarely surprise me." He turned to Asen, his tone conversational, as if they'd met during a stroll in the park. "This is all very typical, in fact. Turning up here, a knight on a white horse, storming the villain's castle—with no one to aid you but a disgraced witch. You never learn your lessons, do you?"

"Actually, I do," Asen said.

Kosara clicked her fingers and a flame bloomed on her fingertips. By its bright light, her twelve shadows appeared beneath her feet. She'd done her best to keep them hidden on the way here. Now, she could let them free. They circled Karaivanov like hungry sharks.

"This time," Asen said, "I've brought reinforcements."

Behind Karaivanov, one of the bodyguards gasped. The other's hand shook, making his gold rings click against the handle of his gun. His jaw hung open.

Not so disgraced anymore, huh? Kosara smirked. She'd never caused such a reaction before. She had to admit, she could get used to it.

"P-please put that fire out," Karaivanov said, his eyes firmly on Kosara and not on her shadows. "Let's discuss things. I'm sure we can come to an agreement."

She'd made Chernograd's most notorious smuggler stutter! She couldn't wait to tell Vila and the other witches.

"What agreement?" Kosara asked.

Karaivanov spread his arms. "Just name your price. Anything you want. You want money? I can bury you in treasure. I can make you the richest woman in Chernograd."

Money? What was it with greedy bastards always assuming you were the same as them?

Kosara pretended to consider his offer, just to watch him squirm for a minute longer. She saw her flame reflected in his wide eyes. It was blue. A bright turquoise, like the Zmey's.

Kill him, whispered one of the witches' shadows in her head.

Kill him, joined another.

Soon, Kosara's head was filled with their screams. *Kill, kill, kill. . . .*

With the click of her fingers, she could incinerate Karaivanov on the spot. The only sign left of Chernograd's most notorious criminal would be a black smudge on the ground. The man forever ready to sell his city for the right price would be gone. The man who'd tried to stop the Zmey from destroying the Wall because it would have affected his profit margins would be no more.

That was what the Zmey would have done.

"I have nothing to discuss with you." Kosara clicked her fingers again.

Karaivanov jumped, a choked sound escaping his throat. When he realised she'd simply made the flame disappear, he gave her a sheepish smile.

"I don't have anything to talk to you about, either." Asen clicked a pair of handcuffs open. "You know who does, though? The trafficking unit at the Chernogradean police."

"Ah, of course," Karaivanov said, visibly relieved. Kosara had been ready for a fight, but the old smuggler obviously knew when it was time to give up. He gestured at his bodyguards to settle down and presented his hands, palms up, so Asen could handcuff him. "You like playing by the book. I should have guessed." When Asen reached forwards with the handcuffs, Karaivanov grabbed his wrists. "But I've never been one for rules."

Asen screamed, stumbling backwards. His body convulsed. On his chest, the brand—Karaivanov's interlocking K's—shone bright red through his shirt.

Kosara swore. She shouldn't have let her guard down. She reached inside her pocket for Asen's wedding ring. In the blur of the previous night, she'd completely forgotten to give it back to him. A stupid, amateur mistake.

She called for her shadows with her mind. In her panic, she couldn't give them clear instructions, and they twirled helplessly in a circle around her. She'd prepared them to fight bullets and fireballs, not whatever magic this was.

Before she'd managed to channel them towards Karaivanov, one of the bodyguards elbowed her in the stomach. Her breath escaped her lips in a painful gasp. She shot a half-formed, misshapen flame towards the bodyguard, and he stepped back, but not before he'd smeared something hot and blinding across her eyes. It itched as it clung to her skin and made a hissing sound as it glued her eyelashes shut.

Kosara frantically tried to wipe the mixture off with her sleeves. Asen kept screaming.

"We'll meet each other again, I'm sure," Karaivanov's soft voice echoed around them, somehow rising above the commotion. "Cheerio."

By the time Kosara's eyesight finally returned, Karaivanov and his men were gone. Through her tears, she saw the bridge: empty, except for Asen's crumpled form. He kneeled on the cobblestones, grasping his branded chest with his hand. It still glowed red, shining bright through the white fabric and out between his fingers.

"Goddamnit," he muttered. Then, louder, "Goddamnit!" He slammed his fist against the cobblestones.

"Careful," Kosara said. She kneeled next to him and unclenched his fists. First, the one he'd used to hit the ground—his knuckles were already growing purple—and then, the one holding his chest. His brand was scorching hot to the touch. "You'll hurt yourself."

"I'll deserve it," he muttered. "What fool agrees to be branded with Karaivanov's sign without protest?"

Kosara shuffled closer to him and let him rest his head on her shoulder. The twelve shadows circled them curiously. "Maybe so," she said. "But if you keep this up, I'll run out of bandages."

Beneath her knees, the ground was cold and wet. But she didn't move until the brand on Asen's chest faded to black.

When he finally spoke again, his words were barely audible, even with his head next to her ear. "You were right, you know."

"Mmm?" She'd grown distracted, watching her shadows float among the snowflakes.

Asen took a deep breath. Then, he pulled away and looked her in the eyes. "You were right. Whenever you called me out on breaking the rules, you were completely right. I crossed too many lines trying to catch him."

"You had a good reason."

"Yes, that's what I've been telling myself. But once you start breaking rules, when do you stop? Where do you draw the line between a good reason and a bad reason? Can I trust myself at this point to even know the difference?" He hesitated, and then he added, quietly, "I was going to shoot him, you know."

"What?" Kosara said, unsure if she'd heard him correctly. "Who?"

"Karaivanov. When I had my gun pointed at him. It took all my self-restraint not to pull the trigger." Asen paused. "I'm scared of myself."

Birds of a feather. Kosara was scared of herself, too. Once she got home, she planned to fold the eleven shadows—all but her own—back into beads. Then, she'd hide them to keep them safe—even from herself—until she found their rightful owners.

She considered Asen, kneeling on the ground across from her. They were lucky an early morning milk delivery cart hadn't interrupted their heart-to-heart yet.

"Maybe you should have shot him," Kosara said. "And I should have burned him. And then, he wouldn't have got away."

Asen laughed. "You don't really mean that."

"I don't." Kosara sighed. "We'll get him. Next time, he won't escape."

Asen raised an eyebrow. "We?"

"Of course, 'we'!' I made Boryana a promise, witch to witch. I have no intention of breaking it. I'll turn every last bloody cobblestone in Chernograd to find the bastard."

Asen finally stood up and wiped some of the puddle water off his trousers with his hand. "I'll do the same in Belograd. Half his network is based there. It's likely he'll go to them, if he wants to disappear for a while in a city where not everyone knows him. Once one of us stumbles on a lead, we'll contact each other." He extended her hand towards Kosara. "Deal?"

"Deal." Kosara took his hand and let him help her up. "Provided it's all worked according to plan."

"Well, how about we check?"

With every step, the Wall's inky shadow grew bigger, looming over them. Whenever the wind died down, Kosara could swear she heard it scream. She recognised its voice. It made her shudder.

"How does it feel to finally be rid of him?" Asen asked, his eyes fixed on the Wall above.

"It feels good," Kosara said. "Very quiet."

It *was* quiet: the monsters had left Chernograd after twelve long days. What's more, her own monster was gone. For the first time in seven years, she didn't hear his voice in her head.

"What about you?" she asked. "Are you ready to go home?"

"I am. You?"

Kosara took a deep breath. She wasn't ready. How could she possibly be ready? But she also couldn't put it off any longer.

The spell to trap the Zmey inside the Wall was the most complicated she'd ever cast. Until the last moment, she hadn't been sure she had it in her to finish the job. She'd never done anything half as challenging before.

What if it hadn't worked? What if she'd managed to trap him in the Wall, but she hadn't embedded him? What if he was still alive, still *himself* in there, waiting to pounce on her as soon as she stepped closer?

"Kosara," Asen said, obviously sensing her fear. "I've seen you waltz into the Zmey's palace as if it was nothing. I watched you weave the spell to trap him in the Wall. You can do this."

Kosara let out air through her nostrils. "You didn't watch me. You were too busy taking a nap."

"Well, I wish I'd seen you. I bet you looked magnificent."

"Stop buttering me up," Kosara said, but she was smiling. She stretched out her hand and touched the Wall's dark surface. It was freezing cold—so cold it burned, but she didn't move. She waited. For a few painful seconds nothing happened.

Then the Wall began to withdraw from her.

Kosara pushed against it. It shifted under her fingers, soft and pliable, until her whole arm disappeared inside it. She felt nothing. It was as if her arm hung in the air.

She inhaled deeply and took a step forwards. The Wall engulfed her. Kosara blinked, waiting for her eyes to adjust to the darkness, until she spotted light trickling through in the distance, from the direction of Belograd.

Before she continued, Kosara turned back. Asen stood behind her in the snow. He was slightly blurry, as if she looked at him through frosted glass.

"You try it," she said, but no sound came out.

Still, he must have read her lips. He placed his palm on the Wall and, slowly, it swallowed him. He looked around, blinking fast. "It seems to be working," he said, and his voice came out muffled, like he was shouting underwater. "Shall we?"

Kosara didn't need much convincing. She felt so vulnerable standing there, with the Wall surrounding her on all sides. As if any minute, it might decide to close in on her, trapping her inside forever. Her heart thumped in the back of her throat, echoing in the quiet.

Kosara took a step towards the light, then another. Next to her, Asen walked casually—he didn't seem to feel the press of the Wall on all sides. Lightning flashed high above their heads. Kosara's breathing grew fast and shallow; she was afraid to inhale too much of the Wall. As if it would poison her.

Just at the edge of her vision, she could swear she spotted the Zmey's blue flames dancing. His face floated behind her eyelids every time she blinked, his teeth bared. She thought she heard him in the distance, wailing and thrashing and slamming his fists against the Wall's surface.

She felt Asen's hand in hers, and he squeezed her hard. "He can't get you anymore."

Kosara's heart rate spiked. How did Asen so often know what she was thinking? Had he spotted the Zmey's fire, too?

No. Asen knew because he was watching her. He'd recognised Kosara's shallow breathing and the fear in her movements.

Calm down, she thought sternly. *The Zmey can't get you now.*

She checked that her shadow still followed her. Then, she stood straighter and kept walking.

Eventually, they made it through. One second she drifted in darkness, the next her heels clicked against Belograd's cobbles. Noise filled Kosara's ears: laughter and chatter from the cafes and restaurants, and loud music from the dancing halls and street musicians on every corner. The moist sea breeze ruffled her hair.

The street was busy, but no one spotted Kosara and Asen walking out of the Wall. No one noted the snowflakes in their hair, even though it was a mild evening in Belograd. No one paid attention to the pile of snow falling off their boots.

Or, if anyone did, they said nothing, too afraid their friends would think they'd gone mad. "You saw a man and a woman walking out of the Wall? Just how many did you drink?"

Kosara wondered how long it would be before people started to cross the Wall freely. She planned to phone a few newspapers and maybe the radio, to spread the happy news, but she suspected it would be a while before anyone else was brave enough to attempt it.

However, Kosara knew that, once they were certain it was safe, Chernogradeans would flock to Belograd's busy streets. Travel between the two cities would go back to how it had been before the Wall. Crossing the barrier would be as normal as catching the train to Phanarion or the boat to Odesos.

"It worked," Asen said, releasing her hand. "Thank God."

"Thank God." Kosara didn't remind him they had no one to thank but themselves. "Glad to be back home?"

"Very. Chernograd is a beautiful city, don't get me wrong, but I can't wait for a proper cup of tea."

Kosara turned to face him. For a while now, she'd been wondering which one of them looked the worse for wear. Her, with her bad haircut and wounded face, or him? Asen had kept his hair, but the bags under his eyes were deep enough that he could keep his small change in them.

But now, he smiled brightly at her, and she decided it was definitely him who'd fared better. Damn him, he had a nice smile.

Her gaze flicked to his eyes, then back to his mouth. What she really, truly wanted was to kiss him. But she couldn't do that. Not after how it had gone the last time.

"What?" Asen asked, completely oblivious.

"Nothing," Kosara said, looking away from him, feeling the heat rising to her cheeks and forcing it back down. "It's too warm here."

"It's nice, isn't it?" Asen took his coat off and hung it from his arm.

Kosara shuffled uncomfortably, not wanting to remove her coat despite the heat. She'd only come across to check if her spell had worked, and to ensure Asen made it back to Belograd whole. She didn't intend to stay long.

She opened her mouth to make her goodbyes, when Asen interrupted her. "So, are you coming to my mum's for dinner?"

"Sorry?" Kosara was sure she must have misheard him. No one ever took her to meet their mother.

"Do you want to come to my mum's for dinner? I'm sure she'd love to meet you."

Kosara very much doubted Asen's mum wanted a grumpy, tired witch as a dinner guest. "I can't. She hasn't been warned to expect guests and—"

"Oh, don't worry, she always cooks way too much. She could feed ten of you."

"I . . ." Kosara turned back to the Wall. She couldn't dally. There was so much to do back in Chernograd: she had to pay Vila a visit. She had to figure out who the owners of the eleven witch's shadows were, so she could give them back. She had to decide what to do about Roksana and Malamir, and she had to track down Karaivanov.

And besides, she and Asen had clearly spent too much time together recently. They both needed space. Maybe if she didn't see him for a while, she'd stop thinking about his goddamned smile and blushing like a schoolgirl.

"Maybe some other time," she said. "I have other plans."

Asen looked doubtful. "You do?"

I'm going to take a long bath, drink half a bottle of wine, and sleep for a thousand years. "Yes, unfortunately, and they can't be postponed."

"Oh. Oh well. Some other time."

For a moment, Kosara stood there, unsure what to do next. A handshake? Too formal. A hug? Too friendly.

She settled on patting him on the shoulder. "I'll see you around."

"Right," Asen said. "I'll see you."

Kosara's gaze drifted behind him, to Belograd's brightly lit shop windows and the colourful lanterns swinging in the wind. She inhaled the smell of seaweed and brine, spices and citrus fruits, expensive perfume, and cheap street food.

And then, just as the Wall had almost glued itself together behind her, she turned on her heel and rushed back to Chernograd. Back home.

EPILOGUE

Once Kosara got back to the house, she couldn't put it off any longer. She had to finally quiet the little voice in the back of her head, constantly asking "what if?"

What if she'd failed? What if the Zmey's imprisonment hadn't been enough?

Kosara paused for a second to calm her heartbeat before walking to the end of the hallway and knocking on the red door. Without waiting for a reply, she pushed it open.

The room was empty. Not like before, when the wind rustling in the trees outside sounded like whispers, and the dust particles in the air spelled messages if you looked at them just right.

No, the room was *empty*. The distant smell of Nevena's perfume was gone. Her silhouette didn't appear in the corner, only to disappear again when Kosara tried to focus on it. Her screams didn't echo in Kosara's mind.

Kosara wiped the tears streaming down her cheeks with the back of her hand. She curled up on the bed, hugging the pillow, and let herself cry until her throat felt rough. She felt such overwhelming relief. Finally, she'd done right by her sister.

But she also felt so, so alone.

She didn't realise she'd fallen asleep. When she woke up, the room was freezing cold, the pillow damp beneath her cheek.

She lifted herself up on her elbows. The wind outside was so strong it snuck through the poorly insulated windows and made the curtains billow. Frost flowers bloomed on the glass, distorting the gas lamps outside. For a second, Kosara could swear she spotted the horned silhouette of a karakonjul on the roof opposite.

Then she blinked, and it was gone.

She chuckled to herself. Silly. The Foul Days were over. Chernograd was safe—until next New Year's Eve, at least. Her tired mind was playing tricks on her.

Kosara yawned and stretched. Her bare feet hit the freezing floor. She'd never had that hot bath she'd promised herself earlier, and now was the perfect time, before her toes fell off from the cold.

"Bye, Nevena!" Kosara said cheerfully before she left the room, out of pure habit.

Nevena was gone. Finally, irrevocably gone.

But as Kosara's fingers landed on the door handle, the curtains moved, caressing her bare forearms. The wind whistled in the chimney, *Kosara.*

Kosara froze.

It couldn't be. It *couldn't.* And yet, it had sounded exactly like Nevena's voice.

Kosara, please don't leave me.

The Chernograd Witch and Warlock Association

P R E S E N T S

A PRACTICAL GUIDE
TO MONSTERS

(Foul Days edition)

Dear denizens of Chernograd and visitors to the city,
The Foul Days are nearly upon us! And what better time is
there to re-familiarise yourself with Chernograd's monsters:
from the common upir to the cruel samodiva; from the prophetic yuda to the bloodthirsty karakonjul. I know what you're
thinking--everyone knows the monsters of Chernograd. Everyone
has a story of how their great uncle's cousin's friend defeated a karakonjul with a clever riddle or fought a varkolak
with their bare hands. However, at the WWA, we believe a quick
refresher is never amiss. We have deliberately written this
guide to be accessible to all ages and levels of knowledge,
and we encourage you to distribute it widely among your family and friends. Remember: to be safe is to be prepared. (For
those looking for a refresher on the Foul Days themselves, we
recommend you turn to the "Back to Basics" section below the
monster listings.)

Upir

WHAT IS IT: The restless spirits of the dead who rise from
their graves to torment the living. Can be encountered year-
round but are especially active during the Foul Days.

HOW TO RECOGNISE IT: Upirs resemble walking corpses in various
stages of decay, often with partially decomposed flesh and
bloodshot eyes. Upon encountering a living person, an upir
will attempt to puncture their body with their needle-sharp
teeth and drain the person of blood. During the Foul Days,

they tend to rise from their graves en masse and are more
likely to move in groups.

HOW TO PROTECT YOURSELF FROM IT: To prevent your loved one
from rising as an upir, be sure to follow the appropriate
burial rituals. Being vigilant begins at the wake: it is
imperative not to let any household cats walk over the body
of the deceased! The burial includes the following precautions: placing a coin in the deceased's mouth, burying them
face-down, trapping them with a sickle or other agricultural
implement, cutting their head off, placing an aspen stake
through their heart, and severing the tendons of their knees
to prevent them from rising. It sounds like a lot, but it's
better to be safe than sorry!

In the event that a person is bitten by an upir but manages to
get away, they should be treated by a professional as upir teeth
often contain venom. Upirs possess a unique brand of illusory
magic by which they are able to make their victims believe they are
hearing or seeing people or scenes from their own memory. This
magic is intensified when many upirs gather in a single area.

There are many stories, some of which you'd have undoubtedly
heard in your local pub, about upirs returning from the dead
and attempting to resume their normal life, going home and
greeting their family as if nothing has happened. If you suspect your recently buried but now mysteriously resurrected
relative to be an upir, do not panic. Upirs hate garlic and
holy water, so it is especially important to keep these substances on-hand during the Foul Days to serve as a repellent.
If worse comes to worst and you have to fight, an aspen stake
through the upir's heart or cutting their head off has proven
sufficient to kill them.

Varkolak

WHAT IS IT: Varkolaks are people who transform into large
wolves during the full moon. Lycanthropy is a contagious disease, transmitted through biting, and there is no cure. There
are folk stories recording cases where angry varkolaks caused

an eclipse by biting off a piece of the moon, but the authors have no conclusive evidence to either prove or disprove such occurrences. While varkolaks are a common threat during the full moon all year, they become particularly aggressive during the Foul Days.

HOW TO RECOGNISE IT: Varkolaks tend to be larger than normal wolves, and besides, there have been no wolves in Chernograd for hundreds of years, so spotting one is a pretty good indication you need to stay far, far away.

HOW TO PROTECT YOURSELF FROM IT: If you suspect a friend or a relative has been bitten by a varkolak, you have to follow the appropriate quarantine procedures. First, lock them in a cage in the basement. Secondly, immediately contact a licensed witch or warlock.

If you suspect you've been bitten by a varkolak, hand yourself to the nearest witch or warlock's workshop. It is not wise to attempt to hide your condition as keeping varkolaks contained requires rune circles and talismans only available to licensed magic practitioners.

REMEMBER: Varkolaks have superhuman strength, sight, sense of smell, and hearing. You can't outrun a varkolak. You can't hide from them. Their one weakness is silver, but we recognise in those trying times, access to the precious metal is highly limited. Singing has been found to temporarily distract them, but it does not work for long. The best thing to do in order to keep yourself and your fellow citizens safe is to remain vigilant and watch out for signs of the varkolak infection in your immediate circle. A varkolak bite doesn't have to be the end of one's life if all appropriate precautions are followed. In fact, many people have gone to live long, fulfilling lives after having been bitten, with their condition only a minor inconvenience during the full moon.

If all else fails, a varkolak can be killed with a silver bullet. The WWA would like to make it clear that this should be a last resort. Varkolaks are humans and they deserve to be treated as such.

Household spirit

WHAT IS IT: Also known as 'stopani,' the household spirits
are the echoes of a family's ancestors, trapped between the
realms of the living and the dead due to their love for the
family home and their desire to protect the household. While
their presence can be felt year-round, they are usually only
spotted during the Foul Days.

HOW TO RECOGNISE IT: Household spirits resemble the dead an-
cestor they've originated from, but with exaggerated features
related to their abode. Thus, hearth spirits often have fiery
red hair and eyes like burning coal while the spirit of the
stable might be wearing riding clothes and be armed with a
crop. Some spirits can transform into snakes, which makes it
particularly important to be gentle with any snake found near
the threshold.

HOW TO PROTECT YOURSELF FROM IT: They are generally benevolent
if prickly. The best strategy is to keep on their good side by
making sure the house is kept clean, tidy, and well maintained.
If they demand food, feed them. If they want a drink, pour them
one--they tend to like milk. If the spirits like you, they're
known to help with household chores, such as keeping the food
from spoiling too fast. Never, no matter what happens, laugh at
them, as it angers them. While household spirits can't generally do much harm, they can cause enough minor inconveniences
in your household to make your life miserable.

Kikimora

WHAT IS IT: The spirit of a murder victim rising from the pool
of spilled blood. Their weapon of choice is their long nails,
which they use to dig into people's chests and pull out their
hearts. Kikimoras do not technically have to eat, but when
given the chance, they are quite partial to a human heart. Due
to the general rise in violent crime during the Foul Days,
kikimoras rapidly increase in frequency during this period.

HOW TO RECOGNISE IT: Kikimoras resemble the murdered person, except often covered in copious quantities of blood and with long, strong talons.

HOW TO PROTECT YOURSELF FROM IT: While kikimoras are the victim's anger and hurt personified, and are thus very volatile and aggressive, they usually aim their wrath at their murderer and anyone else standing in their way from reaching said murderer.

If you find yourself cohabiting with a kikimora, it is important to leave it plenty of space, as they are prone to violent fits. Never fall asleep in the same room as a kikimora: they have been known to enjoy sitting on their victims' chests while asleep, getting progressively heavier and heavier, until the victim wakes up and discovers they are unable to move.

Karakonjul

WHAT IS IT: A small, vicious creature with an omnivorous diet, which more often than not includes human flesh. Karakonjuls are only found in Chernograd during the Foul Days, when they are a common sight, rummaging in rubbish bins and chasing stray animals up the streets.

HOW TO RECOGNISE IT: These are small monsters, the size of large dogs, with thick fur, yellow gleaming eyes, and curved horns. They have donkey-like ears and flat snouts with protruding curved fangs.

HOW TO PROTECT YOURSELF FROM IT: Karakonjuls are, notoriously, the least intelligent of the monsters, and it is tempting to treat them as nothing but rabid dogs. However, their capability for understanding human speech should be kept in mind. In fact, your best weapon against karakonjuls is to ask them a riddle: due to their limited intellectual capabilities, they can rarely come up with an answer, which means they tend to freeze, with their small brains overheating, allowing you to run away. At the same time, there is something to be

said about the very human reaction of becoming petrified on
spotting a pair of lantern eyes staring at you from a dark
alley and being unable to come up with a riddle. We suggest
preparing a few before venturing outside after dark.

There have been reports of karakonjuls being able to transform into common objects, such as shrubs or large boulders. At
present, the evidence remains inconclusive, but we nevertheless
recommend not approaching suspicious large boulders after dark.

Rusalka

WHAT IS IT: The spirits of drowned people, rusalkas are omnivorous creatures which sustain themselves on a diet of
fish, seagulls, and lost sailors. Rusalkas are only encountered in Chernograd during the Foul Days.

HOW TO RECOGNISE IT: Rusalkas are generally human-shaped but
often have fish-like features, such as tails, scales partially covering their bodies, and hair resembling seaweed.

HOW TO PROTECT YOURSELF FROM IT: Stay away from water, any
water—running or stagnant, including canalisation and sew-
ers. Rusalkas have an unusually long arm span, which means
they can reach their victims easily. If you do need to go near
water, remain vigilant: do not allow yourself to be tricked by
lights flickering in the distance. Those are not the lanterns
of lost fishing boats, but the spotlights hanging from the
foreheads of rusalkas. What makes rusalkas particularly dangerous is their ability to steal a person's voice: if you hear
someone crying for help from the water during the Foul Days,
chances are, the person is long dead, and the only thing that
remains is their voice, stolen by the rusalkas to use as bait.

Yuda

WHAT IS IT: Yudas are monstrous birds who feed on carrion
and have prophetic abilities, commonly spotted in Chernograd
during the Foul Days.

HOW TO RECOGNISE THEM: Yudas resemble large birds with human faces and a beak instead of a mouth. They have a crown of feathers, large feathery wings, and taloned feet. Similar to the samodivas, they are almost always female, for reasons we can only speculate: for example, some theorise the female yudas are the only ones who leave the nest while everyone else stays behind to look after the young, somewhat similar to the bee social structure.

HOW TO PROTECT YOURSELF FROM IT: Yudas are largely harmless to the living as their primary source of nutrition is half-spoilt human meat. They can, however, be rather distressing and it is highly recommended that they are avoided, especially by children, the elderly, and those weak of heart. They have the ability to foretell the future and a penchant for screaming the names of people who are soon to die, sometimes accompanied by other gruesome details, such as the time, place, and cause of death.

Samodiva

WHAT IS IT: Forest spirits known for their cruelty and bloodthirst. Unlike other monsters, they tend to kill not to feed, but for fun. Thankfully, these vicious monsters are only able to cross the boundary between the monster realm and Chernograd during the Foul Days.

HOW TO RECOGNISE IT: Samodivas resemble young women, long-haired, usually barefoot and dressed in white linen, with a semi-transparent veil covering their faces. They have bright, impossibly white skin, gleaming hair the colour of moonlight, and large completely black eyes with no whites. When on the hunt, they ride gold-horned deer and are armed with bows.

HOW TO PROTECT YOURSELF FROM IT: The first and most obvious thing you can do is to avoid the places where samodivas dwell. Those are usually recognisable, as they resemble thick forests, sprung among the city overnight. Whatever you do, do not play music or sing near a samodivas' den. They adore music, and have been known to kidnap musicians, forcing them to play until they drop dead from exhaustion.

If you ignore this advice and meet a samodiva, the rules are
simple:

• Don't drink the wine she offers you;
• Don't look her in the eyes;
• If she calls your name, don't answer;
• Don't accept her invitation to join the samodivas' dance,
  as once you dance with the samodivas, you can never return
  home.

Music is a way to attract a samodiva's attention, but it is
also a great way to distract her if you've been captured.
While you play or sing, the samodiva will not kill you. If
you find yourself trapped by a samodiva, the only way to free
yourself is to take her 'bulo' (her veil) and hide it, so she
can't retrieve it. This is where she keeps her power. However,
care should be taken when attempting this, as samodivas do
not take kindly to attempts to steal their power, and their
arrows tend to be very, very deadly.

The Zmey

WHO IS HE: The Tsar of Monsters

HOW TO RECOGNISE HIM: When he descends to Chernograd during
the Foul Days, the Zmey usually takes on the shape of a handsome man with bright blue eyes and golden hair. In his monster
form, he is enormous, with a body covered in golden scales,
wide bat-like wings, and a horned head. It is best not to encounter this form, as he only shifts into it when angry. This
is also the form capable of breathing fire.

HOW TO PROTECT YOURSELF FROM HIM: Young women between the
ages of 16 and 20 are at particular risk, especially those who
have been conceived or born during the Foul Days, and those
who show penchant for witchcraft. Women moving in groups are
safest. The Zmey tends to lurk in places where he might catch
his victims alone and unprepared: near the water fountain so
he'd offer to help her carry water back to the house; near

the library so he'd assist with her books. He is charming to
a fault and often, no amount of prior warning makes a difference. It is possible he enchants his victims, though no
conclusive evidence has been found.

Once the victim has been taken to his palace, your chances of
recovering her are drastically lower, especially once she's
drunk from his moon wine and eaten the enchanted fruit he
offers her. Do not let him take her to his palace. Once the
Zmey marries his victim, you might as well consider her dead.
She most likely will be within forty days.

Back to Basics

What are the Foul Days? They are the twelve days between midnight on New Year's Day and the first rooster's crow on Saint
Yordan's Day, after the new year has been born but before it
has been baptised, when monsters, ghosts, and spirits roam
the streets freely. Here are the fundamental rules to ensure
your survival during those twelve days:

1. Do not go outside after dark, as this is when the monsters
are awake;

2. Do not wash your clothes (the water is unbaptised!);

3. Do not wash yourself (yes, for twelve days . . . do you
want to protect yourself from the monsters or not?);

4. Do not host a wedding, an engagement, or a funeral--
essentially, any large gathering is asking for trouble;

5. Make sure you do not conceive, as any child conceived
during the Foul Days will become a drunk and a rascal, and/or
will catch the eye of the Zmey.

For the WWA, prevention comes first. Our advice will always
prioritise making sure you avoid the monsters as much as
possible. However, in order to account for all possible turns

of events, we've also added tips for distracting the monsters
so you can run away, or, if all else fails, for fighting them.
May God help you.

! IMPORTANT NOTICE !

Please remember the witches and warlocks of the WWA are available for hire to cast protective wards on dwelling places.
Contact your local witch or warlock for more information.

ACKNOWLEDGMENTS

Foul Days took six whole years, from when it was a vague idea that popped into my brain while half-frozen, waiting for the train to work one morning, to it becoming a real book. With such a long, winding path to publication, naturally, the list of people I need to remember to thank is longer than my arm.

Firstly, enormous thanks to the team at Tor, including my editor, Sanaa Ali-Virani, for seeing straight to the heart of the book and helping me shape the manuscript into the best version of itself. To my cover artist, Rovina Cai, and jacket designer, Jamie Stafford-Hill, who brought Chernograd to life. To interior designer Greg Collins, managing editor Rafal Gibek, Emily Honer in marketing, production editor Jeff LaSala, production manager Jacqueline Huber-Rodriguez, publicist Caroline Perny, copyeditor Sarah Walker, proofreader Tania Bissell, and cold reader Rima Weinberg. I feel privileged to have had the chance to work with all of you.

Thanks to my wonderful agent, Brenna English-Loeb, for her hard work and unwavering support, as well as to the rest of the team at Transatlantic Agency and co-agents, including Laura Cook from the Transatlantic contracts department, Theresa Lang and Leonie Kress at the Liepman AG Literary Agency, Renata Paczewska and Martyna Kowalewska at Book/lab Literary Agency, Mira Droumeva at A.N.A. Sofia Ltd., Megan Husain and Sarah Dray at the Anna Jarota Agency, Katya Ilina at the Elizabeth Van Lear Agency, and Júlia Garrigós Martí at the Foreign Office.

Foul Days wouldn't exist without my mentor, Rebecca Schaeffer, the person who sent me my first edit letter and taught me how story structure worked. For seeing something in this book before anyone else did, thank you.

Thank you to Ed McDonald, Marie Brennan, Allison Saft, Lilith Saintcrow, Maelan Holladay, Frances White, Kamilah Cole, Hana Lee, and Laura R. Samotin for the lovely blurbs. It means a lot that authors I look up to—both seasoned industry pros and fellow debuts—took the time in their busy schedules to read and enjoyed the book enough to recommend it.

Thank you to my amazing beta readers, Ashleigh Airey, Mili Tekelieva, Teodora Georgieva, Shirlene Obuobi, and Gwenyth Reitz.

To all the author friends who've been cheering me on and providing a much-needed space to vent in various group chats and discords, and especially the Edinburgh SFF group, the Salon and the Corner, and the 2024 debut group. I also owe thanks to the r/pubtips community for reviewing my query letter and remaining a valuable source of publishing knowledge, and huge thanks to Anna Klop for helping me settle on a title.

Finally, to my partner, Kenneth, for listening to me complain about how this is the worst book ever one minute, and boast that it's the best book ever the next; and to my family—and especially my brother Martin (who's read *Foul Days* more times than anyone else other than me), my grandmother Mara, and my mother, Sofia, for being the best alpha readers anyone can ask for, never hesitating to give it to me straight, and never, ever doubting this book.

ABOUT THE AUTHOR

Julie Broadfoot

Genoveva Dimova is a fantasy author and archaeologist. Originally from Bulgaria, she now lives in Scotland with her partner and a small army of houseplants. She believes in writing what you know, so her work often features Balkan folklore, the immigrant experience, and protagonists who get into incredible messes out of pure stubbornness. When she's not writing, she likes to explore old ruins, climb even older hills, and listen to practically ancient rock music.

X: @gen_dimova
Instagram: @gen_dimova